THE TALES OF ZREN JANIN

THE WRENS FLY AWAY

BOOK 5

M. L. DUNKER

Publishing Services provided by Paper Raven Books LLC
Printed in the United States of America
First Printing, 2022

Hardcover ISBN: 979-8-9850536-8-5
Paperback ISBN: 979-8-9850536-9-2

She was never quite ready.
But she was brave.
And the universe listens to brave.
–Unknown

Only when we are no longer afraid
do we begin to live in every experience,
painful or joyous, to live in gratitude for
every moment, to live abundantly.
–Dorothy Thompson

TABLE OF CONTENTS

Chapter 1 – Dreams and Plans 1

Chapter 2 – Problems and Possibilities 16

Chapter 3 – The Trick of It.................................... 25

Chapter 4 – Choices.. 37

Chapter 5 – A Secret Revealed.............................. 46

Chapter 6 – The Messenger Boy............................ 59

Chapter 7 – Kid Tells Some but Not All.............. 68

Chapter 8 – Heroes with Feet of Clay 81

Chapter 9 – Two Views, One War 93

Chapter 10 – Kid Tells More................................ 105

Chapter 11 – Surcease 112

Chapter 12 – Strangers Bearing Gifts 122

Chapter 13 – Thank You for Your Service......... 130

Chapter 14 – Empty Spaces 140

Chapter 15 – Kid Meets His Future 142

Chapter 16 – A Hunt Through Juisiti................. 148

Chapter 17 – All Who Wander Are Not Lost 161

Chapter 18 – Oro and Linna................................ 170

Chapter 19 – While You Were Gone 179

Chapter 20 – The Cost of Kindness.................... 183

Chapter 21 – Siba tells a Story 197

Chapter 22 – A Resolution – of Sorts................ 199

Chapter 23 – Josef Looks for a Place to Belong 205

Chapter 24 – The Value of a Life 216

Chapter 25 – Cio Claro! 221

Chapter 26 – Things That Were, Things That Are,
Things That Will Be 229

Chapter 27 – The Apprentice 235

Chapter 28 – Letters 245

Chapter 29 – To Matasi 254

Chapter 30 – Softfoots 266

Part II – The First Dry Season After the Settling of
Orsuarlerpaa, Vikland 275

Chapter 31 – Orsuarlerpaa 277

Chapter 32 – Adventuring 281

Chapter 33 – Josef Writes 283

Chapter 34 – A Letter to an Old Friend 285

Chapter 35 – Rell Returns to Vikland 288

Part III – The First Wet after the settling of Orsuarlerpaa,
Vikland 297

Chapter 36 – Hello, Old Friends! 299

Chapter 37 – My Heart is So Full 303

Chapter 38 – Good News! 306

Chapter 39 – Expect the Unexpected 312

Part IV – The Second Dry after the settling of Orsuarlerpaa,
Vikland 317

Chapter 40 – Family is Family..319

Chapter 41 – One Softfoot to Another........................324

Chapter 42 – A Long Journey for a Short Answer 326

Chapter 43 – Gratefully 334

Chapter 44 – Zren Goes Traveling..............................337

Chapter 45 – A Viklander, A Conrosan, and ?...............340

Chapter 46 – A Gift..349

Chapter 47 – Nearing the End of the Second Dry.............352

Chapter 48 – Softfooting Among Friends......................360

Chapter 49 – Misdirection and Maskovestos....................368

Chapter 50 – Softfooting for Practice and Pleasure............376

Chapter 51 – Keepers of Secrets 387

Chapter 52 – The Search for Falan 393

Chapter 53 – The Meaning of Things..........................395

Chapter 54 – The Hunter is Home from the Hills..............408

Chapter 55 – The Sailor is Home from the Sea...................411

Chapter 56 – Full Circle..420

Acknowledgements..424

Reading Guide 429

Contact the Author 435

Bonus Story – Fighting Monsters 437

Bonus Story – A Day to Live or Die...........................469

CHAPTER 1

DREAMS AND PLANS

Axefield had been a small town blessed with a perfect location on a low-level plain. It was a half-day's ride from the palace at Juisiti on a smooth road. South of Axefield the road branched into four directions: southwest to the border with Kerek and the Vikland garrison Nebulin, south to the estates and the Conrosan refugee camp at Rishka, southeast to the orchards and fields of the Selena Plains, and east to the Summer Plains, the breadbasket of Vikland.

Raul Huena had grown up here, the son of a hostler who had a small station boarding and hiring out horses to those coming to and from Juisiti. Like many of the children who grew up spending more time working with their families and on business than on their schooling, he had arrived at the academies far behind the others who came from backgrounds of tutors and coin. He worked hard to catch up, but he'd left in his second year to complete his military service.

That was his real education. He had traveled. He had been experienced enough to handle the high-spirited horses used for ceremonies by the diplomatic corps and ambassadors in the West Islands, the Spice Island, Kerek, and Matasi. It was in Matasi he had met his wife, Melia, another Viklander in the last year of her military service. After, they had returned to Axefield.

Armed with the wisdom of their travels, they built the first Huena Inn. They started a family, planted gardens, increased the stables, and they were blessed with commerce and each other. Melia had an eye for beauty and a palate for the flavors of the known world. Raul had the gift of hospitality and a sympathy for those coming from the outlands to the larger cities. He shared his knowledge freely, and he worked with other people in town to pass along business to wheelwrights, carriage makers, teachers, and tailors who knew how one needed to dress and act at the palace, and provisioners who knew what one needed traveling from the city to the Selena and Summer Plains.

And now his only daughter, Rell, had given him a gift like no other. He had wanted to expand for years but knew his talents were not up to the task. Then, during the war between Vikland and Kerek, Rell introduced him to Piffik Qanaq, a young man with the mind of a scholar, the will of a general, and the hands of a skilled builder.

At first, Raul and Melia hadn't known what to make of Piffik and of Zren Janin, the other young man Rell had brought to meet them. Piffik was a man who thought deeply, read widely, and acted on his convictions.

Piffik had been running his family business since he was far younger than their son Dylis, and he was responsible for many at Manumina. Piffik spoke three languages and the language of business, Melia told her husband, and it was clear to anyone who had eyes in their head, Piffik thought their daughter was a cherished gift. He would not try to bend or break her. Rell had chosen well and could have chosen far, far worse.

Zren Janin, on the other hand, was cheerful and friendly and never stopped talking. He asked questions immediately if he didn't understand something and said whatever he thought. At first it was a little disconcerting, and then it was just refreshing to meet a man so completely without guile. He was funny, appreciative of every little kindness, and had the same gift of well-turned words Piffik had. If these two were indicative of the other Conrosans of Manumina, well then it was good the Empress had offered them a home.

***

At first, Raul had faltered when Piffik and the Conrosans arrived to build the second inn. Melia had asked him if he was sure he knew what he was in for when they set up their tent city, built long, wooden sheds for their cooking and dining halls, laundries, and tool shop. But within days, he realized his good fortune. By bringing his own people, Piffik didn't waste time trying to find people, hiring the wrong ones, and fixing expensive mistakes. Piffik had told Raul their terms: they would work for five and a half days, be paid at midday on the sixth so they could do their shopping, and have a Rest Day. After the seventh day, they would start all over again. It was the Conrosan way and the way they worked best, Piffik explained.

The people worked as fast as the lumber and supplies came in. Women and men dressed in shabby Kereki pants or faded and patched Conrosan clothes. And they worked. When Piffik paid them after midday, they shopped. Soon Axefield business owners knew if they stayed open in the evening of the sixth day, their tills would equal the previous four days. On the seventh day, the workers played, they rested, they walked along the streets of Axefield, they picnicked in the gardens after visiting the street vendors. And even though his daughter Rell was far away in Kerek working with the Diplo at Evensong, Raul Huena blessed her every day.

And so it was, when Falan, one of the Kereki children traveling with the Conrosans, came to him and asked to have a room for the Wrens to meet for a little while, he gave her one of the private dining rooms, and only asked to have the room empty a decon before the end of day meal.

***

Falan watched as Ross and Nelo were the last to enter the room. The other Wrens were scattered about: some sat at the square tables; Josef and Kid stood, backs against opposite walls; Arden sat in the left corner with Mother flopped on the floor to the right of him—the dog just out of the way if Arden would need to leap to his feet for a fight.

The room was tense, not in anticipation of a fight, but in response to Ngahuru's news. The Empress of Vikland had given them a soldier's pay—enough coin for a year—and an invitation to make a home in Vikland. There were no plans to educate them, help them find shelter, or prepare them for a position to make enough coin to feed and clothe themselves in the future. The generosity of living in Vikland was supposed to be enough. They had been told this by Ngahuru and now they gathered to talk about it—without Ngahuru.

"I found Ross in the kitchen with Mother Huena. I told him we had been given this room to meet and when we were finished, he could return to her," Nelo offered.

"Oooooh, did you bring fingersweets?" Josef called out. "I cannot believe Falan would call us all together like this and not serve us coffee and fingersweets."

Ross said nothing, and Nelo gave an exasperated sigh. "Ross, I *saw* her give them to you. Don't stand there pretending you don't know what Josef is talking about. I am not going to let you keep them all for yourself." Ross slowly drew out a cloth napkin and put it on the table. Callis unwrapped it, and the Wrens eagerly reached for a treat.

"Now we are all here," Josef said, "and now we have been fed. Tell us, Falan why *did* you insist we drop our tools and plans and spend time with you?"

Falan gave him a troubled look. "I wanted to talk with all of you about Ngahuru's generosity and what you all plan to do."

Dica crossed her arms. "I am not going back into service." Then she gave a deep sigh. "But I speak too little Vik for another position."

"I'm not sure Vikland is a good place for us." Arden looked at the others. "Anyone who looks at our faces will be reminded of someone who did not come home from the war. Others will narrow their eyes and assume—correctly, I might add—we are living in Vikland because we betrayed Kerek, and so how trustworthy can we be?"

"So Vikland's out?" Callis questioned. "A soldier's pay is not going to go far if we must travel across the known world."

"Maybe so, maybe no." Kid pushed himself off the wall. "My plan is to find the family Ulani. I know our Jenny is there, and I have saved one of their boys twice. I have no interest in becoming an heir, but I wish to be tutored as Jenny is, to go to the academies in Juisiti when I am able, and join the Vikland Diplo service to become a softfoot. If I must serve three years of military service as all Viklanders do, so be it. If I must repay the Ulani family for the cost of my education *after* I am in the Diplo service and a softfoot, so be it. But I know how heavily the Viklanders took losses in the war, and my fine face will fit in well as a softfoot for the Viklanders in Kerek City."

Josef gaped at him, and then laughed. "That's bold. That's beyond..." He didn't finish his sentence. "I like it though. Perhaps we all have been thinking too small."

"What if they say no?" Tyra asked.

"Then they say no, and I am no worse off than I am at this moment standing in front of you." Kid shrugged. The room was silent while everyone matched their own expectations against Kid's plan.

Falan waited for a few moments and then looked about her. "Did anyone hear the argument between Piffik, Rygee, and Ngahuru yesterday?"

The Wrens broke out in sly smiles.

"I've never seen Piffik angry before. I didn't know he *could* get angry," Tyra said in a small voice.

"I saw him furious at Zren once, but he took it out on a Kereki traveling with the Sary Justice. This was much better—Rygee roared back," Josef said cheekily. "Tell everyone what they missed, Falan."

Falan said she had been fetching tools for the builders when Rygee had come flying out of the bakery yelling for Piffik. Ngahuru had been trailing behind, unable to keep up with Rygee's long legs. They had stepped away into the tack room in the stables, but anyone who wanted to—and Falan had wanted to—could hear them.

"It seems Piffik and the Council of Wisdom negotiated for the Conrosans, and received almost an entire district of land in the back of beyond to settle and build a deep-water port, and Ngahuru sold us all for coin and dumped us on Vikland's doorstep, but no one spoke for poor Rygee." Falan shook her head in mock dismay.

"He said it was his coin that bought our houses and settlements, his neck he risked for Nelo, and his farming knowledge that kept Manumina and the Wrens from starving. He said Ngahuru's wish for revenge and Piffik's wish for peace made them blind to what was needed, not just wanted. He expected them both to think over what they could do to repay him. He wasn't leaving Vikland empty-handed."

The room was silent.

"I don't think you gathered us to tell us this story as casual talk, Falan. What is it you want us to know?" Nelo leaned against the doorframe.

"Today I learned Piffik has offered all of the property and homesteads he, Rygee, and Ngahuru purchased from the forfeited tax rolls. Rygee now owns the places Linna, Callis, Josef, and Nelo lived in, and the settlement south of the Northern Track between Balza and Huk. He can sell or lease them as he wishes."

Falan took a deep breath. "Callis and I have talked it over. We are going back to Kerek. The house in Cloa is the only one in a town. We are going to ask Rygee to lease or sell it to us if Callis can apprentice with the healer there. I will try to take the position in the general store, which Linna held during the war."

Everyone sucked in their breath and a few snuck furtive glances at Arden.

He blew out a noisy sound. "You can say her name, people, you can talk about her. I'm not made of fairy dust and dew drops that I am going to fall to ashes at your feet. Please, stop pretending Linna didn't exist. I'm sure wherever she and Oro moved to in Juisiti, they talk about all of you."

"Yes, but…" Josef joked, "I rather liked the idea of using Linna's name as a curse whenever Falan vexed me." He shot Arden a wide grin. Arden shook his head, but a small smile played about his lips.

Falan rolled her eyes. "Does anyone else want to say what they are doing? Or where they are going? Or must we feed Josef's desire for an audience all day?"

Nelo cleared his throat. "Ross, why don't you say what you were doing when I found you?"

Ross shot him a mulish look. "Why don't you go first?" he shot back.

"I will and thank you." Nelo paused. "I am going with Piffik. I like building things, and I like working for him. I am going to move with the Conrosans to build a harbor." He nodded at Arden. "I think you are right—the Viklanders won't love me, but I plan to tuck myself into all of those Conrosans and see if my past can be forgotten."

Tyra gave him a serious look. "I am planning to go also. I am too young to live on my own, and like Dica, I do not want to be a servant in someone's great house. Siba Namikk said with the Conrosans, I can learn what I want in their schools, and not be concerned with food and shelter." She dropped her eyes and then looked at Nelo again. "Is this all right with you?"

Nelo smiled. "Of course, it is. Piffik is not so little a man that he can only manage one of us at a time. I believe Therin is staying with the Conrosans as well. The family that cares for him wishes him to remain."

Tyra looked relieved.

Falan nodded her head at Ross. "You said you wanted Nelo to speak first. He spoke. Now what were you and Mother Huena planning?"

"I'm going to stay at Axefield and raise rabbits. They get first pick for the table. A son, I forgot his name, will build me more rabbit hutches and I can sell my extras and keep the coin. I'll have a small room in the old inn and I won't have to share with anyone. When her boys go to the academies or for their military service, I can pick up their extra work for coin." He looked at the room defiantly.

"Well done, Ross!" Callis smiled. "You may be the most successful one of us all."

His face softened, not smiling, but not glowering either.

Falan looked about the room. This was not a surprise to her, to hear all of the Wrens had started planning as soon as Ngahuru had told them of her meeting with the Empress. They had survived the war by making plans as soon as they had news. She was relieved the littlest ones, Tyra and Therin, would be with the Conrosans and not her responsibility. Dica was still too young to live on her own, which it seemed she knew, but didn't have an answer for.

"Dica? We know what you don't want to do, care to share what you do want?"

Dica stiffened. "I want to be a shop girl. I don't want anyone telling me what to do."

Falan gave her an incredulous look. "That's all anyone does, Dica! The Patron who owns the shop tells you when to work and when you can finally go home. The people who shop think you exist only to magic whatever they want at a price they want to pay." She waved her hand. "You'll find that out soon enough. You'll go to Juisiti then?"

Dica shook her head. "I only know a little Vik."

Callis gave her a troubled smile. "Falan and I think Cloa will be safe enough for us because the Matasi army now guards the Northern Track. Even so, the two of us plan to travel together. I would not go to Matasi or Kerek alone."

Dica said nothing.

Callis looked to Josef. "You have been silent about your plans. Or is there to be three in the bed in our house in Cloa, and Falan has not yet told me the news?"

Josef smiled broadly. "As much fun as that would be, Callis, I will have to turn down your invitation. I have been thinking of Kid's words ever since they fell from his mouth. I thought I wanted to buy and sell horses, but I could not work out how I could make that happen. So, I am going to ask Rygee for his thoughts on how this could be done, and I hope he offers me a position with him when he returns to his father. I remember he said they had horsebreakers on their farm. It was how he knew what happened to Zren when he broke his collarbone and rattled his brain. So, if they have horsebreakers, they have horses."

"Ah, Zren," Falan snorted. "Does anyone know what the half-wit is doing?"

"He's not a half-wit, Falan, his mind just works differently than anyone else's does," Arden said quietly.

Callis gave him a long look. "I never thought I would hear you defend him."

Arden shrugged, but it was Nelo who spoke, "Arden's right. Zren asks too many questions to be lacking sense. His brain is odd, it's true, but he's a hard worker, there is not a cruel bone in his body, and he does what he's told. As long as he is fed often and given a story to puzzle over, he'll be happy wherever he goes. We needn't worry for him."

Dica looked at Nelo. "Is he going with Piffik or Ngahuru?"

"Don't know," Nelo admitted.

Tyra turned to Arden. "Where are you going?"

Arden smiled. "I am going to travel for a bit. I thought I would like to see Matasi. Perhaps after Mother and I have wearied of that, we will sail to the West Islands, or to the new port of Vikland. But I tell you, my friends, sometime between this world and the next, I hope to show my face at each of your doorsteps and we can share tales of our adventures."

Dica stared at him. "How will you earn coin?"

"A little of this, a little of that. A manabout during the Dry, a carpenter during the Wet, an orchard worker, a goatherd, a groom in a stable, a tracker of the lost. I have done all of that before, and I can do all of it again."

He leaned back against the wall. "I promised Piffik I would stay until the Huena Inn is finished. Now that Oro and Linna have moved to Juisiti, he has asked me to trade places with another manabout and work as a carpenter on the inn. I agreed to do so."

Josef nodded. "I will stay as well. But I think I will still talk to Rygee soon. I don't know when he plans to leave for his home."

Others started talking then and soon the room was a warm hub of voices. Falan rapped her knuckles on the table to get everyone's attention. "This is good to know where people are looking and what they are thinking. I had no plans to tell anyone what to do," Josef snorted at this, "but I wanted to see if there were those of like mind. Thank you."

There was a scrape of chairs and a chatter of voices as everyone hurried back to work.

CHAPTER 2

PROBLEMS AND POSSIBILITIES

Dica waited until she heard the soft sighs and slow breathing from the other Wrens letting her know they were asleep. She slipped from her bed and carried her boots in her hand as she crept outside. Once she slid her boots on, she picked her way across the ground to the stables. She knew the Huena grooms and visiting manabouts slept above the animals in the lofts. She also knew she only had one chance to get this right without being embarrassed.

At the far ladder, Dica put her foot on the bottom rung and was relieved to hear a soft whoof—Mother. She confidently climbed up.

Just as her head reached the top, she heard, "Say your name or I throw this knife."

"Dica! Arden, it's me, Dica," she hissed.

"Stay where you are, I'll spark a light so Mother can see you."

She heard the fumbling of bedclothes and the snick of a lucifer. In the growing flame, she could see Arden gently let down the side of the night lantern and set it on a spot of floor carefully swept clean. Mother was standing on all fours, alert but relaxed. Behind her, Arden was sitting up, a blanket over his legs, his brown hair unbraided and falling over his bare shoulders. He had a deep furrow of worry between his brows.

"What's wrong?"

"I need to talk to you, Arden, don't send me away."

He tipped his head to the thin curtain setting apart each manabout's meager space. "Should we walk outside?"

She nodded and climbed down the ladder to wait for him.

There was more rustling above, soft commands to Mother, the lantern went out, and Arden started down the ladder. He jumped lightly down the last two rungs. She started to speak, but he held his finger to his lips. He circled his narrow fingers about her wrist and led her out of the stables.

They walked in silence and Dica realized he was taking her to the flower gardens in the back of the inn. The moonlight was faint, but he was able to find his way to one of the wooden benches scattered about for the guests to rest and enjoy the sights and scents.

Arden gestured for her to sit down and then sat at the far edge of the bench. He waited for her to speak.

Now that she had him beside her, she didn't know how to start. How to say the words to make sure he would take her with him.

"I'm fourteen years old," she started in a rush.

He raised an eyebrow, and stretched out his legs. "More or less."

She nodded in agreement. "Arden, I want you to take me with you when you leave here to go to Matasi."

"No." The answer was swift and sure.

"Arden, I don't want to go back into service, I can't speak Vik well enough to work in a shop, and I am too young to strike out on my own."

Arden took a deep breath and looked out over the garden. He didn't say anything for a long while and Dica felt the first stirrings of hope. He would change his mind. She would be able to go with him. She wondered if they would take a wagon or horses or walk. She would be all right with any of those choices, but she rather hoped for a wagon. She didn't consider herself a strong rider.

"Dica, you are smart and resourceful. Weren't you one of Nelo's Lost Girls in Kerek City? And when you were too old for that, he taught you to be a pickpocket rather than just chasing you away to find a new protector."

She pulled back in surprise. "Are you going to go back to being a thief?"

"I don't want to, no," he admitted. "But if I have you along with me, then what must I do to feed us if I don't find work? Mother doesn't complain when we sleep rough." He gave her a mocking smile. "I am not so sure about you."

Dica considered his words, then spoke carefully, "So, you won't take me with you because you don't want to take care of me?"

Arden was silent for a long time. "Dica, I don't want to take care of anyone else for a while. During the war, we had to convince Viklanders to let us close enough without getting shot by a crossbow by the very people we were trying to help. I don't want to go to sleep at night anymore wondering what the other Wrens are doing, and if they are in danger while I am sleeping in a soft bed. I just want to see the beauty around me and enjoy the day ahead of me."

Dica looked at the silhouettes of the shrubs and flowers around her. The moonlight edged them in shadows. She could smell the night jasmine. She tried to understand Arden, and she puzzled over his words. She *had been* one of Nelo's Lost Girls, but she remembered how Nelo had frightened her if she didn't bring him enough coin every day. She remembered when he told her she was no longer little enough or pretty enough to be a Lost Girl, and she would need to learn to be a pickpocket—and a good one—or he would sell her back to the Orphan Master. How his last plan was to pretend to sell her and Jenny to sailors and then when she led one to an alley, Nelo would be waiting for them and together they would rob the bodies. She had hated Nelo then, and yet knew she would be dead without him. She didn't know if Arden knew that, and she didn't have the words to tell him. She let out a huge sigh to try to keep the tears from overwhelming her.

Arden stirred beside her. "Can you do sums? Read? Write? Do you know enough Vik to go to school here in Axefield? Can you attend the evening or day school at the worksite with the other apprentices?"

"No." Her voice was thick with unshed tears. "I mean, I know my letters, and to write my name, and how much was supposed to be in my paypacket at Regno." She paused. "Arden, I have no coin here. I'm treated as the other children, the apprentices, and given food and a place to sleep is all."

Arden huffed. "Do you think you could learn enough before the Huena Inn is completed? Falan and Callis know how to do sums and read and write well enough to be shop girls. Kid knows how and could teach you. There's Ngahuru or Siba the healer. You wouldn't have to be in a schoolroom with little children."

Dica turned away. How could she say she was afraid of Falan's sharp tongue and too angry at Ngahuru to ask for her help? She knew Callis hardly at all. How do you ask a stranger to teach you something you should already know?

As if Arden had read her mind, he asked, "Do you remember when we pulled you in, Oro and I?" He was still looking out into the garden.

Dica's face flamed in shame, and she was glad the darkness covered her. She had gone to the hiding place after gathering her things and stealing food for their journey only to find it deserted and no evidence Oro had ever been there. She had heard horses and had pushed herself quickly into the rhododendrons to conceal herself. From deep within the leaves, she watched as Oro was beaten and tied to a horse by two Kereki men. She followed the horses' tracks, but she was on foot, and she knew she was falling behind. She tried to think what else she could do. *How long could she track him without being discovered? Once she knew where they had taken him, what could she do then that she couldn't do on the way? Oro said they were all supposed to meet at Nelo's holding and flee to Manumina. Would she get to Nelo's in time to have the other Wrens help her? If the others had already left, could she find her way to Manumina? How long would it take her to walk there if she didn't have a horse?* She remembered how she had sobbed as she walked, trying to do it so silently her throat hurt.

And then Mother had found her. Nearly running, nose to the ground tracking the horses, Mother had almost passed her when Dica called her name. The black dog hesitated, and Dica sat down in the middle of the road and held out her pants and boots to be sniffed. The dog came closer, wagged her tail when she sniffed the familiar soap, but stayed carefully out of reach. Dica had shuddered with relief.

Mother circled a number of times and then headed south expecting Dica to come along. The dog slowed her pace to match Dica's, but Mother was clearly in a hurry to get back. At last, the two of them had stumbled into the clearing where Oro, now untied, and Arden were hitching two riderless horses on a trailing line behind a Matasi-style wagon. By then, she had been too emotionally and physically exhausted to do anything but hug Arden like a little child, in gratitude and relief, and crawl into the back of the wagon.

"I remember," she said stiffly. *Was he going to mock her?*

"Look how clever you were," Arden began. "You slipped back into the great house after Oro told you all our plans. You grabbed clothes and food and coin. You gave Oro a safe place to sleep and rest for the day so he would be ready to walk all night. The fool didn't listen and got captured for his stupidity. But you didn't give up on him, instead you tracked him to learn more and make new plans. I interfered with your rescue by finding two riderless horses and untying Oro. You forgave me anyway and rode back with us to Nelo's place. You fed all of us with the food you had taken. You used Ngahuru's pots of paint to turn Nelo—the fairest man I have ever known—into a swarthy Matasian. You dressed the part of a missionary wife so well we passed unchallenged to Manumina. In Sary, when Inezi overheard the Conrosan settlement had fallen and was taken over as a Matasi garrison, you agreed with the others we should continue to Manumina in case the rumors were false, or if the others were cast out or hurt along the way and needed our help."

Dica was silent. She remembered the story quite differently. She *liked* the way Arden told it, but she knew it wasn't true and she said so.

Arden gave her an odd smile. "You think you need a protector when what you truly need is time. Building the Huena Inn, staying here during the Wet, gives you time. Learn to do sums, to count coins, to read and write well, Dica. That is the most important. If you do not want to help build the inn, ask Piffik if you can work somewhere else—the kitchens, the gardens, the laundries, the school, the other inn. Gain a skill that can earn you coin beyond Axefield or Rishka. A tool runner is helpful to the Conrosans, Dica, but it is not helpful to you. We can talk again at the beginning of the Dry. But for this night, my answer is no."

He was quiet then, letting his words sink in. "Your future has endless possibilities, Dica. The worst days of your life are all behind you." He paused, still not looking at her, and then added softly, "You should know, I do not believe that is true of all the Wrens."

Finally, he turned and smiled. "I need my bed, I am an old man."

She snorted. "You're two years older than I am."

"Three." He flashed her a grin, and she smiled as she knew what he would say next, "More or less." He leaned forward and arched his back and then stood and stretched again. "Find your way back?"

Dica nodded. She wanted to stay and think about what he said.

He disappeared into the dark.

CHAPTER 3

THE TRICK OF IT

Josef stood at the foundation and looked up…and up. The framing for four stories of the new Huena Inn was in place. Now the strongest workers were muscling the trusses to be hauled up to the top. Scaffolding had been built along the outside edges of each story. Two children, with leading ropes tied about their waists, were climbing up the framing on each side like the building was nothing more than an apple tree with wide-spreading limbs. Josef shuddered.

Piffik had said this was how the houses at Manumina had been built. The old men who had built Manumina were standing about Piffik now, giving him the benefit of their experience.

Josef watched as Arden and Zren—"roof walkers," Piffik called them—took the leading ropes from the children and inched their way out onto a narrow boardwalk over empty space. They threw the weighted ropes over the roofline and watched as the ropes slithered to the ground below. People grabbed the leading ropes and pulled as Zren and Arden grabbed on to the boardwalk to keep their balance. The leading rope pulled a dozen other ropes over the roofline and now the truss stood vertically.

An older woman with a mallet pounded rhythmically on a wood block as the crowd chanted with her, "pull, reach, pull, reach, pull, reach." People perched on the scaffolding on the sides carefully guided the truss at an angle so it wouldn't swing wildly and hit the internal walls of the building. Once it reached the top floor, guides on the scaffolding walked the truss over to the boardwalk where Zren and Arden now stood in the middle between the two end carpenters with squares and hammers. The truss was lined up until all four carpenters called, "Square!" There was a rapid pounding of hammers, another measurement, and then, "Done!"

Josef held his breath as Arden and Zren stepped on the newly secured truss and used the vertical brackets to balance as they walked their way back to the scaffolding on the side. The second truss was moved into place on the ground and everyone readied to do the same thing all over again. As the workers pushed out the boardwalk for Arden and Zren, Josef heard footsteps behind him. It was Falan.

"I told Callis if she wanted to see a good man go splat in the mud, she should leave her needle and thread and watch this," she began without preamble.

Josef felt his chest hitch and tried to wipe his sweaty palms out of Falan's view. He watched as the weighted lines were handed over to the roof walkers and the two men inched their way out again. Josef shuddered as they threw the lines over the roofbeam and grabbed the boardwalk to balance while the truss inched its way upward to the sound of "Pull, reach, pull, reach, pull, reach."

"I see Piffik decided Conrosans were too valuable to risk. Of course, Zren is up there, but I thought Arden had more sense," Falan snapped.

Josef angled his gaze down at her. "Falan, it's me, Josef. You can drop the nasty sarcasm for a moment and just be afraid with me. Both Zren and Arden volunteered. Arden says heights do not bother him—I think it was the years of climbing about the rooftops of rich men's houses in the Flower District—and Zren would do anything Piffik asked him to without questioning whether he would live through it."

There was the sound of rapid hammering on wood and then the second truss was secured.

Falan sighed. "Are you planning on watching this all day? I am asking because some of us have work to do, and I thought you might want to come with me to talk to Rygee about the house in Cloa. You could ask him about traveling with him at the same time."

"Shouldn't Callis know if she could apprentice with the healer there first before you try to secure a house?"

Falan gave him an exasperated look. "Oh, how silly of me! Let me just ride my magic horse I've borrowed from one of Zren's fairy tales, and I'll fly to Cloa and back in the blink of an eye!"

Josef reached over and pulled her close. She held herself rigidly as he slowly rubbed her arm. "It's not you against them anymore, Falan. You don't have to save me or Callis or anyone else." He wrapped both arms around her and rested his chin on her head. "Just let your guard down for a while and breathe." She didn't move and he rubbed her back while he watched over her head as the next truss went up.

The difference between roof walkers was obvious. Anyone not knowing the two would be able to tell Zren didn't understand the danger. He boldly reached for the truss, called out when his corner was square, and confidently pounded in rhythm with the others. He wore his fall rope loosely about his narrow hips. Even Josef knew if either man was knocked off the boardwalk by a swinging truss, the sharp jerk of the rope as it broke a fall could cause as many internal injuries as the four-story drop.

Josef dropped his eyes to the three old men gathered around Piffik. They were the roof walkers of sixty years earlier, when Manumina had first been built. Now, they had designed the tests everyone had taken to be the new roof walkers. All of the Conrosan youth had tried balancing on a narrow board wobbling between bricks stacked knee high, stopping a section of a swinging truss, measuring and squaring up wood, and hanging by the hands from a crossbeam and pulling up the body until one lay flat on the boards above. Josef didn't even want to *think* why that skill would be needed.

In any case, he had deliberately slipped off the wobbly boardwalk. Dica had done well until the swinging partial truss knocked her off the narrow ledge. Nelo had refused to try and walked away. Thankfully, two handfuls of Conrosans, girls and boys, passed all the tests. The old roof walkers were delighted to have so many. The stress and concentration needed for the job tired the roof walkers out quickly. With so many rotations of workers, the trusses could still be done in a day and a morning.

Josef continued to hold his breath each time the two inched out on the boardwalk and released it slowly once the truss was hammered into place. He felt Falan slowly relax into him, and he suspected she was trying to get her tears dried without actually wiping them on his shirt.

Another team of roof walkers readied themselves and climbed up the open framework to the top scaffolding. Arden and Zren were done. They would not need to go up again until the next morning. Josef watched as they handed themselves down, Zren crabbing sideways to reach around the long open spaces, Arden dropping to the bottom first. As Arden drank from a dipper at a bucket, Zren said something that made him laugh. Looking around, Zren saw them, waved, and started over. Arden followed more slowly, probably trying to figure out who he was holding, and whether or not it was a good time to interrupt.

"Falan, others are coming. If you wipe your face on my shirt, you'll completely destroy your harsh reputation, and nothing I can say will save it. Nothing. You will be ruined completely," he mockingly whispered.

He heard Falan choke back a laugh. But she turned away from him, wiped her face on her sleeve, and then turned and scowled at the two walking toward them. Zren took one look at her face and peeled off toward the stables.

"I'll get the horses ready," he called over his shoulder. Arden was still laughing when he reached them.

He nodded to Falan, and then asked, "Nelo is stuck on the pull crew for the day, but do you want to go out and hunt for the table?"

"Sure," Josef agreed. "I'll get my short bow. Meet you and Zren at the stables?"

"Only me, I'm afraid. Zren is going to find Kid for some reason or other." He looked at Falan. "I am sorry you were so frightened on my behalf. Next time you can throw yourself at me," he held out his arms and gave her a mocking smile.

Falan sniffed. "You wish."

Arden chuckled low in his throat, and started to walk away. "I'll find Zren and let him know his silence on what he saw is worth his life."

"You all right, now?" Josef asked Falan.

"Of course, I'm all right. It's just sometimes…"

"I know. You don't need to explain anything to me." He reached out his hand but dropped it before he touched her.

"Go on. Arden's waiting on you." Falan pulled her features into a scowl and crossed her arms about her chest.

He squeezed her shoulder and walked away.

***

Zren watched as Josef and Arden rode easily to the east with quivers of arrows over their shoulders, Mother trotting alongside. He liked both Arden and Josef, but he didn't know how to ask to go along. He sighed. It was probably better he didn't go hunting with the others. While he knew he would never shoot Mother by mistake, he wasn't sure he was ready to let out his secret of how poor his eyesight was at a distance. And well, he had promised to find Kid after he was done roof walking.

He started looking for Kid by heading to the old town of Axefield and visiting the bookseller. Yes, she knew who Kid was, no, he had not been in for several days. And you are? Ah, I thought Zren Janin was the name of a hero in a book of fairy tales. Yes, I see. Well, could you tell Kid the book of Vikland maps he ordered is here.

Zren said he thought he could remember and wandered back out into the street. One of his favorite food vendors was out on the corner. Zren slipped his hand in his pocket only to realize he had left the worksite so quickly he had no coins with him. He looked about the square, couldn't think of anyplace else Kid could be, and walked back to the inn.

In the third room in the old Huena Inn, Zren found him carefully writing out the Vik alphabet. Kid looked up as he came in.

"Done for the day already?"

"Only the roof walkers. Piffik says it is very important for us not to get tired and careless. The old roof walkers said the worst mistakes always happened when someone was almost done with their turn."

"You're a braver man than I am, Zren Janin." Kid nodded agreeably. "I took one look at that wobbly boardwalk, another look at those massive trusses, a third look at the clouds in the sky, and 'oh, was that the top of the building I would be crawling on up there?' I ran and hid in here."

He grinned at Zren and put his graphite down. "I was hoping you could tell me about the Ulani family. I want to write them a letter so I can be welcomed. I remembered you and Ngahuru did so, and I knew you could tell me what to say."

Zren scrunched up his face as he remembered. "Well, Ngahuru wrote the letter, but in it she said she had heard Solkka was recuperating there and she thanked them for their great generosity to Jenny. She said who she was and asked if they could meet." Zren paused. "Then she got a letter back written in Wester, from Solkka's mother, inviting us both for a visit. And her son, Tedros, would be our guide and host on the way." He shrugged. "Then Tedros came here, and Ngahuru thought it was Solkka. She did not know how you had helped him after Jenny had saved his life."

Zren found he still couldn't talk about the scar that slashed across Solkka's face. "Then they came to the refugee camp at Rishka, and we rode horses to the Ulani coffee farms. You know, you should ask Ngahuru to help you write the letter. She would know what to say. She knew Mother Ulani was the West Islands King's sister. She wrote the letter to her in Wester."

Kid stared at Zren. "The man I saved with Jenny is the nephew of the West Islands King? And he was fighting? Like a common soldier?"

Zren pinched his lips shut. "Not many people know. Solkka has actually never told me. I only learned it because Ngahuru curtsied and called Mother Ulani a princess, and Devi Ulani told me a story of what people have given up to marry an Ulani." He repeated, "Ngahuru could help you more than I could."

"I asked. She refused me immediately," Kid responded morosely. "Now I know why."

Zren looked at him incredulously. "But Mother Ulani wanted to meet you. She asked if you were one of hers— Ngahuru's, I mean. She wanted to thank you. You should go to the Ulani family and say you are one of those who saved her son. Tell her the stories so she knows you are telling the truth. Jenny will be there and she will know you too."

"Oh, and then ask that they educate me?" Kid asked despondently.

"Well, no." Zren considered his words carefully. "The Ulani family is very kind, but they are not foolish. I followed Devi Ulani and his sons and I learned about coffee. Solkka said the farm was not big enough for three sons, but I know now he meant he never wanted to live there. You could help them while Tedros is away at his last year in the military and while Solkka is in Matasi. When you are not working, you could ask Jenny to teach you what she is taught. If they house you and feed you and pay you small coin, you could send yourself to the academies. Rell's father has sent Rell and two sons to Juisiti. He could tell you how much your schooling costs. If you do not have enough coin when Tedros comes back from finishing his service and takes his place on the coffee farm, *then* ask the Ulani family to send you to the academy." Zren grinned at him. "If they say no, you are no worse off than you are now."

Kid was startled. "You heard us?"

"No," Zren admitted. "I saw you all leaving the dining room, and I wondered if there had been a gathering with food, so I asked Tyra. She said there had been a meeting of the Wrens to discuss Ngahuru's news. She told me what people were going to do."

Kid leaned back in his chair. "So, Zren, can you write in Wester? If I wrote a letter in Keresh, would you be able to read it and put the words in Wester for me?"

Zren dropped his eyes to the floor and slowly shook his head without saying anything. He glanced up and saw the look of disappointment in Kid's eyes.

"That's fine, Zren. I understand."

Zren looked up at him. "I never learned the trick of it. I can read and write Conrosan and Wester. But Keresh? I can only speak it."

Zren watched in surprise as Kid broke into a slow grin. "So, you are saying if I write the letter in Keresh and *read* it to you, you can put the words down in Wester? You would do that?"

Zren stared at him with a surprised look on his face. "Of course."

CHAPTER 4

CHOICES

The problem with mending and sewing and tailoring, thought Callis, is it gave one too much time to think. She looked up at the huge drying racks of the makeshift laundry. For as dumpy and crowded as Rishka had been, the laundry there had been vastly superior to this one. Piffik had not wanted to spend the time building the big copper pipeworks, so they had merely put in three sandpoint wells and built firepits underneath the huge cauldrons. Everyone stirring the clothes in the near boiling water had to worry about scalding their hands or burning their feet.

Callis was strong enough to lift the giant wooden paddles of dripping clothes from the first tub to the second to the third rinse, and finally, to the large flat presses where the water would be squeezed out into the shallow square tins which the gardeners would later gather. She had started there, and then when she had told the head laundress she had been a tailor in Kerek City, she was moved immediately to the other side of the drying racks.

The drying racks were in the center, floor to ceiling, nearly the width of the building. On the other side sat the tailors, who would repair the clean clothes, remake those which could not be mended, or carefully re-stitch the family name in the collar and waist. The tailors would talk and share jokes and stories. At least Callis thought they did, for they spoke Conrosan nearly all the time. If one or two would try to translate the joke for her the words didn't match up enough for her to follow along.

Usually, she just waved her hand and smiled. "Oh, please speak Conrosan, it is the only way I will learn." Inwardly she worried, how could people live in a country for generations and not speak the language? How long would it take for her to learn Vik? But whenever Callis thought of having to move back to Kerek and her future home back in Cloa, she found her stitches getting tighter and tinier.

She and Falan would lie awake at night in their bed and whisper about the future. Falan was more confident about returning to Kerek than she was. Callis wasn't convinced Matasi soldiers would necessarily keep the peace so well that they would have the idyllic life Falan described. But she did agree living with the Conrosans, as gracious as they had been, would be stifling. She didn't speak Conrosan, and she could barely guess the meaning of the Vik she encountered everywhere at the inn and in Axefield. If it weren't for the Wrens, and their conversations in Keresh every night, she thought she would cry from the loneliness and isolation. Once they moved to build the new port—"the middle of nowhere," as Josef said—it would be even harder to leave.

Callis reached for the common shears to cut the thread on the mended shirt. She folded it carefully and placed it on the finished stack. She arched her back, smiled at the others and picked up the next bundle on the pile. Ugh, men's pants. At least the tailors all worked with clean clothes.

Callis didn't like to watch the building of the inn as Falan did. She liked Zren; he was like a little kirikiri bird distracted by every shiny bit around him. Until she had met him, she did not know a person could talk so much. She had noticed how others flocked around him at first because he was such a hard worker. But then, when they realized he did not understand the dangers of his work and would not take precautions, they found other places to be until only Arden would be his partner. She trusted Arden, he hardly talked at all, but she didn't want to watch them work so many stories above the ground.

Most of all, she liked to watch Nelo with his shirt straining across his muscles as he worked on the pull crew or lifting heavy sections of walls and ceilings. She played a game with herself to see how quickly she could pick out his tail of white-blond hair— like a flash of sunlight—among all the curly brown-headed Conrosans. She liked how he tipped his head as Piffik talked to him, as if the words falling from Piffik's mouth were the most important in the world. She hadn't been surprised when Nelo said he would follow the Conrosans to build the port on the Northern Sea.

Callis scoffed to herself. Nelo may think he was going to hide among the Conrosans, but he was never going to disappear.

At least, Nelo would take Tyra and Therin with him. She liked the idea of them going to school and finding a home. She wished Dica would go with them as well, but she thought the girl was nearly as strong-willed as Falan. At least, Dica was now studying with Kid in the evenings. She had noticed them in one of the workrooms, their dark heads bent over a book together. Callis was curious if he was teaching her sums, or reading and writing, or information gathering like he had done in Kerek City.

Callis finished mending the trousers and started to fold them on the pile when the others erupted in laughter. She glanced at them uncertainly, but they all had their heads bent and no one looked her way.

There was a commotion at the other end of the laundry and Callis looked up to see those coming in for the evening work. They would be responsible for folding the dry laundry on the racks, sorting it by family, and more mending. She saw Dica hurrying in.

"Callis, can I use your needle please? Josef tore his shirt while he was hunting with Arden. He says he doesn't have another one, clean or not, so this one can't go through the laundry and wait for you. I said I would mend it if I could get a needle."

The two walked out into the late day sun. "I didn't know you could sew. I mean, beyond what we learned at Manumina before we were scattered across Kerek."

"I learned more at Regno. I had to mend all the servants' clothes."

"Then why are you working as a tool runner? We could use you in the laundries."

"This is where Ngahuru told Piffik to put me." Dica wrinkled her nose.

"Huh," grunted Callis as she gave her the needle. She pocketed a small spool of grey thread as they left the laundry and handed it to Dica. "Before you give Josef his shirt back, can you find me in the infirmary? I would like to see your work."

Dica nodded as she hurried off with the needle and thread.

Callis found the healers in the infirmary, along with a handful of others needing attention. Callis quickly washed up and put on one of the aprons the healers used to protect their clothes.

"How can I help?"

It had been the last truss of the day. The pull crew on the ground had lifted the truss to the second floor when one of the pull ropes snapped and the truss started swinging. The people on the right side had been able to grab the truss, but it had pulled two of them off their feet and one had fallen off the scaffolding. The other had been dangling from the truss when one of the old roof walkers had yelled, "Run back the ropes!" until the truss was back on the ground. Those in the infirmary had been hit by the truss—either on the scaffolding or on the ground.

Callis nodded and began washing the bruises, looking for broken skin, feeling for broken bones and sprains. She examined cuts and scrapes and removed slivers. As she bandaged the foot of the last patient, Dica came in carrying Josef's mended shirt.

While Dica explained to Siba what happened, the healer examined the mending of Josef's shirt. Quickly, Callis finished up and tidied up her workspace. She reached for the shirt and felt the stitches.

As she looked closer, she exclaimed, "This is good, Dica! You should work in the laundries as a tailor. We could certainly use your help."

Siba agreed. "This is very tidy work, Dica. You should go to the head laundress tomorrow and offer to help her. If she likes your work, Piffik will let you go. All the children are tool runners, it is why we have a day school and an evening school. So the apprentices do not fall behind while they are learning their trade. Your talents—now we know what they are—would be much better served in the laundries."

Dica was shocked. "You mean all I had to say was, 'I want to be a tailor and not a tool runner,' and it would be so?"

Siba nodded. "The head laundress and Piffik would need to agree, but yes, that's how it works in Manumina, everyone works together."

Callis began slowly, "So you are saying, if Dica takes my place in the laundry, I could come here and work with you in the infirmary?"

Siba said, "Certainly, if that is your wish, but I thought you and Falan were leaving us any day now?"

Callis looked stunned. "This changes everything. Could I really apprentice with you?"

"You can apprentice with my aunt, but yes. We could use you in the infirmary."

Callis was speechless for a long while, and then Dica piped up, "Do you have another shirt? Josef says this is his only one. If you have a damaged one in the infirmary, maybe I can fix it for him."

"I do not. Have you checked the rag and bone wagon? I know during the war we would borrow from it freely when we needed clothes for the injured Viklanders," Siba explained.

Dica looked at Callis.

"I do not even know what happened to it." Callis shook her head.

"I believe the rag and bone wagon and all of its clothes may still be at Rishka." Siba paused. "Here is one of the ways you can do this. Rest Day is three days from now. Two of you could ride down to the refugee camp after our half day, the day after tomorrow. I can make a list of medicines I would like you to bring back. Rygee may want you to make the cheese run so the cheesemaker does not lose so much time traveling. Ask Piffik if he needs anything from his woodworking shop there."

She continued thinking out loud, "Oh, and I don't think Arden has been back since Ngahuru sent for him to tell of the Empress's decision. Piffik asked him to stay and exchange places with one of the manabouts here who was definitely *not* a carpenter. Arden may ask you to bring back some things, or even ask to accompany you."

Siba looked at Callis and Dica. "You can bring back all the clothes from the rag and bone wagon and distribute them as you need among the Wrens. They belong to all of you. Or I think so anyway, Ngahuru may not agree. If Piffik does not need you to bring back a wagon, you can ride back late the same night or sleep there and come back on Rest Day." She paused. "It is not the only way you can do this, but it is probably the easiest—except for the two Wrens who must give up their Rest Day, of course."

Callis and Dica looked at each other. "Let's go find the others."

CHAPTER 5

A SECRET REVEALED

Josef wrinkled his nose at the old Conrosan horses Piffik had told him to use and looked longingly at the Viklander mare everyone called "Rell's horse." He gave a sly look to Nelo and Arden.

"If only you two were better horsemen, I could ride this horse and you two could try to keep up."

Nelo snorted. "You'd be tasting dust before the edge of Axefield."

"Do you know the story of Rell's horse?" A voice in the shadows interrupted their banter, and Zren walked forward. He stepped up on the mounting block at the corner and draped his arms over the wooden stall of Big Bess. "It was the first time Piffik became a horse thief. Although there were others, this story is my favorite because he tricked Rell into thinking she was the only one who could save Manumina."

Josef cocked his head. "Thievery and trickery, sounds like my kind of story."

Zren hesitated. "I could tell it to you on the way. Stories make the journey go faster."

No one said anything for a moment. "You know we are riding horses and not taking a team and wagon, don't you?" Nelo questioned.

"I know. I can keep up," Zren said stubbornly. "And I know lots of stories."

Nelo looked at the other two. Arden just shrugged, but Josef answered mischievously, "He does know a lot of stories."

Nelo gave Zren a mocking smile. "Please join us. We will take the four Fortika horses. If we are going to be hearing stories of trickery and thievery, then we should be riding stolen horses, so we do not get above ourselves with self-righteousness, no?"

Zren looked over at the Fortika horses and swallowed hard. "We are taking a wagon back tomorrow, right?"

Arden relented, "You can drive the wagon back. We'll be your outriders."

Josef had already begun pulling tack for the horses while Zren went back into the shadows and pulled out an oversized travel bag.

"Siba said we would arrive too late to join those who still live there for the end of day meal, so she packed food for us. She said there is a letter for Nelo in here from Rygee. She said to share it with only those you trust."

Nelo scowled. "I suppose you read it since I cannot."

Zren shook his head. "I cannot read Keresh, only Conrosan and Wester. Siba told me to tell you she put a piece of melted wax to seal it so you would know no one has read it from the moment it left Rygee's hand."

***

Zren started the story of how Piffik became a horse thief with the Kereki deserters—boys who just wanted to go home from the war. He cheekily described Josef in his too small shirt taking Zren's rightful place as Ngahuru's *titiro mai ki ahau* and sending Zren back to Manumina with Bima Ritwik and a wagon full of Viklanders.

He described his long night swapping out the five extra horses they had found after they had left the second homestead with six bodies and two graves. He told them about the horror of Kereki Trickster tales, where Greed, or Rage, or Death is so tricksy you are given what you already have, to exchange for the Trickster's heartfelt desire. He went on to say how he had heard Matasi parables the rest of the night to puzzle over and keep him awake until they reached Manumina at dawn. He laughed as he retold of Piffik's confusion at five new horses with no one to ride them because Rygee and Siba had already taken the Viklanders to Ishes, and how the Viklander mare was so spirited only Rell would be able to ride such a fine horse.

"Piffik said he could not speak Vik well enough, and I could not ride well enough, to take the horses over to Vikland and sell them. We could not keep them at Manumina because they were branded and each side would think we had killed for them.

"There was nothing else that could be done. Rell must travel with Piffik to Vikland and sell the horses." Zren chuckled as he looked at Josef. "You should have seen Rell try to dress like a Conrosan married woman. She wore the clothes, Josef, but the moment she was on the horse she only looked like a warrior in disguise. She did not have your skill to be whoever you needed to be." He went on to tell how Rell could not bear to part with the mare, and the horse was bought by the Huenas. How the coin was used for the Wrens and Manumina farm laborers.

Josef laughed and Nelo smiled. "That is a good story."

Arden asked, "Was that your first time meeting Bima Ritwik?"

"No," Zren said somberly. "But, I think it was the one time he let me see him, truly see him." He was quiet for a moment and then grinned. "Let me tell you about the first time I met Bima Ritwik and how he taught me to walk up walls."

Zren continued to tell stories until the four men stopped a decon before the Rishka estate to stretch, drink, and eat the food Siba packed. The sun was setting, and as the men sat around a small fire, they talked about sleeping rough in the woods and the first time they had each gone to sleep without the noise of Lowertown as a lullaby.

Josef told a story of visiting Falan to exchange clothes for a softfooting adventure, and how the widow who owned the house had walked into Falan's room without knocking to find Josef in a dress and Falan tying Kereki ties about the ankles of her trousers. Zren laughed so hard there were tears running down his cheeks.

It was long after dark before the men rode into Rishka. There were only a handful of candles in the windows of the main house. The Wrens' shed looked shabby and deserted. The stables were nearly empty. Only the cheesemaker's pony stood alone in her stall. The four dismounted and cared for their horses in near silence. They were all ready for their beds.

Arden spoke first, "I'll be sleeping in my old room tonight. I want to see if there is anything I want to take back with me tomorrow to Axefield."

"You could sleep in the Wrens' nest with us," offered Nelo. "The girls aren't here to make a fuss and anyway, you don't have Mother with you."

Arden just shook his head.

Josef looked at Zren. "What about you? Above the stables or Wrens' nest?"

Zren looked shy for a moment. "I've only ever slept in the infirmary here, so I will stay there." He wrinkled up his nose. "Unless there is someone dead in there."

Josef barked out a laugh. "Now you've done it, Zren. If you scream, no one is going to come running to rescue you."

Zren pulled off the travel bag and rummaged about. He pulled out the letter and handed it to Nelo. He threw the travel bag over his shoulder and nodded to the others. "G'night then. Don't leave without me and don't wake me up before the sun is this high over the horizon." He stretched out his arms as high as they would go and laughed at his own joke.

***

Arden was still searching his belongings in the loft above the stables when he heard footsteps below. He peered over the edge to see Nelo.

"Something wrong?"

"I thought I could wait until morning, but can you read Rygee's letter to me? Bring your light."

Arden turned and quickly came down the ladder one handed, a lit lantern in the other.

"Josef already asleep?" He stepped off the bottom rung and the two walked out into the sliver of moonlight.

"I think I know what this is about, and I do not want Josef to know…not just yet."

Arden quirked an eyebrow. "This isn't going to be one of those moments where I read your letter to you and then my body is buried in the sand somewhere, is it?" he said drily.

Nelo gave him a startled look and then laughed at Arden's half smile.

"No, it is only…" He broke off and started again, "I have only known Josef as part of 'Falan and Josef.' In Lowertown, Ngahuru gave me coin to use my Lost Girls as drops for her information gatherers and street runners. Falan would whisper secrets to my girls that Josef had heard as he cooed about the gamblers. I did not understand what they were to each other. Josef flirted with everyone, and Falan didn't seem to care. I still don't know what they are to each other, but I believe what Josef knows, Falan knows, even now that Callis shares her bed." Nelo looked at Arden, "but you. You keep your secrets so close."

"It's because I have no friends. Let me have your letter. I will read it to you, go back to my bed, and sleep so deeply I won't even remember it in the morning." Arden held his palm out.

Nelo broke the seal on the letter and handed it over. Arden glanced over it quickly and then began,

Nelo,

Much has happened since you were taken by the crimpers, but I have not forgotten. Piffik and I used the coin for the Wrens, but most of it is still left in the paymaster chest. I took it with us to the shepherd's cottage in Vikland. I buried it again in one of our two hiding places.

I have talked with Piffik. He wants nothing more to do with it. You and I are not such delicate flowers, I know what price you paid for it. Use a traveling bag and take most of what is remaining. You can use the coin however you wish, share it with the Wrens or not, share it with your friends or not. It is enough to provide years without want or care.

I ask that you leave the chest hidden where you found it with the remaining coin. If I return to my father and I am not welcome, if I greet my brothers and am murdered for my inheritance, I want Siba to flee to the cottage and have enough coin to travel to Piffik and the other Conrosans as they build a new home in the outlands of Vikland.

I do not need to travel with you to know you will do as I wish. My Siba, my heart, is safe with you.

Rygee Namikk

Arden handed back the letter to Nelo without comment.

"Huh," Nelo grunted. "I thought the chest would have been buried here. Or Piffik and Rygee would have spent all of it. If we go to the shepherd's hut tomorrow, we cannot be back to Axefield until the very end of Rest Day."

Arden set the lantern on the ground throwing his face in shadows. His voice came out of the dark. "I think Zren, Josef, and I should go back to Axefield tomorrow with the wagon of everyone's wants and needs. You can go on to the shepherd's cottage on your own, and we will tell Piffik you will return when you return."

Nelo looked at him, astonished. "You won't go with me?"

Arden shook his head. "If the coin is ever missing when Siba needs it, I don't want to be blamed. If you return as an old man and the coin is not there, I do not want to be blamed. If I do not know where it is, I cannot ever be blamed for thieving it." He blew out a noisy breath. "You need to learn to read, Nelo. Someday, you could be murdered for what someone writes to you."

"I do not learn as quickly as you. I did not have Linna to teach me every night as you did."

"Now you have an entire Wet. The Conrosans have an evening school and a day school for the apprentices. You could ask Siba or Callis to teach you. Don't let your pride get in the way of what you need to know."

There was a long pause, and then Nelo spoke, "Dica said what you did for her. She told Tyra and me she had asked to go with you, and you refused her. You convinced her she was looking at her future as a problem and not as a possibility."

Nelo went on, "You and I...we did not know each other in Lowertown. I did not know you stole documents and maps for Ngahuru in the Flower District as well as coin and jewels for your own pocket. But now...now, you are one I count closer than a brother."

Nelo paused, but when Arden didn't say anything, he tried again, "I do not know all of your secrets, but I know some. I know you lost your position at the stables long before Kid came to Cloa. I know you are not Kereki, even though you pretended to pass for Linna's brother. Linna told me she mended you after a fight, a bad one. Parts of your body which have never seen the sun are just as sun-dark as the rest of you. I have seen sailors with your light brown skin, and I think, maybe from the Spice Island. The Wrens would never care, but perhaps someone who didn't know— or believed your insistence that you are Kereki—would not be so careful with documents written in Wester. And then I remembered you told the other Wrens you come from a family of thieves—'the family business,' you said—but I think it is more than that."

Arden remained as still as the night. His face was still hidden in shadows.

Wondering if he should say the rest, Nelo stopped for a moment. "When you and Josef acted as Matasi missionaries picking up lost soldiers in the Cold Mountains, the Viklander softfoots all knew who you were, Arden. I think," he took a deep breath and then voiced his suspicions, "I think you were part of the Viklander softfoots before we left Kerek City."

Nelo spoke slowly, "This is why I think so. I know you kept the secret you spoke Mata from Ngahuru until Siba Namikk forced your hand. This also makes sense to me as most Spice Islanders who sail on the seas speak Wester and Mata. Then I ask myself, 'What good is a thief who cannot read the documents he steals?' Unless of course, he is not a thief who cares about Keresh papers, but only those written in Mata and Wester. 'Now what softfoot would care about those?' I ask myself. 'Only someone who is spying on the West Islands and Matasi embasados and staff.' Now who would need such a softfoot who does not look like anyone else?

"Oh, I know it was said you reached out to the Viklander Bima Ritwik and added yourself to his softfoots because we needed more help than just Padro Morto and his coffin wagon and Ngahuru and her cart. But Inezi told me the Viklanders brought you coin to use instead of a paypacket from the stables so Ngahuru wouldn't know. Linna didn't know where you got your coin. No one knew.

"I know you use your dog Mother as an excuse not to live with the Wrens, so they do not know you get up before dawn to worship your Lost God. Or perhaps, it is you are meeting others here at the Huena Inn? Are you still softfooting, Arden? Does Ngahuru know? Do the Viklanders?" Nelo gave a long pause. "You have trusted me with so many of your secrets, Arden, I wanted to trust you with mine."

Arden bent down and picked up the lantern again. "You tell a pretty story, Nelo. I am not clever enough to be a softfoot for the Viklanders and for Ngahuru, even though they fought on the same side in this war. I could not be a softfoot here in Axefield listening in at doorways and also climb to the top of the scaffolding every day to build the new inn. I do not have the gold in my ears and on my fingers to show my Spice Islander wealth. You have never heard me speak Wester as all Spice Islanders do.

"I did not know how to read and write Keresh until we came to Manumina. You heard me struggle with my Keresh letters just as you struggled. Linna will tell you she did not have an easy time of it, hearing me read aloud night after night.

"As for speaking Mata? What people think is my Mata is only a few words of greeting and goodbyes." Arden gave his odd smile and in the poor lantern light, Nelo could not decide if Arden was telling the truth or not.

"I do trust you, Nelo, and because of this trust, I beg you, don't ask this of me, please. I have been a thief, and known as a thief, longer than our friendship. If you go to the shepherd's cottage and you do not find your treasure tomorrow, you will go back another time. And if you still do not find it? Then the suspicion will start in your head and move to your heart and our friendship will be destroyed. I do not have so many friends, that I wish to go on this adventure with you." He paused. "I do not want to waste a friendship on this."

Nelo was silent a long time until he knew his voice was under control. "I will go tomorrow, and the three of you will head back to Axefield. Tell Piffik, I will return when I return."

CHAPTER 6

THE MESSENGER BOY

Raul Huena had never seen the like in all his years in Vikland. The gleaming carriage, which had just pulled up into his courtyard, was gorgeously carved, meticulously maintained, and so old-fashioned as to be laughable. The man on the high seat was a West Islander of middle years, who looked more like a soldier than a mere driver. The carvings were of fish Raul had never seen and crests of sails and stars. It snapped into place for him then. He was looking at a carriage from the West Islands embasado. It made sense now. Nothing so fanciful would ever have traversed the Northern Track while the current King had been on the throne.

Raul looked around to send out one of the various youths he employed to greet the new guests and help them with their arrival. He wanted the Kereki, the one with a smooth tongue and clever wit; he was a favorite with all the guests. But then he remembered he had left with his friends to go to Rishka, the refugee camp, for supplies for the Conrosans. Raul stepped out himself.

The driver placed a wooden block on the ground. He stepped up on it to give himself additional height and opened the door. First one black carved cane poked out, then another one, then a leg in a Viklander black boot and dark trousers.

A young voice called from inside the carriage, "This, my friend, is where I need your assistance."

Raul hurried forward and watched as the West Islander grabbed under the forearm and the bicep of the Viklander. Raul did the same, and together they lifted the young man out and held him while he got both canes under him to support his weight. He had the classic strong features of the Viklanders which looked out from so many tapestries and paintings of the warriors. Raul noted the missing leg below the left knee and snapped his eyes back to the young man's chagrinned face.

"I finally learned how to ride a horse with one leg and now my cousin's aunt decides I need to ride in her carriage. Thank you. I will get this figured out some day, but today is not that day."

A Viklander relative of the West Islands Ambassador? Was the Ambassador doing the Empress a favor? Quickly, Raul folded his hands and began the formal introductions as if the young man were a personal friend of the Ambassador. When he finished, the young man flashed such a gorgeous smile Raul could not help smile back at him.

"You are too kind, Raul Huena of the Huena Inn. I am just the son of a Vikland coffee farmer. My name is Nari Ulani. I am only traveling in such fine accommodations because the Empress of Vikland and the West Islands Ambassador have sent me to Axefield to find Ngahuru of the West Islands. So, you see? I am little more than a messenger boy."

Raul stepped aside and invited him in. "Please come in and take refreshment and rest. I will send a runner to find anyone you seek."

The Viklander used a swinging gait to pull himself forward with the canes. Raul stopped to ask the driver if he wished to have someone put away the horses for him and a boy sent to watch the carriage. The driver assured him he would take care of it all himself and stay with the carriage the entire time they would be in Axefield.

As Raul walked behind the Viklander, he took the opportunity to observe him closely. He was taller than Raul but not by much. His dark Vik clothes were a little baggy, and he was still awkward on the canes. Raul guessed a soldier injured near the end of the war. His sleek black hair was already shoulder length with a very tiny braid, so either he had lost his braid of honor to the bounty hunters early in the war or it had been a hasty hack in battle. His face was classic Viklander—strong and sharp—striking rather than handsome. Raul guessed the soldier was younger than his son Dylis. Raul took two long strides and moved up beside Nari. He led the soldier over to two comfortable chairs in a small alcove.

"Do we have the privilege of keeping you for a few days?" He asked as he flicked his wrist at one of the women standing behind the desk to come join them.

"Only one night, I am disappointed to say. I must return tomorrow to Juisiti with or without one who is called Ngahuru of the West Islands."

Raul introduced the young woman next to him, "This is Claire. She will arrange to have food and drink brought to you here while we prepare your room. I will send out runners to find the West Islander. I know who she is, she stays here at the inn. When your room is ready, someone will come to assist you. What time would you like Ngahuru to arrive at your door?"

"I am also looking for a Kereki named 'Kid.' I am sorry, I do not know his family name."

Raul nodded. "I know of him as well. The Kerekis here in Axefield do not have a second name. Do you want Ngahuru and Kid to come to your rooms together or separately?"

Nari considered. "Separately please, as soon as they are found. If at all possible, could I have coffee and fingersweets served when Ngahuru is shown to my room? My aunt would never forgive me if I mistreated one of her countrywomen."

"Certainly. Claire will have a person outside your room for the rest of today for you to send on any errand you need." He gave a short bow and lightly touched Claire on the elbow to follow him. He spoke low as they walked away, "Give him the best available room on the ground floor. Also send out food and drink to the West Islander in the stables. Have someone find Piffik Qanaq and ask him for a Kereki to stand outside the room and run errands for the rest of the day. I want someone who does not speak Vik, so Nari Ulani's secrets will not be overheard and become gossip. Claire," he stopped and looked at her, "Nari Ulani is your responsibility until he leaves tomorrow. He is here at the Empress's command and is somehow related to the West Islands Ambassador, a sister to their King. I want him treated as near royalty no matter how much he protests he is only the son of a coffee farmer. I trust you to do this."

Claire looked back at the soldier. "It will be my pleasure."

***

Kid hurried down the hall smoothing down his still wet hair. The runner had found him less than a decon ago at the bookseller in Axefield. He had been told to clean up well and wear Viklander clothes to meet with Nari Ulani. Then he was to find the room with the person stationed outside the door. Kid had wasted a few moments looking for Zren Janin to try to learn just where Nari fit in the Ulani family, only to learn Josef, Nelo, Arden, and Zren were gone for the rest of the day and tomorrow. Kid ran up to Arden's cubby above the stables and borrowed his Viklander clothes and boots. He had none of his own, and Arden was his closest size. Now he glanced down at the shiny polished boots, smoothed down his trouser legs and the sleeves of the shirt. He stretched himself as tall as he could, then turned the corner to the room and there was…Falan.

"You!" they both said together.

Falan squinted at him. "Are you here to replace me? I was told to be here until the Viklander went to bed."

"I'm here to speak with him. Do I just knock?" Kid said.

"Ngahuru left not long ago. She had me knock, walk in, announce her, and then wait out here. I don't know if that was because of who she is or who he is. A woman brought coffee a while ago." Falan sniffed. "You're not as important as Ngahuru, but I'm not so foolish as to cause trouble when she already showed me what to do."

Falan gave a huge put-upon sigh and knocked discreetly. A voice said to enter, and she walked in ahead of Kid.

"Nari Ulani, Kid is here to see you."

Nari smiled. "Thank you." Falan turned to walk out. She rolled her eyes as she passed Kid, and he heard the door close behind him. Kid stepped forward and bowed the Viklander short bow. Nari remained sitting in a comfortable chair. On a side table next to him there was a tray with two empty coffee cups and small plates with scattered crumbs.

"Kid! I am beyond glad to meet you. Is it all right if we speak Keresh? I am not so well-spoken in Wester as you are." Nari gestured to a comfortable chair facing his own. "Forgive me for not standing and greeting you in the formal way."

Kid sat. He wondered if he should tell Nari that Zren had translated the letter for him.

Before he could confess, Nari spoke first, "Mmm. You are younger than I expected. Although my cousins insisted all of you Wrens are fiercer than any monster in our Vikland sagas and should be treated as the warriors you are."

Nari looked at the expression on Kid's face. "I did not mean to embarrass you. Perhaps if I had met you when I was fighting in the Cold Mountains, I would not have spent so much time suffering at the Academy of Pain and Misery in Juisiti." He waved his hand at the empty space where his lower leg used to be.

Kid didn't know what to say to that.

Nari tipped his head to the side and continued, "So let me tell you why I am here." He reached down to the travel bag beside his chair and fished out several letters. He sorted out two. "Do you know Zren Janin?"

Kid nodded.

"Good. These are for him. I will give them to you and my duty to my cousin Solkka is done." He sorted out two more. "Do you know the two men who dressed up as Matasi missionaries? They did at least one rescue, or perhaps many, beneath the Cold Mountains. It would have been after the firing of the fort at Earles. Tedros said something about a dog named Mother."

Kid cleared his throat. "Josef and Arden. Josef would have dressed up as a Matasi woman, and Arden had a black-haired dog named Mother he used to track lost Viklanders."

Nari looked relieved. "Good. We are talking about the same two men. These letters are for them." Nari handed them to Kid. "My cousin, Tedros, said he did not know if they spoke Wester like Zren, so he wrote his letters in Keresh. Truthfully? Keresh is the only other language he barely learned besides Vik. But you didn't hear that from me."

Kid looked at the letters in his hand and up at Nari who was now leaning back in his chair.

Nari nodded. "You are wondering, I think, where is your letter from my aunt, Hilanna Ulani? But I see now, you are a man of few words and quiet ways. Perhaps your letter to my aunt was so brief of words, because you did not wish to be a braggart. Or perhaps it was so empty of details because you wished to pretend to have done something in order to extract coin and pity from a tender-hearted woman."

"No!" Kid was shocked into speaking. "No," he said again quietly. "If you spoke with Jenny, and I hope you did, you would know I am the man who saved Solkka's life, and Mother Ulani had expressed a desire to meet me as I wish to meet the Ulani family."

"Go on." Nari waved his hand. "Tell me the story Jenny would have told me."

CHAPTER 7

KID TELLS SOME BUT NOT ALL

Kid looked startled for a moment and then, "This is the story as it happened." He leaned forward in his chair. "I was a Wren of Ngahuru's placed at Evensong, a great house between the Northern Track and the Cold Mountains. In the beginning when I took the position, we did not know how much the master of Evensong would throw his support to the King of Kerek. But over the course of the war, he entertained Kereki army officers. He offered his land for an encampment where the Kereki army would receive supplies, send out patrols, and keep Viklanders from reaching the battles east near Balza. The news I overheard, the dispatches I read, the maps I saw were very valuable to the Viklander softfoots at Fortika.

"Then the owner of Evensong decided he needed to fight himself, and he called up his own militia. He forced all of us in the house and grounds to join and march with him. We had two skirmishes. At the second, his personal aide was killed, and my master selected me to carry all the rosters of the militia, their locations, strengths, and possible battle plans. Once I had the documents in my possession, I deserted my position, circled wide about the battle until I found two Viklander sentries and asked to see their commander.

"They were not fools; they took me to another. I offered him the documents and explained what they were. The soldiers took their knives from my throat and allowed me to show them the maps I was carrying. The contents of my travel bag were taken by one of the soldiers to someone higher up.

"I said if they let me return to Evensong, I could get them more information in the future. I told them to give my description to their softfoots, and I would be their eyes and ears inside the great house. The captain looked me up and down and then agreed. The sentries were told to take me far to the south of the fighting, and then release me to find my way back.

"It is then we met Solkka. I do not say 'found' because your cousin had hidden himself and our Jenny so well, we walked by within a jeong bong length without detecting him." Kid stopped and licked his lower lip. "It is always my business to notice things. I did not notice him. He would not have been found if he had not called out to us."

Nari filled a cup with water and pushed it across the table. Kid nodded his thanks and drained it.

"I knew if I could get them to Cloa—the hub of Ngahuru's Wrens—they could be taken all the way to Vikland. We had no coin to make this happen. Solkka cut off his braid so I could collect the bounty and use the coin to have a healer stop Jenny from bleeding out, hire two horses, and buy a little food. I got them to Cloa. Arden and Linna lived too close to the center of town, but we risked it. Jenny and I showed our faces and without a braid, Solkka can make himself look other than a Viklander soldier. Linna hid us in her house until Padro Morto took them to Ishes. Your garrison helped them to Juisiti. He was not in the battle I was in, but it was when Solkka got the scar which ruined his pretty face," Kid finished.

"You would think so," Nari shrugged nonchalantly, "But Tedros still grumbles the women think the scar looks dashing, and Solkka is so brave. So, they trail him in adoration, leaving Tedros with a cold and empty bed."

Kid snorted in spite of himself and Nari's grin widened. "Good to know you haven't fallen for his charm." Nari thumped his cane on the floor. "Well, that was actually more information than Jenny and my aunt shared with me, so I am going to accept what you say as truth."

Kid stiffened. "I am not a liar."

Nari looked down his nose and smiled blandly. "Did you not hear the words which have fallen from my lips? I said you were not one as well." He paused. "So, tell me the events of the second time you and my cousin crossed paths."

"Jenny was not there," Kid protested.

Nari smiled thinly. "I know. But Quan was, and I met with him in Juisiti before I traveled here. You know of him?"

"Quan was also a softfoot with a parent or a grandparent who was not a Viklander. Because of this, his face allowed him to pass more easily through Kerek." Kid looked at Nari thoughtfully. "It became too dangerous for me to stay at Evensong any longer. The master knew he had a traitor in his house. His suspicions fell on another footman who liked to tell secrets to the pretty girls in the kitchens to make himself seem important. I did not flee and draw attention to myself. Instead, I gave my notice properly and made my way to Cloa.

"Arden had lost his position there some time earlier. He had not learned the trick of being in two places at one time—at his work in the stables and out in the countryside rescuing Viklanders. My plan was to see if I could earn the open position in the stable and then live with Linna and Arden, so Linna would not have to softfoot alone so much.

"The day I arrived, Arden fed me and told me to rest as much as I could. Linna would have a task for me as soon as she came home, he said. He had to leave and find out if Falan," Kid pointed to the door, "was in danger. He and his dog were gone for a long time before Linna, Quan, Solkka, and Falan arrived. I explained to them what I knew, and it was decided Linna and I would drive a cart with the others to Manumina. I watched as Linna arranged the table and the house with pottery and clothes to give Arden a secret message telling him of our plans.

"We went to the stables where Linna knew the stable boy who cared for the horses which came late at night. We were discovered by others—not friends of Vikland—and Solkka and Quan used their bongs to defend us. But there were too many. Next thing I remember is Padro Morto pulling us out of the coffins at Manumina." Kid paused. "I suppose you could say Solkka saved *my* life for without his strength on the bongs, we would have all died."

"Yes, well," Nari responded, "He and his brothers practiced on each other every moment they were not working in the coffee fields. I am not surprised he was able to stand against so many." Nari looked at Kid a long time. "This story too is the truth as I heard it. Are you hungry?"

"What?" Kid was confused at the abrupt change.

"Are you hungry? I am told all I need to do is tell the person outside my door—Falan, you said?—whatever I wish and it will be brought to me."

Kid swallowed hard. He knew if *he* poked his head out the door and told Falan to bring his end of day meal, she would refuse. Or she would bring it flavored with one of Siba's potions of misery.

"Shall I ask her in?" Kid offered. "Perhaps *you* would like to tell Falan what you would like to eat."

Nari's face broke into a slow grin as he understood what Kid didn't say. He nodded.

"Perhaps that would be best."

Kid opened the door, gestured to Falan, and stepped aside as she followed him in.

Nari gave her an amused look. "Falan, I understand the Wrens listen to you when Ngahuru is not in the room." Falan's eyebrows went up, and she narrowed her eyes at Kid.

Then without warning, she smiled blandly at Nari. "Of course."

"I understand tomorrow is the Conrosan rest day." Nari waited for her to nod before he continued, "The Empress of Vikland has entrusted me with the coin to be paid to each of you for the good you did for Vikland." He gave her a thoughtful look. "This is not a surprise to any of you, I hope. Ngahuru negotiated for you many days ago."

Falan curled her lip. It was not a smile.

"We heard. A soldier's pay for a year… and a home in Vikland *if* we wish."

Nari nodded again. "The West Islands Ambassador has sent along a guard and offered her carriage to me to bring your reward to you and ensure it was given to the correct people. Could you bring all of the Wrens here to this room tomorrow a decon before midday? Then with the West Islander who traveled with me and Ngahuru as Witnesses, your coin will be given to each of you. Is this acceptable?"

Falan was silent for a moment, thinking. "We have three who are Wrens who have traveled a half day away from here to gather supplies and medicines for the Conrosans. They will not be here until after midday tomorrow. We have one—Jenny—in the Keopi district, and I do not know where that is or how far away. There are two who have married and moved to Juisiti. If we sent a rider to them now, they could not arrive until tomorrow late."

"Mmmm. That is too late, I must leave tomorrow midday to bring Ngahuru to the embasado on a different matter. I could stop in Juisiti for the two at that time. Is there one you trust—not a Viklander and not a West Islander—whom you trust to hold their coin for the ones who are a half day away?"

Falan looked at Kid and together they said, "Siba Namikk."

"Bring her as well."

The Wrens stood there uncertainly for a moment before Falan cleared her throat and offered, "Is there anything else?"

As if it was an afterthought, Nari added, "Falan, could you find Claire and ask her to send end of day meal? I know it will be busier for her later, and I do not want to be a bother."

Falan gave a half smile. "Certainly."

Nari tipped his head to the side. "When Raul Huena asked you to be available to me, did he say you must only stand outside my door?"

The smile fell from Falan's face, and Kid recognized the look that replaced it. Nari Ulani was about to have his ears abused… and harshly.

Before she could draw a breath, Nari interrupted, "I only ask because I would like to ask you and Kid to join me for end of day. You are quite famous in Vikland, you know. The Empress encouraged stories of your rescues and escapes as proof we were fighting a good fight. I would love to tell those I know, I had end of day meal with some of the Wrens who fought for Vikland. Would that be possible?"

Falan looked uneasily back and forth between Nari and Kid.

Nari nodded. "That is correct. I am asking Kid to join us so no one mistakes our meal for anything but what it is. Or if you would be more comfortable, you may ask another Wren to join us. Would that be acceptable to you?"

Falan nodded a little uncertainly. "I would like to ask Callis."

"Agreed. Please let Claire know there will be four for our meal."

Falan left with a small smile playing about her lips.

Kid stared at Nari in astonishment. "Are you in the Diplo Corp?"

Nari laughed. "Never! I just finished my third year of military service." He tapped on his stump. "A little early. But I have two older sisters." He sobered immediately. "I *had* two older sisters. Lissil died in a battle near the Huk River. She was the same age as Solkka and already a field manager for my father's coffee farm. But when the Empress called for soldiers, she rejoined."

Kid said softly, "May her name live on."

Nari looked startled, but repeated, "May her name live on." He paused for a moment and then added, "And that, Kid, is why I am here talking to you.

"My father is Devi Ulani's younger brother, Gayo. Our coffee fields are just to the east of theirs. My grandmother's house is between the two farms. What I am saying, Kid, is the news from one house travels easily to the other. My father heard of the letter you had sent to Hilanna Ulani. He talked it over with my sister, Nadja, and me.

"At first, we thought it was a trick. We had heard of others who claimed to be Kereki friends and lovers and spouses of fallen Viklanders and demanding land or coin or a place in the family. But Jenny said she knew you, and it was true what your letter said, you were the reason Solkka and she were still alive. Also, in your letter, you knew enough to write to my aunt in Wester, a language she still prefers over Vik. That is not common knowledge.

"So, my father went to Devi and Hilanna and talked to them of what we needed to do to make our farms thrive until all the soldiers in the family could come home. It was decided, I would be sent from the Keopi District to discuss it with my aunt's sister the Ambassador, meet with you, and if I believed you to be full of truth to offer you a possible future."

Kid stilled. This was what he wanted. He corrected himself: he hoped they would offer what he wanted.

"My parents had four children to carry on their coffee farm. My oldest sister, Nadja, runs the business accounts under my father's guidance. On the coffee farms, we would say she is my father's Right Hand. Until the war, Lissil was the field manager, and I was training to join her as soon as I finished my three years in the military. The field managers are called the Left Hands. My youngest brother, Leo, is still in the academies and has not yet decided what he wishes to do after he finishes his military service—it is years away. With Lissil's death and my…" Nari waved at his missing leg, "it is too much for my parents and Nadja, and too much for me to walk in the fields daily to inspect the crops as the only field manager."

Nari paused. "Do you understand what I am saying, Kid? If you will consent to travel with me tomorrow, we can reach my home before the heaviest of the rains. During this Wet, you must learn Vik. This is not a choice. It is the language the coffee pickers speak, and you will have to give them instructions and talk with them. I will teach you to be a coffee farm's Left Hand, as I have been taught. My sister will teach you what she has done in my absence. In return, you will be housed and fed, and you will be tutored at home as Jenny is tutored.

"I have been told your wish is to attend our academies and join our softfoots and work in Kerek." Nari gave a sly smile to Kid's startled look. "*If* you are a satisfactory coffee hand for three years, or until my youngest brother finishes his military service, then my father is prepared to pay for your classes and boarding at the academies. I know this will make you older than some of your classmates. But there are many who start later or drop out and come back, even more so with the war. You will not stand out so much. If you do not like the coffee farm or cannot learn it, my father will pay only your travel to Kerek or Matasi for you to start a different life."

Nari was quiet for a moment. "My uncle Devi offered to help us until my brother finishes his service and can take his place on the farm. But Uncle and Kaede have their own challenges. Tedros still has one more year in the military. Jenny is learning to be a Right Hand and not the Left. Solkka would leave the Diplo for the Ulani family and come home to farm with our fathers if his parents asked, but it would crush his spirit. He is more like his mother than anyone."

Nari gave Kid a thoughtful look. "I believe your letter came to Devi and Hilanna at the time it did for a purpose." He paused. "What do you say? Do you leave tomorrow for the Keopi District?"

Kid sighed in relief. His instincts had been right to have Zren write the letter in Wester. He wondered if Falan had told Nari his plans...and why. It didn't matter. He was going to go.

"I accept. I will pack my bags and books and be ready to leave after our meeting tomorrow." Kid hesitated. "I would ask only one thing. Please do not say anything in front of the other Wrens. I will say goodbye only to Arden, Dica, and Zren Janin."

Nari raised an eyebrow. "Well, that simplifies things. I did not have permission to bring anyone but you home." At the knock at the door, Nari looked over his shoulder. Kid stood up to open it.

"Claire! How lovely!" Nari struggled to stand. "I certainly did not expect you to drop everything to bring our meal personally. That smells delicious! Are you able to join us?" Nari smiled widely at her.

Claire smiled back. "Thank you, no. I must find out what happened to the one posted outside your door, and then I must arrange a meal for the one guarding your carriage. Nari Ulani, the Huena Inn does provide someone to oversee the stables, your man does not need to stay with the horses."

Nari lifted his shoulders and let them drop. "I am only the messenger boy. The carriage and the driver belong to the West Islands Ambassador and her orders outrank mine." He grinned. "But I will share your news and concern when I return the carriage to her tomorrow."

Falan and Callis appeared in the doorway. Both had bathed and changed into Viklander clothes. Callis had braided her brown hair, but Falan's dark hair was so short it barely skimmed her ears.

Claire raised her eyebrows at Falan, and Nari quickly interjected, "It's my fault, Claire. I asked her and her friend to join us. They know my cousins, and I hoped to hear news of them."

Claire gave him a surprised look, but quickly schooled her face. "Of course. Will there be anything else?" She put her hand on the doorknob.

Nari gave a mischievous glance at Falan before he spoke. "If there is, I will send Falan to find you."

CHAPTER 8

HEROES WITH FEET OF CLAY

The next morning Zren wandered out of the infirmary to find Josef and Arden already packing a wagon from the building Piffik had converted to his workshop.

"Have you eaten first meal? Where's Nelo?"

Josef raised an eyebrow. "Good morning to you too! As for Nelo, he left the Wren house before first light, and naturally, I assumed he had crawled into your bed for comfort."

Zren shook his head, confused. "No, I slept alone all night."

Josef chuffed. "I was joking, Zren. I was saying big, strong Nelo crawled into your bed for little old you to protect him against the scary monsters." He sighed dramatically. "My talents are so underappreciated." He fished in a pocket tied about his waist. "Here. Siba gave us a list of medicines she needed. The smart woman she is, she wrote the list in Conrosan. I am assuming she knew that unless she gave you a specific task, you would just hang over the edge of the wagon and watch us work."

Zren scowled. "I don't work on an empty stomach."

"Well then, you should have gotten up earlier," Arden said crossly as he carried out another load of tools. "The cook in the kitchen here is not as good or as generous as Rygee, so you better smile pretty and get there quickly if you don't want to feel your belly against your backbone all day."

Zren gave him a shocked look and then hurried off without another word. Josef looked at Arden.

"So, Nelo isn't with any one of us, you're all persnickety, and a horse is gone. What did the letter say?"

"What letter?"

"Zren doesn't read Keresh he says, and Nelo didn't come to me. That leaves you," Josef pointed out.

"Maybe he is going to wait until he gets back to Axefield, and that's why he left before daybreak." Arden stopped and looked at the wagon. "That's everything on Piffik's list, what's next?"

"The rag and bone cart. I say we just bring everything, and what Callis and Dica can't mend or fix, we pay to have the tailors make over for the little ones. Tyra and Therin look like they are going to grow right out of their shirts any day now."

The two pulled the lightweight cart into the sunlight so they could see more clearly. Arden grabbed an armload and dumped it into the wagon. Josef carefully shook out each item before tossing it into the wagon.

"What are you looking for?" Arden looked at Josef suspiciously.

"Coin mostly. But we probably should remove any papers or knives if we find them."

Arden pulled out a pair of shiny black Viklander boots from the heap. "Ah, Nelo will be sorry to miss these." He sat down and tried to pull them on. "Ah well, maybe he will get them after all." He pulled off the too small boots and slipped his battered leathers back on.

The sound of coins hitting wood had both of them alert.

"It was this traveler's cloak," Josef began, "I shook it and…"

It was Ngahuru's disguise. The faded and patched cloak the Wrens had all described as 'dirt-colored.' Now as Josef held it open, they could both see tiny and large pockets sewn all over the inside lining.

"Why would she have left it here?" Josef questioned.

"Why not?" Arden countered. "She's not going to wear it at Axefield or Juisiti. Since she met the Empress, she has been going about as Ngahuru with fully dyed hair and skin and both functioning hands." Arden paused. "Lately, she is in Juisiti at the embasado more than she is with us."

Josef handed it to Arden. "Let me watch you work."

Arden gave him a long-suffering sigh. "I was a thief, not a pickpocket." But he rapidly searched the pockets, and the contents disappeared in his tunic, up his sleeve, even a delicate stiletto with its needle-thin sheath slipped into the leather thong tying back his braid. He ran his long, narrow fingers along the seams and the folds of the hood and fished out coins and another narrow blade, this one no longer than his finger. He handed the cloak back to Josef who stood gaping.

Arden laughed at his expression. "What? Tiju Tia no longer exists, so this poor cloak and all of its belongings were without a home." He smiled wickedly. "I gave them a home."

Josef nodded. "I'm not disagreeing with your right to the belongings, only in awe of your talent. Truly. Callis told me once she had watched you thieve among the men in her father's tavern. I thought she was over describing your abilities. I will apologize immediately to her."

"Did she also tell you her father paid me never to step foot in his tavern again? He said he was an honest man trying to make an honest living for his three daughters, all apprenticed to make a better living than a tavern owner. He said he had his hands full keeping his daughters and his wife safe from harm; he couldn't keep an eye out for me as well.

"I thought he was mocking me and said so. Then he explained if the men knew they had been robbed in his tavern, they would not hunt for me in the streets, but only hurt his daughters to punish him. He paid me to take my talents elsewhere to keep his daughters safe."

Arden gave his odd smile letting Josef in on the joke, "When I returned a year later to have a drink and take my ease as a paying customer, he pulled out a cudgel as thick as my leg and kept it close the entire time I was drinking. He remembered me, and wanted me to know it."

Josef had to hang on to the side of the rag and bone wagon he was laughing so hard. Zren walked over to the stables and asked what was so funny.

"Josef is amused Callis's father was my Protector and kept me from harm after the Matasi missionaries left Lowertown," Arden said straight-faced.

"Truly?" Zren squinted at him. "Ngahuru said you thieved for her in the houses near the embasados and in the Flower District where the city and court workers lived. It is why none of the littlest Wrens from the Sinner's District or Lowertown knew you."

Josef chuckled. "Well, I guess you won't be going back to Kerek City if even Zren knows where you softfoot at night."

Arden shrugged. "I don't plan on thieving again, but whether my past rides with me on the wagon depends on other people and the stories they tell." He grabbed more clothes, quickly searched them, and dumped them on the wagon.

After getting one of the empty cheese casks for them to collect the coins, papers, and other bits and pieces from the clothes, Zren joined them. Arden emptied his pockets, sleeves, and braid of the knives and tiny blades he collected earlier and poured them into the cheese cask, earning a gasp from Zren.

"You carry all that metal about you even when you are with friends?"

Arden gave Zren a sly smile. "You've met Falan, haven't you?"

Zren shot a look at Josef before answering, "Yes. It's true. She scares me too."

Josef gave a heartfelt sigh. "Zren, she only goes after you so viciously because she knows she can frighten you." He paused.

"Falan doesn't know she can stop fighting everything and everyone. Or she does and doesn't know how to stop. She doesn't know the difference between not fighting and giving up. I don't know if she will ever have soft edges..." Josef stopped talking as he noted Arden staring at him. "What?"

"Do you know any other fairy tales, Josef? Falan is a dragon and you are her treasure. She will fight whoever she must to keep you all to herself." Arden watched Josef carefully. He wondered if Josef's shocked silence meant he understood what had been said.

The rag and bone cart was now empty, and Zren was quickly checking all the hidden compartments by lifting latches, moving levers and locks. Inside one, Zren pulled out a Kereki army chest. It was so heavy, the muscles corded on his forearms.

"Where did that come from?" Josef broke his gaze from Arden and gasped.

"Um. The Kereki army?" answered Zren.

"No. Why is that in here?" Arden snapped.

Zren thought for a moment. "Yes, well. Nobody told me I couldn't tell you." He set the chest on the back of the cart. "When Rygee, Nelo, and Piffik were coming back from getting Nelo free from the crimpers, they saw a Kereki army wagon overrun by bandits. When only two bandits were left and they were taking out this paychest, Nelo and Rygee killed the bandits and took the payroll. Piffik had me bury the chest in the stables at Manumina. Ngahuru saw me, and the three travelers told the story that night at end of day meal.

"When we had to leave Manumina, Rygee packed the chest. Piffik was gone to see the Council of Wisdom and Rygee didn't want to leave the chest behind for the Matasi soldiers.

"At the shepherd's cottage, my head started to hurt so I laid down on the floor inside the cottage. Siba came in and waved some of that good incense under my nose. But I was still awake and saw Rygee move a table and a rug and lift a piece of the floor up. He pulled out some Viklander clothes and some short bongs. Then he went out and came back in with an old blanket. Under the blanket was this chest. Rygee put the chest in the hole in the floor, covered it with the blanket, and then moved the chair and table back over it. Then he swept the floor around me. I pretended to be asleep so when Siba came back, she would give me more of the incense that gives me such nice dreams."

Josef looked confused. "So how did it get from there to here?"

"During the night, Rygee and Siba left before morning to take the food to the refugees while it was still cool out. I found you sleeping with Callis," Zren looked at Josef. "As we were leaving, I remembered Rygee had forgotten the chest and so I told Ngahuru. She said she would take care of it." Zren pointed to the chest. "And she did. Here it is!"

"So, Rygee doesn't know this chest is here," Arden demanded.

Zren looked down at the chest and back at the Wrens. "I don't know what Rygee knows or doesn't know. Ngahuru just told me to come with you today to bring the chest back without all of Axefield finding out about it."

Arden slammed the flat of his hand against the side of the wagon, then turned abruptly and walked away.

Once he was out of earshot, Zren turned to Josef, "What did I say?"

Josef gave him a small sad smile. "You have shown Arden his heroes have feet of clay. I think his head and his heart are fighting very hard right now as he tries to justify that which is not justifiable."

"I don't know what that means," Zren said in a small voice.

"Zren, did Ngahuru write down instructions for you? Or did she just say to bring the chest back?"

Zren looked at Josef with a troubled face. "No, I said I could remember it. I knew all the carts and wagons we used for the Wrens had hidden compartments and I knew how to open them."

"Ahhh," Josef said and fell silent as he watched Arden gesturing and talking to himself with his back to them. "Zren?" Josef began, without moving his eyes from Arden. "Do you and Arden go back on the top of the new inn tomorrow?"

"Yes. Now that the trusses and the roof are done, we are taking down the scaffolding at the very top. Piffik said I need to do a better job of tying my fall ropes because now no one will be my partner except for Arden. If I am so careless, Piffik says, it will endanger Arden and he needs him as a finish carpenter, he is that good."

"I see." Josef fell silent again. "Well, I certainly can't be your partner," he muttered under his breath.

Arden walked back to them. "Change in plans. Zren, gather Siba's medicines. Josef already gave you the list. Josef, ask the baker for a bag of flour and then go to the cheesemaker and see if she has anything to send along to the work camp. You two will have to go back to Axefield with the wagon and horses.

"I will take a horse and go after Nelo. He's headed in another direction, but he is only a decon or two ahead of me. We won't catch up to you, but tell Piffik we will be back tonight and I will *not* disappoint him. Tell no one—no one, Zren, including Ngahuru—we have the paychest with us." Arden looked at Josef. "That includes Falan as well. This is a battle that must be fought by others. We Wrens? We just pick up the broken bodies."

Arden started to walk away, and Josef called out after him, "You better stop at the kitchens and get food for all of us. You can't expect me to travel half the day with Zren without feeding him. I'm liable to reach Axefield missing an arm at least!"

Zren heard Arden's laugh as he turned back and smiled at them. His braid swung easily as he changed direction and headed for the kitchens.

***

Josef had been the tallest of the Wrens, next to Oro, and now he stretched out his long legs resting his new boots on the buckboard. He had found clean Kereki-style baggy pants, billowy shirt, a tunic, and even a pair of Kereki ties—red and brown. He used the end of one of them now to brush off an imaginary speck of dust from a pair of polished, black Viklander boots. He explained how he had, and almost all of the Wrens had, lost their few clothes in the communal laundry because no one had told them to stitch a family mark in them.

Zren nodded. "This was a good idea of Dica's to take the rag and bone cart for clothes for everyone."

"Dica has lots of good ideas," Josef said, "It will be interesting to see how her story will end. She has already made it possible for Callis to leave the laundry and train with Siba. This means Callis and Falan will now stay through the Wet. I'm still working in the inn, so I can befriend the horse master and ride as I wish. Perhaps by the time the weather turns again, we will all be ready to leave."

Josef sighed and looked at his boots. Then he put on a bright smile and grinned at Zren.

"You know, I don't believe I have ever heard the story of how you got your name. Children in Lowertown never have two names. Nelo said you were called 'Red' before you disappeared. I have been told of a Conrosan folk hero named Zren Janin which we were to use in our rescues. Supposedly, Viklanders were well-read enough to know that was an offer of help."

Zren smiled and leaned back against the wagon seat letting the reins rest lightly in his hands.

"First, I must tell you the story of Zren Janin and the Legion of Heroes, and then I will tell you how I met Miyamoto Suki in Ribelo, Matasi and became Zren Janin…"

CHAPTER 9

TWO VIEWS, ONE WAR

Nari Ulani thought the end of day meal would be cautious conversation, a silent measuring of foe or friend. Kid, he believed, was reserved by nature. But while Falan had been wary and cautious, Callis had been open and friendly. Nari had learned the most from her as she had described how the Wrens worked together, and their plans for the future.

She described how she had been a tailor in Kerek City, the daughter of a tavern owner. How, once she had met Siba Namikk and Rell Huena at Manumina, she wished to be a healer. But it would not have been wise to be apprenticed to the healer in Huk, and be under another's watchful eye. and so she had supported herself in Huk through work at the toggery and tailoring. She told how she had been proud Ngahuru had chosen her to be the center of the network in Huk and then had glossed over how the center had somehow moved to Cloa.

Falan had hissed, "Ross," but Callis pretended not to hear.

She had merely shrugged and switched to telling stories of how she and Falan had dressed up as Kereki males to move Viklanders east from the battlefields north of Balza to Cloa where Linna and Arden could arrange transport with Padro Morto and his coffin wagon, the cheese cart when Zren drove it, Bima's Matasi missionaries, or Ngahuru's rag and bone wagon with Zren or Oro as her *titiro mai ki ahau.*

"But how?" Nari had interjected. "How did you know who needed help? How did you not get shot with a bolt or knocked on the head with a bong?" He paused. "Until we Viklanders knew who you were, we were as much a threat to you as the Kereki soldiers."

"Some took greater risks than others. Inezi, one of Bima's softfoots and helpers, taught Dica, Nelo, and Tyra some Vik. Josef would sing your ballads and battle songs when he was trailing Viklanders, trying to decide if they were lost or just on patrol," she smiled slyly, "at least that is what he told me. They were probably naughty ditties he learned from the sentries at the encampments where he passed documents."

She paused, serious again. "Your soldiers were told to trust the friends of Zren Janin. Arden and Nelo would search for lost soldiers and patrols. They took the greatest risks. Usually, you were already in one of our barns or buildings by the time Falan or Linna or I would come to take you to the next place of safety, or to have you travel with Padro Morto.

"It wasn't perfect. We couldn't reach many of you trapped in the Cold Mountains. There were too few who were friendly to us, and we were spread over too large of an area. Sometimes your soldiers on watch were too quick to fire their crossbows, and we had to abandon helping you, or Kereki militia were too close for us to move you safely and still keep our heads attached to our bodies." Callis pinched her lips together. "There were injuries. But they are not my stories to tell."

Nari started slowly, "I have met Jenny. She lives with my aunt and uncle at the next farm over. She was nothing more than a child when Solkka brought her back from the Academy of Healing." He paused. "Were there others so young?"

Falan grimaced. "For many years, Nelo ran Lost Girls and Lost Boys in Kerek City. Jenny, Tyra, and Dica were all his. Dica grew too tall and plain-looking, but she is quite clever and he taught her to be a pickpocket. When Ngahuru told Dica to find the others, she went first to the other Lost Girls. Then, Nelo himself climbed into Ngahuru's wagon. If he would have left them behind…" she faltered and then added, "They were too young to survive on their own."

Falan went on to say how Dica had been a between maid at Regno, one of the northern estates by the Cold Mountains. She had learned how to be a maid in a great house by being a servant for the servants' quarters. Falan had wrinkled her nose then. It hadn't been a nice position, but Dica had been the center in the north. Because the master had been away so much, the other servants were nonattentive, absorbed in their own interests. She was able to sneak away and hide Viklanders, pass messages from Kid at Evensong to Tyra and the Vikland network to the east, and to Nelo and the Wrens to the south and west.

"She is still too young to survive on her own, especially in Kerek. But she is cleverer than most her age. She merely needs a *titiro mai ki ahau* to hide behind until she looks old enough that others do not immediately assume she can be taken advantage of."

Callis continued the story, "Ngahuru and Rygee came to bring us all in. Falan had been discovered. Ngahuru wanted all the Wrens to flee. Ngahuru sent Oro to help Nelo and Arden bring the others in, but Oro was captured for his trouble, and Dica rescued herself."

"Any others? What about the ones who are not here at Axefield?" Nari asked.

"The three, Nelo, Arden, and Josef, are younger than Falan and I, but older than Kid. They have very different skills, and no one would ever mistake one for another. They were not friends in Kerek City. But their talents and territories did not overlap, so they were not enemies either. All three have caused Kereki metal poisoning to those whose only failing has been to be in the wrong place at the wrong time." Callis paused. "More than once I had to trust each of them with my life. It was not misplaced."

"Did…" Nari fumbled for words. "Were there any who will not receive their reward from the Empress? Any who did not survive the war?"

Callis sighed. "We all survived. Those who suffered at the hands of Kereki troublemakers—Tyra, Linna, Falan, Kid—were defended by Viklanders."

"We had two—Oro and Ross—who did not follow the instructions they were given by those who knew the area best. Oro learned from it and blamed no one else." Falan huffed.

"Ross was told to take a longer way from a settlement to return to Huk. He chose not to heed Josef's news of a patrol in the area. He was taken by the Viklanders hiding ghostfire in the area, blindfolded, and forced to run through the woods with them until they abandoned him far west of Huk. As he was walking to Balza to ask me for help, he was found by some others who did not think such a young boy so far from home was a treasure to be protected. Josef found him a day later and brought him to the settlement south of the Northern Track for Callis to heal. His body has recovered." Falan fell silent.

"I would not trust him with my life, either before or after. He is his own worst enemy, although he does not understand that to be true." Callis grimaced. "He is staying here with the Huena family. It will be interesting if they can drag him to the other side of childhood."

Nari said nothing. He was not so naïve or foolish as to believe Viklanders always acted honorably. It was war after all. He also knew those who had lost their braid during the war because of cowardice, crimes committed, desertion, or any other reason would now be able to hide their dishonor because of the bounty. He also knew anyone who had not been in the war would be looking askance at the shorn soldiers for seasons to come, wondering how they were able to return without a braid, but with life and limb intact. The bounty on the braid had been a brilliant and destructive weapon on Vikland soldiers and society by the Kerekis. It would cause distrust and scorn long after the war was over.

He roused himself to change the topic. "Do you have a favorite story, a rescue which you like to tell the others…and would like to tell me?"

Falan smirked. "You mean, like the time I rescued Bima Ritwik, the great Softfoot of Vikland?"

"Is this true?" Nari asked, too surprised to hide his astonishment. "I did not know him. But he was held over us poor soldiers as a man who could walk up walls, listen to secrets, and disappear as easily as smoke. Our commanders would threaten us with a transfer to his softfoots if we failed as soldiers. It was not meant to be a kindness."

Nari paused. "There were always stories whispered about him. He was not gentle to his newest softfoots. But those who survived his training were as formidable as he was."

Falan nodded. "It is true, but you should know I did not know it was him. He was gathering secrets when he came upon a Vik healer helping another soldier. He had a hiding place in an empty malting shed, which I also used for supplies. I found them there and offered him a way to get his information to Ishes and then he could get it to Juisiti. It was Zren Janin who recognized him and said his name. Zren took him back to Vikland, I think, but I do not know that to be true. Tyra said he saved her life. I heard he did not survive the war."

The room fell quiet.

Callis interjected gently, "The only Viklander softfoot I knew was Quan. I did not know his family name. He did not have a braid, and one of his parents was not a Viklander so he could pass in poor light or at dawn and dusk as just another Kereki with parents from different countries. He overlapped Josef's territory, and I know he used the Matasi missionaries to travel from place to place. I think Linna knew him as well. He brought us coin to buy the freedom of the soldiers held at the Huk jail."

Callis explained to Nari, "The Justice and Jailor at Huk were brothers. They took bribes to release the soldiers before the hanging judges came to sell them or take them along to the Kereki encampments. Sometimes, if Quan didn't come quickly enough, we would have to use the profits from the coffin wagon or cheese cart.

"We used Ross to deliver the coin because he could not hide his hatred of the Viklanders. He is small for his age, and the Justice understood he was only the delivery boy. Once the prisoners were freed, Ross would merely point them to the dark of the woods and go on his way. I would be waiting in those woods to take them to Josef, or Nelo, or east to Cloa."

Kid cleared his throat. "Ross was good that way. Nelo cultivated the same disdain and disgust. We always had trouble getting enough clothes and boots for the soldiers to change into as we moved them across the country. Early in the war, Nelo started to wear Viklander boots more than his own. If he was questioned by Kerekis, he would sneer and say, the boots were a reward to himself and still warm when he put them on. Or he would say, the braid was gone and he thought the boots would be worth something. It made it easier for him to give away his Kereki boots to the Viklanders to disguise their footprints."

Kid considered. "Josef did something similar with his dresses. By wearing them when he didn't need to, it was easy for him to be dismissed by others. If he dressed as a woman as he traveled to pick up Viklanders, he could wear their escape clothes underneath his skirts and shawls. It left his hands free to carry weapons. He also wore Vikland battle leathers under his clothes to deflect knives or at least dull them. He would jape that he wasn't as manly as Nelo and Arden and could not kill as easily."

Falan blew out a breath. "Josef's greatest weapon will always be his quick wit. He didn't have the knife skills of the others. His courage is of a different sort." She turned to Nari. "The story I would like to hear before I go to my bed, Nari Ulani, is where were you fighting? Where did you make such a sacrifice for Vikland?" She gestured at his leg.

"If it does not hurt you to tell this story," Callis added quickly.

Nari sighed. "I will tell you the truth as I know it. Perhaps years from now I will be able to think of an adventure story to keep my listeners at the edge of their chairs and cause children, stunned by my heroism, to trail me through the coffee fields. But for now…" He paused.

Callis shot a quick look to Falan and settled back into her chair.

"Most of the fighting took place between Balza and Vingt. The King did not have enough troops to defend his entire country. So, he concentrated them far enough from Kerek City to guard the port without inconveniencing the citizens of the city, but not so far he could not get the supply wagons to them.

"If the Matasi navy would have sailed from their ports at the beginning of the war as they had promised Vikland, it would have been a very different outcome. But we Viklanders had to bring our armies, our food, our wagons, our weapons, and supplies across most of Kerek with a hundred little skirmishes and battles along the way.

"I was fighting for two years. We lost a few battles, we won more. The Kerek army was untrained and unmotivated. We had more difficult skirmishes with the local militias—the landowners who supplied and trained their own men. It was a very different war than we had been taught in our academies. There were no battle lines, no formal exchange of prisoners. Just snipers with short bows, snares, and pit traps in the scrubland, ambushes along game trails under the Cold Mountains.

"I was in a large group of probably four hundred soldiers who had steadily made headway westward. We knew Vingt was to the south of us. We had patrols as far south as the Ring Road. I actually thought we would reach Kerek City by the end of the Wet." Nari reached for his wineglass, found it empty, and refilled it before continuing.

"It had been a miserable day. We had marched since daybreak in a heavy rain with patchy fog. Our commander wanted us to reach a rise just north of us that our scouts told us we could defend easily. We were maybe a decon away when a crossbow quarrel came from behind us and killed the soldier near my commander. He thought it was our own soldiers, and we had somehow worked our way ahead of the main group. He wheeled and yelled, 'Stop.' Before he could say anything more, a quarrel had taken him as well. We dropped low to defend ourselves. The Secondo started yelling to 'stop firing, you fools, we are Viklanders.' She said a lot of other things as well, but then a wall of Kereki men came out of the fog to the north of us.

"It was all hand-to-hand fighting. I pulled my short bong, and luckily for me, I was between skilled fighters. I would have told you we were winning when I felt an arrow hit the meat of my calf. I continued to fight until a riata dropped the soldier next to me, and a pigsticker sliced my leathers on my arm. I don't remember when I fell."

Nari took a long drink from his wineglass. "When I came to, I was in our field infirmary. I reached down to feel my wound on my leg and it was tightly bandaged. My leather guards had parted under the pigsticker, but my arm was barely scratched. A healer saw I was awake and came by. I asked if they were able to get out the arrowhead in my leg, and she said yes. I said I thought she needed the bed for someone more wounded than I was, and if she could help me stand, I would walk to my tent. She helped me sit and had someone feed me some broth first. Then I slept. I don't know how long. Days perhaps. When I woke again, I was dizzy with fever. Everyone in the hospital was.

"Every weapon the Kerekis had used on us, arrows, knives, pigstickers, and pitchforks had been drenched in piss and filthy water and dragged through horse dung. They didn't need to be better soldiers than Viklanders. They only needed to get close enough to wound us and let the filth poison us." Nari noticed the Wrens didn't grimace in disgust or turn away. *How did Kerekis raise their children to have such cruel hearts? Did they know nothing of honor?*

"It was a makeshift infirmary. The healers did what they could, but our Academy of Healing and the Academy of Botanicals were so many days away, we had no chance to reach it and survive. The healers soaked my arm and leg in raw spirits as often as they could. Finally, the arm healed, but the leg was poisoned too deeply. I do not need to describe the rest of it. When the internal abscesses set in, the stench was as unbearable as the pain. They took the leg below the knee. It took many days before our commanders could prepare a covered retreat to take us back to Vikland. We were the farthest west the Viklander army ever reached. We had to give up every bit of ground we bled over."

The Wrens were silent. Nari finished his glass of wine. "If I could have reached any of you and the healers at Manumina, perhaps I would be telling a different story. Don't ever underestimate the role you played in someone reaching their home."

CHAPTER 10

KID TELLS MORE

After Falan and Callis had left, Kid had stayed and talked freely. They talked of the Wrens and some of their escapes which Kid knew. He told of Callis and her strength on the bongs. That she would move Viklanders from their hiding places to the settlement south of the track and heal them. That she wore her hair long and loose because she was fairer than most of the other Wrens and would not be mistaken for a Viklander in the night. She had taught the other Wrens how to mend clothes when they were still at Manumina. It was a good skill, he said, but once they were out in Kerek no one had a fine West Islands needle like Ngahuru had shared with them.

He talked of the work the Wrens had done, for some of them the first time coin had ever been earned, and not stolen or begged. He smiled as he told of the Academy of Treason Manumina had provided when the Wrens had first arrived.

Nari had laughed as Kid described how the Wrens were taught to work in a bakery, take care of chickens and goats, and learned to ride horses with a Viklander shooting dulled arrows at them. There were lessons in cooking, in shooting a bow, and in reading and writing and sums.

"There were those," Kid said, "who had never seen their name written on paper before. You do not understand how important that is, Nari Ulani, but for the first time some of the Wrens understood how names have power. *Their* names have power."

He fell silent and looked at the floor. "There are many kinds of power. Our Viklander taught us how to take any farm tool and make it into a bong, or a pike, or a dagger to live to fight another day. She said defending ourselves or others didn't have to be pretty. She laughed and said a riata was not pretty, but it worked. What mattered was that we lived.

"We all needed to live, she said, to come back to see her someday and put our feet under her table."

"Who was your Viklander? Can you tell me?"

Kid gave him a long look. "She is still fighting for Vikland somewhere in Kerek. She is a bowmaster. I do not tell you more than that because I do not know if her life is known. I am sorry. I respect her too much to throw away her name so casually."

Nari smiled. "Your apology is not needed. If she was a softfoot, I should not have asked. I was merely curious and did not mean harm." Nari leaned forward and poured himself another glass of wine. "Tell me more of Ross."

"I can tell you what I know and it isn't much. I know he was on the auction block of the Orphan Master but never bought, then turned out on the streets. He was too small for his age to have value to any who looked for another pair of hands. He may have tried to be a Lost Child, but I know he was not one of Nelo's. He was too young to be a fancy for the sailors. Truthfully, his days were swiftly coming to an end. He would have died at the end of a forced barter sooner than later. I think that may have made him the child he was. He did not listen to others. He would hoard food once we came to Manumina, and there was all the food we could eat whenever we wanted to eat it. He did not share in the work even though we knew it was helping us to learn a skill and survive back in Kerek. He could not understand beyond the moment.

"There was a woman at Manumina—Siba Namikk—her name I can tell you." Kid grinned. "She was the wisest woman I had ever known. She knew how to teach each of us the lessons we needed to know. Even she despaired of Ross. Rygee said his heart was as hard as his head. The Huenas may be able to drag him to the other side of childhood if the entire village of Axefield helps them. But even now," he shook his head, "I do not trust him, not with my life, my coin, or my secrets. Callis and Falan have the right of it."

Nari asked him why Falan had always referred to the missing Wrens as the 'one-two-three' rather than just calling them 'the six' or 'half of the Wrens' or whatever.

Kid explained, "Jenny is with your aunt and uncle, she was a soldier rather than a softfoot or Wren. The three, Josef, Nelo, and Arden, are only gone for the day, it is unfortunate you cannot wait for them. I think you would find them interesting. They are nothing alike, but we needed all of their talents during the war. The two, Oro and Linna, moved to Juisiti to make their way. They left Axefield when the Conrosans arrived to build the inn. Their absence is on-going and forever."

Kid blew out a long sigh. "Oro had a Viklander grandparent. He was not one of Ngahuru's from before, and he left a home and family in Kerek City. Because of his Vik face, he could not take the same risks as the rest of us. He lived safely at Manumina, only serving as Ngahuru's wagon guard or traveling to your garrison at Ishes bringing news and dispatches and soldiers. There was some resentment from the Wrens at what they thought was his soft life. He seldom had to sleep rough as we did on our rescues, he had food to eat whenever he wished, and he slept unafraid that he would be found out as a traitor and killed.

"Oro was in love with Linna who was the center of our network. She shared a house with Arden who made beautiful things for their house—I have seen them—and said he made them for her because she had grown up in a proper home. She taught Arden to read and write Keresh. They worked well together, and we all trusted them. Some thought Arden and Linna had feelings for each other. He was maybe two years younger than she was, or so he said. In the middle of a war, who doesn't like to believe in happy endings?"

Kid shrugged. "But then Oro and Linna traveled to Juisiti and, without telling anyone, married. Ngahuru believes Oro to be the better man, because she knows him as literate and without a past. Arden was a thief for her in Kerek City. She knew him when he was a child and perhaps, still sees him as not yet a man. Those of us who worked closely with Arden believe Linna chose," Kid searched for a word, "…badly."

"What does Arden say?" Nari was curious. "I have not met the man. You need to enlighten me."

Kid gave Nari a long look. "Arden tells a story like so: he will say he found two riderless horses. He does not tell you the reason they are riderless is because he had to kill the men riding them and bury them where they could not be found in order to save a fellow Wren. I had to learn the truth of the story from Oro and Dica. Arden will tell you he lost his position at the stables in Cloa because he didn't show up for work one too many mornings, making it sound like he loves his pillow too much. He does not tell you it was because he rode all day and all night to bring a Viklander softfoot safely to the Earles garrison to deliver commands to march quickly to battle and save countless lives. Arden will say a Matasi family, out of the goodness of their hearts, provided him with a safe place to hide when he was hunted by a Kerek patrol because Mother had thieved a general's mapcase. He does not tell you he gave the same Matasi family every coin in his purse to take a horse from them the next day to ride hastily to Cloa so the Justice would find him there working in the stables when the Kereki patrol thundered into town."

Kid hummed. "Zren Janin will tell you the dog, Mother, is smarter than Arden, because he hears the words Arden says and believes them as they fall from Arden's mouth. But the rest of us know; he talks like a thief. Coins and treasures jump into his pockets, and who is he to deny them a safe place to be?"

Nari snorted then. "That is good to know. But you did not answer my question. What does Arden say about Linna? Did Oro steal her away, or did he steal her heart and Arden was only a maskovesto?"

"Arden says he is 'only a child' and too young for a woman such as Linna. But he says it in such a way I believe he cared for her." Kid considered his next words carefully. "Yet he is already walking out with a Viklander girl who works at the Inn. I think he has a restless heart and wants more of the world. In time, Arden and Linna would have made each other miserable. It is possible, I think, to have feelings for someone who is not good for you."

Nari nodded. "I hear what you are saying." He paused. "You…understand what you see. You do more than notice everything. This is a good skill on a coffee farm…and for a softfoot."

CHAPTER 11

SURCEASE

The next morning broke clear and sunny. Nari sat with a bowl of water, a looking glass, and his straight razor. It was a mess to shave his face like this, but after nearly slitting his throat trying to balance on his canes and shave, he had learned he could clean up the mess later. Yet another step of independence he had to battle for. He sighed. He wondered if the war would ever be over for him, or if every day would bring more humiliation for the rest of his life.

This is a fairy curse, he decided. A slap alongside the head for the time he and his fellow soldiers had made fun of the firemaster who had come to their training and taught them to use the liquid fire in the pottery jars. Nari and the others had been very impressed with the destruction just one of the jars could cause, whether it was planted near a bridge and shot at with a crossbow or fired into a charging line of Kereki cavalry. But that hadn't stopped the Viklanders for mocking the Matasian and his insect-like contraption of braces and sticks after he had left in his two-wheeled carry cart.

Nari rubbed the stump of his leg. Of course, he hadn't packed enough of anything to dull the pain. The first plan was only for him to ride from his home in the Keopi district to the West Islands embasado and ask his aunt's sister for advice on the letter they had received from Kid. Truthfully, Nari was surprised Hilanna Ulani thought it was worth Nari riding for seven days to Juisiti and speaking with the Ambassador, but Devi and Hilanna both insisted the issue was much larger than what appeared to be on paper. He didn't read Wester; he didn't know.

Then he had arrived at the Juisiti embasado to learn the Matasi Triune and the West Islands King were dancing together in their own political maneuverings. The West Islands King refused to recognize the Matasi Triune's right to rule Kerek unless he could be assured the tracks and trails across Kerek would be open to all travelers— West Islanders, Viklanders, and anyone else who wished to travel them—without paying a toll, without worrying about bandits or thieves or mobs, without a tax on what was carried across.

The King of the West Islands offered a test. In the past fifteen years, while the current Kerek King had ruled, none of the West Islands diplomats, their families, or staff members had been able to travel home to the islands from their postings in Juisiti, Vikland. It had not been safe enough to risk their lives on the Northern Track. Therefore, the West Islands King would now send new people to serve as diplomats and their staff on his personal ship to Kerek City.

It would be up to the Matasi Triune and their army to escort the newly arrived West Islanders safely to Juisiti and then conduct the ones in Juisiti back to Kerek City so they could sail home to the West Islands. The King's ship in the harbor must also remain unmolested during the time the exchange would take. Failure to provide safe passage to all travelers would not only mean failure to recognize the Triune's right to rule, it would mean war with West Islands while Matasi was still trying to pay for and recover from the one with Kerek.

During Nari's trip to Juisiti, he had planned a quiet tea in which he would show the Ambassador the letter his aunt Hilanna had received and entertain her with news of her sister and her family. Then he had thought he would hunt down his friends for drinks and a night in the city. Instead, Nari found himself conscripted on a diplomatic mission to travel to Axefield, find Ngahuru, and bring her back to Juisiti immediately, so she could travel with the others across Kerek and return to the West Islands at her King's command.

To make matters worse, the West Islands Ambassador had sent a message from the embasado to the Empress of Vikland explaining what she had asked Nari Ulani to do. He had been summoned to meet the Empress with so little notice, he did not have time to find a tailor to buy the appropriate clothes. He had begged the carry cart driver to stop at the barracks on the way to the palace to hastily borrow a friend's uniform.

At the palace, Nari learned the Empress needed an emissary to deliver her promise of coin and a home to the Kereki Wrens. This needed to happen before Ngahuru sailed back to the West Islands and told her King the Empress of Vikland had not followed through on her agreement. Nari Ulani was already traveling to find Ngahuru, the Empress had reasoned. He was a Viklander soldier with ties to both countries, Vikland and West Islands—as faint as they were. Would he undertake a mission on behalf of the Empress? And so he found himself at the Huena Inn with a West Islands bodyguard and a chest full of coins equal to a year's pay for twelve soldiers. Nari had never seen coins in such large amounts. He wondered just how easy it would be for a Wren to convert them into food and shelter.

Bah! His leg throbbed this morning. He pulled himself up using the furniture and reached for his canes. He hobbled over to the door and pulled it open to see a startled Matasi girl still at the edge of childhood staring up at him.

"Good morning," he began.

She stared at him blankly. He sighed, and began again in Keresh, "Hello. Good morning. What is your name?"

"Tyra. I am your runner this morning. What do you need?" She swallowed a yawn.

Nari raised an eyebrow. This was Tyra? One of Nelo's Lost Girls? The one Falan said had been injured and Bima Ritwik had defended from Kereki soldiers? She looked like she should be playing in a sheltered garden with dolls and a hovering nursemaid.

"How long have you been waiting for me to open my door?"

"Not long." She gave him a cheeky grin.

He could tell she was lying. He blew out a noisy breath.

"Tyra, fine. Does the Huena Inn have a healer? Or one in Axefield that is any good?"

Tyra appeared to consider his question. "The Conrosans, the people building the second inn across the courtyard, have two healers and an apprentice. I live with them. They say one of them trained at your academies in Juisiti."

"Better and better. Could you find one of them? Tell them I am a Vikland soldier who lost my leg below the knee in the war and my stump is throbbing. If they are at all competent, they will know what to bring to make it bearable."

Tyra nodded. "Would you like me to order first meal for you and your driver?"

"Yes. Why not? I could use the coffee, and he's probably up anyway." Nari turned and lurched his way back to the chair and let Tyra close the door for him. He propped up his leg and tried to train his mind past the pain.

He must have dozed. The next thing he knew, Claire opened the door and pushed in a cart with coffee and something that smelled delicious. Behind Claire, there was a Conrosan, about the age of his oldest sister Nadja. She carried a small tray and a smaller shoulder bag.

"Good morning, Claire! Don't they ever let you sleep?" Nari grinned at her.

"I sleep when you sleep, Nari Ulani." She smiled easily.

"Ah then, after the Conrosan has miraculously healed me, I shall take a nap immediately after first meal and not wake up until tomorrow. You of course, will need to sleep as well."

Claire smiled good naturedly at him and switched from Vik to Keresh, "Nari Ulani, I would like to introduce you to Siba Namikk. She is a healer of quite some skill. Our own Arella Huena trained with her before and during the war. The Huena Inn recommends her highly."

He nodded his head in greeting. "Siba Namikk. You are the one the Wrens named. You will stand for those who will not return today before I must leave with Ngahuru."

She nodded. "Is it all right for us to speak Keresh? I am told by my friends it is rude to speak Keresh to a Viklander. But I have not yet learned Vik. Unless you speak Conrosan?" she asked hopefully.

Nari smiled. "Keresh is fine. There were Conrosan language classes at the academies, but…" He shrugged. "I didn't expect to travel so far. I've only ever wanted to be a coffee farmer like my father."

Siba continued, "Would you like me to look at your leg now or after first meal so you can enjoy your food while it is hot?"

"I could enjoy my food better if I was not constantly reminded of my missing leg."

Siba unpacked her bag. Without looking at anyone, she casually asked, "Claire, will you stay?"

Claire looked startled. "I need to get back. I still need to get first meal to the West Islander in the stable."

"Of course. Could you ask Tyra to step in, please." To Nari she said, "You will need to remove your trousers. If you could replace them with the baggy Kereki pants that would be best, if not, your blanket should cover you to here." She pointed mid-thigh on her own leg. "I will need to massage this in very deeply."

She looked at Tyra, now standing beside her. "You will need to hold him down if he screams too loudly." She gave a smile back at Nari. "I am joking." Then she and Tyra turned their backs so he could take off his uniform trousers. He sighed. They had taken him forever to put on that morning. At last, he told them to turn around, he was ready for them.

As Siba unwrapped the bandages about his stump, she glanced over at the two carved ebony canes leaning against the chair.

"Those bastono are very beautiful, but I do not know those carvings."

Nari looked at them as well. "Bastono," he repeated thoughtfully. "In Vikland, we call them canes. A friend of mine carved them when he was in the long-term infirmary with me. He had an injury of the mind. He said carving brought him some peace. But it was not enough to heal him. Every time I use them, I am reminded not all wounds are visible."

"I regret the death of your friend. May his name live on in your memories," Siba said quietly.

The scar tissue was shiny and still pink with mottling up the thigh. She rubbed her hands together to warm them and then slid her palms through the plate of ointment on her tray. First, she smeared light circles to moisten an area and then she began working her palms deeper into the muscles.

Nari felt the heat and pressure begin to push the pain away. He leaned back in relief. The room was quiet as he lay back with his eyes closed, enjoying the pleasure of receding pain.

"Oh, bless the stars, that feels wonderful."

Siba spoke lightly, "Tyra, could you please pour Nari Ulani a cup of coffee, please?" Nari opened his eyes, and accepted the cup from Tyra. Soon he felt the heat of the ointment and Siba's hands climb higher up his thigh. He concentrated on his coffee.

"What is in that?" He shifted and pulled the blanket more firmly over his lap. He couldn't remember the last time his stump didn't hurt when he wasn't under a fog of potions. He was also very obviously responding to a woman rubbing his inner thigh.

"My aunt made it. Sometimes we need to eliminate pain without putting our patients in a deep sleep. She devised this ointment which we can rub into muscles and joints. Is it helping?"

"Yes." Nari cleared his throat. "Yes, it is. In fact, you should stop now."

Siba massaged her hands again over the stump. "I will leave the rest of this. You saw how I did it. Start with the end, work your way up as high as you feel tightness and then finish with the knee again. It will last for several decons." She looked up with a smile in her eyes. "The pain relief that is."

Nari scowled to hide his embarrassment. "I should have my first meal now before it is completely cold," he said crisply.

"Of course. Tyra, could you help me carry this back to the infirmary?" Siba and Tyra packed up her things and left.

Nari leaned back and enjoyed the pain-free sensation. His aunt Hilanna had graduated from the Academy of Botanicals—first in her class if Tedros could be believed. He wondered if he had enough coin of his own along to pay Siba Namikk to write down the recipe for the ointment in the hope his aunt could recreate it. He smiled gratefully and dug into his first meal still warm on the serving tray.

CHAPTER 12

STRANGERS BEARING GIFTS

When Claire came to clear the dishes away, Nari told her what he wanted. She suggested the ceremony be held in one of the private rooms down the hall, which were larger and more formal. As he asked her to make the room worthy of the occasion, he gave a heavy sigh.

"Claire, I know you and every Viklander will think it disrespectful, but I cannot stand without my canes. If I use them, then I cannot do what I need to do. Can you place a chair in the room for me—one that doesn't look like I am a decrepit soldier who has lost the ability to stand in the presence of a hero? Perhaps the Wrens will understand I am doing my best."

Claire nodded and asked, "Do you have Witnesses?"

"Yes. The West Islanders—the one guarding the reward… and Ngahuru."

She nodded again. "I should see if Raul Huena could attend as well. His daughter Arella was assigned to Manumina as a healer during the war. She is a bowmaster and also trained the Wrens on the bows and the bongs before they were fanned out into the countryside to help Viklanders."

"So *she* was the Viklander," he said half to himself. Nari looked at Claire thoughtfully, "That was not known to me. We will never know every soldier's story, will we?"

Nari thought for a moment. "I have an idea. I am an emissary of the Empress, am I not? She may not remember my name next season, but for today I speak for her. We need to remember all those who did not come home on their own. I know there must be some in Axefield, or perhaps even in this inn, who can say they know someone who is alive or was brought home to be remembered because of these Wrens. Can we find and have them come to see the Wrens after they have been honored?" Nari smiled mischievously. "I think we should have the Empress feed them as well."

Claire nodded. "I should go and get everything ready. I will send out runners to find people. I know of some and word of mouth will bring others. When the Wrens arrive, could you hold them here until I come to escort you down to the room. Is that acceptable to you?"

"Yes."

After Claire left, Nari leaned back in his chair and thought about her words. He had heard of Arella Huena in his weapons training. She had been a handful of years ahead of him. Their crossbow instructor had commented not only on her unusually keen eyesight—which he had told the soldiers was out of their control, but also on her endurance—which *was* in their control. Nari and his friends had joked that perhaps Arella's strength and unerring accuracy may have been exaggerated to serve the purpose of the bowmaster as he taught them to hold, fire, reload, and repeat until Nari thought his arms would fall off.

Nari had never reached the level of a bowmaster nor did he have more than average skills on the bongs. He didn't grow up with built in sparring partners like his cousins did. But he had come home from the war. He had a coffee farm to run someday with his sister, if he could just figure out how to get about in the fields. As he looked at the ebony canes propped up by his chair, he knew his life ahead of him was better than the alternative.

***

Nari was sitting at the table, papers and graphite scattered about. He was working on the words he would say to the Wrens, when Tyra knocked on his door and poked her head around.

"Piffik Qanaq and Rygee Namikk are here to see you."

Nari furrowed his brow. "Should I know them?"

"They just told me to tell you their names and that Siba sent them," Tyra explained.

"Ah, you forgot to tell me that part. Well then, send them in."

Nari had recognized the names as Conrosan from his single language class at the academy, so he was surprised to see a tall, strong-looking Kereki walk in with a number of wooden braces and sticks under his arm. He reached for his canes to struggle to his feet, but the Conrosan following just waved him to stay seated. The Conrosan looked like he was carrying horse tackle.

"Please do not be formal on our account. I am Piffik Qanaq, builder of the second Huena Inn," he paused, "and the future husband of Rell Huena."

"I am Rygee, the husband of the healer Siba Namikk. My wife thought we could be of some assistance."

Nari tried to hide his surprise and dismay. "Oh? And what did Siba say?"

Piffik was already sorting out the bundles into different piles on the nearby table. "Some seasons ago, Chul Swyler came to Manumina and stayed with us for nearly a year. He made many inventions for us which made life easier and better for the Conrosans. One of those inventions was a set of staffs and cradles so those who had injured legs, backs, or feet could still use their hands and be able to care for themselves. He called them, 'bastono.' I have some of his pieces here—our workers also have injuries—and I thought we could see if any of the pieces fit you. We can alter a pair, and you can take them with you."

"The firemaster lived with you?" Nari shot a glance at his beautifully carved ebony canes and back at the wooden cradles Piffik was holding out and tried hard not to cringe.

"Yes, he was part of a Northern Track crossing ambushed before Sary. I wish Zren Janin was here. He loves to tell the story of Miyamoto Suki's thirteenth crossing." Piffik looked up as he buckled the leathers about Nari's arm and smiled. "Actually, Zren could talk the better part of the day, if he thought you would listen." He tapped Nari's arms. "Now these must fit closely to your forearms. Your body's balance and weight will rest on them so they must be comfortable. Do you want to try on narrower cradles for when your arms are bare? Or do you prefer wider, not to crush your uniform?"

For all their ugliness, Nari had to admit the bastono solved two problems. He now had his hands free to carry, grab, or make the formal Vikland greetings. The hinged legs—there were only two of them and not four like the firemaster had in Juisiti—folded back when he raised his hands to his face, tucking themselves out of the way when he was balancing against the furniture or sitting. The canes slid into grooves on the underside of the cradles. Rygee made several adjustments to find the proper height as the Viklander walked up and down the room. Nari could see how helpful these would be on the coffee farm where it did not matter so much to him what he looked like.

Nari felt a greater appreciation for the firemaster. Chul Swyler had been so confident in his talents and mind, he didn't care what others thought about his appearance. Nari knew he wasn't there yet. He glanced again at his beautiful carved canes, and Piffik caught him looking.

"These are only meant to make your life easier. They are not to replace the beauty or the memory of the gift of your friend," Piffik said gently.

Nari gave Piffik a sheepish look. "I am still young and shallow, I'm afraid."

Rygee finished installing a taller stick. "Try this."

Nari was able to stand straighter and still put his full weight on the cradle. "Ah, better. My mother won't scold me for slouching." He grinned and picked up an empty cup as he walked up and down the room on the bastono. "Well, I still won't be carrying my own coffee when it's hot, but at least I can stand and drink when I am out with my friends." He smiled gratefully. "These will make this day much easier. I thank you."

Piffik started gathering his tools and bundled the unused pieces. He nodded to the bastono Nari still wore. "You can take those to your carpenter on your coffee farm. He will be able to make another pair or repair these as needed. The most difficult pieces to get are the hinges. Those are West Islands steel, but even leather would work if you have nothing else." Piffik looked at Rygee who pulled out a paper from within his shirt sleeve and gave it to Nari.

"This is the recipe for the ointment Siba used on your leg earlier. She had asked Ngahuru for help to write it in Wester or Vik, but Ngahuru assured her your aunt Hilanna could translate the Conrosan words into the language she speaks best. Ngahuru didn't know some of the plant names and together, they were worried a bad translation might alter the ointment and render it useless. Siba also said you would feel the missing leg for a long time to come, and she is sorry she cannot do more."

"She has already given me more relief than I ever expected. We have potions to dull the pain but then my mind feels half asleep for the rest of the day." He paused. "May I share this with the Academy of Botanicals? We have many who came back from the war who would appreciate this gift."

Rygee looked uneasily at Piffik, who sighed and looked at Nari. "You said you met the firemaster, Chul Swyler?" When Nari nodded, Piffik went on, "Chul shares his laboratory with a student who studies at the Academy of Botanicals. Her name is

Aajan. Give her the recipe if you please, and ask her to translate it into Vik and prepare some sample ointments for the infirmaries. I think, if you took the recipe like so, written in Conrosan, with nothing to show how it works…" Piffik paused, searching for a polite way to respond, "It would not be well regarded."

Nari winced. "Although I do not like to hear the truth of that, you are probably right." He paused. "Aajan will accept this from me without question? Or do I say 'Siba Namikk the healer sent me' like magic words in a fairy tale?"

Rygee snorted. "Better to say that than to say 'her brother, Piffik Qanaq.' Aajan succeeds at your academies because she can be a little…stubborn."

Nari laughed. "Thanks for the warning. She must be a younger sister. We youngers always have trouble listening to our older siblings even when we know they are right."

Piffik smiled and handed the bundle of extra wood to Rygee. He picked up the extra leather straps. Nari noted it *had* been bits and pieces of horse tackle. The men left, and as Piffik closed the door behind him, Nari saw the runner outside his door was gone. Getting herself ready, he imagined.

He blew out a noisy breath. It would take forever for him to get dressed; he might as well get started.

CHAPTER 13

THANK YOU FOR YOUR SERVICE

"The six of you represent all of those who gave aid to the daughters and sons of Vikland while they tried to right the wrongs of the last Kerek King. There are people who are alive today because of your cunning and courage. We will never know all their stories, just as they do not have the privilege of knowing how your story will end. We use this moment today to recognize you. You who have lost your homeland and your childhood."

Nari gave the deep Vikland bow of respect. He knew the Wrens had never seen a military honors ceremony but every Viklander in the room had, and he wanted to do it right. He blessed the bastono, which he had not even known could exist for him a decon ago.

"Today and today only, I speak for the Empress of Vikland as she expresses her gratitude to you for your actions in the war. Please accept this gift in appreciation. May it help you reach your life's desires and fulfill your dreams. I thank you for your service."

Nari stepped in front of Falan and the West Islanders flanked him. Claire gave him one of the traveling bags from the neat stack on a nearby table. Nari gave Falan the bag and folded his hands together for another bow of respect.

"Falan of Kerek City, I thank you for your service." Falan stepped aside with a large grin on her face. By the looks she was getting from the other Wrens, Nari guessed smiling for Falan was not a common occurrence.

Callis had been standing next to Falan and now Nari used his bastono to click-slide, click-slide in front of her. Last night, Callis told him that when they had arrived at the refugee camp, she had been assigned to the laundries because they needed tailors. She had only recently moved to be an apprentice healer with Siba and her aunt Bett, because Dica had asked to take her place in the laundries and had the tailoring skills to do it.

As Nari handed Callis the traveling bag from Claire, he whispered, "This will buy a lot of potions." She grinned. He finished with another Vikland bow. "Callis of Kerek City, I thank you for your service."

Click-slide, click-slide. Nari winced as he moved to the next Wren. He hated to think what was going through everyone's mind as they took in his missing leg, the bastono, the braid so short it barely passed his shoulder.

"Dica." Slender and awkward, she reminded Nari of nothing so much as a sturdy vine reaching for the sun. She wore her brown hair loose and had such an earnest expression on her face, Nari wanted to tease her growing up wasn't so serious a task. Last night, Falan had told him Dica had been the center in the north. Kid had concurred, saying it had never been anyone's intention, but when Evensong became such a Kereki stronghold and he was woven so deeply into the household, there had been no other choice. Dica had been able to move confidently into the role needed from her. Now Nari looked at her and found it hard to stomach how such a young girl could have done so much.

"Dica, I thank you for your service." He handed her the travel bag from Claire and gave her the Vikland bow of respect.

She gave him a smile in return and folded her hands together. "Thank you for your sacrifice." She glanced at Claire quickly and when Claire smiled approvingly, Dica looked back solemnly at Nari.

"Ross." Nari schooled his face quickly. He had met Tyra, a pixie-sized girl on the edge of childhood. The others last night had talked of Ross, but he had not understood the boy had been as small and young as Tyra. Ross was a smooth-cheeked boy, and Nari would bet his last paypacket his voice had not yet dropped. Ross returned his bow, but then flashed him such a look of hatred, Nari stumbled over his words. He wasn't sure anyone else had seen it. Claire handed him the traveling bag to give to Ross as if nothing had happened. After the final bow, Ross walked over to stand next to Falan with a bland look. Nari was stunned at the transformation and momentarily wondered if he had imagined it. Then Tyra stood in front of him. He recovered quickly and smiled at her warmly.

"Tyra, I thank you for your service." He handed her the travel bag from Claire and gave her the Vikland bow of respect. She gave him a smile in return and folded her hands together. She bowed as deeply as if he was the Empress herself, and Nari heard Claire choke back a sound. He flashed Claire a look of reproach, and smiled smoothly back at Tyra. "You are kind," he whispered.

"Kid." Today, Nari looked at Kid carefully. "Kid, I thank you for your service." He handed the boy the travel bag Claire passed him. Nari hesitated for a moment, and then gave the Vikland bow of respect as an equal. He knew the Viklanders in the room would note it, but the Wrens didn't understand how the depth of the bow conveyed rank. Tyra's deep bow had demonstrated that. But Nari wanted to begin Kid's acceptance immediately. This was the man—boy, really—who would be taking Nari's place on the coffee farm until he could learn to be a one-legged field manager and his brother came home from his service. "Thank you for writing my aunt," he said quietly.

Kid gave him a half smile in return and folded his hands together. "Thank you for listening with your head and your heart." He bowed as an equal in return. The boy was quick, Nari noted to himself.

Nari looked at Claire and she moved quickly by his side as he slowly and solemnly said the names, "Nelo, Linna, Josef, Oro, Jenny, Arden. These six are not with us today here at Axefield. I regret I cannot stay to meet them. But today and today only, I speak for the Empress of Vikland, and I know their courage and cunning saved lives. Let us hear others tell those stories." He nodded to Claire and she walked forward and threw open the doors to a crowd of Viklanders waiting in the hall.

Claire turned and faced the room for her announcement. "I have ordered an early midday for you to eat and mingle, but before the food arrives, I want you to greet people who are very happy to meet you. These are guests at our inn and people of Axefield who all have a story to tell of someone they knew who was helped by you or others like you during the war. As you listen to their stories remind yourself of the good you have done in the world."

For the next decon, Nari and Claire circulated among the Wrens, the storytellers, and Piffik, Siba, and Rygee. They listened, made introductions, and bridged awkward conversations. Ngahuru and Ross had left immediately after the coin had been distributed. Nari wasn't surprised, Ngahuru was a softfoot after all. Already she would never be able to use her Tiju Tia disguise again.

Nari *was* surprised to hear the numerous stories of Padro Morto as he rescued Viklanders. He tried to match those up with the quiet man circulating the room. Piffik was broad-shouldered and slim-hipped with brown, curly hair he wore short at the nape of his neck. His face was not handsome, he had spent too many years working outdoors for that. Nari assumed he was a few years older than his sister Nadja. But it was Rygee and Piffik, he had been told by Ngahuru, who had financially supported the Wrens. Nari wondered whatever had happened to the Kereki to make him side with his wife and the others against his homeland. Another story which would never be told.

Raul Huena came to stand beside him. "This was a good thing you did today. It would have been easy to call them to your room and give them the coin as if you were paying them off to keep a secret. But this? This they will remember and tell the other Wrens who could not be here. This will reassure them when they come to the next hard thing in their life, they have already done hard things, and did them well."

Nari grinned. "It was my pleasure. I especially liked saying, 'Today I speak for the Empress.' I wonder if she knew what she asked when she picked me. All of us in the family Ulani like to be the center of attention." He bent his head close to Raul. "Do you have a safe? I think the Wrens do not have a sense of how banks and coin lenders work. You may need to ask someone they trust to teach them how to care for such a large amount."

Raul nodded. "I will talk to Piffik. He may have Siba Namikk talk to them once everyone is back. You will take the coin to Oro and Linna and Jenny." It wasn't a question. He paused. "The bastono are new? I remember your canes from yesterday, you see. I have seen a Conrosan wear bastono when she fell and broke her leg, but never a Viklander. Although, I was told it was a Viklander who invented them and not a Conrosan."

"Yes. They were a gift from the man who says he is to be your daughter's husband." Nari raised an eyebrow.

Raul beamed. "Piffik Qanaq is a wise man. A scholar without books, a general without a uniform. My family is truly blessed."

"You are not…um…disappointed he is not a Viklander?"

Raul Huena drew back in surprise.

"I only meant, if I remember my studies," Nari faltered, "Mmmm, Conrosans are pacifists."

Raul Huena gave him a long, measured look. "And yet, there are many in this room who tell of a ride to safety in Padro Morto's wagon. It's true he never carried a weapon to defend himself, yet there are many ways to stand up for justice."

"I did not mean offense, Raul Huena. I am young and foolish, and I am grateful for your wisdom. This is not a mistake I will ever make again." Nari talked quickly to cover his embarrassment. "You have been courteous and beyond accommodating for all of my requests. I see Claire is still busy teaching the Wrens how to accept compliments and graciously translating when necessary. But I must leave soon to return Ngahuru to the embasado in time to meet with her Ambassador. I also must meet with Oro and Linna in Juisiti.

"I will tell the driver to hitch the horses if you will send a runner to Ngahuru and tell her to meet in the courtyard." He made a bow of respect. "Please prepare the bill so I may present it to the palace when I return."

Raul nodded and walked towards the door. He just touched Claire's elbow as he passed and she nodded in response without interrupting her translation. Nari sighed. She should be in the Diplo, he thought. But he knew he was seeing years of experience in action and if the Empress could entice her away, she would only be doing the same thing for some ambassador in another country.

Nari Ulani carefully walked his bastono over to Kid standing next to Dica and an older woman talking.

Nari waited quietly while she finished her story of her daughter's escape and the Wrens who had gotten her to Ishes. "I don't even know which of you helped her. She said they were told to call all of you 'Missy' and refer to the others as Wrens." She paused. "But my daughter was captured in a battle near Evensong. During the first night, she said, her captors' horses ran off leaving their unbuckled hobbles behind and the soldiers to chase after them. Then she spent a day and a night in a rhododendron hedge."

"This one." Kid nodded to Dica. "I asked you to tell your story again because I found the one who helped your daughter. Dica was posted at Regno. She and Nelo and Inezi carved out a hidden room in the middle of the rhododendron brambles. That was how I knew it was her. Your daughter was not the only one who spent time there. It was a good place to hide Viklanders until Inezi could take people over the border, connect them with a softfoot from Vikland, or we could arrange transport for the injured with Padro Morto."

The woman looked Dica up and down. "I do not wish to say anything to make light of your courage. I thank you for returning my daughter to me." She turned and looked at Nari. "I thank you for your service…and for your sacrifice." Her eyes glistened with unshed tears, and she softly apologized and walked swiftly away.

Nari sighed deeply. He hated pity. "Kid, it is time to go. I am sorry we cannot wait for Arden and Zren to return for you to say goodbye. I have already asked for the carriage to be hitched and brought about."

Kid gave a small nod. "Dica, could you come with me? I will give you the letters for Zren and Josef and Arden, and a book for you to continue your studies while I am gone." He turned back to Nari. "And I will get my books and my bags and meet you in the courtyard."

The two slipped out the door, and Nari maneuvered through the crowd to thank Claire for her work. He told the Wrens goodbye one by one, to stay and enjoy the food, the reception was for them after all. He thanked Siba again for the ointment, Rygee for standing by Vikland, and Piffik for saving so many Viklanders. At last, he reached his room where a runner was already waiting to take his belongings and follow him out.

Dica and Kid were standing in front of the carriage. The West Islander was stowing baggage in the back carryall.

"Ngahuru is inside," he said tersely.

Nari nodded and turned to Kid. "I will need your assistance. You will need to lift me so I can bend my leg to pivot to the seat. Thank the stars the carriage is enclosed, because this isn't pretty." The West Islander came on the other side. Nari said, "Now," and Kid and the driver struggled to lift him in. The West Islander quickly put away the step and climbed to the front of the carriage while Nari continued rustling and rearranging inside. Finally, Nari called out to Kid to join them. Kid pecked a quick kiss on Dica's cheek, scrambled inside, and pulled the door closed.

There was a sharp rap on the roof from Nari's cane and the carriage immediately pulled away, leaving Dica there in the courtyard with her hand on her just-kissed cheek and her mouth hanging open in surprise.

CHAPTER 14

EMPTY SPACES

Nelo may have started out only two decons earlier, but he had pushed his horse. So, when Arden finally arrived at the shepherd's cottage, he found a dejected friend sitting on the steps. Arden nudged his horse closer and slid off his mount.

"It's not here," Nelo began immediately. "There are two hiding places we used during the war and both of them are empty. It's not in either one," he repeated sadly.

"I know." Arden nodded. "I am sorry. Ngahuru had hidden it in the rag and bone wagon. Zren found it at Rishka after you had already left. There was no way to let you know but to come after you. I am sorry," he repeated.

"Ngahuru! She wasn't even there! Why would she move the chest?" There was a long pause then Nelo added flatly, "Rygee didn't know."

"No, he didn't. Zren had been sleeping on the floor and saw Rygee hide the chest inside the cottage after we fled Manumina. Zren told us, he thought it had been forgotten because Siba and Rygee left so early in the morning. He told Ngahuru and she said she would take care of it." Arden was quiet a very long time.

"Maybe she forgot about it with all the comings and goings to Juisiti," Nelo offered hopefully.

Arden gave his friend a long look. "I have ridden four decons on the way here to think of all possible reasons. 'Forgetting' is not one of the possibilities."

"No, it is not," Nelo said morosely. He picked up a stone and threw it hard into the open scrubland. It startled Arden's horse and it sidestepped away.

Both men said immediately, "Don't abuse the horses," and then laughed.

"Do you think Piffik knows?" Nelo asked.

"About Ngahuru taking the chest?" Arden paused. "I doubt it. I don't want to think so."

"Me neither." There was a long silence. "In those four decons of thinking, did you come up with a plan?" Nelo asked hopefully.

"Of course, I did." Arden grinned. "Here's what we'll do."

CHAPTER 15

KID MEETS HIS FUTURE

As the carriage drew closer to Juisiti, Nari roused himself from his nap. He smiled, realizing the potion Siba had rubbed into his thigh this morning was still working. Ngahuru was sitting across from him, her eyes closed against the gentle rocking of the carriage.

Kid was watching out the window, brow furrowed in concentration at the commotion and colors outside.

"Do you know where Oro and Jenny live?" Nari cleared his throat. "We'll have to deliver their coin, but I do not know if we need to stop at the West Islands embasado first. If Ngahuru leaves tonight, you and the driver may need to serve as Witnesses."

Kid shook his head. "I didn't know either of them well enough. Zren might have known if Oro told him, but he was with the others at Rishka." He tipped his head to Ngahuru. "She would know."

"I don't." Ngahuru said, opening her eyes. She straightened up, arranged her clothes, and looked at both of them. "When they came to pick up their belongings in Axefield, Linna said they were staying in an inn near the Academy of Languages. She asked me for coin so they could find better housing. I gave her what I had, but it wasn't much and she never wrote to tell me where they moved. I hoped they would leave a message at the West Islands embasado. I asked the driver to go there first."

"Well, then, I guess we are going to the embasado first," Nari said lightly.

Kid gave Ngahuru a long look. After a moment, he resumed watching the city outside his window.

***

All embasado streets looked the same, Kid decided. The tall, stately buildings towering over the same high walls and gates. Guardhouses with soldiers in fancy dress watching those on the street and the comings and goings of carriages, wagons, carry carts, and people walking. He glanced out the window and saw the heavy gates made of steel. Of course, what a lovely, and obvious, way to remind all of the passersby and guests of the wealth and might of the West Islands. The horse came to a gentle stop, and Kid began gathering his bags.

"I think," Nari began, "we shall keep the carriage until our errand for the Empress is completed. I do not wish to find a carry cart to drag us about the city while I am carrying enough coin for four soldiers for a year. Juisiti is not Kerek, but I don't need to beg Trouble to dance with me."

Ngahuru raised an eyebrow but said nothing. Kid felt the undercurrents of a power struggle between the two.

"Ngahuru, forgive me. I know you are worthy of far better, but I shall convey my thanks and gratitude here and allow Kid to escort you to your door. Our country is grateful and as you return to your King and your islands, please know you and your Wrens will never be forgotten."

The door opened, and the driver stood there with the step already in place. "Kid, you should leave first and hand down Ngahuru. Please walk her to her door and ensure her belongings are carried in behind her. This is how it is done in Vikland."

Kid leaned out and stepped down first. He stood opposite the driver and mimicked holding out a fist for Ngahuru to rest her hand while she stepped down on the small platform.

"Ngahuru?" a voice said in awe, "Ngahuru of the West Islands?"

Kid wheeled about and saw Rani, the Viklander softfoot, who, along with Therin and Nelo and Inezi, had picked up his messages and codes from hiding places in the Evensong outbuildings and woods.

"Kid?" Rani smiled broadly, "How are you? Why are you here?" He looked back and forth from Kid to Ngahuru and bowed deeply to her. "Ngahuru, I am Rani. You and I met at an ambassador's event in the West Islands while I was posted there in the Diplo many years ago. At the time, you had just returned from your own posting in the Spice Island."

Kid stilled. He knew both softfoots knew he was there, but if he was just invisible enough for them to forget for a moment…

Ngahuru returned the short bow. "I do remember you, Rani. I am glad your skills and talents kept you safe during the past war." She smiled slyly. "I hope you have heard of the efforts of my King to keep the Kerek roads open and safe to all travelers. I am accompanying the staff and the Ambassador's family from Juisiti through Kerek and to my King's ship, which is even now waiting for us in Kerek City."

Rani grinned. "I have. In fact, that is why I was visiting your embasado. One moment, I shall walk you." He turned to Kid and said quickly, "Wait here for me, it's important." As he walked Ngahuru to the embasado, the West Islands driver and another soldier followed behind carrying Ngahuru's belongings.

Kid poked his head into the carriage. "What should I do?" he asked.

Nari smiled. "Well, considering Rani may be your future, I would suggest we wait for him. We also don't have a way to find

Linna, and we should see if she left a message with the embasado."
He paused. "However, it is not necessary for you to wait outside
the carriage like a common peddler showing his wares."

Kid scrambled inside and pulled the door closed.

"I am only a soldier, and not a softfoot like those two, or
as you will become, but let me share with you my observations,
Kid, and you can do with them what you will.

"Rani was more than pleased to find Ngahuru stepping out
of the Ambassador's carriage, but he was not surprised. This tells
me her presence merely confirms what our softfoots suspected.
Ngahuru was helping Vikland during the war. Your value, as
part of her network has now increased. I believe Rani is going to
return to the carriage and offer you an evening of entertainment,
or end of day meal, so he can ask all manner of questions about
Ngahuru and how your network was run.

"You have lived by your wits, Kid, and I would not presume,
but I would suggest you deflect any questions about Ngahuru
or friends of yours still living in Kerek, but freely answer any
questions regarding your own plans. If Rani knows of your
interest in serving Vikland in the future, he may be able to
smooth your way in the academies. Something I cannot do for
you. He may do nothing. He may wait and see how you and
Vikland fit together. In any case, he is a friend to cultivate. Do
you understand what I am saying?"

Kid nodded quickly.

"Now my braid is a tiny one, but it does not change the way I feel in my heart. If you wish, you could ask Rani to join us in our search for the lost Wrens. If you have ideas on where they may be, discuss them with Rani. If you are successful, he will have today locked in his memory, and you will not be forgotten over the next three years. If you are not successful, he may decide his new recruits need a training exercise to ferret out your friends." He paused. "As for me, I would like to be just a soldier along for the experience and watch how you and Rani solve this puzzle. I have no better place to be, and I think it would be good for both of you to know each other a little better. Is this acceptable to you?"

"You would do this for me?" Kid questioned.

"You can think that if you wish, but I have promised upon my honor to deliver this coin. If you and Rani do all the work of finding them, I would love to dance in and make a grand gesture of behalf of the Empress."

CHAPTER 16

A HUNT THROUGH JUISITI

There was a sharp rap on the carriage door, and Rani pushed himself in. He started at seeing Nari.

"I'm sorry, Kid, I thought you were alone."

Nari nodded at the softfoot. "We haven't met, though I have heard your name often enough. Rani, I am Nari. Kid and I are riding together, but if you have this evening free, we would love to have you join us on an adventure of our own." He tilted his head in the barest acknowledgement of the short bow.

Rani grinned. "That fits in with my plans. Ngahuru told me to say there was no message left at the embasado. She said the next steps were up to you, but she encouraged you to think of your future and not your past."

Kid furrowed his brow. "Then let me ask you two questions before you ask questions of your own. Does Juisiti have an area where Keresh speakers would be most at home, either to live or to work? A neighborhood not too expensive where two who are newly married would choose to settle?"

Rani considered the question. "Do they speak any Vik? How old are they? What do they look like?"

Kid explained how he had been a witness to Oro and Linna's wedding and according to their records they said they were twenty-one and eighteen. How they had lived in Axefield while the others were at Rishka, and then they had moved to Juisiti when the Conrosans came to Axefield to build the second inn.

"Oro is as tall as a Viklander, though slender. He had a grandparent who gave him his fine golden skin and his black hair. However, he was bought and sold by the Orphan Master in Kerek City to a Kereki family and does not speak any other language but Keresh.

"Linna is known to your softfoot Quan and probably Lomes. She lived in a house in Cloa with another Wren, a Spice Islander named Arden." Kid watched Rani's face carefully. There was a slight tightening along the jaw. It was true then. The Viklander softfoot knew Arden wasn't a Kereki thief. Kid smiled to himself.

"Linna is quiet and smiles easily. She grew up in the Flower District with a family who owned a business. She reads and writes. During the war, she worked in a shop in Cloa gathering secrets to pass along to the Wrens and your softfoots. Depending on who you are, she is a 'look at me' or your eyes would pass right over her." He paused. "Nelo thought she was pretty."

Rani and Nari both laughed.

"What?" Kid scowled.

"It's fairly obvious you don't. What do you consider a 'pretty' girl?" Rani teased.

"One with a little more spark and snap." Kid thought of Dica with her plain face and dark eyes. When it became obvious to all the Wrens that Evensong was going to be a Kereki stronghold and Kid would be watched too closely to travel about freely, Dica stepped forward and said she could softfoot messages and documents to Nelo and Inezi.

He remembered at Axefield how she had come to him and said she needed to learn to write and read Keresh well, and if he could teach her the letters of Vik. When he had agreed, she demanded to learn it all before the next Dry.

"One who considers what may stand in the way of her plans and then conquers it."

"She sounds formidable," Nari said quietly.

Kid snapped his head to Nari wondering if he was being

mocked. But neither man had a smirk on their face. Embarrassed, he dropped his head and fell silent.

Rani cleared his throat and said briskly, "We can find them. How long ago did they arrive in Juisiti?"

"A season ago, at the beginning of the Dry."

Rani suggested looking near the academies first. Nearly all Viklanders spoke Keresh as a second language, said Rani, and students at the academies would be less likely to take offense when none was intended.

Another West Islander came out to the carriage, saying the Ambassador and Ngahuru had sent him to assist them. Nari explained he was not yet finished with completing the Empress's request, and they would need a driver familiar with the streets and neighborhoods of Juisiti. Rani gave directions. Without another word the driver climbed up and the carriage began to move.

Kid followed Nari's advice. As Rani started asking questions about when Ngahuru had come to Kerek, how she had selected where and how the network would work, and places and families still in Kerek who had helped them, Kid deflected them. He would tell a story of one of his rescues, or a time when the Wrens and the Viklanders had worked together, or remind Rani of information he had secured from Evensong and had passed along.

Twice Rani tapped on the roof of the carriage. Once it stopped, Rani merely said, "Stay here," and jumped out. The first time Nari raised an eyebrow, the second time, he told Kid, "He's checking with his own network."

Kid heard Rani as he gave new directions to the driver.

Before he could ask, Nari murmured, "Another part of the city, not as nice as here."

Rani reentered the carriage. He didn't say anything about the change in location, merely asked if Kid had met Zren Janin. How was he and where was he?

"He is at Axefield, and says he is planning to go to Matasi at the end of the Wet. More than that you should ask him because I do not know."

Rani took the rebuke good-naturedly and asked Kid if he could read and write.

"Keresh, yes. Mata, some. Vik? I know my letters is all."

"What are your future plans?"

Kid looked Rani full in the face. "To be a softfoot for Vikland in Kerek City. Your softfoots took heavy losses in the war. Bima Ritwik died saving others, including one of our Wrens, Tyra. I know the cost of a softfoot, Rani. I was one of the information gatherers for the

Harbormaster in Kerek City. I tracked cargos and captains as they did business and pleasure from the time they docked until they cast off. I was paid in coin and percentages of the taxes collected. It was not in my best interest to miss details. It was not in my best interest to be careless walking about the city. It was not in my best interest to misremember a time or date, a shipment's weight, a captain's name.

"During the war, I served as a under footman at Evensong—which you know billeted Kereki officers. Although my master learned he had a traitor in the house, his suspicion never fell on me. I have lived by my wits and talents for years.

"I have heard Bima Ritwik was a difficult taskmaster. It was how he kept so many of you alive during the war. I would wager that Kerek City, especially Dockside where I worked and the Sinner's District where I lived—was just as demanding."

Rani smiled broadly. "It is good I like my softfoots with a little snap and spark as well." He sobered. "It is true our numbers were decimated during the war. All of us old softfoots, except for Bima, are still around, but few of the young ones had enough training before we needed them in the field. For now, Kern and I are trying to gather all of our scattered bits and pieces and weave them into a whole cloth."

The carriage slowed and Rani looked out the window. "Ah, here we are. Again, I beg your indulgence while I meet with someone. I will be brief." The carriage had barely stopped when Rani jumped out and carefully closed the door.

Kid looked out the window at the evening. The sun was setting behind the carriage throwing a pink glow on the buildings. The streets were clean. There were no iron bars on the windows or doors. The houses were small and pushed up tight against each other, but they weren't falling into disrepair. He was surprised. When Nari said the neighborhood was not as nice, Kid had envisioned Lowertown, or even Dockside. This looked more like the Flower District.

Kid could feel Nari watching him even though both were silent. He wondered if Nari was merely doing his duty as he saw it to be, or if this was something else. Kid knew the formal Vikland greetings, he understood how Nari had disrespected both Ngahuru and Rani by his lack of manners. He wondered if Nari was hiding behind a soldier's disdain for those who spy and pry out others' secrets. Could it be pride in the Ulani name when softfoots used only one name as if they were Kereki street runners? Or something else entirely?

Kid pulled his eyes from the view outside the carriage window and met Nari's gaze. The Viklander merely smiled and stretched his arms above his head. There were voices outside, but still both men were startled when the door suddenly opened and Rani pushed himself in.

"We have a clue!" he announced. "There is a neighborhood near here which has been welcoming Kerekis displaced by the war. Many are from south Kerek, but my friend tells me there are also some who lost everything between the Cold Mountains and the Northern Track. Could you draw a likeness of either of them? Is there any reason why they would not use their names as they are listed in the Central Administrative Offices?"

Kid shook his head to both.

"Ah, one bad, one good. I can live with that." The carriage moved forward again.

"So, tell me, Kid, I can understand why you shared a carriage with Ngahuru. I knew you in Kerek after all. But I would like to hear the story of how you and Nari Ulani decided on chasing about Juisiti for an evening's entertainment."

Rani gave a sly grin. "Ah, Nari, did you really think I would not know who you were? You Ulanis all look like you stepped from a Viklander tapestry."

Rani looked back at Kid. "Could you tell me this story? Are you and Nari only friends for the night or for the future?"

"That is not my story to tell," Kid said quietly. Rani looked at Nari who looked blandly back.

"Obviously it has something to do with the two we are tracking down. Kid, you have known me longer than you have known Nari. I am helping you find your lost friends while Nari merely sits in this fancy carriage and waits for us. Yet, you keep his secrets. Should I be impressed by this I wonder? This Viklander who has no manners and does not treat me with the respect I deserve?"

Kid watched as Nari narrowed his eyes and the smile tightened. But the soldier still said nothing.

"I see." Rani nodded his head thoughtfully, "You have no coin and are selling yourself as a fancy, and Nari can get no one else to share his bed."

Nari snarled out something sharp and nasty in Vik, and Kid dropped his eyes. He hadn't known Nari Ulani for more than one day, and he already knew the man was proud, beyond proud. Rani had gone for blood with his comment that Nari would stoop to buying affection.

Rani switched to Vik and the exchange was sharp and heated. Kid kept his eyes on the floor and listened. It was true, he had told Rani he couldn't read Vik, but the softfoot hadn't asked if Kid understood it, and Kid had been disinclined to share the news so freely. If he had, he wouldn't be listening as Nari said Rani knew exactly why he was in the West Islands Ambassador's carriage or he wasn't much of a softfoot. Rani should be grateful to him since it had been his idea to invite Rani along so he could meet this future softfoot who had enough talent he could save Rani's foolish head someday. If Rani wanted to show off for Kid, that was his affair, but he was too old and too tired to preen for a child. He was going to complete his duty to his Empress as any good soldier would. Then he would take himself and Kid home to the Keopi District, where he could return to his coffee fields and leave the cesspool of liars and false friends of Juisiti far behind.

Rani scoffed saying Kid would hate the edge of the world. Taking him to the Keopi District would only age him and not educate him. He would not learn how to softfoot, to learn languages, to slip through a city and find information, or a person, or an answer to a problem. One season in east Vikland and Kid would beg Rani to bring him to Juisiti and teach him what he needed to know. Kid would hate it in Keopi, giving up the excitement and adventure of the city to do nothing but watch the coffee beans grow.

"And who is going to pay for this?" Nari snapped. "You want him now, but you can't pay for the academies. Wars are expensive, Rani. The Empress has already offered what she will. The Ulani family has offered him a home and tutors and work until my brother Leo or cousin Tedros can help us all in the coffee business. We will pay his fees and his needs at the academy in gratitude, and you will gain an educated man to softfoot. If you take him now, you will have one only partially formed. You know how well that worked out for you in the last war. You and Bima whispered sweet words to every student at the academy who had at least one parent or grandparent who was not a Viklander. You stained their skin, you cut their braid, you had Quan tell them how exciting it all was. And who do you have left?"

Rani gave a chagrinned look. "I need him now. I need faces in Matasi and Kerek City."

"You need them but you have no one to properly run them. Use what you have. My aunt tells me Solkka has been sent to both Alenti and Salisport in the service of the Empress. Because of his uncle, the King of the West Islands, he is invited to any event with a royal or ambassador in attendance. He *says* he is in the Diplo. But that didn't stop Vikland from sending him across Kerek with only First Soldier Joon to find out when the Kerek King fell and what was happening in Kerek City. Let Kid be educated first. Let him learn about Vikland by working for the Ulani family first. Then you will have Kid as a true softfoot and not just an information gatherer. Don't be short sighted on this. That is what cost you the love of my sister."

Kid snapped his head up. He had no idea the men had known each other. They both stopped and stared at him.

"I thought you said you didn't know Vik," Rani questioned sharply.

Kid shook his head. "No, you asked me if I could read and write. You didn't ask me if I could understand Vik. I wasn't a thief in Kerek City, there was no need for me to see the words to steal them. I only needed to be able to hear them and repeat them to the Harbormaster."

Nari barked out a sharp laugh. "Ha! Ah, Kid. I will remember to my grave, the night you bested Rani the softfoot. Rani, I wish my uncle Devi could see your face. He could mimic it for my entertainment every night and I would never tire of it." He continued laughing.

Kid could see Rani replaying his conversation in his head. He nodded. "You are right, you told the truth. I asked only what you could read and write, and you offered more than I expected. I was so glad to hear you say some Mata, I did not pay attention to the rest."

"I am not a liar." Kid bristled.

Nari interjected, "I have been down this path with him before, Rani. Kid will tell the truth. It is up to you to ask the questions the right way. I tell you truly, I think he has been trained by better softfoots than you. Now we just need to get him through the academies before he is turned loose on Kerek City."

The carriage stopped again. Rani scowled. "Well, let's see how well Ngahuru trained him then. Kid, you and I will step out here and see what we can find. Nari, I will let you have the carriage to yourself. Perhaps a nap will improve your disposition, although I doubt it." Rani pushed open the door and stepped down into the street. Kid followed.

This neighborhood was not as nice as the one they left. There were bars on the windows, and the houses crowded up against each other. There were small cooking fires in bowl-shaped pits in the earthen walkways. People walked in crowds up and down the street, carrying small woven bags of belongings or food. It smelled like cooked food, too many bodies, animals, and old refuse.

Rani shrugged. "Most people who live here lost everything in the war. It is cheap, but it is not nice. I am sorry, Kid. I think we will find your friends here."

Kid hunched his shoulders together. "What should we do?"

"You said Linna was a shop girl. It is my intention to stop and visit all the shops and ask if she is working there. If you would look at the faces as they walk down the street? Most are coming home from their work in other parts of the city. It is possible you may see your friends at the end of their walk home. It is the best we can do at this moment."

Kid nodded. He took a good look at the carriage to make sure he could find it again, then he turned to push his way against the crowd of people walking toward him.

CHAPTER 17

ALL WHO WANDER ARE NOT LOST

"So where do you learn all these stories, anyway?" Josef leaned back against the wagon seat.

Zren thought for a moment. "Lots of people. Ngahuru's brother, Koanga, started by telling me stories of the West Islands constellations. I had never heard anything like it. I was so caught up in the make-believe, I didn't understand the West Islanders use the stories to teach the children—well, actually anyone—about who they are as a people and how to find their way."

He paused. "On the Coast Road, Ngahuru told me Conrosan folk tales because she was trying to figure out who I was and if I was a danger to her. She had to tell me I was Conrosan. I didn't even know that much about myself.

"In Matasi, I heard about the parables. I heard more of them from Bima. He told me Kereki Trickster tales too." He paused. "Those are really messed up. If anyone offers you something you think you want more than anything else in the world, run the other way.

"Rell and Ngahuru both told me Vikland sagas. I thought I wouldn't like them because Rell said they teach strategy and battle history, but actually, they are interesting." He gave Josef a sly look. "They have monsters."

"All right, all right. I get it. Everyone knows those stories except me." Josef laughed easily.

Zren looked at him seriously. "I don't think that is true. I don't think many people know all of them. Rell says they teach the sagas in the academies. Koanga is a Storyteller of the West Islands. But Bima Ritwik and Ngahuru were the only ones who told me stories from other countries. Now I wonder if it was because they were softfoots and learned them from the countries they spied on. And if so, why was this important to them?"

He was quiet for a moment and then continued shyly, "I think I should write them all down so people could learn them all together. Some of the stories are so much alike it could be one story learned from the other one."

Josef looked at Zren, who carefully watched his hands on the reins. It felt like Zren had given him the gift of a secret, but with Zren it was always hard to tell. Sometimes he wondered if Zren truly thought the way he spoke, or if he was like Arden—

always telling a story just a little differently so it was hard to know what was the truth of it.

He sighed and looked off in the distance, away from Zren. "Do you ever wonder what people would be like if they grew up in another place? Or with different people to help them grow up? I mean look at us." He paused. "What do you think your life would be like if the Conrosans wouldn't have offered you sanctuary?"

"I'd be dead, Josef," Zren said promptly. "I would have been dead if Ngahuru would not have found me along the road to Aldi. I would have been abandoned in a jail until I was dead if the Viklanders would just have left me in Matasi without coin or knowing the language. I would have died at the Battle at the Bridge, if Chul and Song and Rell had not worked together to save all of us, not just themselves. When Miya left me at Manumina, I would have died of hunger if the Council would not have given us the House of Nations to live in, and sent Siba to come over and teach me how to live in a house, or Piffik to take me along to learn how to work for coin and food. Josef, I know I would be dead if many people—many people—had not said, 'Oh, look, here is a boy worth saving.'"

"And yet, you are going to go join Solkka in Salisport at the end of the Wet."

Zren was quiet for a long time. "Is that wrong?"

Josef said softly, "No. Yes. I don't know." He gave a heartfelt sigh. "Falan is ready to move on with her life. She found Callis. She says I am important to her, but she doesn't think I need to move with them. I think she is trying to give me permission to find my own way, but then we say stupid words to each other, and I don't know. I want to go and see what is ahead of me, but what if I…um…miss you all, or learn that I need Falan to survive?"

"Then you come to see us," Zren said promptly.

"You make it sound so easy." Josef paused a long time.

"When I was a boy in Kerek City, one time a man brought in a creature that he had bought from Spice Island traders. He called it a monkey, and it wore a little collar with a fine braided leather leash. I thought it was only a creature he had dressed in little clothes and let prance about while he was gambling. But then Falan's father said the man was winning too much at the tables and must be cheating. Falan said it had to be the monkey; he had trained it somehow. The next time the man came in, he was allowed to gamble as much as usual. He won a great deal of coin. But when he left, Falan's father had two of his men follow him home."

Josef gave a deep sigh. "It was a long time before the gambler came in again, and this time he came alone. He looked like he hated me. I wondered what I had done wrong. He showed me a fine steel knife and told me, he 'had planned a death for a death—a monkey for a monkey.' But then he shook his head and walked out again. It took me a few days to understand…he meant me.

"Yesterday, Arden said something out loud that I have been thinking about since we left Manumina. Sometimes, I wonder what Falan sees when she looks at me."

Josef watched Zren carefully wondering how he would respond. He had seen Nelo watch him and Falan with a question on his face, and yesterday, Arden had bluntly told him what he thought. He was not ignorant of the whispers of the Wrens. But if there was anyone who would say every thought in his head without shading the truth, it would be Zren.

Zren looked like he had been caught out stealing food. Josef felt a laugh bubbling up but then Zren quickly slipped into a story.

It was a Kereki Trickster tale. One in which Death tricked a young girl into trading a year of her life in exchange for beauty so great her true love would see no other. The young girl foolishly agreed, thinking when she was in her extreme old age, her true love would still be by her side, and age would be too cruel of a mistress to want to linger overlong. Within the year, she had met her love, he had married her, and they kept house in a little cottage filled with bliss.

"But Death is a Trickster," Zren said ominously. A fever swept the village, blinding the young man and carrying off the young woman before the first year of marriage was done. Death had claimed her year at the beginning and not the end as the foolish young woman had thought.

"This cannot be true," Josef said when Zren had finished. "Any woman is going to be beautiful to her true love."

"Yes!" Zren cried out. "That is why they are Trickster tales! She already has what she is asking for, and yet she pays too great a price for it."

Josef let out a slow roll of laughter. "You *should* write down all these stories, Zren. I would read them, if for no other reason than to try to learn more about how to make a pretty girl do more than smile back at me."

Zren shot him an incredulous look. "You don't know?"

"Know what? I know I smile at the Conrosan girls, and they smile back until their mothers shoo me away. I smile at the Viklander girls at the inn, and they look me up and down and smile back, but none will take a walk with me."

"Promise you are not mocking me?" Zren was skeptical.

Josef gave him an exasperated look. "Just say it already."

"The Conrosan girls do not speak and flirt with you because they are afraid of Falan. They know you are not her lover. But as

Arden said yesterday, she looks at you like a dragon in a fairy tale. You are her treasure and she will not share," Zren said earnestly.

"The Viklander girls aren't afraid of Falan and would tumble you, but they do not like boys who are prettier than they are." Zren looked Josef up and down and smirked. "And you are very pretty. It is why they flirt and tease with Nelo even though they know he won't flirt back. Or maybe because of it." Zren shrugged. "I don't know for sure."

Josef stared at him. Zren didn't notice but continued on, "Why would Rygee write Nelo a letter when everyone knows Nelo doesn't read? When Siba gave me the letter to give him, she said the seal was not for me, but for him to know it was so private no one else would know. What did she mean?"

Josef breathed out a long sigh and shrugged. Everyone knew Zren's mind flitted about, landing on anything that interested him. It was why it was so easy to get him to share information he didn't know should be secret.

"I don't know. I've thought about it too. But what I have figured out is no one knows whether Nelo does not read because he *cannot* learn or he *will not* learn. There is a difference. I think Siba is trying to show him what could happen if it is because he chooses not to learn."

"What did the letter say?" Zren exclaimed.

Josef looked away over the horizon again. "I think it has everything to do with why Nelo disappeared before daylight. I think Arden's anger when you pulled out the Kereki army paychest is part of it. I believe Ngahuru is going to regret her sarcasm when she told you to bring the Kereki paychest without all of Axefield finding out. She should have told you specifically not to tell anyone. I think you can figure it out from there."

He paused. "And just in case you can't, I wonder why Rygee and Ngahuru are working against each other and using the Wrens to do it." He looked sad. "This is a battle, we—I mean you and me, Zren—want no part of. Nelo is protective and vengeful and not afraid of Kereki metal poisoning. And Arden would take offense at anyone thieving from a thief. Have you ever noticed he doesn't get angry unless he feels he has been tricked? Even when Falan dumped out his bedding from the Wrens' house, he just picked up his belongings, and he and Mother went to sleep above the stables. But this? If those two challenge Ngahuru? Just tell them you were only doing what you were told."

Zren nodded slowly.

For the rest of the trip, they talked about everything and nothing as people do when they are almost friends. There was no immediate demand for the items on the wagon, and Nelo and Arden were still behind them. They wanted to see some of the settlements just beyond theirs, and so they wandered down a few of the breakaways from the main track just because they could. They did not talk again about the army paychest buried deep beneath the clothes and Piffik's tools.

Zren and Josef reached the Huena Inn stables closer to end of day than midday.

As they pulled into the stables, Zren asked, "I can take care of the horses, but what should I do about the wagon?"

Josef thought. "Stay here. I'll find Rygee and tell him his supplies are here and send a runner to find Piffik. I think we hid the chest well enough behind the latches it will be safe until Nelo and Arden get back."

CHAPTER 18

ORO AND LINNA

At first Kid thought he had imagined him. He had been staring at faces so long that when the tall man in front of him looked like Oro, he nearly passed him by.

"Oro!" Kid cried out. The man stopped but not until Kid waved his arm did he recognize him.

"Kid?" His brow furrowed as if he couldn't figure out why Kid would be standing in the streets of Juisiti.

"We've been looking for you. It's so good to see you!"

"Why would you look for me? For us?"

Kid leaned close to his ear. "I have coin for you. The Empress rewarded us for our service during the war."

Oro jerked up. "Truly? Have you told Linna?"

"I don't know where she is. I have two Viklanders with me. Can we come to your house and give you," Kid looked around at the people pushing by them, "what we brought?"

Oro grimaced. "I hate to have others see, but we have no choice." He followed Kid and explained their living conditions as they weaved their way through the people to the carriage. Kid opened the door and gestured Oro to enter.

Only Nari was there. Kid introduced the two to each other and then asked Nari what they should do.

"They live in a house with other people, Nari. If we take their travel bags in, they will be robbed as easily as if they were in a Kerek tavern. There is no safe place for them to hide their coin. Both Linna and Oro work during the day."

Nari considered. "Would you live elsewhere if you could? Or is this house where you wish to be?"

Oro scoffed. "Of course, I would live elsewhere. This is what we could find with Linna's coin from her shop days in Cloa. I was never paid when I was at Manumina. Here, I work at the academies. I weed the flower gardens, prune shrubs, and pick up after lazy students. Linna and I try to learn Vik to get better positions, but truly? Most days we are too tired to do anything but fall into our bed."

"I can promise you nothing, but I think Rani can help us. Let us have the carriage move slowly down the street. That will let him know you have been found and I have you inside." Nari tapped his cane on the roof and called out the window, "Slowly. Just slowly move forward. Rani will find us."

Kid watched as Nari and Oro took each other's measure. Oro glanced down at the missing leg and then kept his eyes carefully on Nari's face. Kid noted Oro's height, not as tall as Nari, but thinner than he had been at Manumina, his straight, black hair loose to his shoulders.

Kid cleared his throat. "Oro, you should wear your hair back in a braid, even a tiny one is better than none. Because you look like you should know better, you are probably treated worse than if you looked like me."

Nari turned and gave Kid a half smile. "Thank you. I did not know how to tell him."

He turned back to Oro. "It's true. Vikland will seem to you very confusing, just as our women soldiers tell us how difficult it is for them at first in Kerek. It would be best for you and Linna to find Vik friends you can trust to help you, to explain our unfamiliar ways."

The carriage halted. Rani knocked once before he opened the door and pushed himself in.

"Hello!" He sat down next to Nari, across from Kid and Oro. Rani gave Oro a long look. "We met at Manumina. A soldier who had been redeemed from the Huk jail and I traveled in Zren Janin's cheese cart. I saw you there before Piffik took me to Ishes."

Oro nodded slowly but said nothing.

Rani asked, "So where is the carriage taking us?"

"There is a problem." Nari switched to Vik and continued, "They do not live in a place where they can safely receive the Empress's reward. You know as well as I do, Rani, it is a soldier's pay for a year for each of them. Do you have a house, a bolt hole in the city, they can stay for the night with their coin? They can move to a new place tomorrow and keep poverty and starvation from their door while they learn Vik and Vikland's ways. They do not know of banks or coin lenders; they need Vik teachers for almost everything. Is there such a person?"

Rani nodded sharply. Looking at Oro, he spoke Keresh, "Let's go find your wife."

***

It was close by. Oro went inside to get Linna and the two of them came out to the carriage. Quickly, Rani explained what would happen. They needed to go back inside and get their most valuable things; they would not be coming back to live there. He would take them to a place close to the academies where they—all of them—would stay the night. Tomorrow, either Oro or Linna would not go to work but go with him to find a place to live, get the rest of their belongings, and place their coin with a banker.

"I will go," Linna said quickly. "My position in the shop was not a good one. The stores that welcome the Kereki refugee coins are not always…" she trailed off. "I was already looking to find a new Patron," she finished quickly.

"Fine." Rani didn't ask any more questions. "Go get your things, only one of you so the others do not suspect you are not coming back tonight." Oro opened the door and left without a word. Rani followed him out and the others could hear him giving directions to the driver.

"Why are you doing this for us?" Linna asked Kid. He cut his eyes to Nari who looked surprised.

"I gave my word to the Empress the favor she asked of me would be done." Nari scowled. "I lost my braid in *battle*, Linna. I am an honorable man."

She glanced at Kid and then looked out the window of the carriage.

The house Rani took them to was long and narrow with rooms opening into each other. There was a front room with cooking to the side, the next room had two sets of narrow beds stacked on top of each other, and the last room had a bed big enough for two large Viklanders and a walled off bathing room with Conrosan-style plumbing.

"What is this place?" Nari asked as they walked through. His bastono clicked on the hard wooden floor.

"It was a professor's house, one who taught at the academies when your sister Nadja and I were students. He was a Conrosan—very old—so he said he built his vertical house horizontally because he did not want to climb stairs. Viklanders are not fond of this style, and it was empty for a long while. Bima bought it for the softfoots just before the war. He housed the newest softfoots here while they were training with Kern." Rani smiled. "They liked it because the noodle shop on the corner is open late into the evening."

The West Islands driver carried in the last of their belongings and both Nari and Rani walked him out to send him home for the night. The three Wrens stood and looked at each other.

"Why are you doing this?" Linna asked again. "We have done nothing kind for you."

"You earned the Empress's thanks as well as the other Wrens. Two years of coin—a soldier's pay—is no small gift for the both of you." Kid grinned at them. "We Wrens softfooted all through Kerek, you think I couldn't find you?"

"And Ngahuru is not the one who sent you? Nor any of the other Wrens?"

Kid stilled as he heard the unspoken question. He thought she was asking about Arden, or as much as she could, in front of Oro.

"Ngahuru is leaving with the other West Islands embasado staff and the Ambassador's family. They have a Matasi escort tomorrow or the next day to travel across Kerek and take a ship home. All of the Wrens have made plans to either travel to Matasi, stay in Axefield, or move with the Conrosans to build a new port in eastern Vikland. You are the only ones who are making a home in Juisiti."

"And you?"

"I am going to travel with Nari Ulani, the man with the bastono, to his coffee farm in the Keopi District. There I will learn the coffee business for three years while his younger brother Leo is completing his military service. I have been promised help and coin for the academies when this is done. Rani, the other man who is helping us, would like me to join his Viklander softfoots if I prove myself smart enough. Tonight may have a cost involved, but it will not come from you, I do not think. It is something Rani, Nari, and I must figure out."

The door opened, and the Wrens fell silent as Rani and Nari came back into the room. Rani rubbed his hands together briskly. "I have asked the noodle shop owner to send us food when he has some ready. The Empress is paying for all this, so I hope you are hungry. While we are waiting for the food, let us sort ourselves out. Obviously, Linna and Oro have the last room, but if you could permit us to freshen up first, we will get out of your way."

The food arrived and Rani took over as host, chatting and telling stories and acting as if he had planned this evening days in advance. Kid could see how tired Nari was. The soldier grimaced, and Kid realized he was probably in pain as well.

Suddenly, Nari got up from the table and said he was going to bed for the night.

"Enjoy yourselves. You won't wake me. The Academy of Pain and Misery has concocted enough different potions for me, you may need a looking glass to see if I am still breathing in the morning." He had unbuckled his bastono from his arms in order to eat freely and now as he fumbled about trying to reconnect them, he suddenly threw them on the floor. He sat down hard on his chair and cursed.

Kid jumped up. "Let me help you so you don't need to take the time for those now, just to unbuckle them a few steps later." He looked to Oro to help, but it was Linna who stood up quickly and walked to the other side of the Viklander. The others were silent as they moved into the room with the stacked beds. Kid angled to the closest one. "Which bag has the medicinals?"

Nari pointed, and Linna bent down to retrieve it. "Leave me." The Wrens stood there uncertainly. "I said, leave. I can do the rest myself."

They left.

CHAPTER 19

WHILE YOU WERE GONE

Nelo and Arden rode in at nightfall. They brought their horses into the stables, and only the overnight feed boy and two hostlers were still up. The younger one stood to help them, but Arden just nodded to her and said they would take care of their own mounts.

More to make conversation than anything, Nelo asked if there had been any excitement since they had left the day before.

Both the feed boy and the girl talked over each other as they eagerly told the men of the West Islands carriage carrying a Viklander soldier with a missing leg. They described the West Islander who had stayed in the stables. Both thought he was a soldier too—definitely not just a carriage driver.

The girl said she had heard from others the Viklander spoke for the Empress and had met with the Kerekis who lived with the Conrosans.

She gave an uncertain look at Nelo. "I think it was your friends."

The boy blurted in then and said how the soldier had left with the West Islands woman and the ghost.

"What ghost?" Nelo asked.

"The sun-dark Kereki who stands so still you do not know he is there until he speaks. The one who is always reading."

"Kid." Arden stiffened. "Where did they take him?"

"Juisiti, I heard. They had to leave at midday. The West Islander was to go to the embasado." The boy was self-important with his news.

"Did the ones in the carriage have a name?" Arden asked.

"There was only the one. When we asked the driver if he was carrying the Ambassador, he said it was a Viklander from the family Ulani."

Arden answered gruffly. "Tedros, or maybe Solkka. You said he was missing his leg, was he also missing his braid? Did he have a long scar on his face?"

The boy was uneasy at the roughness in Arden's voice. "His braid was tiny, still growing. He had no scar."

"Tedros." Arden sighed sadly.

The stable hands looked at each other and shrugged. They had not heard his name.

"Zren will be sorry to have missed him if he had to leave at midday. There is no way they would have made it back in time." He looked back at the two. "Thank you for your news. It is not welcome, but it is necessary for us to know this."

Nelo walked with Arden to the dormitory building for the workers. They both heard Mother's light woof as they got close.

Nelo smirked. "Better than a wife. Mother complains you're late before you walk in the door. Or is that why you've been walking out with a Viklander girl from the inn? Mother trained you just as you trained her."

Arden just laughed. They walked in to find all the Wrens—and Mother—waiting for them. Josef and Zren were there, Zren with a cheese bun in one hand and a pickle in the other. Tyra started to tell them what they had missed, but Falan said the dormitories were no place for secrets. They followed her out into the gardens and then with many restarts and retellings, the story of Nari Ulani was told.

Josef reassured them Nari was a cousin to the two Ulani men he had met and no one any of the Wrens had rescued. All agreed, better a stranger to bear such scars from the war, than one they had helped and known. Dica slid close and gave Arden the letter from Tedros, and another one from Kid. He raised an eyebrow at her, but she only shrugged, and so he slipped them up his shirtsleeve for later.

Nelo was stunned to learn Ngahuru was gone. No letter, no explanation of why she had taken the chest from the shepherd's cottage. He wondered what would have happened if she had not asked Zren to bring it back for her. If Rygee had not sent the letter on this trip. If Zren could have read the letter to him, would he have said, "oh, the paychest is here," and given it to him?

What if Arden had thought about working on the roof the next day and thought it was too far to come after him? The chest carried *so much* coin. He didn't realize until he had been at the shepherd's cottage and thought it was gone, how much it had meant to him. Even sharing it with Rygee would still mean he would have a future without want.

CHAPTER 20

THE COST OF KINDNESS

Kid had once told Dica the reason he thought he loved softfooting so much was the layers and layers of interaction. There was Linna and Oro in front of him now, warily grateful for the help they were receiving, but concerned about the price they would pay for that help. Of course they were, they had been raised in Kerek City where no good deed was given freely, or as Nelo would say, kindness never goes unpunished.

Kid knew a little more, but not much. He knew this was more than a favor done for an Empress. The interaction between Rani and Nari last night had been all flash and fire, the care and feeding of an old grudge. Today, it seemed the men were reassessing each other. Or so Kid thought. He guessed Rani could be in his mid-thirties, about the age of Padro Morto. Nari on the other hand, was in his early twenties if he was still in his military service. And now he thought Nadja, Nari's oldest sister, was the common link. Perhaps.

Kid also felt both men were not exactly testing him, but definitely looking for him to show them his abilities. Over first meal, Kid had listened carefully as Rani had explained how banks worked in Vikland.

"It is not necessary to hide your coin in secret places in your house or bury it in the dirt for safekeeping," he had said. Oro had needed to leave for work then, but Linna and Kid had continued to ask questions.

Kid had asked Linna if she wanted to be a shop girl. He had learned, on the long ride in the back of Zren Janin's wagon on the way to Evensong, how Aajan Qanaq had earned a place in Vikland's academies. Chul Swyler, a firemaster of Vikland, had taken Aajan Qanaq with him when he returned to Vikland because she could draw what was in his head. Perhaps there were other teachers at the academy who needed such assistants and Linna could work there. She looked the age of a student, and it might be easier to gain friends and learn what she needed to know if others thought she was one.

Nari said he needed to find Aajan Qanaq on another matter. He had a gift from the Conrosans to the Academy of Healing. Rani said he was interested in hearing more of this. Nari told him of the salve Siba Namikk had given him and how it made it possible for him to bear his pain without drinking potions or wine which clouded his thinking. The salve had been given without a cost and with permission to share with Vikland. He needed Aajan Qanaq to translate the recipe from Conrosan to Vik and to make samples for the Academy of Botanicals. He had been told Aajan shared working rooms in the same building as Chul Swyler.

Rani asked Kid how he would go about finding Aajan Qanaq.

"I don't think I would," Kid replied. "I would look for Chul Swyler. He is well known in Juisiti, I think, at least the Conrosans thought so. I would start at the Academy of Healing. They might know of Chul as a patient or as an inventor. Padro Morto—Piffik Qanaq—said Chul Swyler had invented the bastono which Nari uses. This would be a gift he would have shared with other soldiers from the war. I would ask about Chul Swyler and where he has his working rooms. Then I would casually ask about Aajan and if she has been to the Academy of Healing or if they might know where I could find her. If they know of her, and where she lives, that would be best. If not, then I would find Chul Swyler and ask him."

"That is a good place to start." Rani nodded. "Once you find Chul Swyler? And he agrees to see you?"

Kid hesitated and then continued, "And then, while I was visiting with Chul, I would casually ask about places to live and work nearby. I would say it is for my sister, who is now in Juisiti. I would say we are struggling with our Vik; our tutors were not as good as we believed them to be, and ask if he had a remedy for that as well. And then I would repeat this story as many times as I needed to until I find Aajan Qanaq, a place to live, and a place to work. I would not neglect the Vikland greetings of course. I would not want those who help us to think I had been dumped in a field and raised myself."

"Your plan has merit." Rani smiled in approval. "Well, Linna, are you and Kid ready to find your future? I will give you directions to the Academy of Healing—it is quite close to here and then it is up to you. Nari and I will meet you at Chul Swyler's rooms in a little while. You should know, Chul Swyler is a busy man and an important one. If you gave the Vikland bow nearly as deep as you would give the Empress, there are many of us who would not think anything of it. Viklanders are alive because of his clever mind. His inventions of ghostfire and compound bows and other designs saved the lives of many soldiers and softfoots in the war."

Rani told them they would be using the house they were in for at least another day. Their coin and belongings would be safe there—on Nari Ulani's honor. Nari had bristled at that, but Rani just pretended to be shocked.

"What? I said you are so honorable they can leave all of their most valuable possessions here and nothing will happen to them. How does this insult you?" He hid a small smirk as he turned and gave Kid and Linna directions.

The Wrens looked at each other and then let themselves out the door. Before they had even closed it, they could hear Rani and Nari arguing again in Vik.

When they reached the end of the street, Linna wheeled on Kid. "What's really going on here? What is this going to cost us? Two Viklanders who act like they hate each other, and now a man so important to Vikland, Rani all but told you to treat him like the son of the Empress. Kid, we are *nothing* to these people. Why are they helping us?"

"I don't know," Kid answered truthfully. "Last night I thought Rani was helping us because he wanted information on Ngahuru and our maps and the names of our friends in Kerek from the war. Then I thought it was because it was Nari Ulani asking for help. The two men have history together although they acted as though they had never met. But I admit, Linna, I did not expect either of them to do anything more than find your lodgings, hand you your coin, and then wave goodbye as you were robbed by your fellow Kerekis."

He considered his next words carefully. "I knew Rani, a little, during the war. He was the softfoot who moved between the Kereki army encampment and the great houses of the north. His...territory overlapped Nelo, Dica, me, and Tyra, and he had Inezi and Therin at Fortika. He had to softfoot among the militias. I know he is not a casual man. I know he is not treating you as a casual favor." Kid tilted his head. "He said the Conrosan teacher had been there when he and Nadja had been at the academies together. I know Nadja Ulani is now the Right Hand at the coffee farm where Nari and I are going. I have known Nari Ulani for less than two days, Linna, and truly I have never met a man so proud. I know Manumina helped Vikland in the war. But these are all just threads, Linna, and I cannot weave them into a story that makes sense to me."

Linna gave him a thoughtful look and then turned down the street and started walking.

The Academy of Healing knew the firemaster Chul Swyler. They also knew he was far too busy of a man to take time from his day to talk with two Kereki refugees. Linna had stiffened at the insult, but Kid just calmly agreed and asked for directions to the workrooms or home of Aajan Qanaq. They were well acquainted with her brother Piffik, he said, and had letters for her from her family at Manumina, a place of shelter for the Vikland army during the past war.

The woman had looked them up and down and sent them to another. This one looked like a student. He flashed an appreciative smile at Linna. Kid quickly introduced her to him as his sister and a friend of Aajan Qanaq. Then Kid explained they were in Juisiti to visit the academies and were to meet their friend. Foolishly, Kid had misplaced the directions to her home and her workrooms, so now they had come here to see if Aajan was here or if someone could help them. Kid apologized several times for speaking Keresh, he had not known his Vik tutor had been such a poor one until he came here and learned he could not be understood.

The student had waved his hand in dismissal and replied, "You wouldn't believe some of the accents the students come dragging to the academy," and Kid tried not to cringe. The student didn't know where Aajan lived. He knew she wasn't in the women's dormitories with the other students because others commented on it, but he did know she had her workrooms on Fire Way. He could remember it so easily he said, because she had been working with many soldiers who had been burned in the war.

He smiled again at Linna. He didn't know which building on Fire Way because he wasn't foolish enough to ask to walk her home.

"She is not as pretty as you," he flirted.

"You are so kind." She smiled back. "You have already given us more help than we had a decon ago. Tell me, is Fire Way a long street, or are there some type of markings? If I knocked on a door, would people think kindly enough of me to point out her workrooms?"

He gallantly said he would certainly walk her to the door himself if he knew it, but that Fire Way would take a half decon or less to walk from end to end.

Kid gave a short bow. Linna merely smiled and thanked him as he pointed her in the right direction.

In the end, it was easier than that. They had merely turned left on Fire Way when they saw a two-wheeled carry cart with an arched awning and Nari Ulani sitting underneath. Rani was out of the cart talking to the driver who stood by his horse feeding it something out of his hand.

Rani smiled as they walked up. "Well done, we just got here. Our driver is ours for the day, and I took the liberty of asking Chul and Aajan for a decon of their time. They are putting their experiments to sleep for a while, and then they said they would listen to our stories. I ask that you tell Chul the truth, and you answer his questions as well as you are able. He is a far smarter man than all of us together. While I do not know Aajan Qanaq well, he would not be able to tolerate her if she is not as clever as he is. If you have any news of Piffik, I'm sure she would like to hear it."

Linna nodded. "Do I ask them if they know of a place to live, or only if there are positions at the academies which would hire a Keresh speaker who wants to learn Vik as fast as she can?"

Rani shrugged. "I'll let you read the room and make your own decision. Do either of you know Piffik Qanaq?"

They both nodded.

"During the war, Piffik gave me a ride on his coffin wagon to the Ishes garrison twice, allowing me to live to fight another day." He gave a half smile. "His sister is nothing like him. I won't say anything more than that."

The door opened behind them, and Aajan looked out. "Well, don't just stand there in awe of my presence. You want to talk? You need to come in and talk." She held open the door a little wider.

Before Kid had moved to the cart, the driver and Rani had brushed past him and quickly lifted Nari Ulani so his bastono touched the street before his leg. Kid noted how much easier it was when the taller Viklanders handed him down. He heard the click as the wooden legs locked into place and Nari swung forward. Rani carefully stood behind him as he navigated the step up to the building and the four walked inside.

Aajan closed the door and turned to Nari. "If you are trying to impress Chul Swyler by using bastono, it won't work."

Before Nari could say anything to such an outrageous comment, the familiar click-slide, click-slide of another pair of bastono could be heard coming down the hall. Chul Swyler came in the room smiling.

"Come in, come in, and sit down. I have chairs back here which will be more comfortable for all of us." He turned and led the way to his sitting room through his work tables with various trays of rocks and liquids. He turned and faced them. "Now, whom do I have the pleasure of meeting today?"

Nari bowed first. "Chul Swyler, firemaster of Vikland, I am Nari Ulani. It is my great honor to meet you. I lost my braid and my leg in a battle so close to Vingt and Kerek City, we had our patrols on the Ring Road. We never would have accomplished so much without your invention of ghostfire. And now, I am still grateful to you. Piffik Qanaq, the brother of Aajan Qanaq, made a pair of bastono for me when I was at Axefield serving at the pleasure of the Empress of Vikland." He bowed to Aajan and again to Chul.

Chul smiled back. "I see Piffik has refined the design. You have two legs, I have four." He turned over his scarred hands. "I now have the use of my hands, thanks to Aajan here, but I still have problems with the buckles. I need the four legs so it stands alone when I am not in it." He nodded his head. "You said, 'Of the family Ulani?' Are you acquainted with Kaede Ulani?"

"He is my oldest cousin, and the Left Hand of my uncle's coffee farm."

"He and I were in the academies at the same time. We had many classes together until he focused on the Academy of Botanicals. I heard he married and has children. Your family, they are all well?"

Nari bobbed his head. "Yes and no. We lost my sister Lissil to the war. She fell in a battle near Huk."

"May her name live on," Chul said gently.

Rani stepped in the awkward space. "Thank you both for seeing us today. I hope none of your work we interrupted is irretrievably lost." He looked to Kid to introduce himself next.

Kid spoke, "Chul Swyler, firemaster of Vikland, I am Kid, a Wren of Ngahuru, trained at Manumina, who served Vikland during the war at Evensong. It is my honor to meet you today."

He bowed and then turned to Aajan. "Aajan Qanaq, a woman so renowned at Manumina, the four of us have journeyed here from Axefield to seek your wisdom. I am beyond glad to meet you. Siba Namikk, Piffik Qanaq, and Zren Janin send their greetings." He bowed again.

"Zren Janin? Would that be the little stray who shows up here begging to be fed and then talks all night so no one can get any sleep?"

Kid hesitated. He had thought the more names he mentioned, the more likely Chul and Aajan would want to help them. Perhaps he had made a mistake.

Chul looked at the confusion on Kid's face and laughed. "Ah, Kid, Aajan's humor is much too sharp for most of us. She is as fond of Zren as I am, and I am very fond of him indeed. He is a man who will never lose the wonder of the world about him. Who could ask for a better friend than that?" He turned to Linna. "You don't look like Kid's sister, and you seem much too clever to associate with Rani on a regular basis. Do you have a name I can remember?"

"I am Linna, and I am also here to ask for your wisdom and advice."

"Well then, let's sit down and find out if this wisdom and advice will come join our conversation."

Linna told her story first. She explained she was married, and she and her husband were trying to make their way in Juisiti. Her husband Oro could not be here today; he was working. Neither of them knew enough Vik to get a position they were capable of, so she had been working in a shop catering to Kereki refugees and Oro was working as a manabout for the gardens and grounds of the Academies of Philosophy and History. Aajan had raised her brow at that but had said nothing. They had been living in a place with others, but as of this morning they were without a home. It would be better for them to find something closer to Oro's position, so he did not have to walk so far to and from their house every day.

She had liked Kid's suggestion this morning that perhaps Chul and Aajan would know of someone who needed another pair of hands, or someone who was needed to care for children or parents or a house while they were working. She didn't need to work in a shop, it was only what she was experienced in. She would be happy to…

"Shhh," Chul interrupted. "You have said enough." Linna sat back, clearly worried she had said too much, and revealed how desperate she felt. Chul gave Rani an unreadable look. "You would not have brought them here if you did not have a plan. What is that plan?"

Rani smiled. "I know you have Vikland coffee here. Why don't you and I make some for everyone while Nari Ulani tries to charm Aajan into translating Siba Namikk's recipe?" He stood and waited for Chul to get his bastono underneath him and then followed him out of the room.

Aajan flashed angry eyes at Rani's retreating back.

"It is more than a translation," Nari quickly tried to soothe her. He explained what had happened in Axefield and how the salve made each day bearable without drinking potions and wine. He fished out the recipe from a cloth pocket and gave it to her.

"Well, what do you want me to do?" She looked at it.

He smiled at her. "Siba said, this was a gift freely given to Vikland. I am to ask you to translate the words from Conrosan into Vik and make some samples for the Academies of Botanicals and of Healing. If you could give me a copy of the translated recipe I could have my aunt, Hilanna Ulani, who attended the Academy of Botanicals and graduated first in her class, make some for me so I could continue to be a coffee farmer."

"And I am to do this because I have nothing better to do?" She huffed. "Are you sure my brother didn't tell you to ask for this favor?"

Nari's grin grew even larger. "He may have been nearby…in the room…the one who said the words."

"I knew it!"

"He also said, if I took the recipe like that, written in Conrosan, to the Academy of Healing, it would not be so well accepted as it would be with your name and efforts attached." He tilted his head. "Do you know why he would say such a thing?"

Aajan sighed. "Give it here." She read it through quickly. "I cannot have the salves made up for you to take with you, they need to cure and mellow together, but I will have this written in Vik and Keresh before you leave today. I will also give you a shopping list of ingredients you must buy here in Juisiti and take to your aunt. Some are not so common that she would have them in her stillroom." She got up out of her chair and walked out of the room. Soon they could hear her climbing the stairs to her workrooms.

Nari smiled at Kid. "Do you have brothers or sisters?"

Kid nodded his head, but didn't say anything more.

Nari grinned. "The thing about brothers and sisters is some things never change."

CHAPTER 21

SIBA TELLS A STORY

The next day at midday, Arden, Nelo, Josef, and Zren went to find Siba to hear her version of Nari Ulani's visit, Ngahuru's disappearance, Kid's plans, and to get their travel bags of coin. Siba told the story again but said their bags with their reward were in Raul Huena's safe. She answered their questions about Kid, what she knew anyway, and told them Dica might know more and to find her to hear the story.

She explained how the King of the West Islands had told Ngahuru to be part of the group traveling under escort. Ngahuru could not defy her King, and so she had no choice but to leave without saying goodbye.

As they left to go back to work, Siba asked Nelo to stay behind and help her with the medicinals they had brought back from Rishka. Josef had muttered something about not all poisonings are intentional, but they had left Nelo behind and headed back to their various worksites.

The sides were up, the roof was on, and the scaffolding was down. Whether the rains came in seven days or in twenty, the critical part was done. From now on, all the work would be inside and dry. Some of the Conrosans would be returning to Rishka now. The carpenters, the pipefitters, some of the laundry workers, cooks, and bakers would remain. Apprentices would stay behind; school would continue when they were not working.

CHAPTER 22

A RESOLUTION – OF SORTS

Kid and Nari took the carry cart with their little shopping to the military stables. Nari's horse had been resting comfortably there while he was off doing the will of the Empress.

"I'm going to miss this," Nari said easily. "During our service years, Kid, we are able to stable our horses here, and sleep in the barracks for visiting soldiers. At the end of the next season, I will have completed my three years, and then I will have to scramble for lodging and stabling and getting about the city like everyone else." He grinned at Kid. "I think my family will make Leo come to the city, so they don't have to worry about me spending all the coffee profits for the year." As the cart came to a stop, Nari asked the driver to wait until they could transfer everything to the horses. "How well do you ride?" he asked Kid.

"Well enough. I have ridden all night to save a fellow Wren's life, but I don't know if I could do that many days in a row. I don't know if I can keep up with you."

Nari gave him a sharp look. "You can keep up. I have a special saddle, but I still cannot sit long decons. What takes others about seven days will take us a little longer. And I've tried a wagon, the lurching is worse."

A cadet who looked a little older than Kid walked up and greeted Nari. He looked at Nari's bastono, Kid, and then the driver of the carry cart.

He made a short bow to Nari. "I thank you for your service as a veteran of the past war. May I help you saddle your horse and gain your seat?"

Nari nodded briskly. "I will need your help, but first we must find a horse for him." He tipped his head to Kid. "He rides well but not often, and I will need the horse to travel to the Keopi District, so it could be as long as a season before the horse is returned to your stables."

The cadet considered. "Let me check with the hostler and the horse master. I have two in mind that could be out that long. Do you have any objection to riding a Kereki army horse?"

Nari looked to Kid.

Kid shrugged. "A horse is a horse." Both Nari and the cadet choked back a laugh.

Nari recovered first. "My horse is the blue roan in stall twenty-two. Ask the horse master for one who is evenly matched in temperament."

As the cadet walked off, Nari looked to Kid, "You haven't asked any questions about what happened at the firemaster's workrooms."

Kid shook his head. "In Kerek City, children learn very quickly not to be too curious. Asking a question of the wrong person could cost a child's life. You will tell me what I need to know when I need to know it."

Nari quirked a small smile. "That's very trusting of you." He paused. "What question do you most want to know the answer to?"

"What did Rani's help cost you?"

"Since you understand Vik, at least a little, you know Rani wanted you now, without an education, without seasoning and learning of Vikland's culture. He would waste you as nothing more than an information gatherer in Kerek City until you are discovered or killed. I disagreed.

"Instead, I gave him Linna and Oro. Or rather, Rani will tell Linna and Oro the cost of his help is that they must write their families in Kerek City and let them know they are safe, married, and making their way in Juisiti. He will take those letters with names and locations and have a softfoot contact their families.

Maybe one or more of them would be so grateful their children are safe; they will do a favor or two for Vikland. Rani says Linna's family owns an import business; Oro's family runs a shop. The kind of places where things are said and others hear them. Both would be very beneficial to Vikland.

"In a year or so, Rani will visit Oro and Linna again and see if they would like to return to Kerek City and visit their families, perhaps to stay, not in Lowertown of course. But perhaps in the Flower District where the clerks and embasado staff live or even near the embasados themselves. He will remind them of his generosity and kindness when they first came to Vikland. Again, he is hoping they would be so grateful they will do a favor or two for Vikland. He may tell them he would pay them for information if it comes often and is good enough. They have worked for Ngahuru. He will not have to overcome a distaste for softfooting."

"And if they refuse?"

Nari shrugged. "That is not my problem. Rani only wasted an evening and a morning doing a kindness for others."

The cadet and a hostler came up with two horses saddled and ready for travel. The horse selected for him was a buckskin mare with white feet. She was a Kereki army horse, the brand was still on her flank. Kid noticed both horses were not as spirited as the Fortika horses he had been forced to ride, and he sighed in relief. He would not look a fool in front of Nari Ulani.

The hostler was commenting on Nari's special saddle. "Did you have that made here in the city or in the Keopi District? The reason I ask, there are others in the war who thought they could no longer ride after earning an injury like yours. I think it would be good for more saddles like that one to be made and available. A Viklander who doesn't ride a horse? Too much has been taken away from them already."

"I had it made here in Juisiti." Nari gave them the name of the saddlemaker and the street he lived on. "When you meet with him, please tell him, 'Nari Ulani is grateful for his talents. His saddle has made it possible to do all the things expected of a Viklander soldier, including a favor for the Empress.'" Nari looked at the cadet. "Our belongings are here in the carry cart. Could you add them to the horses, please?"

Kid jumped out of the carry cart and helped the cadet arrange his belongings and Nari's shopping on the horses. The hostler cleverly tucked Nari's carved canes into the short bong scabbard, and added another scabbard to Kid's saddle for Nari's bulkier bastono. When everything had been moved over, the hostler, cadet, and Kid lifted, and then pushed and pulled Nari until he was seated on his horse. Kid noted how tightly Nari had his jaw clenched and could easily imagine his fury at being manhandled into position. He quickly mounted his own horse and thanked the men for their help. The cadet looked one last time in the carry cart to ensure nothing had been left behind and then Nari dismissed the cart and driver.

The two men stood awkwardly waiting as Kid and Nari's horses slowly walked out of the stables.

"They're watching to see if I fall off," Nari bit out. "As if I would have left the coffee farms without being able to keep my seat."

Kid said nothing and just followed Nari through the streets of Juisiti to his new home.

CHAPTER 23

JOSEF LOOKS FOR A PLACE TO BELONG

Josef walked across to the infirmary. Just as he reached the door, it swung open and Nelo stood in the doorframe, scowling. As Josef nodded hello, Nelo shifted his face to a weak smile.

"Fair warning, if you aren't bleeding badly enough, Siba will put you to work."

Josef grinned back. "I'll take my chances. If I am following you, all the work will already be done. I'll have nothing to do but talk and see if there is any coffee and fingersweets about."

Nelo barked out a laugh and pushed by. Josef walked in and took a deep breath. He liked the smell of the infirmary. The stringent herbs, the crushed petals and berries, and the earthy roots all worked together to create a fragrance he immediately associated with Siba, and now Callis. As he stepped into the workroom, he stopped short. Every surface was covered in trays of crushed and pounded botanicals. Four pestles in their mortars, one the size of his head, rested on the tables.

Siba came in from the kitchen area. "Ah good, you look like someone who needs a task and not a tonic. Come in, come in." She wiped her hands on her apron and leaned her hip against the table. She waited for him to speak first.

"I heard you are leaving Axefield. That you are not waiting until after the Wet, but instead as soon as Rygee can get everything in order." He paused, and then added in a small voice, "Is this true?"

"It is. Rygee thinks it is best for him to reason with his father and his brothers when they are not distracted by the work that must be done from sun-up to sundown. If he can be woven back into his family before the Dry, then all the farms will do much better. I know it is sudden, but the Wet seems to be late this year, and he wants to take advantage of the weather. Also, Axefield doesn't need him as much as Manumina did, and Rygee cannot bear to be idle."

Josef took in the tables and trays of botanicals again. "This?" He waved his arm about the room with the trays on every available surface.

"No, this was Nelo. He had a lot to talk about, and I have a lot of work ahead of me before I am packed and ready to go with Rygee. If you can sew muslin bags as well as you charm strangers,

I think you and I can spend a decon or two together." She smiled gently. "That's what you came for, yes?"

He gave her a sly smile. "Do you have Vikland coffee? Zren Janin has taught me never to work on an empty stomach."

Her smile grew wider. "I'll see if there is some in the back I can make for us."

***

Josef sewed and sipped his coffee while Siba cut the rectangles of fabric for him to fold in half and stitch up the sides. Then she took the palm-sized bags, measured in the botanicals, and tied them shut.

"Why don't you put them in bigger bags? It looks like the same kind in each one," he asked idly.

"I can't risk some molding and spoiling the entire batch. I can hang them separately when we get to Kerek and air small batches that are already measured more easily than large. I do not know what is grown there, and Rygee says he does not remember much of his mother's kitchen gardens. It may take a while to start my own, and until I know what I have, I must over prepare."

"Are you leaving because of what happened with Ngahuru and the army paychest?"

Siba stopped and looked directly at him. "No. It was always Rygee's intention to return and reclaim his birthright. He told me this from the time we began to walk out together. He said I needed to be sure I could leave everything I had ever known to travel next to him."

"Did Rygee tell you I asked to travel with you? To work on his farm and learn to be a horse buyer and seller?" Josef paused. "Did he also tell you he said he didn't want me?"

"He told me," Siba answered carefully. "Josef, it is not that he does not want you. Rygee has been away for nearly four years. Do you know his story? Rygee's family was angry when Rygee refused to marry the woman and the farm his father had picked out for him. His father and his brothers took him to the nearest fort in a forced conscription. Rygee doesn't know if his family thinks he is dead from the war, and he has no idea how he will be received. What if his return is unwelcome? What if his brothers decide there is not enough land or coin for him? Or, perhaps they are sorry for selling him to the army. Does his father regret his anger at Rygee refusing to marry? Have they spent the last four years desiring to relive those days with a different outcome? We could be greeted with open arms and tears of joy, or not. Sometimes, Rygee thinks he wants to leave me behind too, Josef. For my safety. It isn't you."

Josef kept his head down and kept sewing. He could feel Siba's eyes on him. Without looking up, he explained how he didn't want to stay with the Conrosans. It wasn't just the Viklander and Conrosan girls who wouldn't walk out with him. He liked Piffik well enough, but he thought he would beat his head out of boredom if he had to work in Piffik's woodworking shop for the next how many seasons. He didn't want to be a carpenter like Nelo. He didn't want to move to the end of Vikland and feel trapped in a country where he did not speak the language.

Falan had listened to him, but said if she took him with her, he would never know if he could be on his own. For both their sakes, she had said, they needed to separate. When he had asked Callis to speak with Falan on his behalf, she had said it was something he and Falan needed to work out. She wouldn't interfere.

He knew Arden had already refused to take Dica along with him to Matasi, and he didn't like or trust Ross enough to stay and work together with him in Axefield. He had come to see Siba today because he felt everywhere he turned, people were shaking their heads and telling him they did not want him. He did not know what role he should play, what disguise he should wear, for people to crowd about him and beg him to stay with them. Then he stopped talking. He worried if he said anymore, he would sound pathetic. Or cry. He felt his eyes moisten and the tiny stitches in front of him blurred.

Siba was silent for a long time. He glanced up at her once, but then a tear dropped on his hands and he quickly looked down.

Siba cleared her throat and then asked, "Tell me of your little house north of Balza, Josef. I am told Rygee and I are quite the property owners, and yet I have never seen all these places where I must find coin to pay the taxes." Siba didn't look at him but continued to measure and fill the muslin bags.

Josef swallowed and when he felt he had his voice back under control, he told her of his little cottage. It had been a one room house with a loft to sleep in. Piffik had brought him a rope bed and a basket of linens the first time Padro Morto had made his rounds. There had not been a barn or a separate bedroom such as the settlement south of the Northern Track where Falan and Callis hid Viklanders. And he had been to Linna's house, it had not been as nice as that. But he had liked it.

He made her laugh as he told her the first night he had spent there. Without furniture, without another person, without all of the sounds of Kerek City, he had pulled the latch in and boarded the windows as a precaution. Truthfully, he had been a little frightened to be on his own as he rolled himself in his traveler's cloak. When he had opened the door the next day, he had realized he had made the house so dark, he had nearly slept the day away.

He told her of a Viklander who had stayed there for longer than two fortnights while she waited for a leg wound to heal. She could not walk when he had found her. She did not leave the cottage, of course, but she had told him what to buy and bring her, and she taught him a little of all she knew. She had been a wheelwright's daughter and had used her time of healing to build Josef a table and two chairs, a shelf for his pottery and pot, and inside shutters with leather hinges and wooden slats to let the light in, but keep Trouble out.

She taught him how to dress her wound, make a cane for her to get about within the cottage, and make a second bed so she did not need to sleep on the floor. The Viklander had said she had a younger brother about Josef's age, just off at his first year at the academy. She scoffed at how her parents worried the city was too big, the classes too hard, and his funds too small. She said she knew her brother could not do all the things Josef knew to do. She had reassured Josef when he most needed it that he could do what was asked of him. Then she had offered to teach him to cook a little, saying she didn't know if Josef's biscuits were meant to be eaten or used as weapons in a slingshot.

Siba had chuckled at that.

After the firing of the fort at Earles, he had traveled as far north as the Cold Mountains to try to find scattered Viklanders because Falan had told him to. It was then he was shocked to learn Arden was part of Bima's softfoots and no longer worked at the stables in Cloa. He had not known Nelo worked closely with Inezi and the Viklander softfoots at Fortika, and there were Matasians the softfoots used as a waystation. He had heard Evensong now billeted Kereki officers but instead of fleeing to safety, Kid was stealing ever more valuable information for the Viklanders. He told Siba how Arden was only a year older than he was, but had walked without fear through a Kereki encampment and thieved a general's mapcase.

He asked Siba if she had known Linna would take the dog Mother and wear Arden's clothes and his traveling cloak, to move soldiers from hiding place to hiding place. That Falan's practice of stealing the Kereki scouts' boots after they were murdered was talked about even in the Viklander camps. Ngahuru did not know. There was *so much* Ngahuru did not know. As he and Arden had traveled as Matasi missionaries, he also learned Nelo and Arden did not regard Ngahuru as their friend and rescuer from Kerek City. Until then, he thought it had only been Falan who questioned Ngahuru's motives.

"They were right not to trust her," Josef said sadly. "Falan always said we were bought and sold for Ngahuru's revenge."

Siba sighed. "Josef, there are always many ways to hear a story, to learn the truth of it. We do not have Ngahuru here to tell us her story. We cannot presume to know what was in her mind and in her heart unless she chooses to share this. I can tell you this much is true. She did not think your roles would be so large in the war. She thought you were all much safer than you were. It was not until Nelo was taken by the crimpers that I saw how afraid she was for all of you. She was proud of all you accomplished and went confidently to the Empress of Vikland to ask for a life debt to be paid for each of you. She did not get her wish, but she did obtain a home and enough coin to help you start a new life."

Siba waited until Josef looked at her. "Do not let the actions of her last day reflect on how she trusted and confided in you for years. All of you knew she was Ngahuru of the West Islands from your days in Kerek City. There was a price on her head throughout Kerek, and yet she trusted all of you to keep her secret. Her trust was not misplaced. I do not believe yours is either. We have to remember the good in people."

Josef considered her words but didn't say anymore. They worked together in companionable silence and then, "What will happen to you if Rygee is not welcomed by his family? If he suffers Kereki metal poisoning by his brothers?"

Siba was silent. "Rygee has told me I must go back to Vikland and rejoin the Conrosans. It is another reason he wants to leave now. If Rygee is rejected by his family and cannot protect me, he says I will only have to travel to Axefield. Piffik offered to journey with us, but he has an inn to build. I do not think these precautions are necessary. I think if matters were truly this bad, we would not return to Kerek. But Rygee reminds me I do not understand how a moment's anger can cause a lifetime of grief. He said all the remorse in the world cannot undo a thoughtless action caused by the hardness of the heart."

She paused. "He says his father is not a charitable man, but he is a successful one. Rygee plans to show him one can be successful and kind to others. It was why he couldn't leave here without Ngahuru and Piffik recognizing his worth. Rygee feels the properties we now own from the Wrens will command his father's attention."

Siba continued, "Josef, I had hoped to be able to talk with you before I left. I think you, more than anyone else here in Axefield or who lived in Manumina, know how my heart is breaking to leave my best friend for all of my life, and yet still look forward to the adventure ahead of me with Rygee. I know I will never see Piffik at the moments that mean the most to him: when he marries Rell, when he sees the first ship in Vikland's new harbor, if a child calls him 'Papa.' I think I understand a little of how you must feel to have Falan look eagerly to a future that does not have you in it. Perhaps this wounds you the most."

Josef wasn't sure if that was true, although it could be. He knew Arden and Zren both thought Falan was more than his protector—and not in a good way. Since the two men were as opposite in thought and action as he could imagine, Josef considered their words carefully. He kept silent and sewed.

When he finished, Siba asked him to help her with packing the rest of the trays. He realized it was the most time he had ever spent with her. He had enjoyed her company and now she was leaving. As it grew later, she began to tidy her space. She thanked him for his help and casually asked if he knew how to tell time and location by the stars as the other Wrens did.

"Of course. It was something Ngahuru taught us in the very beginning. She said it would help us survive in the outlands where there are not many landmarks and settlements to mark our travels at night. Why do you ask?"

She smiled gravely. "I do not know how to do such a thing. I cannot imagine how I, a woman on my own in Kerek, would ever be able to find my way back to Vikland, even if it was to save my own life." She gave Josef an indecipherable look. "This should be something Rygee considers."

Josef was puzzled for a moment, and then as he realized what she was saying—she needed him to guide her to Vikland if there was trouble—he broke into a wide smile.

"Thank you." He felt his body soften in relief. "Thank you."

CHAPTER 24

THE VALUE OF A LIFE

It was two days since his talk with Siba—past the darkest of the night, but not yet dawn when Josef woke. There was not enough light to see, but he could hear rustling as someone tried to softfoot in the dormitory towards the end where the Wrens had gathered together. He could sense the others waking, tensing at the unfamiliar sound, remembering where they were, and relaxing. Josef looked to Kid's empty cot and wondered if someone was joining them.

"Josef. It's Rygee. Come help me start the baking ovens." Rygee sounded resigned, and Josef wondered what skill he had that Rygee thought he could possibly be of any use in the bakeries. Nevertheless, he rolled to his feet and reached for his pants. With his shirt in one hand and his boot liners and boots in another, he followed Rygee out into the cool, damp morning.

Rygee didn't say anything as Josef finished dressing outside and both walked silently toward the bakeries. Once inside,

Rygee lit and hung the lanterns so all of the room flared as bright as daylight.

Josef followed Rygee to the first oven and watched how he started it, raking the coals forward, adding the wood so the fire would cook evenly, pouring water into the cast iron pots so once they boiled the bakers would know the ovens were hot enough.

At the second oven, Josef leaned forward. "Do you want me to do this one?"

Rygee smiled. "No, you are here to listen to me. I am still sorting out the words in my head. Give me another moment." He bent down and opened the oven door, and Josef started to feel a flame of hope inside.

Siba had talked to Rygee and he was reconsidering.

"I asked Falan to tell me your story," Rygee finally began. "Then I asked Nelo, whose words I believe most of all the Wrens, if he would trust his most precious belongings and secrets to you and travel the unknown together. He looked at me, surprised, and said he already had. He said you are not as close to him as another, but you have his trust…and his respect."

Rygee paused. "I do not know you so well as some of the others, and to be honest, I thought you were…" He struggled for a word, "more foolish than I cared to have about me. I have been reassured by others I am wrong. That you play any role you are asked to play, and your frivolousness is only a maskovesto to soften Falan. My wife tells me you have not been permitted to be you."

Rygee straightened, closed the oven door, and looked at Josef. "I am honored to be married to the wisest woman I have ever known. Siba tells me you have protected others with your life and your steel. She says you could learn the horse trade, but you could also travel and manage our land leases and our properties. You could be trusted on an errand and not be taken advantage of. She believes you have many skills useful on a farm where one person must do whatever task is at hand. That you understand the value of things and can read and write." Rygee paused. "Do you understand the value of Siba, my heart, my wife?"

Josef cleared his throat. "I have heard Zren tell a tale of Nelo and the crimpers in which Siba went on a moon-bright buggy ride with him to return Kid to Evensong. Zren says he knew if they encountered bandits, or armies, or Trouble in any form, he could not return to Manumina without Siba." He nodded to Rygee. "I understand that also."

Rygee blew out a noisy breath. "I do not know what I will find when I return to my family. My father and I parted in anger, and my brothers are as strong-willed as my father. If I sense Trouble, I cannot risk you arguing with me that you are tired, you do not perceive a problem, and let's talk about it. If I say, 'Go,' you must take Siba and flee back to Axefield."

Rygee gave Josef a measured look. "If we stay, I may not have a fine house to live in until I build it myself. In the beginning, we may share a barn with our animals. If I ask to have you taken on as an apprentice to our horse master, he may have enough apprentices and say to me, 'Not now.'

"On our farms you will find yourself doing many things as a manabout, as an apprentice healer, as one who sits at my table and sleeps under my roof that you did not think you could do or have not done before. It is not like Manumina where you can pick and choose what you will do because there are others who will choose what you do not want to do. I can teach you as my father taught me, I can find others to teach you, but before you come with us, I must know that you can be taught. That you are willing."

Josef felt his heart burst in relief. "I can be taught," he said quickly.

Rygee gave him a wry smile. "We leave in three days. If you have belongings greater than a travel pack, see if Piffik has a wooden chest for you we can take in our wagon. I will talk to Raul Huena about buying another horse. Bring your short bow and arrows. Keep your West Islands steel on your person. You will need to be an outrider with me."

Josef grinned. He made a Vikland bow of respect, and then stuck out his hand as he had seen ship captains and merchants do back in Kerek City. Rygee laughed but took his hand and shook it.

"You can go back to bed. Siba had told me you had done as she asked without fuss or bother. But I had wanted to see if you would get up this morning just because I asked you to help, or if you loved your pillow too much."

Josef walked out of the bakery then and just caught the faintest lightening of the eastern sky. He had no idea even what part of Kerek Rygee came from, or how long the journey would be, but he smiled at a future he knew was his and his alone.

CHAPTER 25

CIO CLARO!

More than one old gossip had wagged Piffik Qanaq would be devastated when Siba Namikk left for Kerek. But Piffik handled the whispers by ignoring them. He knew he would be desolate at Siba's leaving, but not for the reason everyone thought. Siba was truly his best and oldest friend in his world. He had been beyond glad when Rygee had understood that as well and had not been threatened by their friendship.

He *had* been surprised when Siba had told him they were taking the Wren, Josef, with them. Piffik had known Josef to be bold enough and clever during the war, but the boy had not settled down to any one thing since they had come to Axefield. Piffik had wondered if he ever would. What kind of a man would the Wren become with so much charm and a pretty face and no sense of direction or purpose?

And then, when Siba had asked him to keep a special look out for Falan, he had given her a withering look. "It is not enough

I have to build the inn, keep Zren alive, live without you, and now you want me to keep Falan from missing one she has known most of her remembered life?"

Siba had smiled fondly. "I don't doubt you will have it all sorted out by midday. End of day if Zren proves elusive."

He smiled back. "So tell me, what do I need to know about Falan?"

Siba looked at him soberly. "She cannot bear to be loved." She paused. "For her, love is a burden that means she must worry about others, take care of others, do as others want even when their wants are not her wants. If she pushes other people away first, then she doesn't have to wonder if they will love her, or not. She doesn't have to worry what will be the price of that love, or what she must do to pay such a price, or what will happen if she cannot."

Piffik sucked in a breath. "You think I can fix this?"

"Rell and Zren healed each other. She calls him her little brother. She gave him a sense of what it means to love—to sort out affection and caring, and not to mistake it for the actions of a lover. In return, he thrives in her affection and has become so much more than I ever expected because he does not want to disappoint her.

"This is what I want for Falan. She needs to pick apart the roles of sister, mother, lover, protector, within her feelings for Josef. I can take him away and let them both recover. But if they do not..." Siba trailed off. "The war helped Josef realize he is more than just an extension of Falan's thoughts and actions. Josef's interest in other girls has helped, though I do not think he realizes how Falan keeps them away. But I do not think Falan and Josef can do this alone. Zren has mastered this and is so uncomplicated, I would have him talk to her, but Zren and Falan do not care for one another."

Piffik snorted. "Those are mild words for a man who will turn and nearly run the other direction when he sees her." He blew out a noisy breath. "Falan won't talk to me. She barely talks to the Wrens except to tell them what to do. But I will also talk to your aunt when she comes to say goodbye. It may be Callis will confide in her while they are working together in the infirmary."

"Rell needs to come back soon." Siba smiled sadly.

Piffik smiled. "We wait on the will of the Empress. But I wrote to her as soon as I knew you were leaving. I know she will never make it back in time to say goodbye to you. You and Rygee will probably be on the farm before she even receives my latest letter. But sometimes I need to write and let her know that life is still occurring in Axefield and not every letter is a foolish man spilling his heart on paper. She will not linger forever in Kerek."

He took a deep breath. "I will be married to a better person than I have ever imagined, Siba. My heart will not let me believe, she and I will never darken your doorstep. We will all see each other again."

***

On his last night in Axefield, Josef noticed Nelo hadn't come with the others to say goodbye at the end of day meal. But as he was walking under the stars unable to sleep, he saw another approach him in the dark. Nelo appeared out of the shadows, said nothing, but handed him a flat wooden box no larger than his hands placed side by side.

"What is it?" Josef looked at it curiously. "There is not enough moonlight for me to see, and I am afraid to open it."

"It holds paper, graphite, and a promise." Nelo smiled. "If you write me a letter and send it to me here at Axefield, I will know where to write you when we move to build the harbor." He paused, and this time Josef could hear the laughter in Nelo's voice. "If you hear the words falling from my lips, Josef, I am saying by the time you stop having fun long enough to write me about it, I should have learned to read it."

Josef laughed. "I shall never be the scholar Kid is, but I think I can scratch out something. Thank you." He hesitated. "I am beyond glad we met again beyond your Lost Girls in Kerek City."

"I am too." Nelo nodded. "We had no future there. And while I do not think Ngahuru had our best lives planned for us, she did not do us harm."

Nelo was silent for a long time and then exhaled sharply. "Dica and Jenny will tell you they bear no love for me because of what I did as I tried to keep my Lost Girls and Lost Boys safe in Kerek City. In my defense, I will only say I was too young, older than they were, but not yet a man. Falan kept you as safe as she could. But Dica and Jenny and Tyra are happy to plan a life without me, and I am glad to see you plan a life without Falan. Do not judge her too harshly as you learn to live on your own."

Josef drew back, surprised. "Did Falan ask you to say this to me?"

"No, but I know my own struggles and my own heart. As I have talked with Piffik, he has made me see, we all bear the scars of the lives we were forced to live as children."

***

Josef's wooden chest—a gift from Piffik—was tucked safely inside Siba's wagon. It contained his reward from the Empress of Vikland, her Viklander coin now changed to Kereki dias. Josef, Arden, Nelo, and Siba had all been there when Rygee had taken Nelo's army paychest to Raul Huena. He had asked to have the innkeeper act as their banker and exchange Josef's Viklander sols to Kereki dias. No one told the Viklander where the Kereki chest had come from, and the innkeeper did not even look surprised to be asked to handle such large sums.

Raul Huena had explained how coin worked in the different countries they traveled in, and said at the inn they often had coin from every place in the known world. He said it was not unusual for him to exchange coins from one country to another as travelers came and left from Vikland. Then he smiled and said it *was* unusual for the travelers to have all the coins themselves and just use him to determine the exchange rate and do the counting out.

Arden had asked so many questions of how it was determined what value the coins had, how the coin lenders decided how much to charge, how the buying and selling of coins between countries could be agreed upon, Nelo had laughed and asked if Zren Janin was hiding under the table with them.

Josef was glad Arden had asked. Every day Josef seemed to learn yet another thing he didn't understand, and he was relieved he was going to be traveling with Rygee and Siba.

But now his Kereki dias were all jumbled together with his clothes, a spare pair of boots, a knife made of West Islands steel, a silver spoon from Falan—Josef wondered where she had filched it, an apothecary bottle from Callis, a map of Kerek from

Arden, two leather pockets and two cloth pockets with ties to wear underneath his tunic from Dica, a rabbit's foot from Ross, and a feather from Tyra.

He had placed Nelo's gift on top. He wondered if he would ever have been taught to read or write or count cards or the value of coins if Falan's father would not have thought it a useful tool for him to know in order to trick gamblers.

Piffik had threatened to call a rest day on the day Siba Namikk left Axefield to take up her new home in Kerek. But Rygee and Siba wanted to get an early start. As the sun was peeking over the horizon, there were the Wrens, and Piffik, Zren, Siba's aunt Bett, and a scattering of others from the bakery and Manumina. Siba was sitting alone on the settler's wagon. Piffik had added taller sides and now a waxed canvas was lashed tightly over the goods inside. Two army horses were ready to pull it across Kerek, and Josef and Rygee were also on strong Kereki horses; the four Rell had sold to her father and now sold back to Rygee. They were army horses true, but Rygee thought with the war over, it was still better to have Kerekis riding Kereki horses than to be riding Viklander horses with their distinctive breeding.

The travelers were ready to go, but hesitated. This would probably be the last they would ever see the Conrosans and the Wrens. Rygee looked anxiously at the sun, he clearly wanted to be on the road—but Josef thought perhaps Rygee knew what he was asking of Siba—to leave the home and people she had known all of her life. Zren was standing there, eyes filled with sleep, his curls flying about his head. The Wrens were there. Josef noticed Falan was not.

"*Cio claro!*" Arden called out in a strong voice. "May the Lost God travel with you and keep you safe."

"*Cio claro!*" Josef responded. "All is well!"

"*Cio claro!*" cried the Wrens. "All is well!"

Rygee lifted his hand and let it drop. The horses took their first steps, the wagon lurched forward, and the travelers moved south on the road out of Axefield.

THINGS THAT WERE, THINGS THAT ARE, THINGS THAT WILL BE

Falan walked into the infirmary at the end of the day looking for Callis. She stopped in surprise. Callis was there of course, but so was Dica leaning over a table, and so was a half-dressed Conrosan youth standing in the middle of the room, shirtless, and holding up his beltless pants.

"What's going on here?" she snapped.

The youth flinched at the tone in her voice.

Callis merely looked up and said, "I'm helping Dica dress this man." She leaned back down and pointed. "Try this one, Dica."

Dica picked up the fabric pattern piece and draped it over the youth. She placed one hand on his shoulder to keep it in place and smoothed the other over his belly to get a better look at how the shirt would hang when finished. The boy flamed a deep red. Dica kept her head down, but Falan could see her lips upturn in a small smile.

Callis carried over a few smaller pieces and together they pinned and tucked, ignoring Falan altogether. They also ignored the boy who looked as though he was ecstatically miserable, or self-consciously happy as the women touched him to turn him, and rubbed the fabric for the fitting over his naked skin. Falan snorted at his awkwardness. Conrosans.

At last, Callis pulled off the larger fabric with the various pieces pinned and flapping.

Dica smiled up at the boy. "You can get dressed now, Baffin, thank you so much for your time today."

Falan rolled her eyes at the goofy grin he gave Dica.

"Same time tomorrow?" he said hoarsely.

Dica looked at Callis who nodded. "Same time tomorrow, it should be the last one we need."

Falan caught the quick shade of disappointment across his face, but then he smiled at Dica as she handed him his belt and his oversized shirt. "Tomorrow then."

She waited until the youth was gone and then turned on the Wrens.

"What is that all about?"

She looked at Callis, but Dica answered. "I've decided I'm going to run the rag and bone wagon. Only I'm not going to sell cast offs like Ngahuru did during the war—that was only her maskovesto. Piffik says the wagon belongs to the Wrens, and I am a Wren and free to take it. I will travel to the towns and settlements and sell clothes made to order as well as those I already have in the cart. I will buy clothes as well and have cheaper seconds— bits and pieces. I have learned in the laundries how to cut down damaged clothes to make others. Callis is helping me create my fabric patterns and then I will make samples."

Falan was impressed but not quite ready to show it. "And you are just going to ride around Kerek on a wagon without thought to your safety?"

Dica straightened and looked at her. "No, I have a plan for that as well. Arden gave me the idea. He said if I had a skill, a way to support myself, he would consider taking me along on his travels. I know at the end of the Wet both Zren and Arden want to travel to Matasi. It is my plan to offer them a place to rest their feet on my wagon in exchange for their quick wit and bravery."

She slyly smiled. "If they have a skill, *they* can travel with *me*. We can travel together from Kerek to Matasi—to take Zren to Salisport where his soldier boy is, and Arden to see more of the world.

"I talked with Zren. He says it is so safe to travel in Matasi, even a girl of fourteen could do it as long as she remembers to follow all of their many rules. He says if I felt afraid that I would stand out too much, I could let the sun darken my skin to hide my Kereki mother. But then he said if I travel with those who are Conrosan, or have a dog named Mother, then perhaps my *titiro mai ki ahau* will be so handsome, no one will even see me on the wagon seat."

Dica laughed at that and continued, "Although I do not know any words of Mata, perhaps Zren and Arden and I could learn together. If Arden finds a place he wishes to stay, I hope to find another who wishes to travel about. Maybe I will find a home. Maybe Zren's soldier will not be at Salisport when we arrive, and we will travel together to find him. Maybe I will travel back to Kerek and find Siba and Rygee and Josef. Maybe I will see the world and realize I like Vikland best and return to Juisiti and go to the academies.

"I also talked to Raul Huena and he says it is common for Vikland business people to take on travelers as well. That I must stay in a better and bigger inn for a night or two, and ask the innkeeper to see if anyone has asked to travel with another for coin or help. He said it is how Zren traveled to Juisiti when Raul Huena could not afford his son, Dylis, to travel with him."

Dica paused. "I cannot believe in all of the known world there are not more who wish to travel to a new place to test themselves, find a new home, or travel on business."

Callis looked at Falan. "How can you wish us to go back to Kerek and live, when all the rest of the known world is so much better to us than how we grew up?"

Falan narrowed her eyes. "We only have Zren's word for it. No one else we know has been to Matasi. Do you really trust a half-wit?"

Dica bristled and stretched herself to her full height. "I know Zren cannot tell a lie without his face betraying him. If he told me, it is very important to learn their holy days and he felt safe in Matasi as long as he followed their laws, then it was so. If Raul Huena says there is already a way in place for Viklanders to travel together, then it is so. Maybe by the time the inn is finished there may be a Conrosan who would not like to move to the far side of Vikland, or would like to travel a bit first and then rejoin the others. I do not need a protector, Falan. I only need a *titiro mai ki ahau* until my youthfulness is not my enemy. I do not have to have every day of my life planned out. But I have asked those I trust—Raul Huena, Zren Janin, Callis, and Siba Namikk before she left us, and all say my plan has merit."

Falan shrugged. "Well, you obviously aren't running off to join the King's players, or disappearing without notice on a stolen horse, so what does it matter to me? I won't rescue you."

Callis gave Falan a searching look. Dica merely turned and started to gather her fabric pieces together. "Thank you for your help today, Callis. This dream would not be possible without your knowledge. Should I make little cloth bags to keep all of my fabric patterns together?"

"Yes. And make them different colors so you can grab the patterns to hand quickly. If you are making made to order, it will impress your customers that you don't fumble about your goods, but confidently select the ones closest to their size."

Dica grinned. "That is clever."

Callis said her goodbyes and tucked her arm in Falan's as they went out to join the others for end of day meal.

CHAPTER 27

THE APPRENTICE

"So. King's Players? Stolen horses? No notice? Dica is not Josef, Falan, don't scold her because he has done exactly what you told him to. You told him to find his own way. Actually, I think I also remember you telling Dica to find her own path—not a shop girl—because you didn't want to be responsible for her."

Most of the people in the dining tent were already eating. Callis and Falan hurried to gather their platters and find an open spot. Callis looked about briefly for the other Wrens. Tyra was over with her school friends, and Therin was just leaving with a like-sized group of boys. There was no sign of Nelo, or Arden, or Zren, and really, who else was left? Ross had so worked himself into the routine of the first Huena inn he even took his meals in their kitchen with the scrub boys, hostlers, and inn workers. If he passed them in the courtyard, he would nod, but Callis knew he thought of "the Wrens" as his past life—one he didn't care to remember.

"This food is terrible, cold, and I don't even know what it is. If we had our own house, Callis, we wouldn't have to eat here." Falan looked about the room with a look of faint disgust.

"Except neither of us learned to cook well, and we would be eating far worse than this." Callis ignored Falan's mood. "Do you have plans later? The shops in Axefield are open late tonight since Piffik paid his workers today, and I thought I would like to walk about with you."

"I didn't get paid today. Raul Huena only pays us on the first of the fortnight." Falan sniffed. "You know the shopkeepers talk about us while we are there like we are nothing."

"Perhaps." Callis shrugged. They had had this argument before as well. "But if we learned Vik, we may learn they are only talking about their children, or how their harvest was, or how late the Wet is this year."

"Why learn Vik when we will never need to speak it when we go back to Kerek?"

Callis took a deep breath. The more she learned of Vikland, Matasi, and even the West Islands, the less she wanted to move back to Kerek. She was beginning to feel that soon she was going to have to choose between living where she wanted to and living with Falan. However, with Josef gone, now was not the time to talk about it.

***

One morning Callis found Bett in the infirmary taking inventory. She washed up, put on her apron, and asked what they would be working on that day.

Bett smiled. "We will be leaving soon, perhaps the day after tomorrow. There is a healer here in Axefield the few remaining workers can use. But if you are to be my apprentice, I need to get us back to the infirmary and stillroom with all of my salves and tinctures. Most of the Conrosans are at Rishka anyway."

Bett waved her hand at the empty shelves. "I had told Siba to take most everything here. I am now at the place where I must go back to Rishka and bring my things here or go and work where my pots and plants are. So, if it is agreeable to you, I think I can have this sorted out today with your help, packed up tomorrow, and get an early start the day after. That should give you time to say your goodbyes."

Callis nodded. "I'll tell Falan right away. She will need to talk to Raul Huena at the inn and get her paypacket early."

Bett paused. "Are you thinking Falan is coming with us?"

Callis stilled at the tone in Bett's voice. "She's not welcome?"

Bett considered her words carefully. "Callis, she does not have a purpose at the refugee camp. There is no need for a shopgirl, or one skilled in numbers to work in an inn we do not have. At Manumina and now at Rishka, Conrosans believe all must work together in order to live together. If she does not work, she will not be welcome."

"She can do other things," Callis interjected.

Bett huffed, "Like what? Teaching—when she does not speak Conrosan? Perhaps she would like to be a manabout, or work in the gardens and fields." She gave Callis a condescending look. "Falan would refuse all those positions, as she should. She has a place here at Axefield. She should not take work away at Rishka from someone who has no other options."

Callis was stunned. "But I thought we—she and I—would travel together."

Bett looked sadly at Callis. "I do not care if she comes or stays behind. That is not my concern. But I am telling you for her to live at Rishka, she must have a position. She must work with us to live with us. You can talk this over with her today. And I will make sure there is room on the wagon for her things, but I will not take her along for her to be idle."

***

Callis told Falan she would be moving to Rishka to be Bett's apprentice.

"She will take me on, Falan, because Siba is gone and one healer for all of the Conrosans is not enough. Falan, we don't have to leave for Kerek only to find out the healer in Cloa won't take me. We won't have to pay Rygee for the use of his house, if I can stay here and work and live with the Conrosans during the Wet. We have already stayed in Rishka. The Wren's nest is still there, Nelo said, and now there are even fewer who will need to sleep there. We can save all our coin until I learn enough to set up my own business in another place someday."

"What happens when the Dry season comes? Then you will say, 'Oh, Falan! Let's move with the Conrosans! I still have so much to learn!'" Falan gave her a stony look.

Callis took a deep breath. "I do not think I will leave with Bett and the Conrosans for the far side of Vikland. But I do not know this to be true."

"I see. So, our dream of returning to Kerek is tossed aside because it is so much easier to remain with the Conrosans in Vikland."

"It was always your dream, Falan. I want to stay with you. But we must have a way to support ourselves and a home where we are safe. Neither of us have had that. Our fathers kept us as safe as they could in Kerek City, but we knew it would not last forever.

"During the war, we softfooted in the night moving soldiers and maps and documents because we were spread too thin among too many places. Falan, I know you know the feeling of a man you do not know following you. I know you remember the fear of hearing footsteps in the night ahead of you and not knowing if you will cross the path of a friendly man who has had a drink, or a mean drunk with ill intent. And does it really matter which one it is if his ears are stopped up with liquor and he doesn't hear your words begging to be let go?"

Falan gave her a condescending look. "And you think things like that couldn't happen here?"

"I think they are far less likely than if we are two women who live in a house in the center of Cloa. You and I saw that house, Falan. It is nicer than the ones we had in Huk and south of Balza. Arden fixed it up well for Linna. But it is close to the stables and not far from the center of town. Many people would know where we live and if we are alone. It only worked for Linna because Arden left Mother there to protect her."

Callis gave Falan a long look. "I do not think we would have a dog to protect us in Cloa. You would not even let Arden stay with us and the other Wrens when he insisted Mother stay inside too. And when he said he preferred Mother's company to yours? You dumped his bedding out the door."

Falan huffed. "What am I supposed to do in Rishka? Keep house for the Wrens? I am not going to cook and clean and do laundry for the rest of us."

"With Rygee gone, they need another baker. You could apprentice there."

"Too early in the morning." Falan sniffed.

"Ross is not returning with us; you could see if they need another manabout."

"And work with Zren Janin? He talks so much I wouldn't be able to hear myself think!"

"Zren is staying here. As is Nelo, as is Arden, as are Dica and Tyra. There is a chandler and a cheesemaker. Maybe they need an apprentice." Callis paused. "Falan, I am going to Rishka with or without you. This is not something you can bully me to do what you want."

"And my future doesn't matter?" Falan questioned sharply.

Callis turned and walked away.

***

The next day, the cheesemaker came to Axefield to make her deliveries, and Callis nearly sobbed in relief when she saw Falan talking with her. She had been so worried Falan would say no and go to Kerek by herself.

Callis didn't say anything to the others, only asked if they could have end of day meal together. She didn't want attention like Josef needed, she didn't want to sneak off as Kid did. She just wanted to get together with everyone and enjoy the evening. If they all rejoined at Rishka before the Conrosans left for the far east of Vikland, it wouldn't be awkward as it would be if they had all said goodbye.

When Callis entered the dining hall, she saw Dica and Tyra at a large table shaking their heads when others approached to sit down. Then she saw Arden and Zren peel off from the line with their platters heaped high. As they joined the others, Zren said something which made Tyra laugh. She saw Nelo a few people ahead of her in line. She looked ahead of her and behind her but she didn't see Falan. She dished up quickly and sat down with the others.

"Bett came to see me today," Dica started eagerly. "She gave me a West Islands needle. She said it works for mending a shirt or a person, but if I use it to stitch a person, I must be sure to fire it over a lucifer first."

"Eeeewwww," Tyra scrunched up her nose. "You had to say that while we are eating?"

"When did you become such a delicate flower, Tyra?" Nelo smiled at her. "It must be all that book learning you are getting with your friends. I didn't know there were so many giggly girls in Axefield."

Tyra poked her nose in the air. "You could come to school with us, Nelo, and then you would know all the giggly girls' names."

Arden laughed. "You bet on the wrong rooster, Nelo. Better go home while you still have coin in your pockets." He nodded at Tyra. "Well said."

Callis smiled at all of them. "Tonight is my last night with you. Tomorrow, I leave with Bett to go back to Rishka. I will be her apprentice. For a while anyway."

Nelo raised an eyebrow. "No Cloa? No Kerek?"

Callis shook her head. "Not yet anyway. It was not a good plan because we could not see if I could apprentice before we moved there. This way, I can save my coin, learn my skills, and then move wherever I am needed."

"Are you coming to east Vikland with us?" Nelo continued.

"I don't think so, but I cannot say that is true." She smiled at Nelo. "But who knows? Stranger things have happened to all of us since we first met each other in the wagon in Kerek City. So, if I see you again, I'll nod and smile, and we can pass the day with the stories of our adventures. If our paths do not pass again, remember me with kindness."

Before Nelo could say anything else, Zren popped in with questions. "I have heard you are taking Falan with you. Is this true? Piffik said she is going to be an apprentice to the cheesemaker." He looked almost gleeful. "A very old apprentice a very long way from here."

"It's true, Zren." Callis nodded. "If she learns a trade as well, we should be able to travel anywhere and set up housekeeping in a town or settlement who needs us. We can work in the toggery, with a cheesemaker, or a healer, or on our own. I can always tailor if we are far enough from Dica and her cart."

Callis continued, "Falan still wants to move to Kerek and live in her own house, but…"

"But this is good too," Falan said as she came and sat down at the table. "At Rishka, I will no longer feel responsible for everyone." She sighed at the group. "It's a new experience. Not bad, not good, just different." She opened the small cloth napkin she was carrying, "Fingersweets," she said. "I asked Mother Huena for some. Whenever I see fingersweets I will think of all of you."

CHAPTER 28

LETTERS

The Wet made up for its late arrival with days of rolling storms. But the exterior of the second inn was finished and secure against the weather. Another set of workers left for the refugee camp at Rishka and only the most skilled builders, carpenters, and one small kitchen crew were needed for the remaining work. A handful of spouses and Dica remained as laundry workers and tailors. Both Nelo and Arden had the affinity and interest in learning to be builders, not just carpenters. Although they didn't call themselves apprentices or journeymen, they were quick to add themselves to any group command Piffik gave.

Zren preferred the small work of carpentry. He liked the coziness of the woodworking shop, the journeymen and apprentices who prepared the pieces the builders would install, the stories told to pass the time. The business of the first Huena Inn slowed to a tempo which allowed Raul Huena to visit his new inn several times a day—testing Piffik's patience. The innkeeper seemed very pleased it would be done before the Dry.

Piffik was summoned again and again to Juisiti to meet with those planning the blasting of the mountains and the building of the new port. But this last time when he returned from the palace and the central administrative offices, he brought a large bag of letters for those who lived in and around Axefield. He turned over the bag to Raul Huena—who spent the remainder of the day sorting out the papers, news, packages, letters, and documents sent from one end of the country to the other, from Kerek and Matasi across the continent to the hearts of those missed. All day the Wrens watched as runners from the inn made deliveries across Axefield.

Then there was the surprise of the first letters most of them had ever received. There was a letter from Josef to Nelo and one to Falan. A letter from Siba to Piffik, and one for her Aunt Bett. A letter from Kid to Dica, with another to Arden. A letter from Jenny to Ngahuru, a letter from Solkka to Zren. And so many letters from Rell. Many to her family, more to Piffik, and one for Siba, one for Zren. Piffik carefully bundled up the letters of those who were no longer at Axefield—Falan and Aunt Bett would receive their letters when the cheesemaker came to deliver the latest dairy. Rell's letter to Siba would be bundled with all of theirs to the Namikks—now that they had a location to send them at the Brick Family Farms, Lowel, South Kerek. Ngahuru's letter would go back to Juisiti with the next travelers and be delivered to the West Islands embasado. It was a marvel to believe letters could travel anywhere in the known world.

Siba's letter reassured Piffik they had arrived at Rygee's family safely. The father had been heartily sorry for his hasty actions years ago, the brothers were pleased Rygee had returned with a wife, lands, coin, and was ready to take his place next to his father. It was not going to be the easiest of adjustments, Siba had cautioned Piffik, they were all as strong-willed as Rygee, but she was happy to report they were not going to live in a barn with their animals while life was sorted out. It had been the right decision to return. There was enough work and land for all of them, and all was forgiven, even if not quite forgotten. Siba was learning as much and as fast as she could. Rygee was truly happy and busy from sun up to sun down even during the Wet, and Josef was adjusting well. Piffik gave Zren the letter to share with the other Wrens, cautioning him to return it in the same condition it was given to him.

The Wrens gathered in the privacy of the empty infirmary to share their letters. After Zren read aloud Piffik's letter from Siba, Nelo handed Arden his letter from Josef and asked him to read it aloud to the others. The handwriting was large and sprawling, but the words were clear and the spelling was as unusual as Josef himself.

Josef was happy to announce Rygee had grown up on much bigger farms than he had ever imagined, men called Rygee 'sir' wherever he went—although Josef didn't have to, and Rygee had been able to get him apprenticed to the horse buyer and breeder for the farms. He could ride fine horses every day as soon as he was done with his chores, and they were not Conrosan plow horses. During this Wet, he had learned a lot of book work, and he boasted he could probably read as well as Arden or even Kid. He lived in a house with Rygee and Siba, not in the bunkhouses with the farmhands or horsebreakers. Rygee had added running water like they had at Manumina and was building a laundry with pipeworks for all the farms to use. Only now, Josef wrote, did he understand how much Manumina and the Wrens had benefited from everything Rygee knew about farming. He added that as the newest apprentice his worst job was preparing the stallions for stud duty.

Arden looked up from reading the letter. "Do we *want* to know what that means?"

Nelo gave the Wrens a sly smile. "I didn't know what that meant either when I puzzled out the letter for myself. So, I went to find Piffik. When Piffik didn't know, I asked some of the workers at the inn. They laughed at me and sent me to the stables to ask. Finally, the hostlers stopped laughing and explained to me what had to be done.

"Let's just say," Nelo's grin grew larger, "it involves a bucket of warm soapy water, a mare on the other side of the fence, and a willing horse." At the Wrens' shocked looks, Nelo continued, "Such a perfect job for such a pretty face." He smirked. "You know he couldn't wait to tell us this. He knew we wouldn't know and would make ourselves look foolish as we wandered about Axefield asking someone, or many someones, to tell us what it all meant."

Arden just shook his head and handed the letter back to Nelo.

Arden then read parts of his letter from Kid to the others. Jenny was doing well and had changed so much Kid had not recognized her when he arrived. She wore a glove like Ngahuru on her damaged hand, only hers was made of lace. Devi Ulani had carved wooden fingers to be worn inside the glove and the lace was rough enough she could grip things that were not too delicate.

Kid liked the coffee farms more than he expected; there was a lot to learn. He was learning to read and write Vik 'by drowning in it.' The Gayo Ulani family was kind, but still grieving the death of their daughter, Lissil. Nari rode horse with a special saddle and stirrups, and he used his bastono Piffik had made to get about in the coffee barns. It was easy to see, Kid wrote, Nari loved being a coffee farmer.

Nari Ulani would never be a friend, Kid confided, but he was knowledgeable and committed to making his plan work: None of the Ulani coffee farms would suffer just because Nari had been injured in the war. His aunt made a special salve for him which took away the feeling in his stump, and Kid believed Nari now suffered more at the loss of what he could no longer do than actual pain. Although, Kid had written, Nari was such a proud man, he accomplished things no one expected of him because he demanded so much of himself.

Tedros had come home on another short military leave and had graciously spent the time with Kid teaching him how to walk and read the coffee fields. The soldier had asked to be remembered to his 'Matasi missionaries' and wanted them to know he understood their intervention in the Cold Mountains meant the difference between his life and his cousin Nari's circumstances. He was filled with gratitude for them. Tedros thought if he could ever find a woman to share his bed, he might name his sons, Josef and Arden. Or maybe his daughters. Arden paused, took a deep breath, and then continued.

Kid liked Kaede, Nari's cousin, because he was the best teacher of all of the family Ulani. Nadja and Mother Ulani were the Right Hands and ran the coin and books for the farms. Kid considered them very smart, in love with the coffee business, their families, and the land. Grandmother was formidable, but she adored Jenny, he said.

He did not have a tutor for the academies yet, as he agreed with the others he needed to learn to read and write Vik first. He wasn't sure how many Wrens would still be about Axefield, but said he would be happy to receive their letters and he would share them with Jenny. He hoped everyone was well.

Arden folded up his letter carefully and slipped it up his sleeve without any comment.

After a moment, Zren looked at Dica. "You got a letter from Kid too; do you want to read yours out loud next?"

Dica gave Zren a long look. "I read mine privately and it says what Arden's letter says, Zren. There is no need to bore you with the same news twice."

Nelo snorted, and Dica narrowed her eyes at him. She turned back to Zren. "You got two letters, Zren, are you going to read both of them to us?"

Zren ducked his head. "No, I shared my letter from Rell with Piffik to read when he has time. But I can tell you Rell is sorry she never got back to Manumina before the Matasians took it over. She misses Vikland coffee, and she writes, 'Evensong is tedious with old men who do nothing but bemoan their loss of power now that Kerek has fallen.' She says she should be back in Vikland soon and threatens to take me on a very long pony ride."

"And your letter from Solkka?" Dica gave him a sly smile.

Zren gave her a big smile in return. "Would you like to read it?" He fished it out of his sleeve and handed it to her. Nelo snatched it out of the air before she could reach for it. He flipped it front to back and front again and then started to laugh. "Here, Dica, this is how you do it if you want to get letters from a lover." Dica bristled as she looked over his shoulder, but Nelo ignored her. He gave the letter back to Zren. "What language is that? It looks very pretty, but you don't read Vik and I know enough of my letters to recognize it isn't written in Keresh."

"It's Wester. Solkka's mother was born in the West Islands and her boys learned to read and write it as well as Vik. Well, Kaede and Solkka did anyway."

Arden leaned over to look at the flowing script. "Does it have different letters? I do not recognize any of the words on the paper." He reached for the letter and looked at it closely as Zren continued to talk.

Zren bobbed his head from side to side. "The letters are the same in Mata and Keresh, I am told. Some of the letters are the same but have different sounds in Wester or Conrosan, and so the writing of them is not expected. It is only Vik where even the drawing of the letters you use to make the words is different. I think that is why all Viklanders learn many languages even from the time they are young." He paused. "I do not know that to be true."

He started again, "When I first came to Manumina, I could not read or write in any language. I asked Siba and Piffik to teach me Conrosan to understand those around me, and because it was the language of my parents who I do not remember. I asked Rell to teach me Wester because, um, Ngahuru speaks Wester."

Arden had flipped the letter over as if he had been reading it. Now he looked up. "You are telling the truth, Zren, but you are not telling *your* truth." He smiled. "You are among friends, Zren. We know you have a soldier waiting for you in Matasi."

Arden grinned then, and returned the letter to Zren. "You should keep that in a safe place. If Dica learned how to write in Wester, Kid would never stay and learn the coffee business."

Dica gave Arden a sharp look, but Zren chuckled, folded up the letter, and tucked it into his pocket tied about his waist.

CHAPTER 29

TO MATASI

And then, near the end of the Wet, when everyone felt as if they would grow gills and breathe water if there was not at least a little sunshine soon, a group of Viklanders, some soldiers, some in the Diplo, and a softfoot stopped at the Huena Inn for an end of day meal and overnight stay on their way to the Vikland embasado in Salisport, Matasi. They were a large patrol to test the safety of the Old Fort Road and find an alternative route to going over the Silver Mountains before the Dry began.

Zren had been walking through the inn looking for one of Raul Huena's younger sons when he heard his name called. A Viklander waved him over, but Zren hesitated since he wasn't close enough to see the soldier well.

"Zren, it's me. Lomes." The Viklander walked up to him. "How are you and why are you here?"

Zren looked Lomes up and down. This time Lomes walked with a swagger and carried a bong strapped to their back. Zren had seen so many hacked off braids, he was startled to see Lomes still had theirs intact. Now that he was sure it was the softfoot, he asked to hear what had happened since they had last met. Lomes laughed and said it would take too long to say standing in a courtyard, but asked him to share the end of day meal at sundown. Lomes said he should come hungry.

Zren grinned.

***

Zren found Lomes in one of the private dining rooms at sundown. Now dressed as a woman in a night-blue skirt and soft, light grey shirt, Lomes had freshly washed and redid their braid, and Zren could see black Viklander boots peeking out below their skirt. Zren was reminded of the Vikland Ambassador in Kerek City all those years ago. Zren looked at the food on the table and squinted.

"This isn't a moment where you are going to sneak out in the night and I am going to spend two fortnights working to pay for this, is it?"

Lomes laughed. "No, Zren, the Empress has already paid for tonight's lodging and meal. Come sit down and tell me all that happened to you since you rescued me at Regno, and I saw you last falling into your bed at Manumina."

Zren sat down and filled his plate. Between bites, he told of the Wrens and some of their stories. He talked of the crimpers and the night he spent with Siba Namikk traveling to and from Evensong. He explained he knew what a Viklander mapcase looked like, could make his own bee paper for rainproof maps, and could ride a horse but he still preferred a wide wagon seat.

He shared the story of Nelo saving Piffik and him at the burnt out Earles fort. He told of driving the cheese cart, and Callis arranging for the bribes for the Jailor at Huk. He talked of Wrens pretending to be Matasi missionaries rescuing Tedros Ulani and others, and Arden rescuing Oro—even though Oro and Arden loved the same girl. He told of the deserters that were younger than the Wrens, and Falan stealing boots and rescuing Bima Ritwik, although he truly just traveled along to get quickly to Ishes and then over the border to Juisiti.

Lomes laughed. "Oh, I bet that was a night's story. Bima never did tell the rest of us that one." The Viklander was silent for a moment. "He really was an amazing softfoot. Before the war, maybe as many as half of those who wanted to be a softfoot would not meet his exacting standards or would quit at his impossible assignments. But during the war? We all could draw upon our experiences of surviving one of his dastardly trainings to save our lives. The newest ones, the ones who did not have time to do more than accompany us a time or two before we needed them to go alone, hardly any of them survived."

Lomes was quiet for a long, long time and then drained their wineglass.

Zren stilled. "Kern? Is she?"

"She told us how you outwitted the Earles garrison by showing up without being rescued." Lomes nodded. "She survived, Zren. As did Rani and Quan. A handful of new ones, and those with a Viklander heart but not a Viklander face. I cannot speak of those, they are still working for us, but not so much in Kerek anymore."

Zren felt confused. He knew Lomes had just told him something, but he wasn't sure what. "Is that why you are going to Matasi?"

Lomes raised an eyebrow. "There are many reasons I am going to Matasi. You can pick any number of them and I will nod my head and say 'yes.'" The softfoot refilled their glasses. "I'm told you like stories, Zren."

"I love stories!" Zren tipped his head. "Well, some stories are better than others. The Viklander Wisdom of the Warrior sagas are good, the West Islands Constellations stories are better." He smirked at Lomes. "Of course, during the war Viklanders liked the Conrosan folk tales of Zren Janin because then they would be mended and fed and taken to a safe place to rejoin other Viklanders."

"Ah yes, there were so many clever touches about your Wrens. The best part was how everyone suspected Ngahuru, but no one ever saw her until Rani encountered her by chance. She was stepping out of the West Islands Ambassador's carriage on the streets of Juisiti as if she had traveled halfway around the world merely to have a cup of Vikland coffee with her Ambassador before escorting them back to Kerek City and home.

"I know you told Bima Ritwik it was Rell Huena. He told us he didn't want to believe you. But your face is known for not having the ability to tell a lie, and so he could not work it out how Rell could do this without ever leaving Manumina."

"Were all of your softfoots in Kerek?" Zren asked.

"Most were. We had loose territories. Bima was above Balza and in the heaviest fighting below the Cold Mountains. Quan was along the Northern Track from Balza to Cloa because without a braid he looked more Kereki than any of us old softfoots. He stayed at Earles first, and then squatted in a deserted barn just north of Huk. He worked closely with your Callis to redeem the soldiers out of the Huk jail."

"Kern was at Earles," Zren prompted.

"Only for a very little while. She was long gone before the firing of the fort. Kern is a 'look at me' and her talents were not best suited to this war. We used her to train new softfoots in

Juisiti. She also worked along the far eastern edge to help Inezi and your Nelo get soldiers, maps, and plans to and from the Viklander encampments just over the borders.

"I bridged between our east and west, north and south. I probably encountered your beautiful boy, and the Wren with the dog, the most. I drove another missionary wagon with a Matasian sympathetic to our plight. I was not as clever as your Padro Morto, but we limped through the war.

"We were so very dependent on all of you. Rani had the far north great houses, Evensong, and the Kereki encampment. He was usually the first Viklander to see the information Kid was getting. Knowing who was in that house and sitting at his master's table? That was important. Many more Viklanders would have died without Kid in place to send us the numbers and locations of the regiments and the militias that would be fighting. None of us with our Vik faces could have done what he accomplished."

Lomes gave Zren a slow appraisal. "And this brings me to my first question, did any of your Wrens survive the war? Do you know where any of them are?"

Zren looked startled. "They all survived! They all received a reward from the Empress. Some live in Juisiti, some here in Axefield, or in Rishka, or the Keopi district, or in Kerek but they all survived."

Lomes grinned broadly. "And would any of them like to live in Matasi?"

Zren scrunched up his face. "I am traveling to Salisport in Matasi at the end of the Wet, why do you ask?"

Lomes leaned back in their chair. "Really? Why?"

So Zren explained. He said he had gotten letters from Solkka Ulani, who was in Matasi for at least the next year. Solkka had asked Zren to join him. He couldn't live in the embasado, of course, but they would find a small place nearby and the two could explore the city and get to know each other. If they enjoyed each other's company and wanted to see more of the world, Solkka would try to get posted to the West Islands or even the Spice Island, and they could see what there was across the sea that was not in their own country. If they tired of that, perhaps the new port in Vikland would be done and they could sail to the Keopi district to visit the Ulani families and rest their feet under the table for a while.

Lomes laughed. "Well, my work is done then! Rani told me Ngahuru said she left some Wrens in Axefield and Rishka. I was to come here and try to take one with me to Matasi. Can you leave tomorrow, Zren? I'll deliver you directly to Solkka Ulani's bed."

Zren grinned and nodded. The two spent the rest of the evening with stories and laughter, talking of wishes and plans.

Before the two left for their beds, Lomes walked with Zren to get his traveling bag of coin from Raul Huena's safe.

Raul was sitting in his small counting room off the inn's entrance looking over the day's numbers. One of the women who collected the fees from the travelers ushered Zren and Lomes in. Raul listened to the story of Zren's traveling with the Viklanders to Salisport. Zren asked for his traveling bag from Raul Huena's safe so he could have enough coin to live in Matasi.

The innkeeper looked astonished, but recovered quickly. He told Zren he would give him the coin for his travels, but insisted Zren promise not to leave in the morning without talking to Piffik first. Raul Huena then gave Lomes a hard look and muttered about Viklander honor.

The next morning Zren was up with the sun to say goodbye to Piffik and the remaining Wrens. He had packed a travel bag full of coin, another of clothes, and had carefully packed his last gift from Siba Namikk—a new pressed book of paper and graphite to write down his stories.

He looked for Nelo first and found him with Piffik working on the plans to move the last of the Conrosans back to Rishka.

"The Viklanders will take me to Solkka Ulani. I am leaving today."

Piffik looked up, shocked. "You are not going to give me more warning than this?"

Zren hung his head at Piffik's harsh voice. He could hear Piffik blow out a noisy breath.

"I am sorry, Zren. I am not angry. I am just startled. It is good for you to travel with such a large group on horseback. And they will know exactly where you must go." He paused a long time. "This is good for you," he repeated. "It is the safest way for you to travel. You must write me here at Axefield as soon as you arrive so I know where Rell can send you our letters." He started to say something else and stopped.

Zren looked up and nodded. His eyes were bright with unshed tears. Then he had swallowed hard and asked Nelo for one of the Fortika horses.

"You know that's a stolen horse," Nelo reminded him.

"I know, but we won't leave Vikland until we reach south Kerek and no one will know. I can't take one of the Conrosan horses or the Kereki army horses, it could never keep up."

Nelo grinned. "Just be sure *you* can."

Zren looked shyly at the ground. "Thank you for the coin."

"Hmmm," Nelo said noncommittedly.

"When Ngahuru left, Siba told me there had been no coin for me from the Empress. Ngahuru had nothing to repay me for the coin she had used when the Wrens first came to Manumina. That was why Siba thought perhaps Ngahuru had asked me to bring back the army paychest. Ngahuru did not want to leave me without anything to live on when I left the Conrosans. She had wanted to give me a traveling bag of coins like the others and repay my coin I had received from Miyamoto Suki. It didn't make it right, Siba said, but she understood the why. Perhaps, Ngahuru didn't think I would notice the coin was Kereki dias and not Viklander sols." Zren grinned. "I think I would have noticed the first time I tried to buy a pastry."

Nelo blew out a sigh. "All she had to do was ask. Now I will never know if she meant to share, or if Nari Ulani saved me by taking her away before you could get back to Axefield."

Zren was quiet as he looked away to the east. He took a breath and then continued in a small voice, "Siba Namikk says we have to remember the good in people. Like I will always remember the good in you."

Nelo was still. "Aw, Zren," he was quiet for a long moment. "This is why everyone is so willing to listen to you talk all day long."

Raul Huena came out to the courtyard. He looked at the travel bag of coin Zren had asked him to take out of the safe last night and sighed. The innkeeper cautioned him not to spend his reward too freely. Piffik reminded Zren not to forget his friends. Zren said he would be back for Piffik's wedding. He had to learn how these things were done. Piffik gave him a sad smile, but he didn't correct him.

The Viklanders came out of the inn then, loud and happy to be traveling to new places. Raul hurried back inside, but Piffik and Nelo helped Zren ready his horse. Lomes offered to ride beside him and practice Mata.

They left heading southwest on a different track than one going past the refugee camp at Rishka. Zren turned and looked back at Axefield. Piffik and Nelo were standing there in the courtyard with hands raised in farewell. Off to the east the sun was now over the horizon. Zren could see the dog, Mother, and Arden walking back to the inn with his prayer rug under his arm and his long brown braid swinging freely.

Suddenly, he saw two girls, one so short she barely came past Nelo's waist, the other one slender and nearly as tall as Zren, come running out to stand next to Nelo, waving wildly. Tyra and Dica. They would all be staying through the rest of the Wet. Zren waved back.

There was a hole in his heart he had not expected, and he turned quickly to the front of his horse and tipped his head away so Lomes couldn't see him.

Lomes chuckled. "Zren, we all do this. I'm just glad you didn't see me bawling like a newborn when I told *my* parents goodbye." They clucked their horses forward. "Just remember who's waiting for you in Salisport."

CHAPTER 30

SOFTFOOTS

The second Huena Inn was done. Conrosans came up from Rishka to help tear down their tent city, the laundry, the waterworks, and the kitchens. It was noisy and crowded. People were out to enjoy the day and the spectacle. The sun was shining as if the Dry was finally here at last.

Dica was hurrying across the churned-up courtyard when she spotted Kern and Rani, the Viklander softfoots she had known from her time at Regno during the war. They were talking together with Salik Oqina, his son Mikale, and Piffik Qanaq. Dica couldn't figure out why the Conrosans would be talking to the softfoots now. She stopped where she was and stood by the wall trying to figure out what she was seeing.

Kid had once told her that he liked softfooting because every interaction had three conversations going on at once. The words that were spoken, the actions of the people involved, and the casual and not so casual interest of the bystanders. Dica tried to see what Kid would have seen.

Kern was doing most of the talking. Everyone's eyes were on her and Rani would glance about as if he was merely taking in the sunshine. Dica knew better. Rani had softfooted near Evensong, Regno, Fortika, and the Kereki encampment north of Earles. For him to survive the war, working where he had, meant he was never unconcerned about anything.

Piffik had his arms crossed. He looked exasperated rather than angry or upset. Mikale looked puzzled and Salik was answering Kern. It had to be about the Conrosans moving to their new home, Dica decided.

"Your hearing is better than mine if you are listening to that conversation," Arden said easily as he walked up beside her.

Dica waved her arm at them. "Do you know what it is about?"

"The Viklanders seemed to have misplaced one of their softfoots—Inezi. Of course, they didn't care a year ago when she actually went missing, but now they have need of her and she is not where they thought they had tucked her away."

Dica gave him a concerned look. "Are you in trouble?"

"Of course not. Viklanders and I have nothing in common but our braid of honor."

Dica snorted. "I wondered why you braided your hair instead of just pulling it back like Nelo does. I thought it was to make it easier for Viklanders to find you to ask for help." She hesitated and then added, "not a lot of Kerekis wear their hair as a Viklander would."

He said nothing, just watched the others on the courtyard. Without taking his eyes from the group in front of him, he asked, "It's the beginning of the Dry, Dica. What are your plans?"

She smiled proudly. "I am a tailor traveling through south Vikland, crossing into Kerek on the Old Fort Road, and making my way through Matasi. I sell made and made-to-order shirts and skirts from my own cart and horse. I read and write Keresh, know a handful of Vik words, and I know and understand the formal Vik greetings. Before he left, Zren taught me enough Mata sayings so people in Matasi will think I have good manners." She gave him a quick smile. "What can *you* offer me to earn a place on my wagon?"

Arden laughed and turned to look at her. "My belief in you was not misplaced. I would like to ride along and see part of your future. And to earn a place on your wagon, I have skills to provide coin, food, and shelter. I will protect you with my wit and my bow until your age is not your enemy. I read and write Keresh, and know enough Mata to ease our way through Matasi. I will share and share alike as long as Mother and I are welcome on your wagon."

"And the woman you are walking out with? From the Huena Inn?" Dica asked.

Arden shrugged. "She has no interest in the traveling life, and I have no interest in asking her." He paused a long time. "And you? Have you told Kid your plans?"

She gave him a long look. "You know I have. I will travel with you and learn of the world as we can. Kid and I plan to meet again when he is at the academies. If I can, I will join him in his classes. If I am too far behind, or cannot learn it, he will teach me as he is able. We plan to work together—first as friends, then as we grow older maybe we will be like Siba and Piffik, or maybe like Rell and Piffik. I can wait for that day when I am old enough to know my own mind." She paused. "I asked Kid to write you and ask if the rumor was true."

Arden paused a long time before answering. "It was one of the letters you gave me. He said, when it was no longer safe for him at Evensong, he asked Inezi directly if Bima had softfoots he could trust on the Northern Track. She had heard my name often enough from Rani and Kern, and didn't know it was information not to be shared. She told him Quan and I were Viklander softfoots from Kerek City he could trust. She had never been told I had come out to the war with Ngahuru and her other Wrens."

Dica carefully avoided Arden's eyes so he wouldn't see her skepticism. They both watched Kern looking about while Rani was talking with Piffik. She noted as Arden nonchalantly took a step back behind Dica out of Kern's line of sight. "I tell myself Inezi was distracted by Kid's youthful face for her to give me up so easily. Or perhaps, she already hated me, and thought Kid would tell Ngahuru and she would end my life." He shrugged. "At the time, we were on the same side and no harm was done. Kid told me and not Ngahuru, and I lived to see another day." He grinned at her.

Dica blew out a breath. "So you agree? You will teach me what Bima Ritwik taught you? What I did not learn from Ngahuru?"

Arden nodded slowly. "I will teach you. And in two years, maybe more, maybe less, you will return to the academies. Together you and Kid can choose your futures, because sometime between now and then, you will leave me in Vesaport and I will take a ship to the Spice Island without asking the Empress's permission."

"I thought Callis said your family was in Kerek City. That you came from a family of thieves. You don't wish to return to them?"

Arden gave her a pointed look. "I do not know how Callis and Nelo think they know so much of my story if I am not the one who told them." He sighed. "I would like to find my sister before I continue to sail the seas and travel the world. I would like to know all is well with her. I want my family to know all is well with me."

He looked down his nose at her. "But between that day and this day, there are a lot of nights of sleeping rough and cooking over a campfire."

She gave him a look of mock horror. "You can cook, can't you?"

"I think Mother may be..." He quickly turned and walked away. Startled, Dica watched him go and then looked back to see Rani watching them both.

***

The Conrosans left at midday. Nelo had told Dica to stay behind, he would be her outrider on one of the Fortika horses. But now her cart was loaded and she was ready to be off. Nelo was nowhere in sight.

She walked into the gardens looking for him and instead saw Rani and Arden talking together. Both of them were facing east, both had their backs to her. She wondered if Arden was going to be softfooting for the Viklanders in south Kerek and in Matasi. Of course he was, she scowled to herself. Why else had he suddenly asked her about her plans? Traveling with her was the perfect way to travel about and capture news. She wasn't sure how they were going to get it all back to Juisiti, but she was sure Rani and Kern had a plan for that too. Well, she and Kid had said they wanted to be softfoots, so she would learn from a softfoot as he did his work.

Dica turned back and headed to the inn to see if Nelo was there. She had just reached the door when she recognized Falan sitting inside the open area where guests were greeted.

Falan scowled. "I thought all the Wrens had already left with the Conrosans."

Dica hid her surprise quickly. "No. Nelo is going to be my outrider, and Ross is going to stay here. We are all that is left. Why are you here?"

Falan sighed. "I am here to ask Raul Huena to hire me for the second inn. I am not a cheesemaker's apprentice anymore. I cannot live in Rishka anymore." Falan gave her a suspicious look. "And since you would not ask, I will tell you. Callis is traveling with the Conrosans to build the new port. She has abandoned our dream of returning to Kerek. But it doesn't matter to me. I won't have to take care of her."

Dica was going to ask her if anyone else knew she was in Axefield, but then Claire, the Viklander who had helped Nari Ulani give them the thanks and coin of Vikland, walked over.

"Hello! Which one of you spoke to Raul Huena a few moments ago? He asked me to talk to you about what we need and what you could do to help us."

Dica turned and gave her the short bow. "Claire of the Huena Inn, it is good to see you again. It is my friend Falan who wishes to share her knowledge and experience with you."

Claire smiled and returned the bow. "I remember you now. You were the one who asked me for the proper responses for the honor ceremony with the soldier. It is good to see you again. Your manners are better than mine, for you remember my name, but I cannot recall yours."

"Dica." She bowed again. "But you have business together, and I am looking for Nelo. I will not steal any more time from you." She nodded to Falan and walked out into the sunshine.

Nelo had hitched a horse to her cart and was mounted on another horse. He was looking around and she waved to catch his attention. He waved back and wheeled about.

"Arden will be bringing the last Fortika horse when he comes later today," Nelo said.

Dica pulled herself up into the cart and released the brake. Together they gave one last look about Axefield, their home for the past season. Then Nelo nodded to her, and she snapped the reins. The future was waiting.

PART II

THE FIRST DRY SEASON AFTER THE SETTLING OF ORSUARLERPAA, VIKLAND

CHAPTER 31

ORSUARLERPAA

To: Piffik Qanaq, now residing at the Conrosan settlement in Orsu, Vikland.

From: Siba Namikk, healer at the Brick family farms, southeast of Lowel, South Kerek.

I am writing this letter as soon as I received yours. I am glad the Empress of Vikland allowed you and the other Conrosans to name the new settlement, Orsu. Did you tell her the entire meaning in Conrosan? "Orsuarlerpaa — She pours oil on water so it becomes calm, then she can see what lies in the depths."

Or did she just roll the sound on her tongue and say 'A name that will please the Conrosans and still sound a little Vik'?

I am teasing you, my friend.

I know you are still gathering your people and Salik Oqina is still convincing the reluctant ones to leave Rishka and join you. But letters take so long to travel from here to there, I do not doubt all of you will arrive at your new home and build your tent city before this letter even reaches Juisiti and the Central Administrative Offices. There some poor clerk will be forced to look at my letter and find the map of Vikland to learn what box to store it in until someone can carry it forward.

I heard the sorrow in your letter as you described Zren's leaving for Salisport. I know you have already convinced yourself Zren was not leaving you, he was merely embracing his future. We both know Zren is an unusual man. It is why, I think, everyone flocks to him so quickly. And then, when they realize the entire world will always enchant him, and he only looks forward and never to the past or to the ties of others, then his friends must decide the cost of their friendship. I don't know how Tiju Tia/Ngahuru knew how to name him so well. He truly is our Conrosan folk hero come to life.

But I know even now, how the other Wrens need you. I feared for Tyra at first. My friend, Kalina Pitse, came to me and said she had quickly asked to have Tyra join their house to help her with the coming baby, and then realized Tyra had no idea how to care for one. She hid food and fought with the other children when they found it. My friend felt she could not keep her because Tyra frightened her little ones with stories from Kerek City. Kalina said her man scolded Tyra for lying, and the Wren would scream it was all true.

Then when Falan and Callis cleaned out the shed and said it was the home for all the Wrens, I thought Tyra and Dica would never overcome their beginnings. I had not counted on Tyra's desire for friends and school and a life without want. Rygee has since told me she would come by the bakery several times a day. Not for fingersweets, but for a slice of bread, a piece of fruit meant for the pies, or a sliver of cheese or pickle from someone's midday. Once she knew she could have food whenever she wished; once she felt safe, she found those schoolgirls and made friends with others who helped her claim a childhood.

I am beyond glad to hear Callis is moving with you to Orsu. She already has the skills of a tailor, and I think she will make a fine healer someday. I remember those nights during the war when Rell and I would take turns caring for the wounded, burned, and broken you found for us. My aunt alone would never be able to care for as many Conrosans as lived at Manumina.

I am glad for another reason as well. Callis needs to know who she is before she can care for another. All the Wrens need this. I think she and Falan found comfort in each other because they knew no one else like them. It was a lack of others, rather than desire for each other. I think you and I saw enough marriages at Manumina where this was true. I believe you recognized it as well. Miyamoto Suki's thirteenth crossing saved us both from making the mistake of settling for those who would not make us happy.

Life continues here at the farms. The heat of the Dry is much stronger here than in north Kerek, and Rygee has taught me to rest in the covered porches to catch the breezes. He told me when he was a child, his brothers and he would wrap their sheeting about the posts to keep out the creatures and bugs and sleep outside to catch any movement of wind. I am not there yet. I do not yet understand how much more freedom I have here than I did at Manumina. But I am learning quickly.

Your devoted friend,

Siba Namikk

CHAPTER 32

ADVENTURING

To: Kid, an apprentice at the Gayo Ulani coffee farm, the Keopi District, Vikland.

From: Dica, a tailor, now traveling through South Kerek.

Well, didn't you fill my head with a lot of stories of other places and other people! I know the information you heard and gave the Harbormaster only increased your own appetite for adventure. So, since you are there and I am here, I will do what I can to tell you how I am adventuring. (I asked Arden if that was a word, and he said you would know what I meant.)

Neither Arden nor I spoke enough Vik to linger in Vikland, so we crossed over early into Kerek. Instead of traveling all the way south to the Old Fort Road and crossing over at Neblin, we set out for the Southern Track. We camp rough most nights. Arden is a fine cook over a campfire—except for biscuits. He claimed he never learned how since Linna grew up in a proper house and knew how to take such good care of him. He says it with his odd smile so I do not know if he is joking or not. He doesn't talk a lot.

I know you can't write me back, even I don't know where I am going to lay my head from one night to the next. Arden has asked to be in charge of our maps and destinations. I can't say more than that, but you are a smart boy, you will figure it out. He has a book of pressed papers like Zren had. He writes a little every day. I asked to see it and he showed me. I didn't recognize the words. It could be Mata, it could be Conrosan, it could be Wester. It could be something he made up. But I grew up in Kerek City where it is best not to ask any questions.

I know you will think I am young and foolish, but I would like to ask you to save my letter and write a letter in response even though you cannot send it to me. Keep them all together and when I come to the academies to study, I will be able to read the whole of my story from beginning to end.

Dica

CHAPTER 33

JOSEF WRITES

To: Nelo, a builder at the Conrosan settlement in Orsu, Vikland.

From: Josef, apprentice at the Brick family farms, southeast of Lowel, South Kerek.

Ah, Nelo, I am trying to decide if you are going to read this Letter yourself or find someone to whisper the Words to you. And if so, what naughty Words should I write so the others refuse to read to you again and you must Learn to read it for yourself?

I told Siba I didn't know if I should use big Letters and little words or big Words and little letters to write you. She just shook her head at me. Ha! I will laff at my own Jokes since you are not here to Laff with me.

It is already Hot Hot Hot. Rygee says this is south Kerek and what did I expect? I asked him if Matasi was hotter yet and he said he didn't Know. But he said they grow fruit and Vegetables much larger there, so it is possible. We have a Matasian horsebreaker here and he wears a funny hat with a cloth on the back of it that touches his shoulders and protects his neck from the sun. It looks like a Woman with her hair unbound. It is bright Orange and I asked him once if that was to help the other Horsebreakers find him in the Dust when he has been thrown. It took Rygee and two others to hold him back. My sense of Humor is so underappreciated here!

I wonder if you are tired of building things yet. I do not have time to get tired of doing things, I just get tired because I am doing things. I work with the Horses early in the morning before the heat is too much. Then when we are all Resting inside at midday, Siba has me help her in her still room and her ~~infermy~~ ~~infrom~~ sickroom. I do not have to cook here, but Rygee asked if I would like to Learn to make south Kerek's version of apple jack. For medicinal purposes, Siba says. And then she frowned at Rygee. Ooooh, this will be Fun!

Siba says I must Practice my writing so everyone can understand my Letters and not just those who Know me well. So you can Write me as often as you want. I will find the time to read your Words. Probably at the cool of the night when Rygee wants me to help him with something heavy to lift or hard to do.

Josef

CHAPTER 34

A LETTER TO AN OLD FRIEND

To: Ngahuru, daughter of the Tailor to the King, The Royal Palace, West Islands.

From: Zren Janin, now receiving letters at the embasado at Salisport, Matasi.

My Ngahuru,

I am writing this letter in Wester because Solkka says he will send it either with a West Islands ship heading home or from the Matasi Central Administrative Offices and not through the Vikland Diplo pouches. I do not know what that means, but he said you would understand and approve. Do you?

Do you remember Lomes? They were one of the Viklanders we rescued at Regno during the war. They had been trying to get a group of soldiers to Fortika but Inezi had already left taking others. Dica had found them and hid them, and then Piffik and I brought them to Manumina and then to Ishes. You should know, Lomes and some other Viklanders came to Axefield and took me to Salisport with them. Piffik said it was good for me to travel with a group, and they would know exactly where to go.

Solkka was surprised to see me, but very happy. He found a room for me in a house where I live with a wife of a soldier posted at the embasado. Did you know married people cannot live in the embasado except for the Ambassador? Doesn't that seem strange to you?

I am learning Mata—a little. Solkka has to work most days and so we spend evenings walking the streets and learning the city. I would eat at a baboy every night but Solkka laughs and says I would run out of coin in a season. So, I showed him my traveling bag of coin, and he frowned and asked to manage it for me. He gives me coins for midday and if I need more, I only need to ask. He says he needs to teach me not to buy a horse when all I want is a pastry. I remembered Rell told me so too, and I said to Solkka I knew that was a Vik joke. He laughed and said it was true. He is very kind to me. He says it is because I love him for himself and not who he is and what I think he should do for me.

One time when we were walking, I recognized a statue in the circle in the street. I told him how Bima and Lomes and others tried to make me lost without coin nor friend before I sailed for Kerek City. He said Bima Ritwik did that to everyone and then tried to talk the successful ones into becoming softfoots. The ones who were *not successful spent a night in Matasi jails for breaking curfew. I know Bima did many nice things for me, and some not so nice. I still don't know if he was a friend or not to me.*

But I know you are my friend. You found me injured on the road to Aldi, then answered my plea for help at Manumina. Solkka says we will see you again someday. He said for me to tell you when Matasi and Vikland are finished posturing for each other, he hopes to be posted to the West Islands. He has some cousins he wants to get to know better and he is beyond grateful you have made that possible.

Solkka is here now and ready to take this letter to the docks to be posted on a ship to you. I will write again.

Zren Janin

CHAPTER 35

RELL RETURNS TO VIKLAND

To: Solkka Ulani, a diplomat of Vikland now posted to the embasado at Salisport, Matasi.

From: Arella Huena, formerly of Axefield, now residing in Orsuarlerpaa, Vikland.

Greetings and good health to you, Solkka Ulani.

We are not so well known to each other, but we have met at Manumina and I have helped you and yours. Although I am well aware Zren Janin, a hero of Manumina, cannot live in the Vikland embasado, I have no doubt you are well acquainted with his whereabouts. I am enclosing a letter for him. I would be grateful if you could ensure he receives it.

I know you appreciate the treasure that he is, Solkka. There is nothing deceitful or unkind in his heart. He is braver than he thinks and loves fiercely and faithfully. He is so curious about the world he never had a chance to learn about as a child. Remember that when it seems he never stops talking. Be kind to him.

When the new port of Orsu is completed, I hope you and Zren will sail to Vikland for a visit and put your feet under our table. Your family in the Keopi district is not so far that you cannot see us all in your travels home. Take care and take care of Zren. He is very dear to me.

Arella Huena of Orsu, Vikland

The enclosed letter

To: Zren, a hero of Manumina, and a very fine carpenter to the Huena family inns.

From: Rell Huena, formerly of Axefield, now residing in Orsu, Vikland.

My little brother!

I cannot believe the lengths you would go to avoid a pony ride with me! I was sorry to arrive back at Axefield and find the inn had been built, the gardens planted, and my other little brothers (so many I cannot remember all their names) quick to tell me of all the adventures I missed. But now the Matasi Triune and Vikland Empress have decided the Kereki great houses (and I) have been punished enough, and I have returned to Vikland.

Piffik and I are married. My parents insisted we marry before we traveled across to the 'edges of Vikland'—my father's words. Unfortunately, my mother forgot to inform Vikland's Empress. A military attachment arrived to lead the Conrosans to their new home before we had planned the wedding. There was not time to do everything Vikland tradition demands, and I believe Piffik was grateful. It was more than a Conrosan meeting with the Council of Wisdom and less than a traditional four-day Viklander ceremony. The best of both worlds.

Even with only one day's notice, Chul Swyler, Kern, Rani, and Aajan, all came down together from Juisiti. We left an open chair for Siba and Rygee, Zadah, and you. We plan to travel and see all of you when the port is finished and we can sail from Vikland's own harbor.

The trip to Orsuarlerpaa took twelve days. It was the heavy settler wagons that slowed us down. And the goats. Many of the Conrosans walked beside their wagons. It was awkward for those in the military who accompanied us since Viklander horses could have done the trip much faster. But the trip is behind us now, and no one will be moving away anytime soon.

Do you remember Ceri, Kern's wife? She is from the far eastern parts of Vikland, and we have many from her district who have come to help us build the port. For now, we all live in a tent city while our houses are built. Piffik wants to build our house where he can watch the sea every day. He says he wants to be the first one to see his brother's ship sail home for a visit or perhaps to stay. Everyone here calls the new city Orsu. It sounds like a Vik name, doesn't it?

Chul and Aajan will be sending us the ingredients we need to blast through the mountains, but there is a lot of work to be done first. Piffik and the others have started to survey and lay out the path to the harbor. The Empress's daughter has a mind for such things and has sent along many plans and maps and people to help Piffik. Chul sends letters as well and when Piffik reads them to me, I feel as if I am back in the academies. It is good those two met at Manumina. Minds like that need to find each other.

Those you know and care for are doing well. Nelo continues to work with Piffik and is training to be a builder's Left Hand. He sorts out crews and decides what work will be done. Nelo has a good memory for names and faces and remembers their skills. He is protective of the newest apprentices. He sounds just like Piffik when he praises their work and points out their opportunities to do better!

Nelo is learning Vik as fast as he can and continues his studies with me so he does not need to sit in the classroom with the little children. He does not like to read the Wisdom of the Warrior sagas—too many monsters—but likes sums and the numbers and problems used for buildings. For today, there are others to do the numbers and coins. The Empress has sent three for such a task. I think they are meant to watch each other so every sol is accounted for!

Nelo has asked me for a book of Conrosan folk tales. He likes the tales of Zren Janin that some of the woodworkers tell. But I cannot find one—written in Vik or any other language. I think you should write one for us.

We are three days ride—two on a fast horse—from the Ulani coffee farms. Shortly after we arrived, Kid, Jenny, and Nadja Ulani came to see us. Nadja said they came to talk about coffee and explain what warehouses and storage would be needed by the coffee farmers for their shipments. She was older than me and attended the Academy of Botanicals so I had never met her before. She looked over the harbor plans with Piffik and determined where to buy land and how much. Jenny and Kid both say they are glad to be at the Ulani farms. Tyra and Jenny were happy to see each other. Kid asked after everyone who did not have their feet under our table.

Callis remains with us here at Orsu and continues her apprenticeship with Bett. She is cheerful and kind and will be a fine healer someday. She is still practicing her short bong. We have some Viklanders here for their military service, and she trains with them to improve her skills. She and Nelo also spend a lot of time together talking through their past and how they will learn from it. I think they will be close friends like Siba and Piffik because of their shared experiences. Truthfully, I do not know how any of you lived through your childhoods.

Tyra and Therin are in school and learning to be children again. I never see either of them without a group of friends. We hear nothing from Ross, or Falan, Oro and Linna. Callis believes we may never get letters from them. They have put the war, and all of us, behind them.

It seems both Kid and Nelo receive many letters from Dica and Arden although there is no way to return the news. Kid and Nelo do not circulate their letters as the rest of us do, but Nelo reads to us and Kid writes their news in his notes so we learn what they wish us to know instead. Dica and Arden are both very vivid writers, and we enjoy their stories and descriptions. The letters talk about new places they are seeing, foods they try, and people they meet. They are doing well. Dica writes Arden doesn't talk much, but he always has an answer for her questions. She writes he has mended a broken harness, fixed a wobbly wheel, and seemed to be able to do anything except make biscuits. Nelo tells us Arden likes to hunt for the stewpot. He has always found work for a day or more when Dica sets up for a few days in a settlement for her tailoring.

According to Dica, they do not wander without a purpose. Arden is in charge of the maps and where they put their heads to rest at night. Mother is such a great titiro mai ki ahau, *once they arrived at a settlement already known as 'Mother and her children!' They write that south Kerek is very different with such a great Matasi presence. There are soldiers and guards for the orchards and estancias everywhere. Far different than what north Kerek was before and during the war. I can't imagine what they are going to think when they reach Matasi.*

Nelo takes our letters from Orsu to the Ulani farms to be carried along to Juisiti. Some of the coffee farmers have suggested with such a large presence here at Orsu, there should be a regular route—perhaps a military or civilian cart—to go back and forth to Juisiti once every few days rather than hiring a messenger or waiting for someone who has business at the palace or in the city. I can't imagine such a thing, but I think the possibilities would be wonderful! I take a turn and travel once each Dry season stopping at every home and settlement along the way and then visit my parents in Axefield for four days before returning to Juisiti picking up the packages, letters, documents, and orders and doing the same route in reverse. I ride my mare, Wishes, and she makes it feel like a pony ride!

Siba and Josef send a letter every fortnight. Because of the distance the letters must travel, they have sometimes written two or even more before we get the first one. Sometimes, I must piece together their letters to follow the story properly.

Siba says she is so busy she does not have time to miss Manumina, but she misses her dear friend Piffik and her aunt, Bett. She spends her time learning from and teaching Rygee's mother and sisters by marriage about her way of doing things and they share with her as well. She is the healer for all the farms in the area, and Rygee has made her a medicinal garden so large, they hired a girl to help her tend it. Occasionally, Rygee adds a few lines as well or includes a separate page for Nelo.

We asked Piffik's mother to move in with us, but she has chosen to live with another widow whose children are not here at Orsu. There are many who have not heard from their distant children since they were forced to leave Manumina. I wonder where those letters are going. How will they find us?

How will we find you, Zren Janin, when Solkka Ulani is done with his time in Salisport and you two sail to the West Islands? Continue to write to us. Together we can look up at the stars at night and know we are all looking at the same constellations and thinking of each other and our adventures of the past and our dreams of our future. Write down your stories, Zren. Someday when your feet are under our table, we will ask you to tell us of all you have learned.

You are missed, you are loved. You are still my favorite little brother.

Rell Huena

PART III

THE FIRST WET AFTER THE SETTLING OF ORSUARLERPAA, VIKLAND

CHAPTER 36

HELLO, OLD FRIENDS!

To: Kid and Jenny, the Ulani coffee farms, Keopi District, Vikland.

From: Dica, now traveling through South Kerek.

So, Arden told me to write you together because apparently the many letters I have been writing both of you have been taxing his poor muscles as he carries them about until he can find a place to send them on to you. I pointed out his books of pressed papers that he sends to Juisiti are much heavier. He never responded. I think that meant he didn't know what to say.

In Kerek City, there are many lessons we are forced to learn early to avoid a dance with Trouble. Run fast, lie convincingly, and never show curiosity or ask questions of the wrong people. Ha! This has not served me well, as Arden has taken me over all of south Kerek using his maps and drawings. As the Wet began, our waxed overcloth was losing its waterfastness. (Is this a word? Arden says you will know what I mean.) I asked him to build me a canopy over the cart like the one Rygee had on the settler wagon before they left Axefield. I was worried my patterns and clothes would be ruined by the rains of the Wet. He said he could do better than that, but said nothing more. And of course, I didn't ask!

Three days before yesterday, he took me through the tiny town of Lowel. Arden said he needed to stop at the stables and pick up a new piece of leather for one of the bridle bits. I shopped and bought some food. As we stopped for midday in yet another drizzle, he unhitched one of our horses and rearranged the cart to be pulled by one horse. He took the other and saddled it for an outrider. I was worried, thinking he knew of bandits in the area, although I couldn't imagine it with all of the Matasi soldiers and guards we have seen. He cleaned Mother's paws and dried her fur with his extra shirt and had her ride on the wagon seat under our tiny awning with me to stay clean and dry. We headed southeast and after a decon we came to a beautiful valley with orchards, fields, horses, and animals of all kinds in fine fences. No brambles like we used for the goats at Rishka anywhere! There were tidy farms all about and a large house in the middle with a front porch like the houses at Manumina, only on all sides. Arden grinned at me and said that was where we were camping for the night, and I better be ready to do some mighty fine tailoring.

There were fancy wooden posts and an arch saying BRICK FAMILY FARMS over the dirt road leading down into the valley. We didn't drive up to the one in the middle but a nice settlement to the west with a garden so big it was almost as large as one of *the barns. And who should come out of the house to greet us? Siba Namikk! She cried when she saw us, she said she was so happy. 'It is so good to see someone from home,' she said. Arden looked at me and said to use my sleeve to wipe my face before Josef saw me.*

That speck of moisture on the paper that made the graphite run was from the drizzle. You know the Wet.

That first night at end of day meal, Rygee and Josef told us of the work they do and what has happened since we saw them. Arden asked if they could use a manabout for a few days in exchange for a place to lay our heads. I said I could do some tailoring for them or help with Siba's gardens or stillrooms if she told me what to do. Josef said I could sew muslin bags for her herbs to hang to dry, he was much too tired to keep his eyes open to thread the needles.

That night I slept in a bed so fancy I didn't want to get out of it the next morning. Josef has a room nearly like it and before we came, he had it all to himself. Arden and Mother are sharing with him now.

Arden got up earlier than I did on the first day. He and Mother went with Rygee to talk with his oldest brother. After two days of showing his carpentry skills by fixing things about the farms, he has been offered work through the Wet. They will be finishing a new barn on his brother's farm.

I am to learn to make baby clothes. Siba says her sister by marriage is having a baby and doesn't know how to sew a stitch!

Her baby will be born first but after that, my plan is that Siba's and Rygee's baby is going to have so many clothes she can change it every decon of the day!

The room I am sleeping in will be the nursery, but Arden tells me we must be gone before the baby is here. Siba still looks like Siba mostly and nothing like her sister by marriage who looks like she swallowed a pillow.

Write quickly and your letters should reach me here before we leave at the beginning of the Dry!

Dica

CHAPTER 37

MY HEART IS SO FULL

To: Siba Namikk, at the Brick family farms, southeast of Lowel, South Kerek.

From: Zren Janin, of Manumina, now receiving letters at the embasado at Salisport, Matasi.

Greetings and good health to you, Siba Namikk,

Solkka says that a man who uses words as often as I do should write more letters to give everyone the benefit of my stories. He smiled when he said that, but said he wasn't joking. He smiles a lot and has a laugh Jenny once said just sounds 'joyful.' Isn't that a beautiful word?

When Ngahuru and Koanga and I were traveling through Matasi on the way to Salisport, I told the West Islanders I thought I could live in Matasi. Koanga had scoffed asking if I was so willing to sell my freedom for comfort. Even Miyamoto Suki, when he was here, would stay out until the very last moment before curfew. Ngahuru said it was to 'assert his independence.' I am not sure what all of that means, but I do know, I like it here very much. I told Solkka people are so kind here. He said people can be kind everywhere; they just need to be treated with respect and dignity. I told him he has never lived in Lowertown. He gave me a sad look and said he wouldn't last three days in Lowertown, even now as a past Viklander soldier.

He will be leaving in a few days to go to Alenti again. I cannot go with him as he will be traveling with the Ambassador and First Soldier Joon. He says he is invited, not because he is smart and good with languages, but because he is a nephew of a King. He says it doesn't matter, he is still learning to be a good diplomat and someday he may be an Ambassador himself. But I think it matters very much to him.

Siba, you will be happy to know I have been filling the book of pressed paper you gave me with stories and stories and stories. I found a Matasi missionary who is living on the next street over. She is very old, and I help her with her errands and her gardens, and she tells me stories which I write down. She speaks Keresh with a thick tongue, but I can understand her. She is trying to teach me Mata too.

Solkka and I look through bookshops—did you know there are places where they sell nothing but maps and books and papers? We are looking for a book of Conrosan fairy tales like Ngahuru had. I think we may need to go to Conrosa to find it. Or maybe Ngahuru will still have one when we go to the West Islands and Solkka can help me write the stories in Vik. I want to find it for Nelo. He told Rell he would read it if I sent it to him.

I miss you very much, Siba. Many people here in Matasi ask to talk to me and want to know about Conrosa. I say I was dragged to the other side of childhood at Manumina and could tell of what I learned there. Sometimes they ask me to speak a few words of Conrosan. Solkka says not to do it. If he is with me, he gets mad at them and says I am not a trained bird from the Spice Island. I told him they just are curious about Conrosa and they don't mean to be unkind. I like to learn things too, I said, and he never gets mad at me for asking questions.

I miss you very much, Siba. I see I already wrote that once. But my heart is so full I thought I should say it again.

Zren

CHAPTER 38

GOOD NEWS!

To: Piffik Qanaq and Rell Huena, now residing in Orsu, Vikland.

From: Siba Namikk, at the Brick family farms, southeast of Lowel, South Kerek.

My friends,

This Wet has been full of so much good news I hardly know where to begin. First of all, thank you for your letters. Congratulations on your marriage! I am sorry, more sorry than you can imagine, to miss such an event, but I also failed to tell the Vikland Empress I would need at least two fortnights notice for us to travel there. The empty chair was a thoughtful gesture and one that touched me deeply.

Rell, you should know, and I believe Piffik has already told you, many times, he believes he was marrying a far better woman than he had ever imagined. I agree. While I would not wish what you went through at the Battle at the Bridge on anyone, I am forever grateful the remnants of Miyamoto Suki's thirteenth crossing ended up at Manumina. All of our lives have been enriched by those who chose to call it home, even if only for a little while.

And speaking of those who choose to stay for a little while, Dica and Arden surprised us with their presence almost a fortnight ago. Arden said he had asked Rygee to mark a map for him before we left Axefield. I thought it was the map he gave to Josef so he would know where he was traveling. But it seems Arden marked a second map as well. We are beyond glad to see the both of them.

Arden is helping Rygee's brother build a gathering barn. I say helping, but truly you have trained him well, Piffik. Rygee says none of his brothers have the patience, the carefulness with small details, and the building skills that Arden has, and he hopes they are paying attention.

Dica has been helping me in my stillroom and gardens, and tailoring. My sister by marriage and I are both expecting babies, but hers will be coming within two fortnights and mine has only just quickened. Some of the compounds and salves I need to make aren't good for me to touch now or I cannot stand to smell them at this time. Dica reads the directions to me, I point to the bottles and drying sacks and she mixes them for me. In the evenings, when the men are snoring in their chairs after their days working outside, she and I sit together and sew and listen to the rains. She is clever and curious and asks such interesting questions. I have her read to me in Keresh, and we have an old battered book of Matasi parables that came from who knows where. She will sound out the words and Arden will correct her pronunciation if he is only half asleep. I like the sound of Mata, but Rygee says I already have baby brain and cannot learn a new language. Hmmmf!

Rygee has told the Wrens they need to pick a family name. That only orphans and bastards have one name. Nelo and Callis and Tyra may wish to consider this also. Dica said softfoots have only one name, but Arden said they have two. They only use one to protect those they love, but they never lose their family's name or honor.

Josef asked to know Arden's family name and he refused to say, but said if we ever sail to the Spice Island, his family will host a feast to celebrate. Is this a surprise to you? Our Kereki thief who led everyone to believe he was born unloved and unnamed on the streets of Kerek City, is a man of the Spice Island with a family, a family name, and family honor. Neither Dica nor Josef even blinked at this news. Truly, our humorous little boy only responded that he refuses to go unless Arden can promise there will be Vikland coffee and fingersweets.

It is sometimes difficult to believe Arden and Josef are merely a year apart in age—if either one of them can be certain. Josef still asks permission for nearly every decision he makes, or he waits until someone makes it for him. It is heartbreaking to see the result when a child's will and boundaries have been stripped away and replaced with emotional manipulation and fear. I cannot imagine a man like Falan's *father. Josef still has so far to go. And yet I would not trade away any of the Wrens, or the lessons I learned from them, from my life.*

I know Dica said she sent letters to all of the Wrens, but now you have a place to send a response. We hope to keep them through the Wet and possibly even until the baby comes.

My heartfelt wishes for peace and joy for all of you.

Siba Namikk

This additional page was written by Josef Brick.

Dear Everyone — Nelo, Callis, and Tyra — at Orsu, Vikland

Siba only gave me one page of Paper to write all of you and She said I should make My letters smaller. I suppose that means Nelo can read Big words now.

There are still Chores to do during the Wet, but I don't mind it since it is cooler and the daily Rain is almost warm like a bath. Siba told you all the Happy news. There is going to be a Baby in the house. Dica is sleeping in the nursery for now and Arden has finally been house-broken enough he and Mother can sleep inside and not in the lofts above the Stables like he did at Rishka and Axefield. I share my Room with them. Mother sleeps between us to protect me.

He and Mother get up before it is even Morning. He is so very quiet most Mornings I do not even hear him—unless I put my Boots in his way. There are four Matasian workers on the Farm, and they meet Together on the porch at the big House. They silently sit facing South on their prayer rugs until the Sun rises.

Callis, if you are at Orsu, where is Falan? I do not know where to write her. I am anxious that if You and I are not with her, there will be no one to Joke and make fun to smooth away Trouble when she has blistered Others with her scalding tongue. I need for her to know she is not Alone, so please Tell me where she is.

Tyra, if you are still reading Nelo's letters to him, please let me know and I will stop putting in so many Naughty words. Unless you like Reading them, then I will leave them in. I learn them all from Arden when he trips over my Boots. He says he is merely praying in Mata.

Siba says I can pick any day of the year to be my Birthday and they will celebrate it. She says I have had at least two birthdays since she has known me, yet I still tell others I am Sixteen. I think I will be like Zren Janin as he says he is between nineteen and twenty-two and then says he will be whatever age we need him to be. I think I need to be twenty-one and here is why.

Rygee said I needed a family Name. I said since he wasn't using his, I would like it. He told me to ask his Papa for permission. I did, but

I asked Siba to go with me. His Papa said he didn't think I could mess it up, but he could always have a Horse drop me on my head if I did.

He asked if I was sure I was Sixteen because in Kerek a man had to be twenty-one to own his own Farm, and I was so Tall he thought I might be older. He thought my pretty Face might get him a nicer farm. Then he said there could never be too many Bricks in the world and he would be Happy to share his Name with me. So now I am known as Josef Brick.

How did I get to the bottom of the page already? I barely said anything!

Josef Brick

CHAPTER 39

EXPECT THE UNEXPECTED

To: Rell Huena and Piffik Qanaq, friends at Manumina, now residing in Orsu, Vikland.

From: Zren Janin, of Manumina, now receiving letters at the embasado at Salisport, Matasi.

Greetings and good health to you!

A pony ride! You think I left for Salisport because you were going to take me on a pony ride? Rell, did you forget you spent a whole year of your life teaching me Wester? Piffik, did you not spend decons with me in your woodshop telling me I needed to hold you in my heart when I left Manumina? A pony ride! Ha!

Solkka has watched me write this letter and asked what has me so upset. So I showed him your letter and he said you were trying to be funny. That sometimes when people care for each other a lot it is hard for them to show it, so they use sarcasm or funny jokes or sharp words to hide it. I am not good at hiding things, so I will just tell you I care about you both and miss you. You are still my best friend, Piffik.

I have looked in so many bookshops for a book of Conrosan fairy tales for Nelo. Solkka says I should just write down the ones I know in Wester and then he will rewrite them in Vik for me. He said Nelo might like them in both Wester and Vik to help him learn his languages faster. But he said it is just a thought he had and I can do as I wish.

I think that feels right. I will begin writing the book for Nelo and still look for one when we walk out and see the city of Salisport. Would he like some Matasi parables and West Islands Constellation stories too? I truly like the Constellation stories, but maybe because they are the first ones I heard and I heard them from Koanga, a West Islands Storyteller. In the West Islands, the stories are so important, they have people who do nothing else but learn them and pass them on to others. In Vikland, you study the Wisdom of the Warrior sagas in the academies. Why doesn't everyone think their stories are important? Why doesn't Nelo like the Warrior sagas? They have monsters, true. But the monsters always lose against the Warriors!

Several days ago, we had a visitor at the house I am living in. Solkka was over and we were reading together. He was reading a book in Mata to me, and then he would stop after a little bit and ask me what I thought he said. It is a children's book so I have already learned lots of the words. There was a knock at the door and it was

Kern! Our Kern! The one that was on Miya's thirteenth crossing with us! She said she was in Salisport on her way to the West Islands and Lomes had told her I was here. She is still very tall and has a smile that makes you want to smile back. The first thing she said was, "Zren Janin! I should have learned by now to always expect the unexpected where you are concerned!" That's what she said at Earles too!

We had fun visiting while Solkka went out and got food for us to eat. She asked me if I was happy and I said of course. She said I should watch my back. There were a lot of unhappy women who were going to have to settle for Tedros now that Solkka had declared for me. I said I didn't know what that meant. She just patted my cheek and said Solkka was a lucky man. Too many people wanted to be Solkka's friend for what they thought he should do for them, while I loved him for himself. I said of course I love Solkka! He loves stories as much as I do!

Then Solkka came back, and we ate and told of our adventures until very late. I was worried she was going to miss curfew and Matasi soldiers would find her and make her spend the night in jail. But she said she was just brushing up her softfooting skills.

She kissed Solkka on the cheek when she left and then said, "To think such beauty will never wake up on a pillow beside me." He laughed so she must have told a joke. It was good to see her again.

I wish I could see you both again too. Solkka says as soon as the Orsu port is open, we will sail there and put our feet under everyone's table. I can't wait for that day to come.

Your little brother,

Zren Janin

PART IV

THE SECOND DRY AFTER THE SETTLING OF ORSUARLERPAA, VIKLAND

CHAPTER 40

FAMILY IS FAMILY

To: Nelo, Callis, and Tyra, members of the Conrosan settlement now residing in Orsu, Vikland.

From Arden, a carpenter at the Brick family farms, southeast of Lowel, South Kerek.

It is the beginning of the Dry, and Dica and I are moving on. You may have heard Josef has chosen a family name—Brick. Dica has also chosen one—Namikk. She says it is because Siba taught her to listen to her own dreams and not the voices of others who tell her what she cannot do. She's a determined one and only grows stronger and cleverer by the day. Siba told her to pick a day for her birthday and we would celebrate it. We had samiss—a Conrosan delicacy. Dica is quick to remind everyone she is now fifteen. I have enjoyed watching her grow up this past year.

Thank you, Callis, for all you have done to teach her to be a tailor. Thank you, Tyra, for being her friend in Lowertown and in the Kereki strongholds of the north during the war. Thank you, Nelo, my friend, for keeping her alive and safe in Kerek City where little girls like her were worth nothing more than a few coins from the Orphan Master.

I only meant us to stay a few days at Siba and Rygee's home, but the steady coin I earned and the evenings with Josef and all of them has been good for us. I am behind schedule in my tasks and will need to keep an eye on the days and distance ahead as we travel across Kerek. We should be in Matasi in a fortnight, or possibly two.

If you wish to send us letters, please use the same delivery as Zren Janin in Salisport, Matasi. I have gotten his whereabouts from Siba. Dica has written him in care of Solkka Ulani to let him know of our plans and to hold our letters for us. We should be there before the next Wet. Nelo, if you could let Kid know as well the next time you carry letters to the Ulani farms? Although I am sure Dica has written him by now and told him herself.

Dica is spending her coin she earned on books. During the Wet she talked to Siba of all manner of things at night as they sewed, and I know Siba helped her with her book learning. Siba says I must keep up her studies while we are traveling, so she is ready for the academies in Juisiti. I told her that is what I thought the academy was for. She smiled at me and said, 'Why, Arden, I think you just joked with me!' It is clear Josef has been a very poor influence on Siba, and I tremble at what damage he may do to the baby's humor.

Tyra, I tell you truly. All the things you learn in school with the Conrosans will make your life better later. It will certainly save you years of your life bouncing about on a wagon seat with a dog that smells of Wet and a girl who asks as many questions as Zren Janin.

Until we see you face to face, may our letters always find you safe and free from harm,

Arden

A letter from Dica Namikk enclosed

Arden says if I write quickly, we can deliver this letter to Lowel as we pass through and it can be passed on the grain trains headed overland to Vikland on the Southern Track. Arden says they drive night and day by switching out their horses often and can get a letter to the Vikland garrison in five days!

We have to leave. It has been fun to be at Siba's, but Arden said he has made promises and we must go on to Matasi. He said if I can help him, we will try to spend the next Wet in Salisport near Zren Janin and not on a wagon seat soaking up the daily rains.

I helped him with another project as well. Arden built a wooden cradle that stood on legs as tall as mine and rocked on leather straps tied through the top. I had never seen such a thing, but he says that is how cradles for babies are built in the Spice Island. The parents do not have to bend over so far and the cradle is up off the floor so nothing can slither in and harm the baby. He showed it to me when he was still working on it and hiding it in Rygee's brother's barn. He would work on it after his prayers and before the men started work on the barn for the day.

I asked him if I could make quilts and bedding out of some of my scraps for it. I worked on it when Siba was taking a nap or in the evening after she went to bed. The night before we left, I gave him the bedding and he showed me how to make it up as if there was a baby in it. We gave it to them and Arden said, "Family is family." and this cradle and bedding was 'in thanks and gratitude for their hospitality.'" (Is this a word? Arden said you would know what I meant.) Rygee's eyes got wet and Siba cried.

Josef joked and asked where was his gift? He had to share a room with Arden and Mother after all. Arden smiled, went out of the room, and brought back a wooden box with slatted shelves and little doors. It was for Josef's boots—and Arden showed us how it could hold three pairs of boots if Josef is ever so rich to have so many. He said it was made so the boots would never be left in the middle of the floor again to be tripped over in the dark. Josef didn't know what to say. Rygee said it is the first time he has ever known the boy to be speechless.

When we got to the cart, I saw Arden had made a change. He had made another wooden box for me, like Piffik made for each of the Wrens for our belongings. But this one is lined with beepaper and covered in wax on the outside to make it watertight and dustproof to protect my books as we travel. He had also rewaxed our covering cloth on the back of the wagon to protect the clothes I have ready-made, the fabric, and my patterns. Between all the wax needed for our travels and the wood and things for making the cradle, he must have used up all his coin he earned from building the barn!

I stored all my letters from all of you in my new box. They are as precious to me as my books which I own all by myself.

Dica Namikk

CHAPTER 41

ONE SOFTFOOT TO ANOTHER

To: Rani, a member of the Vikland Diplo now posted to the embasado at Juisiti, Vikland.

From: Arden, formerly of Kerek City, now traveling in South Kerek.

I know I am behind schedule, but here are my books of notes for the travels we agreed to. The code begins on page 54 of the book I gave you before I left. Additional letters have been sent to your future in the Keopi District. You may wish to visit him and he will share what he, and only he, can piece together for you. This should not be too difficult for you—it is the way we were both taught. Something you have and something you know. I know people.

I plan to be in Salisport before the next Wet. I am reminding you again that if my sister does not come to greet me, there must be someone who knows of her whereabouts. My father may be many things, but he is not a liar. If he said, she was in the Viklander embasado when war was declared in Kerek City, then someone must know where she went.

Let someone know I am coming so I do not stand at the embasado gates like a beggar.

Arden

CHAPTER 42

A LONG JOURNEY FOR A SHORT ANSWER

It was late at night, and Rani just finished decoding the last of Arden's journals. He was stunned. The Matasi military presence in South Kerek was greater than he—or anyone else in Vikland—imagined. Arden had been careful to differentiate between those who were obviously still serving in the military by wearing a uniform and those who appeared to have military or militia training. He had also loosely described Kereki ex-military and militia working with the Matasi Triune and Matasian army: "I am doing this based only on appearances: clothes, style, language (when heard), and faces. And we all know how appearances can be deceiving."

Arden noted how the grain trains traveling from Matasi to Vikland through Kerek were the most reliable forms of transportation and heavily guarded. They also carried letters and dispatches and how he was able to pay a fee to ensure a letter or a package could get to Vikland in just five days.

He described the huge logging and ore wagons with their teams of many horses coming from Vikland through Kerek on their way to the Matasi ports. He asked if Rani knew Vikland had to pay sinner market fees. Arden had heard Matasi was making extra coin at the ports. He could possibly find out how much more when he reached Otalport or possibly even Vesaport.

He wrote how larger Kereki farms such as the one he had worked on over the Wet were able to prosper although their Matasi competition was only five days ride away. The land and businesses along the Southern Track were solidly Kereki owned and managed. When they had dipped down closer to the Old Fort Road in the southeast of Kerek, the infrastructure had tilted to Matasi owners and managers.

There seemed to be little difference in the price of things, Arden said, so Matasi was not throttling goods to make South Kerek more compliant.

Banditry and thievery were nearly non-existent. Hostlers and shopkeepers said nothing non-flattering about the Justices in the small towns and villages. In the entire area they had traveled was a sense of omnipresent oversight. Not menacing, just...everywhere.

Arden wrote he would not be able to slip over the border as originally discussed, it was too closely guarded for that. Instead, he would be crossing into Matasi in two fortnights and needed papers. He knew Rani would agree with him that the papers should be for non-Kereki citizens because of the recent war and to raise less suspicion. Arden thought he would like his to be for a Spice Islander. And since he was traveling with a *titiro mai ki ahau*, he would need another set for Dica Namikk, a Conrosan tailor.

He requested them to be left for him at a place he had heard about from Zren Janin in one of his many stories, an olive estancia in the borderlands owned by the Potenco family. Arden added he knew Rani would appreciate his efforts on the enclosed letter Arden had written to bind the traveling papers together. A translation in Keresh was enclosed for Rani's convenience.

Rani scowled. Bima Ritwik had always praised the Spice Island family as completely unconcerned with right and wrong since they had first come under his wing all those years ago. They had thieved from the best houses. They had traded or sold information at other embasados in order to give information to Vikland. The children were so light-skinned and light-fingered, they easily convinced others about them they were nothing more than just "Kereki thieves."

The entire family was sharper than sharp and occasionally, like now, Rani had the uneasy feeling that the Viklanders were being deceived as easily as the Spice Islanders had tricked other countries' softfoots.

Rani could read Mata just fine. He wondered when Arden had learned to write Keresh. The boy had always seemed more interested in learning Bima's trickery than in any books laying around. Now Rani wondered if the boy's father had lied about anything else regarding his very talented children, and if there were other skills the Viklanders should have known.

Rani picked up the corner of the paper and read again the letter Arden had enclosed.

Greetings and good health to you, the family of Ebla Potenco!

We have never met, you and I, but I spent my favorite night in all of Matasi at your father and grandfather's table in Anarkio, Matasi. I was a Conrosan traveling with a Storyteller of the West Islands and his sister, and our Storyteller spent the night telling tales of the West Islands Constellations. In the morning we were joined by Miyamoto Suki, your grandfather called him a Prince of Vikland, and we spent the morning enjoyably together talking of his family's olive groves and the pride in his daughter and grandchildren who now run the estancia. Your family is truly blessed by the Lost God.

I am sorry to presume upon our acquaintance, but I have a request of you and yours. A young woman under my care and coin, a tailor of the name of Dica Namikk, is traveling to see more of the world. You will note she carries a Conrosan family name although regrettably she has failed to gain a Conrosan tongue and uses Keresh in her every day dealings. She is clever for all that and speaks some Mata.

Now she writes me and tells me of her desire to see Matasi, especially your great cities of Alenti and as far south as Vesaport, and to marvel at your libraries and round churches. I find I am quite unable to deny her anything; her love of learning is so great and should be encouraged.

But she left our home without her traveling papers to cross over another border. I could demand she return to me and take her papers, but she would lose too much of the Dry traveling over lands she has already seen.

She is traveling under the protection of a man I trust completely, a Spice Islander named Adah Onbek. He is fluent in Mata and will travel as her translator in Matasi as she will no longer have a need of a male protector as is required in Kerek. (Such a backward country!)

So here is my request. My respect for your father and grandfather is so great, I have trustingly enclosed their traveling papers for them to cross the border and a small gratitude for you and yours for holding the papers until they claim them. They will be there in a matter of days as I had asked them to stop and purchase olive oil from your estancia as a remembrance of my travels. Remember me to Ebla Potenco. Never again have I had biscuits so light they floated off my fingers. He is truly a man of many talents!

Please, if I can ever return the favor for you, let me have the opportunity.

I remain in your debt,

Zren Janin, a Conrosan and friend of Koanga, the Storyteller to the King of the West Islands

Rani waved the letter in the air. What was Arden playing at? Who were the Potenco family? And why would he use Zren Janin's name? Rani had deliberately not wanted Arden to have Vik papers to cross into Matasi, so Vikland could deny any knowledge if he ended up in a Matasi jail for breaking one of their many, many rules. And now Arden was asking, no demanding, Rani have false papers made for a Spice Islander and a Conrosan. At least he chose countries unusual enough the border guards wouldn't be suspicious. Thank the Lost God for small graces. He sighed. Working with all the Matasi regulations gave everyone a headache. How could anyone stand to live there and have so little freedom?

Rani glared at the stack of journals in front of him. He had coerced the boy into softfooting for him by telling him he had news of his sister. Rani had promised Arden she was alive and safe, and waiting for him in Salisport.

Truthfully, Rani only knew she had disappeared with Bima and the other softfoots from the Vikland embasado in Kerek City on the day the war had been declared. Quan had remembered that she had led them to a West Islander, a printer in Aldi who had helped them. And she had been left behind when the printer had hired a cart driver to take the Viklanders to the border. In hindsight, Rani now wondered if she had been softfooting for the West Islands. How had she known they would be safe in Aldi? Why had Bima trusted her? Who was she loyal to? Or was the plan to sail with the printer's family only one of desperation and survival? If only he could ask Bima. But Bima was dead. And truly, did it matter? Once Rani had the journals from the boy, he could worry about the consequences later.

Right now, he felt that Arden was not as compliant as Rani thought he should be.

Arden's journals had been missing a key component: the names of every person who owned the lands, the people encountered, their political leanings, and the locations of the militias. Rani knew exactly what he would find when he visited Kid at the Ulani coffee farms, handfuls of letters chatting easily about people Arden had met and the dates he had met them in his wide-eyed wonder at playing visitor to south Kerek. Kid and Rani would be able to match them to the journals, date by date. It had been a common trick of Bima Ritwik and one taught to all softfoots—communication codes must always include something you have and something you know. Anything else was simply too easy to break.

What hadn't been a Bima touch was the seven-day journey he would need to take from Juisiti to the Keopi District, staying in family inns along the way, being bored senseless by the rustic quaintness of it all. And there was the embarrassment of seeing Nadja Ulani.

Rani was sure Arden didn't know about his encounter with her little brother, Nari. To his knowledge Nari and Arden had never met. But it was just one more complication when all he wanted was hard numbers and information about Matasi violating the truce signed between Vikland, Kerek, and Matasi.

Rani sighed. Kern had laughed in his face when he had suggested she take Bima Ritwik's place. Then she had outmaneuvered him by speaking with First Soldier Joon who had the ear of the Empress. Rani was learning just how quickly he had to beware of other Viklanders as much as threats against the empire. Rebuilding Vikland's network of information gatherers and softfoots was going to make an old man out of him. No wonder Bima Ritwik had been such a difficult person to know and to like.

CHAPTER 43

GRATEFULLY

To: Siba Namikk, a healer at the Brick family farms, southeast of Lowel, South Kerek.

From: Callis Penny, a healer trained at Rishka, now residing in Orsu, Vikland.

Greetings and congratulations to you, Siba Namikk!

Your aunt is sending some presents for her newest family member. We are delighted to hear you and Rygee will be parents to more than just Josef. You have touched so many of us with your wisdom, I cannot imagine any child in better care than yours.

Your aunt says I have the insight of a good healer. Rell Huena continues to encourage me to work on my bongs and make friends with the Viklanders who are posted here. She reminds me people learn most when they travel and since I can't easily move about the world from here, I must take advantage of those who come to build the port and create the city of Orsu.

I am also writing you on a more difficult matter. Josef has asked me for the whereabouts of Falan. Truly, Siba, I do not know. We parted in anger, and she left early in the morning from Rishka without telling anyone. She did not take a horse. She walked, or found a ride in a wagon. In any case, we did not see her go, and we did not have Arden with us to send Mother to scent her. I cannot imagine she would travel to Kerek alone, yet I cannot fathom she would stay in Vikland since all of her words were how much she hated it. Please tell him gently. I am too much a coward to say any words in a letter.

I am gratefully in your debt,

Callis Penny — I have taken Rygee's words to heart and reclaimed my family name.

***

To: Rani, a member of the Vikland Diplo posted to the embasado at Juisiti, Vikland.

From: Arden, formerly of Kerek City, now traveling in Matasi.

Your package arrived and was waiting for us as requested. Your generosity to the family means you have another drop in South Kerek. You are welcome for my efforts on your behalf to extend your reach and contacts beyond Vikland. I accept your thanks and appreciation.

I received a letter from Kid at the same stop as your package. He wrote how you arrived in a timely matter to review the journals and read his letters, but your feathers were a bit fluffed. I am truly sorry, I did not know you had been jilted by their oldest daughter, Nadja, for refusing to call the Keopi District home. Of all the Ulani families, I have only met Tedros Ulani, and I thought of him with all the substance of a light sea breeze. I did not learn, until I received Kid's letter and talked a little with Dica, how Nari and his sister, Nadja, are made of steel and not silk.

Ngahuru has said Viklanders could trip over their own noses looking down on others. I shall remember more of her advice in the future. I shall not send you to the Keopi District again.

We have crossed the border. I hope you enjoy the two journals I have enclosed for you. They will complement your set beginning on page 86. Have you by chance read a book of Matasi parables? Do you remember the one of three stewards and whom they serve?

I remain gratefully appreciative of our traveling papers,

Arden

CHAPTER 44

ZREN GOES TRAVELING

To: Rell Huena and Piffik Qanaq, my friends at Manumina, now residing in Orsu, Vikland.

From: Zren Janin, formerly of Manumina, traveling through Matasi.

We are traveling! Solkka and Lomes have been tasked with traveling to all the embasados in Matasi to see what is happening and how the Triune is saying one thing but doing another. It will take the entire Dry to journey through all of the country. I am so excited!

Solkka had told me I would not be allowed to travel with them, but Lomes came to end of day meal to tell us they are specifically inviting me along and will say nothing, or they would say I am a traveling aide. Solkka said that seemed a little dangerous if we are found out and Lomes laughed. 'Softfooting is meant to be dangerous and that is why I like it,' Lomes said, 'and perhaps Zren's handsome Conrosan face could find information our Vik faces could not.'

I said, 'Please, I would like to go,' in my best manners voice like Siba taught me. She was right, manners are important because Lomes said they couldn't turn down a face like that.

Dica sent us a letter before we left. She and Arden might come to see us for the next Wet! Can you imagine? First Kern and now Dica. I did not know how easily the world traveled before Ngahuru found me at the side of the road. And now I am traveling too!

I have written down many stories in my book of Conrosan fairy tales for Nelo. Solkka said he never learned to read Conrosan at the academies and could not translate to Vik for me. So I wrote them in Wester so he could read them too. I will take the book with me, and Solkka says he can work on the translation at night when we are shut up for the day in our Matasi accommodations. He told me to buy three more books of pressed papers and bring a handful of coins to take with us. Then he is going to lock my travel bag of clothes and coins at the embasado. The Empress will pay his bills, he said, and he will pay mine.

I asked how Lomes would be traveling with us and Solkka said it didn't matter and I shouldn't ask. Lomes was Lomes and knew how to do softfooting well. If they could, they would tell us ahead of time what part we should play, but if not? Solkka was glad I was so smart I would be able to figure out what to do. He was beyond glad I had traveled with Ngahuru and understood these things. My face hurt I smiled so much.

I am sorry to say goodbye to the woman who owns the house where I slept in a room to myself. She was very kind to me. She said she was sad to see me leave. She has had others who are the friends and family of the soldiers at the embasado and they are not as quiet as I am.

Did you see what I wrote, Rell Huena? She said I was quiet! She did not say I talked all the time! She did not roll her eyes and say there are no more questions in all the known world! You have asked them all!

I do not know when I will get to read your next letter. Solkka says we can't have the letters sent on to us, we have to let them wait for us here and as soon as we return, we will spend the day in his room at the embasado and do nothing but read all the stories everyone has sent to us. I can't wait for that day to come.

Your little brother,

Zren Janin

CHAPTER 45

A VIKLANDER, A CONROSAN, AND ?

Zren didn't know they would be riding until the morning they went to pick out their horses. Dismayed at the news, he immediately explained to Solkka that when he had traveled with Ngahuru and Koanga through Matasi before, he had walked. It had been a wonderful journey listening to Koanga tell stories. Ngahuru taught Mata phrases and whatever else she wanted them to know so people would think they had good manners. When Solkka didn't immediately agree, Zren thought he might not have understood at first. He tried again to explain all the advantages of walking over bouncing about on a horse.

Solkka only smiled and told him to talk to Lomes.

When they arrived at the stables, Zren repeated his request to avoid riding horses and reminded Lomes that walking allowed for stories, and stories made the decons pass quickly. Walking with Koanga and Ngahuru meant they had always found a safe place to sleep anywhere the travelers chose in Matasi, well, except for the night they spent in the Subversiva jail.

Lomes and Solkka just looked at each other and grinned.

Lomes cleared their throat. "Zren, it sounds quite lovely, it really does, but a Viklander will never walk if there is a horse within shouting distance." The softfoot shrugged and looked around the stable where they were standing, "And there are quite a number of horses here within shouting distance."

"Do we need a wagon? A cart for all of our many belongings?" Zren offered hopefully.

"Like a peddler?" Solkka wrinkled his nose.

"Like a *titiro mai ki ahau*?" Zren answered.

Lomes paused. "Wait a moment. Let's talk about this. Tell me your idea."

"Solkka said you softfoot very well and I don't need to worry about you…"

"Thank you, Solkka."

"…but Ngahuru had her bags of pots and paints, and Koanga carried all of his tailoring kit and clothes to change her appearance. Now there will be three of us to change who we are. That's a lot of bags and maybe the horse would like it better if we had a cart to carry it all. I could drive it. We could still have an outrider and then somebody could ride away if we couldn't travel together for a bit. We could take turns so sometimes people would see one thing and then another. During the war we had this very blue traveling cloak Tiju Tia would take on her rag and bone cart. Different people would wear the cloak when they were riding with her, even a Viklander once, but people only saw the rag and bone cart, Tiju Tia, and a lump of bright blue traveling cloak." Zren paused for a breath. "It was Josef's idea."

"I'm listening," said Lomes.

"During the war, Solkka stained his skin darker and he had already lost his braid so his hair was curly. When Piffik brought him to Manumina after he had lost the fight in the Cloa stables, he looked like a West Islander," Zren hesitated, "a very tall West Islander."

Solkka winced. "I prefer to remember that day in Cloa as 'defended those in my care until I was overcome by an entire village.' And yes, it is true, First Soldier Joon and I tried to look like West Islanders."

Lomes laughed. "I hear what you are not saying, Zren. If we are *truly* softfoots, then sometimes we should be a woman and two men, three men, a Viklander, a Conrosan, and a West Islander, two Viklanders, a peddler, and anything else we can think of."

Zren nodded quickly. "We definitely need a cart for all those people."

Lomes squinted at Solkka. "How long has he been preparing this speech?"

Solkka just shook his head. "I didn't tell him until we were almost here. I needed you so I could catch my thoughts between his questions."

Lomes looked back at Zren. "Let's pick out a *tiny* cart. We are going to need to repack."

Lomes gave Zren the map of Matasi. As he retraced the path Ngahuru, Koanga, and he had traveled, Zren realized how little of the country he had actually seen. Now they would be following the coasts from Salisport to Otalport, then Thodport to Vesaport. From there, Lomes showed Zren where they would go north through the heart of the country to Alenti and then west to Salisport. There was another group of travelers—when Zren asked who they were, Lomes said he did not need to know—traveling through the north of Matasi and gathering news, names, and numbers of soldiers for Vikland.

Zren felt anxious about the journey. He had not been scared the first time he had traveled because he had been surprised by the lack of danger. He loved Matasi.

But both Lomes and Solkka said they had been chosen for this task because of their looks and skills. Now that Zren knew they would be playing a part, he worried he would not know what was expected of him. What were his skills? If Lomes had invited him along, did they expect him to play a part as well?

The three left Salisport as Viklanders in their dark, closefitting clothing. As they had dressed that morning, Zren had watched Solkka attach a false braid to his hair. Lomes was dressed as a he, but all Viklander soldiers dressed so much alike, Zren would not have known except Lomes asked Solkka and Zren to say 'he' and 'him' if they encountered any Matasi guards. When Zren had questioned why, the softfoot interrupted.

"We need to be unremarkable Zren, we aren't out to confuse them."

Zren was driving the wagon with Lomes beside him. It was smaller than the cheese cart at Manumina and it could only take one horse. Solkka was the outrider on a beautiful horse he called Batali. Zren was wearing Vik clothes too, but Solkka had found a black cap like Piffik owned and Zren was wearing that to hide his wild curls. Lomes said they were to leave Salisport looking like three arrogant Vik soldiers resenting an early morning patrol.

Once they were decons down the road and no one was about, they stopped and changed into the Matasi wide-legged pants and brightly colored shirts. Lomes dropped their braid down between their shirt and neck and wore the hat with the cloth in the back like a Matasi field worker. Solkka took off his false braid, and

Zren took off his cap. The two fluffed their hair until Lomes laughed and said they looked like berry bushes. Lomes rode Solkka's horse, and he climbed up on the wagon with Zren. The travelers told stories to each other to pass the time.

If Zren asked a question Lomes didn't want to answer, they would ask him why he wanted to know. Lomes might not answer or even ask what he wanted to eat for midday, but they would not be angry. When Solkka apologized once on Zren's behalf, Zren asked him why.

"Because you were being rude," Solkka said. "There are times that every question in your head doesn't need to fall from your lips."

"Shush, both of you. There's a difference, Solkka, and you know it as well. How can Zren learn about the world if he doesn't ask questions?" Lomes turned to Zren. "You grew up in Lowertown so you understand this. When I tell you to call me 'she' or 'he,' it is not how I think of myself, but how I want others to misremember me. When I dress in skirts, or in clothes other than myself, it is only a maskovesto. You cannot say you know all about me by how I act and dress and ask you to call me. Remember, I am a softfoot. I have to have secrets. You allow me mine, and I won't ask what you scribble in your books when we send you off to the shops and village greens to entertain yourself for a decon or two."

Lomes paused. "Still friends?"

Zren looked surprised. "Of course, we are still friends."

Every time they passed a checkpoint, Zren was supposed to greet the soldiers and ask them questions, while Solkka and Lomes counted soldiers, and watched for other things. They did not tell Zren what those other things were. Later when Zren asked Solkka to show him what he was writing in his book of pressed papers, he did. Zren couldn't read it. It wasn't Vik, although the letters kind of looked like it.

Solkka said it was a code, and that Kern in the West Islands and Rani in Juisiti had the books needed to read it. Zren asked if Solkka could teach it to him, and Solkka looked sad and said he regretted that he could not. Zren pretended to understand and said it didn't matter. But it mattered to him very much.

By the seventh day, Lomes said bringing Zren along was the best idea they ever had. Once the three of them had checked into the administration building and gotten the travel passes and accommodations, they would wander about and find a noodle shop or food cart in order to eat. They were home long before curfew, and Zren was supposed to tell stories to the hosts, and the other guests if there were any, until it was time to sleep.

Lomes reminded Zren to say 'he and him' so the three could share a room. Solkka explained Lomes could not risk being sent to sleep on the second floor with the women. Most nights, Lomes needed to crawl out from the ground floor windows and sneak about after curfew.

Zren told Solkka how worried he was the softfoot would get caught by the soldiers and spend the night in jail. Solkka shrugged and said if Lomes wasn't there by first meal, they would just go along to the jail and pay the fees before they picked up the horses at the stables.

Zren told him he remembered how scared he had been when he had been with Ngahuru and Koanga, and spent the night in the Subversiva jail the year before the war.

"I hope Lomes is braver than I was."

"You were not afraid of the jail. You were afraid because you didn't understand Mata and what the soldiers were saying. You were afraid because you didn't know what would happen to you the next day. There is a difference." Solkka reminded him, "There are many kinds of bravery, and you are brave when you need to be."

Lomes called Zren the best *titiro mai ki ahau* the world had ever known and said Kern should take lessons. Zren reminded them when Kern was happy, she could make a room so bright nobody could see anyone else but her. Lomes shrugged and said Zren had the same gift with his stories. He would make a fine softfoot.

Solkka reminded them Zren had a face that could not lie. Lomes said that was regrettable. Then Zren said when he was very frightened, he could not move or talk. He told them how he and Mikale Oqina had been the only two men of conscription age on the Manumina green when the Tax Collectors came looking for coin and conscripts. Mikale was smart and funny, Zren said, but no one outside of Manumina ever looked beyond his withered arm. Every year Mikale stood on the green along with a handful of others while his friends and classmates and others walked to Vikland to escape the Tax Collectors and their forced conscription.

"I cannot believe how brave he is, Lomes," Zren exclaimed. "He has stood on the green with his father to greet the Tax Collectors for ten years, every year since he was twelve. I did it *once* and I was so afraid I was mistaken for a half-wit!"

Lomes nodded and said there were many kinds of courage. Sometimes just waking up and facing a difficult day took more courage than fighting a Vikland dragon.

Then Zren asked Lomes to tell a story with a Vikland dragon in it, and forgot all about being a softfoot.

CHAPTER 46

A GIFT

To: Nelo, Piffik Qanaq, and Rell Huena, now residing in Orsu, Vikland.

From: Zren Janin, a traveler in south Matasi.

Greetings and good health to you!

Nelo, this gift of two books is only a small measure of the gratitude I have for you. It is the Zren Janin stories I learned from Ngahuru and at Rygee's Fourth nights in Manumina, all the West Islands Constellation tales I know, and four Matasian parables. There are no Kereki Trickster stories! The book in Wester is in my own writing. I still have not learned to write Keresh. The book with Vik letters is the very same stories written by Solkka Ulani. Rell Huena can tell you this is true. She can read and write both languages. Solkka said to tell you it is a translation of the beauty of the story and not word for word. He said Rell would be able to explain this better.

We are traveling in south Matasi and I have been to Otalport and Thodport. Neither city is as large as Salisport, but I still spent my days looking in bookshops while Lomes and Solkka counted soldiers. Solkka said I am not to talk about that, so I won't.

We have been to three baboys since we started traveling! I think roast pig is my favorite food! Lomes and I like to sing and dance at the baboys. Solkka says he likes to hold down our table so it doesn't run away. That is a joke. Tables can't run away.

I am so glad we are traveling with a cart. It is fun to travel when my feet are as fresh at the end of the day as at the beginning. Lomes and Solkka take turns riding with me. Sometimes Lomes takes the horse, Batali, and goes on a different road than we do, and we don't see them for a day or two or three. I asked Solkka how will we know if they are taken by Matasi soldiers after curfew? Does he know Matasi soldiers are called the 'Fist of God?' Solkka says Lomes will be fine, and he doesn't worry about anyone else but me. His hands are too full.

I practice my Mata every day and now try to tell some of the stories in the evening in both Keresh and in Mata. This next part is written by Solkka in Vik, but he won't tell me what it says.

Dear Arella Huena,

If there is anyone who takes more joy and gratitude in the world around him than Zren Janin, I have not met him. I do not always understand how his mind works, but truly, by saving his life, you have given me a gift like none other. You have blessed me immeasurably.

– Solkka Ulani

CHAPTER 47

NEARING THE END OF THE SECOND DRY

To: Piffik Qanaq and Rell Huena, now residing in Orsuarlerpaa, Vikland.

From: Rygee Namikk, at the Brick family farms, southeast of Lowel, South Kerek.

Siba will write a longer letter when she is able, but I wanted to be the first to say, we have a daughter. Her name is Kay. Although she came earlier than expected, she is healthy, of good weight and color (or so I am told), and has a very strong voice (which I did not need to be told). Siba is in fine health she says and everything went as she expected. Even though my mother agreed, I still worried. But after the third night without sleep, I have decided that any baby who can cry that loudly must be strong and strong-willed. She is my daughter, after all.

Josef moved to the bunkhouse with the others—to get some sleep, he said. He was back three nights later with a black eye. I asked him if someone needed to leave the farms since there is to be no fighting in the bunkhouses. But he said it was an Oro lesson—one with less consequences than getting hauled off to a Kereki encampment. Siba and Josef both said to let it alone. So, I have.

I am blessed my wife and daughter are healthy. My mother has been over a handful of times already bringing one food or another. Siba says she is going to stay in bed for one more day and then she will be up and about. She says we are treating her like a Conrosan queen and she wants to savor the feeling.

My father now has four grandsons and two granddaughters from all of his sons. He is already talking of what farmland he will give them when they are of age and ready to marry. He has asked me to reclaim my family name, but I told him that man is dead and gone when he sold me for tithes and taxes. I will always be,

Rygee Namikk

Josef will be sending along a letter for the Wrens.

The enclosed letter

To: Nelo, a man still without a family name, and a builder at Orsu, Vikland.

From: Josef Brick, apprentice at the Brick family farms, southeast of Lowel, South Kerek.

Siba told me no one Knows where Falan is. I asked Callis in my last Letter. She didn't answer me. She wrote Siba and said they had an argument and Falan left the next Day without telling anyone where she was going. How can I find her, Nelo? Where do I even begin to Look? She could be lost or hurt or scared and no one would know. It is like the War all over again.

The Baby never seems to stop crying. I am so tired I can barely drag myself out of bed in the morning. I tried to move to the Bunkhouse, but the men think I am there to tell Rygee or his papa what they are doing. I tried to make a Joke about it. One of the Matasians told me not to tease the one giving me Trouble. I wanted to show I wasn't scared of them, so I said it again and…he hit me.

All I could think of as I went down was "That was such an Oro." Remember when he borrowed the Horse and rode to Cloa and tried to climb in the window and Arden and Mother nearly killed him? Well, maybe not Killed him, but I'm sure it felt like it to Oro. Then just when he gets to be the Hero for Linna and rescue Dica from Regno, he gets himself captured by Kerekis and rescued by, of course, Arden and Mother. You know that had to hurt his Pride.

I guess what I am saying, Nelo, is I don't think I fit in here. I like living with Rygee and Siba, and I think I have Learned a lot from them, but I don't seem to get on with the ones Who make the farms run. I will never be a Rygee or any of his brothers.

When Arden was here building the barn, the other workers listened to him. If someone mocked his braid or made a Joke about him getting up before sunrise to pray with the Matasians, he just gave them a long look and didn't say anything. Even Dica seems more like him. While she was here, she was so serious about reading her Books. She made Baby things for Siba, and earned Coin from Tailoring from those in Lowel to buy her own feed for her Horses even though they were content in Rygee's stable.

And now it is too late. I could have ridden with Dica and Arden and traveled with them. They had two horses. But I just stupidly waved goodbye to them because I didn't think the Baby would change anything. I didn't think I would change. Now what do I do?

Where is Falan?

Josef Brick

***

To: Kid, an apprentice at the Gayo Ulani coffee farms, Keopi District, Vikland.

From: Dica Namikk, a tailor, now traveling through Matasi.

We reached Kaoso. It took us much longer than we expected. I thought I had asked Zren enough questions about what it would be like to travel through Matasi. I did not. We had trouble getting over the border. The soldiers questioned our papers. Arden took a long time explaining who we were and why we wanted to be in Matasi. I learned he is much more fluent in Mata than just a few pretty words. But all the time we were in the war, he called himself a Kereki thief who could not read nor write, and so that is what I believed. I wonder if Nelo knew? Did he hide this news from those of us in the great houses or didn't he see this Arden either?

His traveling papers call him a Spice Islander and now I wonder how I ever thought differently. I should have suspected as much when I realized he was reading Zren Janin's letter written in Wester. Who would learn to speak Wester but Islanders and diplomats? And it is as common for a Spice Islander to know Mata as a second language, as it is for a Viklander to speak Keresh. Now that we are in Matasi, Arden even found two gold rings to wear in his ear like a Spice Islander would. I never saw him buy them and now I wonder what else he is hiding in his wooden chest from Piffik.

We are not used to traveling so slowly here. We have to stop quite early to register in each town, and we must use our coin to lodge our horses and ourselves every night. We have had some trouble with Mother. At first, we didn't know to ask for accommodations that would take small children and animals. The first night we were refused at the door, and Arden had to hurry back to the Administrative Offices and find another place for the night. They did not give him his coin back for the first house, because they said it was his fault, he did not explain he could not sleep there. How would we know to ask?

Arden and I cannot share a room to save coin, I am shooed off to the second floor in almost all the accommodations to lay on the bed and stare at the ceiling until it is time to sleep. I asked Arden how he can stand it. He gave me a blank book of pressed papers and told me to write down everything we saw, ate, people we met, and how long it took to travel from place to place. To write down how much things cost, even if we do not buy them. I should note how many soldiers are at each checkpoint. He said if I could recreate every day of the trip, others could read my book and know important things without being there. He told me to test my memory and write down as much of the trip through South Kerek as possible and he gave me a map of our journey so far. I rolled my eyes at him, and he asked if I wanted to learn to softfoot or not? Well then, why didn't he just say so?

I have watched people look at him and sometimes their eyes narrow although they still use kind words to his face. I asked him if he noticed, and he just shrugged. He says it could be because the Kerek King sailed to the Spice Island for his exile, and Arden's King did not refuse him. Arden said it was because the Kerek King's wife was a Spice Islander and family is family.

Then he tilted his head and said, 'Or perhaps people do not like me because I am a Spice Islander who does not wear gold on my fingers. They assume I am poor and may beg them for coin.' Then he paused and said, 'Or perhaps it is they don't like my braid, or my smile, or that I am a plain man traveling with a pretty girl.' I was so surprised I just stood there and gaped at him until he reached over and used his finger to push up my chin and close my mouth. He grinned at me and said he was going to try the same thing with Zren Janin and see if it stopped his questions too. He was joking, Kid, I do not ask as many questions as Zren!

Arden said there are so many reasons why someone would not like him, he doesn't have time to think of them all, and so he doesn't think of them at all. Then he gave me one of his odd smiles, you know the ones, where you think he just told you something important and it will take you all day to figure it out. Truly, I cannot imagine how Linna could bear to live with him!

People are very kind here. Everywhere I am asked if I need help or if I am finding everything I need. Arden says it is because I look so unusual. I have dark brown hair but not as curly as a West Islander or straight like a Viklander, I am lighter than a Matasian but darker than a Kereki. I speak a little Mata but with a Keresh tongue (or so I've been told), so people want to talk to me so they can learn who I am. I asked Arden if it was a good thing or a bad thing. He said if you are doing the softfooting, Kid, I would make a good titiro mai ki ahau. *If I need to be the one softfooting, he said you must give me lessons to make me disappear.*

Zren Janin had told me I needed to go to a baboy while I was here. Last night I made Arden take me to one. It was music and dancing and I liked the roast pig—delicious! The music was fun and happy even though Zren had said it was all about their religion. I didn't sing along like the others did, but I could see how the baboy was one of Zren's favorite parts of traveling in Matasi. There was food after all.

I like to imagine Zren dancing.

I wish you were here. I miss talking to you. I know I am seeing so much about me I don't understand. I would like to listen to your voice as you explained a book you had read or a story you had heard which would make sense of what is all around me.

I would love for you to go to a baboy with me.

Dica

CHAPTER 48

SOFTFOOTING AMONG FRIENDS

Dica and Arden had ridden into Anarkio just after midday. As they were registering their presence at the Administration building, he had requested to stay at the accommodations of Ebla Potenco. Dica had been shocked when the clerk had announced the cost of their home stay. It was the same price of two of their stays just days earlier. As they walked out of the building and down the steps, Arden explained what she would be doing.

"You are softfooting tonight and tomorrow in the arms of friends," Arden began. "You must pretend to be under the care of Zren Janin, a man Ebla Potenco, our host, has met before."

Dica stopped in the middle of the street and stared at him. "Our Zren Janin?"

"Yes," Arden said. "Our Zren Janin. According to the stories Zren told, this was his favorite stay in all of Matasi. Our host loves Conrosans and West Islands Storytellers. I think I can tell one or two Constellation tales he may not have heard before. As for you, tonight your beauty is because your father is Conrosan and your mother Kereki. Try to be charming, Dica, it was this man's family who made our traveling papers possible."

"Arden, I have no idea who my father was," Dica protested. "I only know my mother was Kereki because the Orphan Master told Nelo a Kereki woman brought me to him. I was five, Arden. I called her 'mother,' because what else would I have called her?"

Arden blew out a breath. "For someone who wishes to be a softfoot, you sure seem to have difficulty with the part where you cannot be yourself. We should have Josef with us to teach you."

Dica answered sharply, "For someone who *is* a softfoot, you sure seem to have difficulty explaining the *why* of anything. You just say, 'do this, do that' and expect me to understand how your mighty mind works."

Arden suddenly smiled. "Let's stable the cart and horses. Before we find our host, we will find a noodle shop and I will explain *exactly* how my mind works."

***

When Josef had explained to Siba and Rygee why he didn't think he could live there anymore, they had just nodded their heads, asked him not to make a decision or go anywhere for two days.

Then Siba had rushed off to care for the crying baby, and Rygee had left to check on the far fields because, he told Josef, 'There is nothing out there louder than a cricket.' Josef had wandered about for a little while and then gone out to the horse breeder. He had been told to exercise some horses on a few long rides.

He wondered if anyone had been listening.

But then, at first meal the next morning, Rygee asked him if he felt safe enough in Kerek to visit all of the holdings bought during the war for the Wrens. The places had been leased and Rygee wanted someone to meet all the tenants and bring back concerns and rents, meet with the Justices and find out if there had been any trouble, and pay the taxes. Rygee felt he couldn't leave now; he didn't want to leave Siba and the baby. Since Josef had been to all the places during the war, there was no one else he trusted to do this as well as Josef could.

Josef was nodding his head 'yes' before Rygee had even finished talking.

Together Rygee and Josef marked out the map of trails and tracks to take and where to visit the Justices. Rygee showed Josef how to estimate the taxes, and together they looked over the tenant lease papers. Rygee also asked to have Josef learn about any new Justices hired since the war, and note how many Matasi soldiers he saw in the villages. While Rygee had been told banditry had been eliminated everywhere, that didn't mean the Matasi soldiers didn't create trouble of their own.

Almost as an afterthought, Rygee mentioned Josef would be able to look for Falan if she had decided to live anywhere along the Northern Track.

Josef took a deep breath and thanked the wisdom of Siba Namikk once again.

***

To: Kid, an apprentice at the Gayo Ulani coffee farms, Keopi District, Vikland.

From: Dica Namikk, a Conrosan tailor, now traveling through Matasi.

Greetings and good health!

Oh, Kid! I love my maskovesto! Yesterday after we reached Anarkio, Arden asked me to be a Conrosan tailor (or at least one with a Conrosan father) and a friend of Zren Janin to a man who had met Zren Janin before. Arden had told me how he and Josef had pretended to be other people during the war. It was as important as a good titiro mai ki ahau *or being good at softfooting and stealing secrets, he said.*

He spent the time after midday teaching me what he called an origin story, and then I was able to perform in front of Ebla Potenco. Arden told some West Islands stories—he isn't as good as Zren Janin, but he told them in Mata and our host was appreciative. Senor Potenco remembered Zren and the two West Islanders, and the Prince of Vikland who had come the next morning. He said it had happened before the war, but he remembered so much of that visit, I felt like it had been very important to him.

Arden was very kind and got up early to pray with him. The place was nice to stay in although I was not sure it was worth so many cals. Arden explained later it was important for us to stay there, so when the Potenco family in the borderlands and Ebla Potenco in Anarkio met and talked about their lives, the stories would agree. It is also important for me to have people in my network, he said. Everyone needs a safe place or people they trust in any country.

Arden said to tell you Ebla Potenco will not betray Matasi, but he will help and not harm. He told me to say nothing more in this letter but you will be able to explain when I see you. You truly need to save all my letters, as I will never remember all these questions I have for you!

Today, we should reach Salisport. We will try to get as close to the embasado as possible and leave a message for Solkka Ulani, or Lomes, a softfoot Arden knows. He explained Zren Janin won't be living in the embasado, but without the others we have no way to get past the checkpoints to find him. I asked about the letters Siba had sent and received from Zren and he said they had been in care of Solkka Ulani at the embasado. I didn't realize it was going to be so difficult to reach Zren. What if Solkka refuses to see us? Would Zren know to look for us?

I look forward to reading your letters soon. There better be a stack of them!

Dica

***

Kid watched Rell Huena as she rode away from the Gayo Ulani coffee farm. He had given Rell nearly a dozen letters of his own to take to the Central Administrative offices for sorting and sending on. There had been two to Rani, one to Siba Namikk, one to Zren Janin, two Rell would need to carry back with her to Callis, Tyra, and Nelo, and the rest to Dica and Arden.

Well, mostly Dica. He knew the letters were shared among all the Wrens and the Conrosans so he tried to conceal his thoughts, but Arden had written him and said he would never read Dica's letters to or from him and to write things twice to them rather than assume he and Dica talked freely about Kid. Arden had assured him it was the best way to keep all their secrets safe. Dica was the one person he could write to without reservation.

Arden had been equally blunt in his last letter.

"As we travel about Matasi, I think how easy it would be to take the papers Rani created for me, travel to Vesaport, board a Spice Island ship, and sail home. By the time Kern and Rani knew I was gone, I would be far from their grasp. Inezi was able to do it, I will too. But Rani has promised me news of a sister in Salisport, and I remember my promise to you. We will conceal Dica's age from those who would do her harm until she is old enough to stand alone.

Dica chose a day at the end of the last Wet and declared it a birthday. A season later and she now says she is fifteen and a half which is so nearly sixteen as to be almost nothing. She is smart enough, and Siba Namikk has taught her things I could not. She has gained enough in height and strength not to be confused for a child any longer. She is no longer the skinny plain girl Nelo rescued from the Orphan Master. You will have a hard time to teach her to be invisible.

I do not know that I am doing enough to help her with her bookwork. She learned Mata by hearing it everywhere; she studies her books in the evenings at the accommodations. She studies and yet neither Siba nor I are sure she is studying the right things. I hope when the two of you meet again at the academies you can help each other and both succeed.

My plan is still to meet Zren Janin and his soldier boy and to remain in Salisport or near there during the Wet. I hope Zren will be able to prevail upon someone who has actually been to the academies to help Dica with her book learning. Perhaps he will be ready to return to Vikland for a visit or for a while and can accompany her through Kerek. He is fierce enough to protect her life if the stories about him are true.

Here is another set of journals for you. A matching set has been sent to Rani. I found a coffee pamphlet in a bookshop here. I am sharing it with you for a future correspondence.

May our letters find you free from hurt or harm,

Arden

CHAPTER 49

MISDIRECTION AND MASKOVESTOS

Zren was watching the sky anxiously. The first rains had begun yesterday, just a soft drizzle that had lasted no more than a decon. But he remembered Dica had written and said they would be coming to spend the Wet with him, and he didn't want her to come to Salisport and not find him.

Solkka wasn't worried. "We've already been everywhere, Zren, even Alenti is behind us. We should be reaching Salisport within the next few days. If Matasi didn't have so many rules about how early we had to check into their infernal offices, we could ride long days and be there sooner." He sighed dramatically. "How awful if a clerk had to be late for their end of day meal!"

Lomes had laughed at that. "Are you insulting our hosts again, Solkka?"

"Always." He grinned.

Zren wiggled uncomfortably. He *liked* Matasi. He didn't like that he was going to be late to see Dica, but he saw it as their own fault. They had spent too many days softfooting in Alenti and not traveling to Salisport. Yet every Viklander and West Islander he knew seemed to think Matasi was unbearable. He wondered why that was so.

Lomes tipped their chin. "Another checkpoint. Look pretty for their soldiers, Zren."

The softfoot was rearranging their skirts on the seat next to him and missed his scowl. Lomes said that *every* time, and he didn't like it. He had said so before and wondered if he should complain again. He huffed. Lomes glanced up and gave him an earnest look.

"Zren, if a soldier looks at me and takes offense because he isn't bright enough to decide who I am—as if it is any of his concern—and another looks at Solkka and decides such a beautiful man should have all his baggage fondled, you would be forced to stand alone to save us all from a treasonous death. Now I don't doubt your abilities, but why should you have to pull out your Sword of Courage, when all you have to do is keep all eyes and ears on you until we pass through and get our little papers stamped—yet again—and we can all live to fight another day?" Lomes had cuffed him on the shoulder. "Now think of me as your big sister, we don't want to tax their little Matasi brains too much."

The checkpoint was full of soldiers. Zren looked around and tried to guess why. They were in the middle of the track, no town nearby. He could see a far-off estancia, and what Lomes had called a vineyard, a field of grapes close to the track, and that was all.

"Hello, hello!" he began, "Are those grapes? Shouldn't they be harvested by now? I felt the first rains yesterday, and I thought grapes had to be harvested while the sun was still shining. Did you know there are Conrosan folk tales about grapes?" He reached in and took his papers out of his pocket tied about his waist as he continued, "Everything good and tasty I have had on my travels has been grown in Matasi. Who could imagine you are responsible for feeding all the known world?"

The soldiers watched him as one of them took Lomes and Solkka's papers. A soldier gave a second look at Lomes. He whistled and more soldiers came out of the checkpoint. Zren felt his nervousness grow. He talked faster. "Could you tell me what is the best place to eat nearby? We haven't stopped for our midday yet, and I don't know what the next town is. Do you have a favorite food? I like baboys. I am told those started in the West Islands, but Matasi made them so much more fun."

"Stop talking."

Zren stopped talking.

"Get off your horse." The soldiers gestured at Solkka.

Solkka dismounted and stood holding Batali's reins.

Two soldiers reached forward and started to unsaddle Solkka's horse, but the gelding wasn't having any of it. Solkka lost his temper.

"I'll do it. All you are doing is making Batali so feisty, he'll be fighting with me the rest of the day." Solkka walked up to the horse and spoke softly as he stroked its nose. Once the horse gentled, he moved slowly back and unbuckled the traveling bags. "There is no need to remove the saddle, although I will do it if you wish. Everything is in the bags or in the cart."

The soldiers swiveled to the cart. Four soldiers approached and Zren jumped off quickly. He turned to help Lomes with their heavy skirts, but a soldier nudged him aside and handed Lomes down. Zren walked up to the horse in front of the cart and spoke softly as Solkka had. Two soldiers held pikes leveled at the travelers to keep everyone separated from each other and the cart. Zren risked a quick glance, but Lomes was just standing there with a small smile and hands clasped demurely in front.

The soldiers were thorough. Zren thought they were as good as the scavengers in Kerek City. He remembered how he and the other children would search the bodies found the next morning after a night of drunkenness or death. These soldiers were also going to make sure not a coin or a small piece of metal was going to slip through their fingers.

While the soldiers carefully went through their bags and then spitefully dumped them on the ground, the first soldier looked at Lomes. "Who are you and where are you going?"

"We are travelers on the way to Salisport," the softfoot said casually. "Our papers are in order, if you stamp them, we will be on our way."

Another soldier narrowed his eyes at Lomes. He held up their papers and said, "Tell me what these say."

"Certainly. The one written in Conrosan is for our friend on the peddler cart. His name is Zren Janin, and his occupation is a Storyteller. He is quite famous among the storytellers not only in Conrosa, but also in the West Islands. And you know how *they* adore their Storytellers. That muscular West Islander over there is Harti Kabul. You will find his papers written in Wester. Obviously, his role in life and on this journey is as our bodyguard and protector. Have you ever seen such a tall West Islander before?"

Lomes leveled a long look at the soldier holding the papers. "You have two sets of papers left in your hands, both written in Vik. Obviously, the ones referring to a female would be mine. The other Viklander—a male? Bah! He abandoned us for the nightlife of Alenti. Good riddance, I say. I hope when his coin runs out, he remembers how badly he treated his friends and hangs his head in sorrow for his shame. Truly, he could visit your round churches for a while." Lomes shook their head in mock dismay.

The soldier looked at Solkka who looked back without any expression. Zren wondered if he was going to pretend not to understand Mata. But then he remembered Solkka had already spoken Mata when he snapped at the soldiers. Then he wondered if Lomes needed *him* not to know Mata. Oh. He had already responded when the soldiers had told him to stop talking. He looked to Lomes. *What was he supposed to do?* The softfoot was smiling cheerfully as if the wagon was searched at every checkpoint.

One of the soldiers held up Zren's pressed books of papers and crowed. "You were right, I found them!"

Zren screeched, "No! Those are mine; those are my story books! When I hear a story I write it down, see? Those are mine!"

Another soldier pushed his way up. "Let me see them." He paged through them. "These are in Wester. *I* can read Wester." He looked smugly at the other soldiers as he began reading aloud. Zren recognized the story as one of the Matasi parables he had heard when he had visited a round church in Vesaport while Solkka and Lomes had been counting ships and soldiers in the harbor. The soldier read just a little longer and then flicked ahead a few pages.

This one was a West Islands Constellation tale Zren had read about in one of the Alenti bookstores while Lomes had been meeting with her network and Solkka had delivered one of his coded books to the embasado. He wasn't even to the good part, Zren thought, when the soldier snapped the cover shut and started paging through the next book.

"The same, the same," the soldier muttered. He dropped the books ungracefully on top of their disheveled belongings on the ground. "These are not the spies we are looking for." He flicked his hand over the wagon.

Zren rushed forward to save his books. He cradled them in his arms and watched as the first soldier stamped their papers and handed them to Lomes.

Except for the papers for the male Viklander. "If you have no one with you with this name, these papers are useless to you. We will keep them here."

"You could." Lomes shrugged, and then their smile turned sly and cunning. "Or you could stamp them and our friend who is no longer a friend, could have more than a little difficulty traveling through your beautiful country. It's only fair since he left me completely without coin in Alenti." Lomes kept looking at the soldier. "I think the Lost God would find justice in that, don't you?" The soldier wavered for a moment and then stamped the last set of traveling papers and returned them to the softfoot.

Lomes helped Zren stuff their belongings haphazardly back into the wagon. Solkka mounted Batali and watched the soldiers watch the two tidy up just enough so bags and books wouldn't fall out as the cart moved down the track. Zren helped Lomes up on the wagon seat. With the many skirts crowding him, he could feel the bulky pockets sewn inside the layers. The code books hidden in the many skirt pockets jostled and bumped his leg. He quietly unwrapped the reins about the brakes and moved forward through the checkpoint.

CHAPTER 50

SOFTFOOTING FOR PRACTICE AND PLEASURE

Dica had followed Arden's map carefully and now she found herself in a curve in the road with a wall of bright pink fuchsia ahead of her. Arden had asked her to walk up the pathway until she could see the front of the Matasi checkpoint. She could. Just as she could see the Viklander checkpoint beyond that and the Viklander embasado up the hill from the two checkpoints.

Once she had returned and said it was just as he described, he had jumped out of the wagon. He grinned at her, an honest to goodness grin, she noted, but he only said, "Well done!" He reminded her not to mention him by any name unless she was speaking to Zren Janin. He reminded her to stress she was a *Conrosan* tailor. Maybe even those who couldn't find Conrosa on a map would try to have her meet Zren since all Conrosans obviously knew each other.

"They do?" she had asked incredulously.

Arden sighed. "Why did I promise Kid on my braid of honor to keep you alive for two years? I was being sarcastic, Dica."

Dica snapped back. "I'll be sixteen at the end of this Wet, Arden. Your unbearable hardship of traveling with me to see the world is almost over."

He just smiled at her, lifted Mother gently off the wagon, picked up his traveling pack, and waved cheerfully as he and his dog turned and walked down a small alley.

Dica blew out a hard breath. The next task was simple, Arden had said. Meet with someone who could give her Zren's location. Arden would buy them some food and be waiting for her an alley or two away. It required no softfooting or pickpocketing, no sleight of hand or defense skills, he said. Just simple pretending to be someone else to get something from someone else. How would she become a softfoot if she never practiced?

She blew out another breath, picked up the reins, and drove into the curve of the road.

***

Dica marveled how easily she had crossed the Matasi checkpoint. She had merely held up some dark colored Vik pants and shirts she had in her wagon, and said she was a tailor returning her work to get paid. One of them *had* asked if she was carrying any weapons to defend herself. She had only laughed and said 'nothing larger than a steel needle that had come all the way from the West Islands.' They laughed with her, took her name, and let her pass.

The Viklander checkpoint was another story. She had offered her same tale of a tailor, and they asked her name and checked their lists. She was not on the lists and could not enter. Of course not, she replied, she had not known she was going to finish the work early. She thought if she could deliver it today, she might get larger coin in gratitude. The soldiers shook their head. She could not be admitted.

If she could not be admitted, then could she have a note sent up to the embasado to have someone meet her at the checkpoint and stand Witness for her? No, they were not delivery boys, they were soldiers and could not leave their posts.

She tried again. But surely, when another embasado sent staff to visit the Ambassador, there would not be this same lingering about just for the chance someone from the Vik embasado would look out a window and check to see who had come calling. Well, no. It wasn't the way it was done, but she was hardly from another Ambassador's household, was she?

Well, she would wait, she told them. If she was truly lucky, one of the people whose tailoring she had done would walk by on their way in or out of the embasado and she could be paid. If she was not lucky, she would be here until one of them realized he had nothing to wear and walk down past her to go to her shop and get his clothes.

"You can't wait here. We can't have you here. No one in Matasi can just sleep rough."

"But I am not in Matasi," Dica pointed out. "I am on the grounds of the Vikland embasado. I will wait here until I can be paid."

She paused and then wondered aloud, "Can a Viklander have their braid cut if they are so dishonorable, they do not pay their tailor?"

One of the soldiers sighed. "Write your note. I am to be relieved within the decon. I will give it to the Secondo and she will harshly deal with whoever has ordered clothes from you. You will be paid, but you will never be allowed to come here again," he warned.

Dica tipped her head to the side, "I can agree to that." She rummaged about her cart and took out one of the books of pressed papers she had been filling with notes and observations on the towns they had traveled. She looked at the numbers, dates, and locations of guards and soldiers about the estancias in southern Kerek and northern Matasi and tore out a page at the end.

She wrote her name, Dica Namikk, carefully in Keresh, and said she had more information if she was invited into the embasado.

Then she tucked her note into her book, and tied her book in a square of brightly colored cloth and presented it to the soldier.

He stood about for a few moments and then said, "Oh for all the…" and took off briskly walking up the hill.

Dica bit the inside of her cheek to keep herself from smiling.

***

Zren waited at least a decon—in his mind anyway—before he asked a single question of Lomes. "We are the softfoots they are looking for, aren't we?"

Lomes smiled and shrugged. "I think there are lots of people walking and riding about Matasi trying to understand what the Triune is promising other countries and what they are promising their people. We may need to leave our cart behind at the next settlement, become someone else again, or even split up and meet again in Salisport. They came out to look at us even before they had our papers, Zren. It may be the cart, the outrider, one of us, or the three of us they had been warned to look for."

"But they didn't find anything," Zren replied smugly.

"And they won't." Lomes paused as if trying to decide something. "Zren, you are very good for us. I could not have taught you the reaction you had when the soldier took your story books. It was exactly what was needed. You are so genuine you can make others believe what they know cannot be true, solely because you believe it. You even misled Bima Ritwik—a man who trusted no one—into thinking Ngahuru was not in Kerek, even though his information and instincts said otherwise. But to keep you so effective for us, sometimes I must not tell you everything."

Zren squinted. "Did you just call me a liar?"

Solkka tsk-tsked and Zren whipped his head around.

Solkka had moved his horse so closely to the wagon he had heard their conversation. "Zren, you know how Kern softfoots. She walks into a room and smiles. She has the ability—the gift of charisma—to make everyone feel so admired and desired, they just open up their hands and their pockets to give her whatever secrets Vikland requires."

"Is that why she was so sad your face would never wake up on the pillow beside her?"

Now it was Lomes turn to laugh. "Oh, Solkka. You didn't tell me this one."

Solkka gave them both a long-suffering look. "Zren, Kern practices all the time so she can be ready when she must turn on her charm to others who have something Vikland needs or wants. All of us in the Diplo know this, and so we do not take her seriously when she is so…"

"Forward? Outrageous? Bold? Flirtatious?" Lomes laughed again. "What safe word are you looking for?"

"…Charming," Solkka said firmly. "I am looking for the word charming." He sighed. "You have the same ability, Zren. Only you don't need to flirt and flatter to do it. It's like you radiate joy. You are so happy to be alive, you look at the world with such wonder and curiosity. But to keep you so…" Solkka fumbled for a word again.

Lomes laughed. "If this is how you behave when you are in love, Solkka Ulani, no wonder your bed stayed empty for so many years."

Lomes turned to Zren. "You are like Kern in that you can light up a room, especially when you are telling everyone a story. But think of the world of softfoots as a barren field in Kerek at the end of the Dry, and you come along like a long, cool drink of water. In that sense, you are the opposite of Kern. We know she is only playing a part, practicing on us to keep her skills sharp; we also know if we want the truth about anything, including ourselves, we only need to ask Zren Janin."

Zren nodded slowly. "I am not sure about everything you said, although I heard all of the kind words about me." He smiled mischievously. "I do know it is long past midday, and I do not remember stopping at a wayside to eat." He tipped his chin ahead to the left. "Oh look! A wayside with a table and shade to have a midday!" He grinned at Lomes and jiggled the reins to encourage the horse to hurry along.

***

To: Nelo, Callis Penny, and Tyra Languak, also Piffik Qanaq and Rell Huena of Orsu, Vikland.

From: Josef Brick, formerly of the Brick family farms, southeast of Lowel, South Kerek now traveling about the Northern Track.

Greetings and Good Health to Everyone!

I forgot to pack a book of pressed papers and a graphite to write others and let them know where I am. Since Rygee had told me I was to send him Progress Reports from every property he owned, I had to use my own Coin—not to buy Fingersweets—but to ensure I kept my position as Agent. Did you even know there was such a thing? A Person who travels about the country conducting business on behalf of an important man is known as an Agent.

Siba says in the country of Matasi, that person is known as a Steward and there are many parables about good and bad stewards. She hoped I would be a Good Parable and not a Lesson Learned. I had replied, 'In Conrosan stories such a man would be known as

Piffik Qanaq and he is such a Good Parable, perhaps we all needed a Lesson Learned.'

But then I reminded her, when we Wrens did something which caused us harm because we did not listen to the wisdom of another, we called that mistake an 'Oro.' She tried not to smile, and I reassured her I had every intention of coming home, preferably after the Baby was old enough to talk and no longer cried to make its needs known.

I traveled up the Harvest Trail and spent my first night in Sevno. The inn there is owned by a Widow, her man died in the war. I did not ask for which side. The food was nothing like Rygee's—more like the bits we cooked for ourselves. As she served me, she told me to keep my Head down and my eyes on my own business. There were two guards—Matasian—who were there to keep the Peace. She said she did not have to Pay their keep, and they caused no trouble and kept others from causing trouble. I was flattered to think she considered me Manly enough to cause Trouble, but then I overheard her tell another the same thing and he was a man so old he could only drink his Soup.

I slept in the common room with so many who snored so loudly I thought I might be roosting with the pigs back on the farm.

I have a Plan—I am looking for Falan. If what you say is true, Callis Penny, and I feel the rightness of it, if Falan returned to Kerek she would only travel where she knew her way about. I am convinced she is in one of the towns or settlements where we had one of our Houses.

I have already been to the little settlement where Falan and Callis took their injured. There is a Family there now, they have planted fields, and the Bubbler still keeps everyone and everything alive. They are farming on shares, but asked if the Namikks may consider selling to them. I said I would take it back to Rygee and We would consider it. I think I like this position of Agent very much, as he called me 'Sir' twice before I left the property, and he is probably as old as Ngahuru.

I stopped at the old Cottage where Zren had gained five horses as he took the Viklanders to Manumina. The place has since fallen to pieces, only the Chimney stands. I had thought I would sleep rough there, but then I remembered the two Deserters buried there who Ngahuru had said were only boys and the four Kereki soldiers killed by Viklander bolts. I slept rough farther down the road. I blame Zren for telling me too many stories with monsters.

I should reach Callis's home north of Huk tomorrow and my old House the day after. Falan knows I can read. Do you think she would have left a letter there for me to find? Where could she be? Where will I find her?

Nelo, what is taking you so long to take a Family name? You should be a Qanaq and be done with it. Tyra, I read your letter—the Keresh part anyway. Why did you write the Vik words underneath if you know I do not read Vik?

I do not know this Teacher named Languak. You are so fond of her, you have asked to carry her name? Is she as pretty as I am? Younger than Siba? Rich as the Empress of Vikland? Will she walk out with me?

Continue to send your letters to Siba and Rygee Namikk at the Brick Family Farms in Lowel as I am much too busy as an Agent to linger in a place to Wait for your response.

The Agent of the Brick Family Farms

and Property Owners Rygee and Siba Namikk,

Josef Brick

but you can call me 'Sir'

CHAPTER 51

KEEPERS OF SECRETS

Dica was trying to decide if she should go find Arden and tell him what she had done to try to get inside, or wait a little longer, when she saw a soldier hurrying down the hill.

"Are you Dica Namikk?" he asked.

She nodded.

"Leave your cart and come with me. The Secondo said bring any other books you have."

Dica hesitated. She knew Arden had his code books in the cart as well. She didn't know whether she should bring those or not. Were they only meant for Rani? Would she get them back?

She pointed to the wooden chest Arden had made, still heavily waxed against dust, bugs, and the Wet. "It's too heavy to carry without my cart. You will need to bear Witness there are more I can share with her." She started confidently up the hill hoping he would follow. He did.

The Embasado was far fancier than Dica had imagined. She was led into a large room and told to wait. The Secondo would see her soon. She wandered about looking at the lavishness of tapestries and paintings of Viklanders defeating monsters and looking heroic. Over the entry were large letters painted directly on the wall proclaiming Viklanders as defenders of the defenseless in many languages. The room gave her such a sense of security and safety, she felt the Secondo would immediately be able to help her.

She remembered Zren Janin had been here as well. He had said it was where he first met Bima Ritwik and Solkka Ulani, and little did he know how important they would be to his life.

Then she imagined Arden's voice whispering in her ear, 'Appearances are never what they seem,' and how 'everyone in Vikland's care could be used to hurt or harm.' She wondered if Arden and Mother were sharing a noodle bowl right now and how much easier this would be if she had him to explain to her what she was not seeing.

"Hello!" The Secondo entered the room. Dica noted she was a woman above the age of Siba and Ngahuru, almost the age of Mother Huena who ran the inns at Axefield. Her braid was long but streaked heavily with silver. She was dressed in the dark

Viklander clothes and carrying Dica's code book. "Thank you for seeing me so quickly. When I first received your gift, I was worried you had already left our checkpoint. Please sit down. I have ordered food and drink for us. We will not be disturbed." She guided Dica to a pair of soft chairs and gracefully sat. "It is good to meet you, Dica Namikk. That's a Conrosan name, isn't it? Do you have your traveling papers and your Matasi passes with you?"

Dica nodded. She wondered why the Secondo had not used the formal greetings and thought it may be because they were in Matasi. She reached into her cloth pocket and carefully pulled the papers Rani had sent for her, and her Matasi passes to show the route she had traveled. She handed all the papers to the Secondo.

The food and drink arrived while the Secondo was still reading her documents, but she stopped to serve Dica.

"Do you drink coffee? Would you like something else?" Dica felt she could have asked for anything and the Secondo would have been able to provide it. Instead, she ate the food placed in front of her while the Secondo went back to reading her traveling documents. Finally, the Secondo looked up.

"So, you are one of Rani's softfoots," she mused. "He certainly didn't waste any time."

Dica startled. "I didn't say anything of the sort."

The Secondo waved her hand at the papers. "These are good enough to get through any border crossing, possibly even Conrosa, although I wouldn't recommend it. But all of you who have a Viklander heart but not a Viklander face need something to help us identify you. We wish to assist you appropriately when you come to our door. Your papers have a mark on them so we know you are one of ours. So, Dica Namikk, what would you like to tell me?"

"I…I don't know. I was told to come to the Vikland embasado in Salisport before the Wet began and ask for the whereabouts of Zren Janin. I assumed he, or someone he knew, would help me with the rest." She didn't think she should tell the Secondo *who* had told her this. Dica wondered if this was why Arden had told her not to tell anyone he was here.

The Secondo leaned back in her chair. "I see. Would this be the Zren Janin of the Conrosan fairy tales or a real person?" She gave a sly smile. "I know this name has been used by some of our softfoots. I think one of them is the one you are looking for. Unfortunately, this one has not yet returned from a journey about Matasi." She paused. "There is also a man who uses this name, but he does not stay here in the embasado."

The Secondo thought for a moment. "Do you have a place to stay here in Salisport?"

Dica shook her head.

The Secondo looked at Dica's book again and frowned. "I think we will host you here at the embasado, I will confirm with the Ambassador on this. I would like to provide you with another book to make a copy of yours. We will send the original to Rani with the others, I think he is not so patiently waiting for them. The copy will help us here. Is this agreeable to you?"

"I travel with a cart and horses. I am a tailor. I cannot leave my things about," Dica protested weakly.

"Yes, a Conrosan tailor. That was a very clever touch. It was yours, wasn't it? A Viklander would never choose a peddler as a disguise. We can be so shortsighted that way."

"How long before Zren Janin returns?" Dica tried to take control of the conversation again. She wondered how she could talk to Arden and let him know what she had done.

"I am expecting him any day since no one likes to travel in the Wet. More than that is not your concern. If you wait here, I will have someone show you to a room, you can refresh yourself and I will have an aide bring you materials so you can begin copying your book."

"Please, I need to return to my cart, and I need to deliver a shirt to a business just three streets away. I truly am a tailor. It was not just a maskovesto." *She needed to talk to Arden.*

The Secondo gave her a long look. "I see. Well then, I will have someone accompany you through the checkpoints and beyond to your delivery, it would not do for you to get lost in Salisport after you have come all this way to see us."

CHAPTER 52

THE SEARCH FOR FALAN

To: Nelo, Callis Penny, Tyra Languak, Piffik Qanaq and Rell Huena, residing in Orsu, Vikland.

From: Josef Brick, the Agent for Rygee and Siba Namikk and the Brick family farms, southeast of Lowel, South Kerek now traveling on the Northern Track.

She is not here. I have been to Huk, my little house, Linna's house in Cloa, and your House in the woods, Nelo. Falan is not at any of them. When I met with the Justices to pay the Taxes, I asked about Falan and if she could be living anywhere in their area. No one remembers her, no one has met her. I don't know what to do. I know she would never go to Manumina; it is a Matasian garrison now. I know she would not return to her father in Kerek City.

I left Axefield before she did. I think maybe I should go there, or the refugee camp at Rishka. I remember we walked from Manumina to the Shepherd's Cottage in Vikland, and then we walked to Rishka.

Each was only a half day walk on a Track, and I think I could Find the paths again. If she is not there, then I could go to Axefield and ask Raul Huena if he knows where she traveled. Maybe she went to Matasi, although that does not feel right.

I know Siba and Rygee are expecting me back in a while but they won't worry, I don't think. I have collected all the Rents and paid all the Taxes, and so I am not carrying too much coin. I am sending Rygee his last Progress Report on the properties and I will tell him of these same Plans.

If Falan should ever write you and say she is Traveling or would like to, please give her my whereabouts at Siba's and Rygee's home. I realize now, I do belong there. I just needed to travel the Northern Track to remember what our Lives were like before we fled to Vikland. A crying Baby is nothing.

There are no bandits anywhere. There are Matasian soldiers everywhere. North Kerek still looks like it did immediately after the War.

I met the People who have your house, Nelo. They like the house and the Woods and said there is good hunting there. I said I knew the man who built the furniture in the House and they said to say Thank you.

So. Thank you.

Josef Brick

CHAPTER 53

THE MEANING OF THINGS

Before the Secondo left, Dica asked for paper and graphite. She did not think Arden could reach the Viklander checkpoint, but she thought she could leave a message for him at the Matasi checkpoint. She knew the soldiers would read the message—she certainly would—but she wanted to say enough for him to know what she was about to do.

She took a deep breath and began, *Remember how the Conrosan fairy tales always had Zren Janin traveling on an adventure? Some things never change. He may come tomorrow, he may come in three days, but Zren Janin always comes when people need him.*

I have always liked fairy tales and I am living one now. For the price of a magic book—one of mine—I have been given a place at the table, a room in the castle, and my own dragon to protect me until Zren returns. My books are with me so I can continue studying. The horses and cart are in the stables. We are all tucked up tight! If I can, I will travel to smell the flowers after midday every day until the sun sets. - DN

An aide poked her head into the room.

"Hello! Are you Dica Namikk? I am to walk you to your cart for your things. Someone else will take the horses to the stables and care for them."

Dica quickly folded the paper in her hand and followed the aide out of the room and down the hill. The aide chatted easily. She was a new cadet on her first rotation. She liked Matasi. It was boring, but after all of the horror stories she had heard from her older brothers about Kerek, she thought boring was fine. There were things to do: visiting the city, and reading, and weapons training, and the food was good. Different from Vikland, but she liked it.

Dica told her about the baboy. The girl said she had heard of them but had never been. Maybe the two could go together. There were some not very far away.

At the Vikland checkpoint, one of the soldiers chuckled. "Back already?"

Dica gave him a disparaging look. "Just gathering my things."

The aide gave the soldiers the paper from the Secondo. "She is a guest of the embasado for the next three days, if she leaves, she must have someone with her, she is a stranger to Salisport. Have her cart and horses stabled with us."

The aide faltered. "Is that a dog?"

Dica whirled about and saw Mother just outside of the track under a tree. "It is! Let me see if it is friendly." She approached it slowly. "Hey, Mother, shhhh, can you take this for me? Can you take this to Arden?" She carefully positioned herself to block the view of the dog from the others. She held out her fingers with the paper sticking between them.

Mother turned her head and ignored her. Of course she would, Dica scowled. Arden had trained her not to take anything from anyone else so the dog could not be poisoned. Dica grimaced, she needed another plan.

She carefully untied the pocket from her waist. The secondo had not returned her papers and so the little cloth bag was empty. She carefully rolled the note inside and tied it about Mother's neck. The dog trembled at Dica's touch. Even after traveling a year and a half together, Mother still responded best to Arden.

"Shhhh, good girl. Go find Arden." The dog turned and bolted through the grass.

Dica stood up and turned back to the others. "Not so friendly after all."

"Well, it better step lively. The Matasi soldiers see it wandering alone and some child will be crying tonight over a missing pet."

Dica ignored him. "I need this box delivered to my room. It has my schoolbooks." She put her hand on the wooden box Arden had made.

The aide tried to lift it and failed. "Woof, what do you do? You can't be stronger than I am, I have been training with my brothers on my short bong for years!"

Dica wondered. Arden had carried it into his room every night at any place they had been assigned. Of course he was on the ground floor, but it still would have been a task he had done before he had taken the horses and cart to the stables to be cared for—all before curfew.

Dica shrugged. "Let the soldiers carry it—the old soldiers," she clarified, "You and I? We have a city to discover!"

The aide laughed. "Yes, we do, but now, you need to get back to the embasado. You smell like horse and dust. Just to give you fair warning, the Ambassador here runs the embasado as if he is still in the military."

***

Zren listened to Lomes' plan to return to Salisport. They had only two days, maybe three left. The city seemed so close he thought they should go on as they had. But Solkka and Lomes disagreed and said it was too risky. They were obviously marked and would be searched again. Misdirection and maskovestos would only work so long. They needed to get back quickly.

The new plan had all three taking different tracks. They would abandon the cart in the stable. Lomes would take the male Viklander traveling papers the softfoot and Solkka had shared, take the cart horse, head south and pick up a different horse track, and ride back to Salisport. Lomes would carry nothing but male clothes and be there in four days.

Solkka would ride Batali, use his true Diplo papers for traveling and turn north on a track only used for horses. He would take all the code books. If challenged, he would show his papers and demand that as a courier of the Vikland Diplomatic Services, his bag could not be searched. It would be up to him to be convincing. He should be in Salisport in two days, sooner if he was allowed to buy travel through passes. If he was not in Salisport before Lomes returned, the softfoot would tell the Ambassador, and Viklanders would search for Solkka in the Matasi jails.

"You will get your wish, Zren. You wanted to walk through Matasi. We need you to carry a light travel bag with your story books and your clothes, stay on this track and no other, and walk the rest of the way to Salisport. You have the greatest risk, this is the track we were noted on. You should be able to get there late the second day. Go to the embasado. Tell the guards you need to speak to the Secondo and have them take this message to her." Lomes handed him a small paper and a heavy coin purse. "She'll let you stay there for one night once you explain what happened to us."

"How will I find a place to sleep at night? What if I spend all your coin by mistake? What if I break a rule I don't know about and spend the night in a Matasi jail?" Zren questioned, even as he tucked the note and the coin purse into his pocket tied about his waist.

Lomes grinned at Solkka. "I'll leave Zren and his questions to you. I am going to go through the cart and our belongings and make sure there is nothing left behind to hurt Vikland."

***

To: Kid, an apprentice at the Gayo Ulani coffee farms, the Keopi District, Vikland.

From: Dica Namikk, a Conrosan tailor, at Salisport, Matasi.

Greetings and good health!

I cannot write you everything that happened while I was a guest at the embasado, but I will tell you enough so when I read this later, I will remember to tell you the rest. Oh, Kid, if only you could have been here! You could explain all the layers I didn't see or understand!

On the second day of my visit, I was going to leave the grounds with my 'guide' and look for Mother and Arden when a tall West

Islander rode past us on a horse. He wheeled about and asked me for my name and who I was. When I said Dica Namikk, a Conrosan tailor, he got off his horse. He told the aide with me to go to the embasado and tell the Secondo, "Solkka Ulani is back with news and numbers." She left, and he asked me why I was there. If he was not mistaken, he said, I looked very much like a Wren from Kerek. I told him I was there to find Zren Janin, and if he was truly Solkka Ulani, he would know where I could find him. I said I knew Solkka Ulani was Zren's soldier boy, but I thought he was a Viklander. He smiled and said he was a Viklander. His pots of paint and mannerisms (is this a word? Arden said you would know it) must be exceptional if he could fool one of Ngahuru's Wrens.

He paused a long time and then asked me who was I softfooting for? I said Rani had given me my traveling papers, but the Secondo had taken them when I arrived, and so I couldn't go anywhere that would require passing a checkpoint. He had raised his eyebrows at that. He said he had used all travel through passes to get to Salisport as quickly as possible. He needed a bath, food, and a nap, but asked to have end of day meal with me as we had a lot to talk about. I asked him when Zren Janin would return. He smiled and said if he walked as much as he talked, we would see him the next day.

I said I needed to get a message to someone. He asked if it was another Wren. I didn't know what to say to that, so he told me to go look for them while the aide was gone. He would stable and care for his horse and then come back to the checkpoints to be sure I *would be able to get back in to the embasado. If I couldn't find my friend within a decon to please come back, he truly needed a nap. He promised me we would look together later for the person if needed.*

I trusted him, Kid, because I didn't know who else to trust. He said he knew Zren Janin, he said he knew I was one of Ngahuru's Wrens. He said Ngahuru, Kid, not Tiju Tia.

I couldn't find Arden and Mother.

When I returned to the checkpoints, Solkka Ulani was there at the first one. The Matasians joked with him and said he didn't waste any time, he had only checked in. He grimaced, but he signed me in and we passed through.

The soldiers at the Viklander checkpoint said I wasn't supposed to wander about without someone from the embasado, and they would have to tell the Secondo of the violation.

Solkka had huffed and said he had been traveling the entire Dry on behalf of the Ambassador. Obviously, they were all such new cadets, they needed to wipe the sleep from their eyes and the snot from their noses to recognize he had been posted to this embasado for two years! They could tell the Secondo anything they wanted, but he had been my escort as they could read from the register at the Matasi checkpoint down the hill—if they could walk that far without someone holding their hand—and if they could read the pages all by themselves.

They let us in. As far as I know, the Secondo didn't hear a word of it.

That evening, Solkka came to my room. He looked like a Viklander again. He has a scar that runs from his ear to his chin, but when he was in his maskovesto as a West Islander, it was completely gone. It was how I had tried to cover up Nelo's scar when we were trying to get back to Manumina. Solkka still doesn't have any braid almost two years after the war, and I asked him about it. (Should I not have?) He said he is not going to grow it back, but that is a story for another day. He said we would go out to the city to eat and to look for my friend.

The soldiers at the checkpoints were different ones from earlier and only had us sign in and out.

Solkka had asked me to describe my friend. When I would not tell him what Arden looked like, he blew out a hard breath and said he was only trying to help. That if he knew what constraints a softfoot was working with, it would be easier to pinpoint his location.

I said I didn't know what that meant. He asked what would be the first thing anyone would notice about my missing friend. I said his dog. It was his titiro mai ki ahau.

"Aha!" he said. "He will be lingering in the gardens because anywhere else Matasi soldiers would be pointing to a sign that says, 'no loitering.'" Kid, he tells jokes likes Zren does. Only he doesn't laugh at his own jokes like Zren will.

We found Arden and Mother in a garden near the embasado. Arden and Solkka exchanged formal greetings, but there was no grace and beauty in them such as you taught me. Then they looked at each other a long time and didn't say anything. I think they knew each other, but I do not know why I think that is true.

Finally, Arden said he was one of the Matasi missionaries who had rescued Tedros Ulani in the Cold Mountains. He asked for news of him. Solkka smiled then and said Tedros was alive and well. On behalf of the Ulani family, he thanked Arden and the other missionary for returning his little brother to him.

Solkka said his grandmother reminds the boys in every letter she writes that they are lovely decorations she likes to see about her table, but she knows it is up to those who love them to make sure that happens. Arden laughed and asked if Solkka had plans to return to Vikland soon to see this grandmother. Solkka said he couldn't talk about that.

Arden explained it was his intention to stay in Salisport through the Wet, and to find a tutor for me—someone who had gone to the academies in Juisiti. They were looking for Zren Janin for such a place and a name. Solkka relaxed a little and said Zren would be returning tomorrow, but he had just the place for them. It was where Zren had stayed until this last Dry.

They talked a little more. Solkka asked if Rani had given Arden his papers as well. Arden stiffened and then said yes. Solkka said he was going to wander about the garden and give us time and space to talk. He told me to find him when I was ready to get something to eat. He said to take pity on him because he was an old man.

Arden and I talked and made plans. Kid, I will see you someday and talk to you for decons about this. Arden said he would stay at the same place and then meet me in the garden tomorrow. If I was not there, he would know Zren Janin had not returned, or Solkka could not bring me. He said to make copies of all the books of pressed papers in my wooden chest and not to allow the chest or any of the books to leave my room for any reason. He said they were his only jewel to exchange for his sister.

I gave him a leather pocket of coins because I knew most of his coin was locked in my wooden box. He said he was supposed to be looking out for me. I said we look out for each other. I didn't want Mother to go hungry. He gave me my cloth pocket back and said it was just like a good softfoot to write the note before I needed it—to plan for every opportunity. He said he did not worry about me because I was so clever. Then he told me to find Solkka and ask him to take me to a baboy. I said I would wait until Zren was back so I could watch him dance.

Kid, I think I may be coming back to Vikland with Zren Janin and his soldier boy. It is nothing said in words, but if you have anything you want Arden to know, you should write quickly in care of Solkka Ulani at the Salisport Embasado.

I will be sixteen at the end of this Wet. I am just reminding you.

Dica Namikk

***

Zren couldn't believe he had ever suggested walking through Matasi. His feet hurt, his head hurt, and there was nobody to talk to. He had tried chatting with the soldiers at the first checkpoint into Salisport and even offered to share his fruit with them, but they had just given him a hard look and told him there was no loitering.

He had found the house and host last night without any difficulties. Truthfully, he had watched Lomes and Solkka register so often during the Dry he would have cuffed himself if he couldn't remember how to do it. The host and guests were appreciative of his stories—he told two—but it wasn't as much fun to sleep alone in a room. He never realized how much Lomes and Solkka listened to him, talked about their impressions of what they were seeing, and asked what Zren was doing. He thought maybe Lomes talked out their thoughts as much as he did.

At last, he could see the streets with all the embasados lined up. He decided he would just rest in the garden a moment. Then he would climb the hill with the wall of brightly colored fuchsia that made him smile whenever he passed it.

He gratefully sat on an open bench and sighed. He looked at the 'no sleeping,' 'no loitering,' 'no eating or drinking' signs and wondered how many signs it took before it was considered littering. He leaned back and closed his eyes.

CHAPTER 54

THE HUNTER IS HOME FROM THE HILLS

To: Piffik Qanaq and Rell Huena, now residing in Orsu, Vikland.

From: Siba Namikk, at the Brick family farms, southeast of Lowel, South Kerek.

Josef has returned with quite the adventure.

He served as our agent and visited all of the properties used by the Wrens during the war and deeded to Rygee. He met the tenants and heard their concerns, collected the rents, introduced himself to all the Justices, paid the taxes, and dragged himself to the other side of childhood. Rygee said he is a late bloomer, but he bloomed and that is all that matters.

When he did not find Falan anywhere along the Northern Track, he decided to look for her in Vikland. Without traveling papers, he secretly crossed the border near our shepherd's cottage. It is good the chest now owned by Nelo was no longer there. After two generations of abandonment and occasional use by Conrosans, the property is now occupied by a family displaced by the war. They raise goats, and Josef said he spent the better part of the morning with them sharing all of the goat stories he knew.

He followed the path up to Rishka, not realizing there was a direct track to Axefield. There are only two handfuls of Conrosans still at Rishka, those who would not or could not make the journey across Vikland. Josef says their lives are simple, but no one is in ill health or poverty. Mikale Oqina serves as the head of their Council of Wisdom. There are so few, only three are asked to mediate for them. Mikale is only a year or two older than Rygee, but was trained from birth for this role. They graciously invited Josef to share their food and their shelter. Josef left the next morning for Axefield.

The Huenas greeted him as if he had traveled across all the known world. They truly have a gift for hospitality. This is where he found Falan. She is working at the Huena family inns in Axefield. It appears both inns are thriving, and Raul Huena has clerks who speak every known language so the guests feel welcome and appreciated.

This is our Falan's role, can you imagine such a thing? Josef says she is responsible for many tiny details when Kereki dignitaries come to do business in Vikland, and she makes sure no one unintentionally insults another traveler. Josef says she speaks a little Vik and does the formal Vik greetings, but she is still Falan once the door to her room has closed at the end of the day. She lives in the new inn along with some of the other workers. She is not walking out with anyone. She says she does not have time to take care of anyone else. Josef spent nearly four days with her and said that was enough.

He spent a decon with Ross. According to Josef, since we have left, the boy has grown the length of Josef's forearm, and no longer has the voice of a child. He seemed well liked by his friends, and Mother Huena said she has no complaints. But Josef says the boy had no interest in carrying on a civilized conversation with him, and so he cannot tell us anything more.

Josef has returned home just as baby Kay has outgrown her colic. All of our lives have returned to a little more calmness just as the Wet begins. Rygee loves the Wet and sleeps in until sunrise.

May your lives have quiet nights and peaceful days until we meet again.

Siba Namikk

CHAPTER 55

THE SAILOR IS HOME FROM THE SEA

Zren felt the shadow cross his face and a gentle pressure on the bench as someone sat down quietly. He slowly opened his eyes, but his mind took a moment to understand Arden was sitting beside him. *What was the Wren doing in Salisport?*

Arden grinned at him. "Hello there, when I asked Dica yesterday to meet me here after midday to tell me when Zren Janin was going to arrive, I did not know she was going to make you appear in front of me. How are you and where have you been traveling?"

Zren grinned. "Ah, Keresh! It is so good to hear Keresh again! It is so good to see you! Dica wrote us and told us you were coming. I was so worried we would be too late. Where is Dica? Where is Mother?"

"Mother is laying near your feet if you could open your eyes just a little wider. Dica seems to be locked in the Vikland embasado. Do you know why that would be, Zren?" Arden looked a little worried.

Zren sat up straight. "No, I haven't been back since the Dry began. I have been walking the last two days on the track, and I thought I would just rest here for a moment before I started climbing the hill."

Arden explained he and Dica had reached Salisport three days ago. He had sent Dica alone to the embasado checkpoints. It was meant just to be a friendly softfooting task—try to get Zren Janin's whereabouts from someone in the embasado.

"We knew your letters came here, Zren. We thought we just needed to ask for you or Solkka Ulani and you could come to the checkpoints for us. But when you were not here, Dica offered one of her books of gathered information to the Secondo. She was invited inside. Dica says she has a room and food, and they asked her to make a copy of her book. But she cannot leave without someone to follow her about and watch her. Solkka found her yesterday…"

"Solkka is back? Already? Thank the Wester stars!" Zren leaned back in relief.

"Your Solkka has been helpful to us. He is going to talk to the woman where you lived before and see if we can live there during the Wet. I need to find work to earn coin, and Dica needs to find someone who has been to the academies to help her study."

Arden paused a long time. "When are you returning to Vikland? Are you going after the Wet? Be sure, Zren. Are you and Solkka Ulani going back to Vikland after the Wet?"

Zren slowly shook his head. "We talked about it. Solkka would like to see his family again before he is posted out, but his next posting is the West Islands—just a short sail from here. The journey to the Keopi District and back would take us two fortnights and that is just in traveling time. And the Wet is beginning. Solkka said it is better for us to go to the West Islands now and then go see our friends and families during a Dry. He promised me we will not wait until the harbor in Orsu is built."

Arden looked disappointed. He blew out a breath and said nothing for a long while.

Then he gave Zren an odd smile and asked, "What were you and Solkka doing on your travels in Matasi? Counting soldiers? How are our code books getting to Rani, Zren?"

Zren looked surprised. "Were you and Dica counting them in the north of Matasi? We only had to go from Vesaport to Alenti. Lomes said someone else was doing north Matasi. I didn't know it was you! Are other Wrens helping Vikland here in Matasi?"

Arden shook his head. "How are the code books getting back to Rani? Juisiti is a long way away, and I cannot believe everyone is using the grain trains."

"They're not." Arden startled at Solkka's voice. He turned to see Dica and Solkka standing behind him. Dica came around the bench and tried to give Zren a hug.

"Zren, it is so good to see you!" She pulled him off the bench and hugged him properly. "It is so good to talk to someone besides Arden! Did you know we stayed at Siba's during the last Wet? I am a tailor, Zren. In the Dry season we drove the cart and horses and I tailored all over Kerek and Matasi. Did Arden tell you? He taught me some Mata, and Siba helped me with my studies. At the end of this Wet I will be sixteen, and I will not need a *titiro mai ki ahau* on the cart with me anymore." She sighed happily.

Solkka shook his head. "I think the three of you all pretended to be someone else's look at me." He paused. "Lomes will be back in two, maybe three more days. They will need to talk to both of you. They may be able to talk with you more about what is happening. But for now, we won't talk any more about this."

Solkka looked at Arden. "I had promised to find you a place to stay. I did talk to the woman Zren has stayed with before. She has two rooms, so either I can find Zren another place or I can find Dica a place where she can also be tutored. It is not the cheapest lodging in Salisport, but it is clean and well cared for in a nice part of town. It is very close to here and the embasado. The woman who runs it is the wife of a soldier and knows not to ask too many questions if this is a concern. When I saw Mother last night, I asked her today if she would accept your dog as well. I said it is better behaved than most soldiers I know. She would like to meet the dog but thinks it will not be a problem.

"I thought for tonight," he continued, "it could be Zren and Arden with her since Dica still has a room in the embasado. I want to find out more of why her traveling papers were taken. This has not been done before to my knowledge."

Dica looked thoughtfully at Solkka. Then she wrinkled up her nose and whispered in Mata to Arden, "Can I talk to you alone?"

Zren crowed at her, "We all know Mata now, Dica, you must pick another language to whisper your secrets!"

Arden took her carefully by the elbow and they moved away.

Solkka watched them, but spoke to Zren, "Last night, when I talked to her, I thought he was more than her friend, but that is not true, is it?"

Zren shook his head. "Arden was walking out with a Viklander girl from the Huena Inn when I left to come here and join you. I do not know what happened to her. The Wren at your cousin Nari Ulani's house, Kid, and Dica have plans to go to the academies together, if they can get accepted."

"Arden is teaching Dica to be a softfoot? Why?"

Zren tipped his head. "Is that a bad thing?"

Solkka smiled down at Zren. "No. I was just wondering what country he is teaching her to work for."

Zren frowned. "You will need to explain this."

"Later." Solkka grinned. "Both Bima and Ngahuru and a missing Spice Islander are part of Arden's story so it may take a while."

***

To: Kid, an apprentice at the Gayo Ulani coffee farms, Keopi District, Vikland.

From: Dica Namikk, a tailor, traveling to Vikland.

Greetings and good health!

I am sending you this letter on the first grain train we find, but it is possible I may still reach Juisiti before it arrives at your door! I will be traveling during most of the Wet, but Lomes says it will only be unpleasant and not deadly as it used to be when they had to go over the passes of the Silver Mountains.

At first, Zren and Arden and Mother and I were living at the home where Zren lived before the Dry. The dommastrino only had two rooms and so I said I would share with Zren. I said he tells better stories. I still think she wonders about all of us since Solkka and Lomes are over until curfew almost every end of day.

Solkka Ulani and Zren are leaving for the West Islands within a fortnight. Solkka has completed his two years here and he is very ready, he says, to spend time with his cousins and live and dream in 'Paradise.' Zren has been busy buying blank books of pressed papers. Solkka just shakes his head at him and says there will be plenty of paper there for him to write his stories, but Zren says he needs to be prepared. He says Koanga knows a lot of stories.

Lomes and I will be traveling to meet Rani in Juisiti as fast as we can with all the books gathered from the travelers during the Dry. The softfoot added a West Islands steel lock to the wooden chest Arden made for me, and we will carry them all in there. We will take the tailoring cart as our maskovesto, but we will not stop to tailor anywhere.

Arden and Mother are now gone. No Spice Island ships sail out of Salisport. So we do not know what ship he took out of the harbor. I thought perhaps he and Mother were walking to Vesaport where there are many Spice Island ships to choose from. But this did not feel right.

Solkka says Rani would have given Arden a marked set of papers which would have alerted the Vikland embasado if he would have tried to leave on a ship owned by Viklanders or Matasians, or gone through certain checkpoints where the Viklanders had friends. The West Islands ignores the pettiness between Vikland, Kerek, and Matasi and would have refused to notify the embasado if they had noted the marked papers *at the Harbormaster's office. Maybe Arden knew this and maybe he was just lucky. Solkka says he may have had his own papers and never used them until now, or he may have sailed on a West Islands ship out of Salisport. It is more than possible, Solkka said, that Arden will take a ship to the Spice Island after he has visited the West Islands. But you should know this, Kid, he and his dog have disappeared like sea smoke.*

I did not tell the others Arden told me he was leaving. He had asked Lomes for news of his sister, saying Rani had entrusted the information to the softfoots at Salisport. Lomes and Solkka shared a long look. They said she had left with the others on the day the war was declared and had traveled as far as Aldi. Quan had said she had stayed there with a printer from the West Islands. Her plans were to sail home to the Spice Island and try to contact her family from there. Lomes told Arden they had no news of her since then. Solkka said he was sure she had been successful. Arden left us in anger and did not return back to the house until the next day. I wonder, if he had not have left Mother with us, if he would have returned at all.

Arden gave me three letters—one for you, one for Nelo, and one for me. I am to give them to you in person, and not risk them to the winds or prying eyes. I do not know this to be true, but I think the three letters are very different.

I know you will not be in Juisiti and you cannot come to the academies until your three years with the Ulani family have ended. So I have decided to drive my cart across Vikland to Orsu. Lomes says it can be done, even during the Wet, and even by a girl who is almost sixteen. Many students at the academies are responsible for traveling from home to Juisiti and back again. The softfoot will help me find a map, and try to find someone who is traveling to show me how it is done. Then Lomes smiled and said perhaps Rani would think it would be a good idea to have someone find out what all those Conrosans are doing in their new city, and they could travel with me. I think that would be nice. Lomes has been very kind to me and talks as much as Zren Janin. Oh! And the Viklanders took me to a baboy! Lomes and Zren taught me how to dance! Solkka and Arden did not join in because they said they had to hold down the table and watch over Mother to keep them from dancing away. Ha!

Kid, when Arden asked me to open the wooden box so he could take his coin and his books of Matasi parables, he also took all of the rest of his code books of pressed papers with him. He said it was not a gift freely given. I do not know what that means. He says if I ever need a new home to come to the Spice Island. Family is family.

I will tell you the rest of my adventures when I arrive. I will send a letter to the Ulani coffee farm as soon as I reach Orsu, Vikland. Maybe Nelo will ride with me to deliver it? I look forward to seeing you again. Oh, Kid, the world is full of so many possibilities!

Dica Namikk

CHAPTER 56

FULL CIRCLE

To: Solkka Ulani, of the Vikland Diplo now posted to the Royal Palace, West Islands.

From: Arella Huena, formerly of Axefield, now residing in Orsuarlerpaa, Vikland.

Greetings and good health to you, Solkka Ulani!

I do not know the protocol for the West Islands. I do not know if Zren is in your house or in Ngahuru's tender care. But I ask you as a great personal favor to give the enclosed letter to Zren Janin.

The enclosed letter

To: Zren Janin, a hero of Manumina, living near the Royal Palace, West Islands.

From: Rell Huena, formerly of Axefield, now residing in Orsuarlerpaa, Vikland.

My little brother,

I was disappointed to read in your last letter you and Solkka Ulani traveled directly to the West Islands for his next Diplo posting without stopping for a visit with family and friends in the Keopi district of Vikland. It wasn't much out of your way at all! (That is a Vik joke. How can you spend so much time with Solkka Ulani and still not understand Vik humor?)

You will be surprised and amazed to learn I saw Dica Namikk in Axefield! She and Lomes were traveling from Salisport, Matasi to Juisiti and had stopped to spend the night in my father's inn.

I had taken letters and documents from Orsu and all along the track to the Central Administrative offices in Juisiti. I needed to wait for coffee contracts to be signed and registered before returning to Orsu, so I decided to visit my family in Axefield for three days. (It is only a pony ride from Juisiti after all!)

Dica and Lomes trotted in on a clever little tailoring cart the second day of my stay. It had an awning over the front to protect them from the Wet and a waxed covering over the wagon bed. I had end of day with them (actually, they joined my family and me. You know how that is.) I said if Dica could wait in Juisiti for me, she and I could ride together to Orsu. I could show her how to do the courier route for all the letters and packages and introduce her along the way.

It rained every day of the journey. Some days I didn't even ride Wishes but stayed under the awning with Dica as she told me of her adventures in Kerek and Matasi. I cannot believe everything she has seen and done. She is only going to be sixteen at the end of the Wet!

Dica is living with Piffik and me for now. She studies with me since she does not yet know either Vik or Conrosan. Her Mata is better than mine, and she has asked to learn Vik first. I think Piffik was disappointed, but it makes sense as all of her classes at the academies will be in Vik. She will be fine in some studies but very far behind in others. She has never read a Wisdom of the Warrior saga! I am tempted to ask Nelo to read them aloud to her.

Nelo loves your books by the way. That was a very good and generous thing you did for him. I understand why you could not write them in Conrosan as Solkka was writing the translation in Vik for you. But if you do not mind, I would like to take your Wester and Vik words and translate them into Conrosan for the people here. Piffik and I will work on them together. I know, when will he find time? But he always does. I am blessed to be married to the kindest man I know.

Callis says there will be room in her boarding house soon and then Dica will move there. Dica says it is nothing about us, it is only she wishes to know she can live on her own before she goes to the academies. She is so eager to grow up, and I smile to think what she will be able to accomplish. Callis and some of the Viklanders posted here are teaching her the short bong. She asks as many questions as you do. No, that could never be possible. You asked every question in the known world!

We wish to see you soon. I miss you very much. Do not forget your friends here,

Rell Huena, Piffik Qanaq, Nelo, Callis Penny, Tyra Languak, and Dica Namikk

ACKNOWLEDGEMENTS
(BUT I PREFER TO CALL THEM GRATITUDES)

Writing five books in three years is not quite what it seemed. I had notebooks and notebooks of ideas, written impressions, short stories, and mementos from my work as a global auditor. As I reread my memories of the pearl markets and beaches in the Philippines, the palaces and pilgrimages in India, the beauty of Korea, and the medieval history of Japan, the worldbuilding that peppered these pages sprang to life nearly fully formed.

But while Asia provided the backdrop, it was the trips to South America that provided the plot and heartbreak. It was during a 2015 trip to the Falkland Islands that I witnessed military troops still disabling landmines that had been laid by Argentina during the 1982 Falklands War. You read that correctly: Thirty-three years. An entire generation has grown up with the remains of a war that lasted just seventy-four days. The seeds of ghostfire were planted.

As for my other travels in South America: Uruguay, Argentina, Chile, Columbia, Guyana, Nicaragua, Costa Rica, Mexico, Guatemala, Panama, Honduras, and Belize, the amazing people I met all provided history and heroes which morphed into *The Tales of Zren Janin.*

The world is a big place and a passport is a magic ticket. But books and an imagination can stir our hearts when we must remain in place. While my feet reside in Minnesota, and my heart resides in the Waitaha (Canterbury) region of New Zealand, I am reminded over and over again, none of us are on this journey alone.

Thank you to the team at Paper Raven Books. These books would not be in their current form without all of you. I learn so much and there are so many people to keep me focused on the end goal! A special call out to Ashley Swanson—editor extraordinaire. You understood the story I wanted to tell, and carved it out of the pages and pages (and pages) I submitted. I am so grateful for all of you!

A huge debt of thanks to my beta readers and writing group. When I flipped book 5 at you and asked if it could be a standalone, you didn't blink—merely said, "Yeah, no. We need the arc of the Wrens to understand their choices." When I wanted to fix plot holes and character flaws by asking you who were your favorite Wrens and why, I got enough feedback to plot out the next books. As the characters continue to unfold in all of their imperfections, in stand-alone books of their own, I hope you continue to cheer them on. Thank you.

Angela Lawson, Stephanie Dodge, Gary Dunker, and Florence Dunker – Such an amazing team of first readers and reviewers. I owe you all so much.

Elizabeth Schoenenberger – When I was buried under too many responsibilities and deadlines, you jumped in and said, "I got this." I could never have finished these books without you taking on the rest of the world for me. The world is a better place with you in it. Thank you!

As always, David and Bridget (and Sylvia), Ryan and Briana, Jenny and Zach, Katie and Nelson, Almond, Brandon, Liz, Kaeden, Callie, Peyton, Philip, Lauren, Ryla, Rinoa, Gunther, Lark, Hayden, Max, Nordica, Penelope, Cory, Catherine, and Hallie – Stand proud and live loud.

And finally, and most importantly, Steven – Thank you for everything.

He was quiet then, letting his words sink in. "Your future is endless possibilities… The worst days of your life are all behind you." He paused, still not looking at her, and then added softly, "You should know, I do not believe that is true of all the Wrens."

- Arden to Dica in *The Wrens Fly Away*

"There is a difference." Solkka reminded him, "There are many kinds of bravery, and you are brave when you need to be."

- Solkka to Zren in *The Wrens Fly Away*

READING GUIDE

Book club/ Book review?
Try using these questions to start the conversations!

1. There are many sides to every story. The Empress believes she is generous in giving a reward to the Wrens for their assistance during the war. Ngahuru feels the coin is worthy of their efforts. The Wrens are dismayed there are no plans to help them become who they want to be. Discuss how perceptions and biases have created this lack of understanding between all participants.

2. During most of *War and Wrens* (book 3) and *Exile: A New Beginning* (book 4) the Wren, Kid, stays in the background. We learn of his talents and exploits mainly through the stories of others. However, in *The Wrens Fly Away*, he plays a pivotal part in getting the other Wrens to think beyond their immediate needs. He helps others (Dica, Oro, and Linna) get past limitations. Think of a person in your life who has stepped in and helped you think beyond any obstacles to achieve your goals.

3. Ross was disregarded for much of the war by the other Wrens. However Josef is uniquely able to see Ross in a different light. Josef tells Zren, *"…we needed him in Huk and he understood that. I do not know what it cost him to stay and help us. I do not know if he believed he could not walk away. But I do know what it is to feel trapped in a life that is nearly unbearable to live."* As young as Ross is, he understands that his healing will only come once he put the Wrens and the war behind him. How do the other Wrens accept that this is the path he has to take to recover himself?

4. Callis and Dica are both extremely competent Wrens during the war between Vikland and Kerek, yet at the beginning of *The Wrens Fly Away* they don't understand how to reach out for their own dreams. How does Siba teach Callis to have a voice in her future? How does Callis help Dica achieve her own dreams? How do both women find their voices and move confidently forward? How can we help others find their voice?

5. Rygee's entire story arc through the series is based on an interpretation of the Old Testament story of Joseph and his brothers (Genesis 37-50). What other epics and mythologies tell a similar story of banishment, a quest, and return to glory? (Think of Odysseus in the *Iliad* and *Odyssey*).

6. How did Piffik's and Ngahuru's gifts from the Empress
   and Rygee's gift from Piffik and Ngahuru all reflect what
   they needed? How does this demonstrate the Matasi
   parable of the *Gifts of the Father* (told in *War and Wrens*
   Book 3, Chapter 23). (Trick question!)

7. During the meetings with the Empress, no one spoke
   for Zren Janin, even though it was clear he could not
   advocate for himself. Why do you think this is? What
   assumptions do you think the others made? How can we
   be better advocates for those who need us?

8. Nelo and Falan bore tremendous responsibility before
   the war trying to keep others alive and unharmed. How
   did this affect their own growth and well-being? How do
   you think this impacted their choices after the war? How
   does Nelo show that he is still taking care of others? How
   does Falan deal with the loss of responsibility for Josef?

9. Nari Ulani is the non-royal cousin to the nephews of the
   King of the West Islands. He is described as an ordinary
   soldier, average student at the academies, and an injured
   war veteran. He is proud to the point of arrogance. Yet,
   he listens to the Wrens, and ensures other Viklanders
   acknowledge them as heroes. Why do you think Nari
   is able to provide such validation? How can we provide
   support to those in our own community?

10. Josef and Linna both portray a very different personality to others than their own truth. It isn't until Josef spends the day with Siba that we learn of his fears of being left behind, of not having a place, of not knowing who to be. Linna is a quiet leader driving her own future. She brings Oro out from Kerek City, works with Arden as the center of the network, stands up to Ngahuru, and then Rani, marries and settles in Juisiti. Did either of their destinies surprise you? Why or why not?

11. Ngahuru leaves abruptly to return to the West Islands. She has been a catalyst throughout the series, putting people on a path to a future they would not otherwise be able to achieve. Yet, the Wrens don't always see what she has done for them. Without knowing why she did what she did, the others create their own story of her actions. How do you see her? How do you interpret her actions?

12. *The Tales of Zren Janin* occur in a time and place where information cannot get from place to place without someone physically bringing the news either in person or by letter. How does the inability to quickly communicate with others impact the story arcs of so many of the characters? (For example, Josef's search for Falan occurs because he left Axefield first. Dica was the only Wren to see Falan working in Axefield.)

13. The last third of the book is written in letters as the various Wrens discover new adventures. How do the personalities come through in their letters? Give examples.

14. As the Wrens take Rygee's advice and adopt new last names or regain their family names, Nelo retains one name. What do you think this represents to him?

15. As Solkka, Lomes, and Zren travel about Matasi softfooting for Vikland, Lomes carefully sets up Zren to be a *titiro mai ki ahau* for them. What examples can you give that Lomes and Solkka understand Zren's neurodivergence and accept him for who he is?

16. Siba provides additional insights to Tyra and Therin and expresses relief that they are regaining a childhood. How do you see Orsuarlerpaa providing the same environment for them as Manumina provided for Zren Janin?

17. Kern outmaneuvers Rani to force him into Bima Ritwik's role. As he sorts through the talent that he has and the talent that he could have, how do we see Rani's own strengths and weaknesses? As he and Nari Ulani snarl and snap at each other over the past, what insights do you gain into both of their personalities?

18. We, the readers, are given the information that Arden is softfooting for both Vikland and the West Islands early

on. One by one, the Wrens start to learn this too. When Solkka shares with Dica and Zren that he thinks Arden traveled to the West Islands and Dica tells Kid that Arden took his code books with him, what foreshadowing do you see?

19. Does your favorite Wren have the adventure you wish for them? What would you choose differently?

20. What Wren's future surprised you the most? Why?

21. Which Wrens do you think will see each other again?

22. Which Wrens would you like to see again?

FIGHTING MONSTERS

When the coffee farmers had suggested there be a regular route from Orsu to the academies, palace, and Central Administrative offices of Juisiti, Rell Huena had thought how wonderful it would be to have such a reliable way to transport letters, documents, taxes, and all manner of packages. What she didn't imagine was she would be in charge of it.

Because no matter how the Vikland Empress claimed to have opened the borders to everyone, the bitter truth remained, when the costs and care of the overland transportation route was decided, the Empress insisted the position had to go to a Viklander at Orsu, the current end of the road along the northern coast. The military attachment assigned to Orsu rotated over the seasons, but the Empress wanted someone who would be invested in the project for years.

First Soldier Joon warned the members of the Diplo stationed in Juisiti that someone might have to relocate to the back of beyond. He had—together with his softfoots—located every name on the Diplo roll, their current duties and residences, and given the Empress the list.

Rell Huena was on that list. When the Empress learned the Viklander bowmaster and healer had married one of the Conrosans and now resided at the soon to be port city, she had declared Rell Huena the logical choice. The Diplo staff in Juisiti sent up a fervent thank you.

Rell took the assignment graciously if not necessarily willingly. She still had younger brothers coming up in the academies and their military service, and she didn't want to make their lives difficult with the decision makers in Juisiti. She also knew she would need tact and knowledge to codify a process that had worked on social trust for generations.

From the beginning, she had asked the Ulani families for guidance. She had been in the service with Lissil and in the Diplo with Solkka. The Ulani family had been a part of the many along the road who had been informally running a delivery for years, and she wanted to learn from their wisdom.

The Ulani families had entertained her at end of day meal and hosted her because there had been no inn within a day's ride. Perhaps because all the land within a day's ride belonged to the Ulani coffee farms, but Rell had said nothing about that, and thankfully accepted their offer.

She had learned more about all of the coffee farmers' needs and wants for the traveling courier and their desire for the port and what they hoped it would accomplish. At first, she had been surprised at how much Devi and Gayo asked advice from their adult children, but then she realized this was how they were teaching them to take on the responsibilities of everything that would rest on their shoulders someday.

She liked Nadja's and Kaede's seriousness. They had been years above her in the academies, and seemed even older now as they managed the coffee farms and the businesses with their parents' guidance. She had hoped either of them would accompany her to meet with all the families and settlements, to formally introduce her to others and discuss the plans for the traveling courier. But as they had talked over the details, she realized she had picked the wrong time of the year for them to take fourteen or fifteen days away to travel to Juisiti and back.

It was Nari Ulani, a son of Gayo's about the age of her younger brother Dylis, who had offered to introduce her to all the families along the way and help explain to them how the routes and costs and timings would work. She had not met him before; she had already been banished to Evensong—at least that was how she thought of it—when he had come to Axefield. But she had heard from Piffik how he had come in the West Islands Ambassador's carriage at the request of the Vikland Empress. He had honored the Wrens by acknowledging publicly the role they had played to help Vikland. He had seen them, Piffik had told her, truly seen them for who they were and who they could become, and that was no small thing to any of the Wrens. Again, she regretted she had not been in Vikland when so much had happened.

Now she noted how easily Nari Ulani moved about on his bastono, as if they were an extension of him. His humor was as sharp-edged as Aajan's, and he was as casual with his Vikland greetings and manners as students in the academies when adults weren't around. But his prickly personality— which Piffik had graciously attributed to never-ending pain on his still healing body—was gone. Rell thought she could spend a fortnight in his company. She had smiled and accepted his offer to accompany her.

A few days later, when Rell had come to gather him together, she had been riding her favorite horse, Wishes, the Viklander mare Bima Ritwik had left at Manumina. Nari had an equally well-trained horse with a special saddle and stirrups. The gelding had stood patiently while Nari loaded his own traveling bags and a short bong scabbard. She watched as Kid and Nadja unbuckled his bastono and handed him his cane to balance himself. Nadja showed her how to hold the horse so Nari could lean and pull himself up. How she would have to pick up his dropped cane and slide it next to the other one into the scabbard as the bastono could not be used with mounting and dismounting a horse.

Nari had looked down on her. "This isn't going to be a problem for you? I thought you seemed bright enough to handle it, or I would never have volunteered to be your guide."

Rell responded sarcastically, "It's obvious you have never met another Viklander before." She mounted her horse and smiled at Nadja. "I will return him in fifteen days with better manners."

Nadja snorted, "Good luck with that."

The first day Nari had been quiet. She had attempted to carry on a conversation by asking about coffee farming. He had just looked down his long nose at her and asked if she was applying for a position as a coffee picker or just talking. Because if she was just talking to hear herself talk, he would ride on ahead and meet her at the first farm. She pinched her lips together and said nothing more.

He had been more cheerful when they stopped at the first coffee farm at the other side of his uncle Devi's. He greeted the groom who came out to meet them, nodded to the stable boy who was sent to tell the house they were there. He carefully handed down his canes to another who came out. Rell watched closely and soon realized this had been done before at this house. One groom held the horse, the larger man circled his arm about the back of the saddle, ducked his head, and braced himself. Nari swung his damaged leg around and balanced his body using his arms while he pulled his good leg from the stirrup. The larger man caught him and acted as his balance until he could get the canes underneath him. Rell was impressed. There was no clumsy grabbing and pushing and pulling as if he was a sack of flour, and Nari hadn't been handed down like a child. Within moments he had his carved black canes under him. He moved on his own to the house where the rest of the family waited to greet him, his dignity intact.

Rell followed Nari's lead as he completed the formal Vikland greetings and introduced her. They were invited inside and another child had been sent to the fields to bring in the Left Hands. Rell had been trained in the Diplo. She knew the value of small talk. She carried on a comfortable conversation until everyone was assembled and she could explain the Empress's plan for the mail courier.

"This was an idea brought forth by all of you along the track. There is so much social trust here, we know this is why it has worked for so many years, but it is difficult when a schedule is not known. We would like to propose a courier who would begin in Orsu, move along the track at these houses, businesses, and settlements." She pointed at the map. "We estimate it would take about eight or nine days. Then there would be two or three days in Juisiti to take care of all the business entrusted to the courier. Those two or so days, the courier and horse would be housed and stabled in the military dormitories near the palace. This expense would be borne by the Empress. Then the courier would pick up all of the documents, letters, packages, and travel the route in reverse. There would be fourteen or fifteen days in between and the route would begin again. This would not mean you could not send your own messenger for items which must move much more quickly. And I am sure there are those who are on their way to and from the academies who will stop and pick up our needs out of courtesy and kindness. But this is a consistent schedule. You would not need to hire a messenger at full expense just to learn your neighbor had done the same."

Rell laid out more maps, the dates, and the locations that would be included. If something was meant for someone along the track yet to come, it could be delivered there. Nothing had to go to Juisiti just to be delivered back along the route again. Rell watched as the family talked it over and then addressed their questions to Nari. Sometimes he deferred them to Rell and sometimes he answered them himself.

He offered his opinion that the Ulani families thought this would be especially helpful during harvest when it was hard to have someone step away to be gone so long. Coffee contracts could be delivered and signed in the two or three days in Juisiti and returned within the travel loop. No more harvesting based on the hope—but not the certain knowledge—the contracts had been signed and registered at the Central Office with the prices agreed upon.

He pointed out now it was quite easy, so many of the families had someone in the military with their home leaves, and students at the academies coming and going at the term breaks. But that would not always be the way of it. He also thought there might be another benefit to have someone who knew the city so well accompany the children who were going to the city and the academies for the first time. Not everyone had been as lucky as he had been with two older sisters who had guided his first days settling in at the Academy of Botanicals.

The room suddenly felt oppressively silent. Finally, the woman said, "May their names live on."

Nari nodded. "I am sorry for your loss. I think of your son every day." He touched his canes gently. There was another moment of silence and then the man cleared his throat and asked to see the maps again.

Rell asked them about the cost of staying overnight in the inns to Juisiti and said how this cost would continue to be borne by everyone on the route and now would be much less for each of them. But the Empress was very interested in paying for much of this, as this route would be the first one in the country. If it went well, it would be expanded to other areas. Rell was already hoping it would go from Juisiti to Axefield and her own family.

"I can imagine a day," Rell said earnestly, "when I can send a letter from Orsu to my family and receive one from my mother within three fortnights. Now? I am lucky to see one twice a year."

After the business was concluded, coffee was brought out in small cups. The family visited a little more and asked after Nari's family, his grandmother, his uncle's family. At last, Nari rose to leave and Rell quickly gathered her maps and papers. They were walked out to the dooryard and the horses brought to them. Nari grabbed the pommel, put his knee in the special stirrup in the back, his foot in the stirrup in the front, and laddered himself up and his damaged leg over the saddle. Rell reached for his dropped cane, but the other man picked it up first and slid it easily into the open scabbard. Rell quickly mounted and the two waved goodbye and cantered down the road.

"When you stopped on the way to the academies before, did the visits usually take this long? I am wondering," Rell said quickly, "if we need to adjust the timings of the routes."

Nari shook his head. "We visited longer today because they lost their son to the war. I had served with him, and I wanted them to know they were not alone in their grief."

"I am sorry."

"Why should you be sorry?" Nari snapped. "You didn't cause his death."

Rell sighed. It was truly going to be a long trip.

At the end of the third day, Rell Huena knew three things. The courier system was going to be successful. Everyone she and Nari had met with so far was pleased to have such a regular travel route to and from the palace, military dormitories, the academies, and the Central Administrative offices.

Secondly, she had been right to ask the Ulani families for guidance, they were well known by everyone she met. People asked after Nari's extended family by name, just as he asked after theirs. In fact, Nari Ulani was so thoughtful and so well-mannered to everyone they met, she could only assume the third thing. That for whatever reason, he truly disliked her to the point of nearly constant rudeness. And this she could not decipher. What had she done to him? And why would he volunteer to travel with her if he could not bear to be in her presence?

Before they turned into the lane to visit the last family scheduled for that day, Nari asked her to stop and listen to him. He said they would not stay, even if the family offered end of day meal. He said they were a family whom Trouble embraced as a dear friend, and were barely keeping their holding together. He said to treat them as if they were kin to the Empress, they were very proud, but during the meeting he would promise they had a prior arrangement to eat and sleep elsewhere. If they stayed, he warned her, they would be taking food from the mouths of their children and the bed from the backs of the parents, as it was the only one they had.

"Do you understand, Arella Huena?" he said in that haughty tone she had come to detest.

She nodded, because she didn't trust her voice to answer him civilly, and they turned into the lane. The house was large and meant to be quite beautiful, but it had a look of neglect as if someone could not keep up with all the demands of fields and home and outbuildings. Rell wondered if the parents were foolish with their coin to live in such unkempt surroundings, or if the family was too small to have the many hands needed to do everything, or if the hands were not capable. Then, as Nari hailed the house, the family came to the door to greet them.

The Trauo family was kind, very kind. Rell estimated the parents' ages about those of her own parents. They were delighted to invite them inside, listen to the news up and down the road, and hear about the mail courier. As Rell explained the places that would be serviced, and the dates the routes would run, she noticed Nari slip the pages talking about the shared costs and expenses under the ones she had already mentioned. She had glanced up at him then, but he had only given her a bland look in return.

Then she had talked about the couriers themselves, how they would be from the military attachment posted to Orsu, but she would accompany the first one, and that one would accompany the next one, so there would be always two soldiers, and one would be a known face to them. They were to demand a receipt to be given them for anything accepted by the couriers, just as they would be asked to sign a receipt acknowledging it had been delivered when they received anything.

Then Nari had turned to the mother and explained how this would be the first route set up, and the Empress would undertake the costs of everything. That the Right Hands in the Central Administrative Office needed the receipts only for their recordkeeping. It would help them as they set up other courier routes across the country.

Rell said nothing to the lie. She decided she would confront Nari later.

As Nari had anticipated, the father asked them to stay for end of day meal and perhaps even the night since sunset was not far off. Nari demurred saying how he now regretted his earlier decision to accept at the home of another.

"Perhaps another time. You are always so gracious to offer us travelers a place at your table whenever we pass through." The mother hurried off to make coffee for them before they left for the evening.

Rell began gathering her papers together, and looked up when she heard a noise in the doorway. She had expected it to be the mother returning with the coffee, but instead saw three children about the ages of the youngest Wrens when they had first come to Manumina. They looked thin, but not as underfed as Zren Janin when she had first met him. It was more the pallor of their skin, the sense of fragility about them. Each of them had a wrapping about either an arm, a foot, a hand. At first, she wondered if the parents were the kind of monsters who hurt their children, but then she knew Nari would never be kind to those types of people. And Nari Ulani was much too sharp to be taken in by the smooth words of others.

Her thoughts were interrupted by the mother returning with three coffee cups. She smiled as she handed them about and apologized to Nari again how she hated to insult such an important coffee farmer by not drinking the fruits of his fields. She explained to Rell she had never learned to like the taste of coffee. Rell smiled and assured her it was not so unusual. She knew a man she called her little brother, who did not like the taste of coffee either, although it seemed he could eat or drink anything else that was placed under his nose. She was going to say more about Zren Janin when she saw Nari deliberately push his cane off the chair and to the floor. As both the father and mother reached to pick it up for him, he looked at her and shook his head. She hid her confusion by taking a drink of coffee.

She nearly spewed it out. It was so weak; it was barely colored water. She hid her grimace and silently thanked Nari for taking their eyes from her. She was not sure she could have hidden her distaste in time. It wasn't that the mother didn't like coffee, Rell realized, but she had diluted what little they had to serve their guests so their poverty would not be obvious. Rell noticed the father never set down his cup. She realized it probably held only water.

They chatted about this and that, and Nari asked about their plans for the children's school. Somehow, both Rell and Nari were able to swallow every drop in their cups. Nari was a far better actor than she was, Rell decided, and they took their leave.

There was no one who had seen Nari mount and dismount before to help him now. So Rell curved her arm about the back of the saddle to brace herself and Nari used her shoulder to balance and push off. The children watched him wide-eyed.

"Quite the trick, isn't it?" he called out to them as he settled into the saddle. "You will learn as you grow older, there is nothing you cannot do if you set your mind to it."

Rell quickly mounted and in a flurry of goodbyes they started down the lane. "Stop here," Nari commanded. Rell pulled up. "Turn back and wave as if you are saying goodbye one last time. Now see that little fence surrounding that small stand of trees?"

Rell nodded as she waved. He continued, "Each tree was planted when a child of theirs died. My aunt, Hilanna, says it is a disease the parents carry but do not die from. If you or I get a scrape, a cut, or a bruise, we complain about our clumsiness, or weapons training, or whatever caused us harm. If their children get a scrape or a cut, they can bleed out before anyone can come in time to help them. Of all of their children, only the youngest three are left. You noticed they all had bandages wrapped about them? It was probably no more than a nip from a goose, a stubbed toe, something you and I would never even notice. Yet the parents are forced to worry night and day if those they love will reach the other side of childhood." He dropped his hand and wheeled his horse about. "I will pay their costs for the courier. Not the Ulani family, me. Send their bill directly to me."

He trotted ahead leaving Rell to stare after him.

The next few days were the same. Rell and Nari introduced the scheduled courier plan to settlement and home and business and drank countless cups of Vikland coffee as they chatted with their hosts. Mostly they stayed with the families. When she complained about the lack of inns along the way, Nari had just shrugged and said they didn't need many of them. Everyone on the track took care of each other.

It was the evening before reaching Juisiti, and Rell thought the day couldn't possibly get any worse. They had been caught in a cloudburst in only the second decon of travel. Midday had been non-existent as they had arrived too early at one house to join them, and had just missed another. As sunset approached, all Rell wanted was a hot bath, a dry bed, good food, and not another word or question about the traveling couriers.

And now the innkeeper politely told them he only had one room left. He cheerily announced there were two beds in it, but if it wasn't satisfactory, they would have to go back a decon to another inn. There was nothing ahead of them except Juisiti and three more decons of travel. She looked at Nari and she could see his exhaustion.

But when he caught her looking at him, he stiffened and archly replied, "It's not acceptable. Have our horses resaddled."

"Nari, stop, just stop. We are tired, our horses are tired. There are two beds. It is just like the military all over again. You are not so old you have forgotten those days." She turned back to the clerk, "We'll take it."

The innkeeper flicked his fingers at one of the children loitering in the reception area. A boy quickly came over and picked up their traveling bags. He led them across the common room and down the hall. Thank the Lost God for small graces, thought Rell, it was on the ground floor. She stepped back and let Nari walk in the room first.

"Have food and drink sent here, I do not want to go back out tonight." Nari told the boy. Then he looked at Rell, "you can do what you want."

She sighed. "The same for me, please." The boy barely nodded in acknowledgement; he was so excited to show the attached bathing room—"just like a West Islands inn!" Rell knew the boy heard her, but she wondered what would be on the platters when the food arrived.

Nari sat on one of the beds and twisted his canes about. He looked at the floor. Then he looked at the ceiling. Finally, he cleared his throat. "You may want to use the bathing room first. My…efforts, my routines, take me a long time." He looked at the floor again. "Everything takes so long."

"You know I am a healer. I have seen worse injuries than yours, I have helped…"

"I don't need your pity," he bit out.

Rell snapped back, "No, you do not. But it appears you were a less than competent student at the academies. Nari Ulani, what is the difference between pity and compassion?"

He threw himself back on the bed. "I will not play your childish games."

"Then I will tell you. Pity is 'I see your pain and am relieved it is not mine.'" Rell paused and then went on, "Compassion says, 'I want to relieve your suffering and pain because I can.' I know you know the difference. I saw you all along the track. The family of the man who carved your canes. The family who is barely scraping by and whose bills you would pay. Even the concept of the mail couriers themselves will significantly decrease the cost and the inconvenience for each family on the track. As much as you try to hide it and pretend otherwise, Nari Ulani, you are a compassionate man.

"Now I am going to take a bath. When the food comes, I will join you in your meal, and I will tell you a story that you will listen to. Then you can tell me all manner of things, and I will go to sleep knowing I have said what I wanted to say for the last eight days." She grabbed her smallest traveling bag and stalked into the bathing room.

***

Rell hurriedly stepped out of the tub and let it drain when she heard the food arrive. She dressed quickly in clean clothes and left her hair unbound to dry. Nari had older sisters; he wouldn't fall over from shock from seeing unbraided hair. She stepped out of the bathing room just as the boy closed the door to the hall behind him. At the table, Nari was seated at one of two heaping platters of food.

"Are you joking with me? This is all just for the two of us?" Rell asked in astonishment.

Nari sighed. "Yes, along with the words, 'Thank you for your sacrifice.'" He cast Rell a long look. "If they only knew that sacrifice was not freely given, and I will wish it back for the rest of my life." He shrugged. "There. You can't think any less of me, now."

Rell stilled. She had wanted to get to the root of why Nari was so difficult to her and her alone, but right now she was so hungry. Food first, she decided. Maybe then, she would know how to say what needed to be said.

Before she was finished eating, Nari left her to take his own bath. She wondered how he would manage the tub. Then she remembered how he had used his arms to balance himself as he mounted and dismounted his horse several times a day. She couldn't imagine the strength he had built up in his upper body.

She took the empty platters and set them out into the hallway on the small table, brushed out her hair, and changed into her favorite long shirt of Piffik's before crawling into bed. She blew out the lantern, thinking Nari would want the darkness to cover his movements. Almost immediately after, she saw the light in the bathroom go out as well and then the door opened. She heard the canes drop to the floor once Nari sat on his bed. There was a fumbling and then she heard the sounds of rubbing. She had been in enough military dormitories to associate that sound with action, but in such close quarters, she couldn't imagine Nari…of course! He was probably rubbing painkilling ointment in his leg. Sheesh. She was such a fool.

Rell lay on the bed and stared into the dark. She felt she had one chance to get this right. But if she waited too long, Nari would be asleep and the moment would be lost. She smiled as she remembered Zren saying how it was always easier to talk in the dark.

"Nari, I would like to tell you a story," she began a little tentatively.

"Oh, for…" She heard him give an irritated sigh. "I am sorry my handsome face has confused you to the point you have mistaken me for a child waiting for a bedtime story. I didn't realize you were married to such an old man."

That did it. He could insult her, but not Piffik. "It was your actions and behavior actually, that convinced me you needed a bedtime fable and a lesson learned." She took a deep breath and began, "I am Arella Huena of Axefield, Vikland."

"I know exactly who you are. Your name and skill with the crossbow were name-dropped all through training. You are Rell Huena, her eyesight is so keen she can send a bolt through the center of a target across the weapons yard. Rell Huena, a warrior full of strength and endurance—she never faltered in battle or lost her braid to the enemy. The sole defender of Manumina, not just a Viklander waystation, but also the home of the intelligent creator behind a network of softfoots and helpers of nothing more than Kereki throwaways scraped together.

"The rest of us poor soldiers? We weren't good enough since we came home without our braids. My sister wasn't good enough, since she fell at a battle north of Huk. My friend and neighbor wasn't good enough since he died by his own hand, after carving my canes, because he could not live with his failures." Rell thought she heard his voice catch, but she wasn't sure. "*I* wasn't good enough since I came home with part of my leg missing and my braid gone.

"Now a system that has worked for generations based on social trust and the kindness of one neighbor to another is handed to you at the Empress's patronage. Because *you* are Arella Huena of Axefield, Vikland."

Rell was stunned. This was the root of his anger and animosity? This was why he could treat everyone else with the good manners and grace she noted in all those who bore the Ulani name, but not her. Because he thought she had not failed, had never failed.

"I see."

"No, you don't. You just look at all of us who came back with injuries and tsk-tsk that we didn't do better, that we are not better. That we will never be the defender of the defenseless again. We will never stand for justice because so many of us can no longer stand at all. You see the missing braids. Do you ever wonder, 'Did we truly lose them to the bounty and in battle, or were we cowards and thieves who were caught and punished by having our braids of honor cut to show our disgrace?'"

Rell inhaled sharply. "I have never wondered. Not on any soldier, any softfoot, anyone I have ever met who has traveled beyond Vikland's borders."

Nari huffed and then fell silent.

Rell waited. She wondered how to rip off Nari's misconceptions and still keep her heart intact. She wasn't sure she would survive if she told of her monsters, and he didn't believe her. Or worse, laughed at her.

She thought back to her days living with Zren and how he would casually mention some horrific aspect of his daily life in Kerek City. It would be so far from her reality she would have to bite her tongue to keep from calling him a liar. She remembered when she would experience some appalling behavior from Zren, and realized he had no idea he was rude or selfish or casually cruel, because no one had taught him differently. His unique ability to repeat stories nearly word for word, while he was still counting on his fingers for any number greater than five. Her initial confusion over his delight in stories, mere stories, and the time he would spend puzzling over them, pulling out insights, and sharing them with anyone who would listen to him.

But Siba and Piffik and Chul and Rygee all had told her how to help Zren grow into the man he was meant to be. He could learn anything, they assured her, but he had to be taught everything. Everything that all of them had learned by instinct, just by living in a family.

Zren was desperate for approval and acceptance, they said, but he did not know enough to ask what he needed to know. His entire life until Manumina had been survival. He did not learn by observation, Chul said, because he didn't understand what he was seeing in front of him. But pouring words into him was like filling an empty jug with water.

Rell learned she could tell her own stories of her brothers for Zren to learn the lesson without humiliating him. Praising him for taking his dirty pottery from the table to the sink meant the next time, the table had been cleared. The others had been right. He could learn anything that would give him security and a sense of family and a home.

But Nari Ulani was not Zren Janin, and she had no idea how to reach him.

"Well, you said you wanted to tell me something that you have kept back for eight days. I cannot tell you all manner of things in return if I am fast asleep because you did not tell your story before the moon was halfway across the sky." Nari sounded exasperated.

"Nari, did your cousin Solkka ever tell you *why* I did not return to Vikland? Why I was at Manumina in the first place?"

There was a long pause. "I thought you were there as an assignment from the Diplo. I had heard they were a settlement, a walled settlement that had thrown in with us. When war was declared, the Conrosans and Kerekis who lived there needed a Viklander defense. They did not know how to fight. That you used their children and their people as your softfoots and helpers to save a lot of Viklanders. Everyone was told that if we were lost or separated from our units to try to reach the encampment north of Balza, the fort at Earles, or the walled city of Manumina. We were told any child, any person, who said they were a friend of Zren Janin was a friend of Vikland." He paused again. "But Solkka said nothing."

Rell smiled in the dark. "I truly like your version better. If this is the story that is told about me, I would not be ashamed to walk the halls of the palace again."

She huffed. "But it's not. I'm glad Solkka kept my failures to himself, but I want you to know them."

She could hear a small smile in Nari's voice. "My cousin doesn't say much about his work in the Diplo. Nadja and I think he may be other than just a pretty face at the negotiating table. It is nothing any of our friends in Juisiti have said, but more of what they do not say. We keep our thoughts to ourselves, however. His mother has enough to worry about with Tedros."

"Then I will say nothing more about Solkka." She paused and then continued, "I was with Miyamoto Suki's thirteenth crossing.

We had four crates of West Islands weapons and Chul Swyler, who had brought his inventions to the Kerek City riots. One of his pots of chemicals had exploded near him, and he had been burned badly. We also had the paychest for the garrison at Earles and four Kereki soldiers who had been sent along to guard it." She added drily, "This was after Vikland had already taken over Earles."

Nari chuffed in the darkness.

"We also had Zren Janin. He was this small, skinny boy, a Conrosan, no taller than me. Miya told me he had saved Ngahuru's life as she fled Kerek City, and Zren was along to help us protect the cargo. I laughed in his face, Nari. The stories we heard of Ngahuru? I didn't know what she was thinking to push him on us, but Miya didn't seem concerned.

"The very first night we camped, Zren asked to borrow my red cloak for his watch. I woke up to a scuffle, and my first thought was we had been struck by bandits. Chul said, 'Stand down, the fight is over. Zren won.' When we had light, there was Zren in my cloak, and the Kereki army captain dead at his feet with a dagger-sized rip in his belly and slashes across his face and throat. Zren, that skinny little boy half the size of the army captain, had killed him."

"But I thought Conrosans were pacifists." Rell heard the confusion in Nari's voice.

"I had never met Zren before that day, but Kern told me Zren Janin had been raised in Kerek City and had no knowledge of who he was. She had softfooted with him and said he seemed bright enough but was very naïve about the larger world about him." She laughed softly in the dark. "He had a face which could not lie. Truly, Nari, you had to see it. False words would be falling from his lips, but his face would go through these strangest contortions..."

"After the death of their captain, the Kereki soldiers avoided him. It was a rough trip. We rode armed at all times and kept full watches at night. I saw traders or bandits on the hills watching us pass. We saw the aftermath of a massacre of Kereki families."

She sighed. "I just wanted the trip to be over. At least, Miya talked the Kerekis into deserting so they would not report to Earles. It would have been hard to have their deaths on our hands as well.

"Then when I thought we were still two days before the Vikland border, we crossed a small bridge with high stone sides. There were children underneath hiding in the shallows. I don't know how they remained so still none of us saw or heard them. But we had been arguing about where to camp for the night, and none of us were as aware of our surroundings as we should have been. Our outriders were trapped between the two wagons at each end of the bridge.

"The children swarmed us. Then maybe ten archers stepped out from the trees. They had bad bows and poorly fletched arrows.

Miya and Rygee tried to keep the children away, so Kern and I could hold our horses steady to fire at the archers. Chul mixed his chemical pots, and Zren made something he called 'riatas' and threw them at the archers and the children to explode in their midst." She inhaled sharply. "There were so many children…

"Song Yao died. So did two of the Kereki soldiers. Chul and I were too damaged to return to Juisiti with Miya and Kern. Neither of us could walk. Chul couldn't use his hands. We lived in the infirmary at Manumina for the entire Wet." Rell tried to keep the emotion out of her voice. "My mind broke." She said nothing for a long time. Neither did Nari.

"My mind broke, and I lived the battle over and over trying to find a way that Song would live. That we could win without killing children. That we could reach the Vikland border without crossing the bridge at all." Her voice caught, but she pushed on, "And in the end, nothing changed. I still fired on children, and Song Yao still died."

Rell listened for Nari. She knew he wasn't asleep, but he was as quiet as a softfoot. She continued, "Later, when I was well enough to leave the infirmary, I moved into a house with Rygee and Zren. Me, living in the same house as a Kereki soldier. A deserter. A man we as Viklanders have been taught to sneer at. During the war, he acted as the face of Manumina with the Justices and the settlements, so Piffik and the others could help the Viklanders without too much curiosity from others. Rygee Namikk was a traitor to Kerek. He was everything I was taught to despise. And yet, I called him my friend.

"The house we lived in had stairs. Piffik and Zren built bars along the wall so I could pull myself up. I practiced on those stairs every day until I could walk without a limp. People at Manumina watched me as I worked to regain my crossbow skills. They were a community of pacifists, and they would watch me, not in judgement and condemnation because I was not like them, but in acknowledgement for who I was, a Viklander bowmaster, healing in their midst.

"There were others, Nari. Siba Namikk was a healer, and until the Wrens came, she had never traveled more than a half day from Manumina. Piffik had dropped out of their school to take over his father's business. Yet Chul Swyler and Piffik became great friends, and talked about everything because Piffik had such a curiosity about the world, he continued to read and study. Zren was so illiterate he didn't know how to count without using his fingers and thought coins had value based on their size. Siba taught Zren how to read and write in Conrosan. It was like he had a lifetime of words bottled up inside him. While I was healing, he would come to the infirmary and tell me what he had learned that day and what he had done as a manabout. He was so pleased to master any task they taught him; nothing was beneath him.

"It was almost a year later when Bima Ritwik and Solkka Ulani came to Manumina. It was clearly a scouting expedition. Solkka stood as Witness as Bima asked Chul and me to return to Vikland. Chul returned. I refused. Bima didn't cut my braid then, although I expected him to. Instead, he told me there was no shame in what happened at the bridge and when I was ready to return I should. I didn't know it then, but he and Solkka did not report me as a deserter, not then, not ever." She smiled in the dark. "I probably shouldn't have told you that.

"Then the war came. The Kereki army tried to burn out the Conrosans at Manumina. The army failed, the settlement stood, but they took all the animals outside the walls. After the Wet all but a handful of the Conrosans left for Vikland. The Empress gave them Rishka, one estate for so many. She could have been better to them. The ones that stayed behind planted the fields in preparation for when the others could return. No one thought the war would last long." Rell fell silent for a moment before continuing, "We were so wrong.

"And then one day an old Kereki woman and a settler wagon full of children came to Manumina. She called herself Tiju Tia and called the children, the Wrens. They were her information gatherers, softfoots, and thieves in Kerek City. In all the time I was there, Nari, I saw her as a Kereki boy and a very old Kereki woman with white hair. I never saw her as a West Islander, not once.

"Now of course we Viklanders know it was Ngahuru, in Kerek for revenge on the Kerek King for the murder of her ambassador. But Zren Janin hid her identity, if he knew it, and in return she built us a network of safe houses, guides, and transports to keep Vikland fighting long after we knew Matasi had betrayed us. She was not at Manumina when the Kerek King's son was murdered. I would not be surprised if she had driven the King from his throne, although I haven't been able to work out how.

"It was never me, Nari. I don't know how Zren and Ngahuru and the Wrens managed it, but somehow Bima Ritwik and the others didn't understand that Tiju Tia was Ngahuru. Any of the Wrens could have told the Viklander softfoots, but they kept her secrets. Rygee was the *titiro mai ki ahau* for the Kerekis, and I was used as the distraction to dangle in front of Viklanders. I have often wondered how many times Ngahuru wins because she plucks at our prejudices, and we Viklanders believe what we want to believe. Even now, with the Empress…"

Rell let the weariness roll over her. "I did not ask to be the one to manage the overland mail service. If you and the other landowners along the track want someone else, I will go to First Soldier Joon myself and ask him to intercede with the Empress to pick your choice instead. But I have younger brothers still in the academies and the military. I will not make my brothers' lives difficult by telling the Empress, 'No, thank you,' and have it said,

I thought I was too good to help Vikland. I will not have my brothers bear the mockery as they serve their years.

"I know Chul Swyler, Bima Ritwik, and Solkka Ulani knew I was a deserter, and I should have my braid cut in disgrace. I know what had happened to me at Manumina. I know the cost of surviving when others did not."

She cleared her throat. "I fight my monsters every day, Nari Ulani, just as you do. You drive yourself harder and demand so much of yourself to prove you are worthy. But the rest of us? We all know that already. The only person you have left to convince is you."

Rell fell silent again. She didn't care if Nari answered her or not. She had said what she wanted to say. He didn't laugh at her at least. Even if Nari took what she said to heart, he wouldn't change overnight. She knew that too, but as long as his heart listened to what his ears had heard, he could recover himself. She rolled over and turned her back to him.

She had just begun to drift off to sleep when she heard the barest whisper, "I hear your words."

Rell heard it and she smiled. She knew the path to forgiveness was such a very long journey, but she felt, for Nari Ulani, it had finally started.

A DAY TO LIVE OR DIE

Nelo had been gruff as he had walked Dica to her corner that morning.

"No more carelessness, Dica. You do not collect enough coin this morning, you do not eat tonight. It should not be the littlest ones who feed us each day."

"It's because the littlest ones are able to best play on the pity of others. You do it yourself, Nelo. If there is only enough bread for some of us, you give the food to the little ones and tell Jenny and I to work harder," Dica retorted.

He stopped in the path and twisted his face away. She could see the scar outlined by the light. "A fist had kissed his cheek," he had told her once. A fist with a piece of metal or a rock.

He turned back to her and scowled. "This is a city full of fools, Dica. You can either find a few to beg for coin, or pick their pockets, or sell yourself as a fancy. I don't care. You need to bring in coin or food. I'll be back to check on you." He turned and walked away before she could answer.

She watched him disappear into the crowd, his white-blond hair bright against the grey clothes and sour faces of those forced to live and work in Lowertown.

"So," she had muttered under her breath. She pressed herself up against the wall as two men looked her up and down. They said nothing and walked by. Dica sighed in relief. She knew Nelo had not been serious about selling herself as a fancy, but she also knew she was too old to beg for help as a Lost Girl. He had tried to teach her to pick pockets, but she thought she wasn't good enough. She was terrified of losing her hand as punishment if she was caught.

It was all so different now. So much harder.

She remembered the days when Nelo had first placed her in the Sinner's District and told her to cry until strangers would give her food or coin. There had been more to eat then. He had given her one of the better markets and prettier dresses—just as he did for the littlest ones now. Sometimes strangers had given her small pieces of paper or strange objects with a small coin and hiss, "For Ngahuru" before hurrying down the street. Sometimes other street children or messengers would whisper their information instead.

One time, when she had been careless about remembering all the words she was to tell him, Nelo had gotten angry. "Think of every message you collect for Ngahuru as one day having enough to eat. Don't be stupid, Dica. I know you can remember this." He didn't strike her though. That was something she remembered.

Dica couldn't read. When she asked Nelo what the messages meant, he had told her not to ask any questions. He reminded her that those who survived best in Lowertown avoided a dance with Trouble. Dica understood that to mean the messages she was receiving meant someone's life was no longer safe.

Then Nelo brought Will to her one day. The boy looked like he was on the edge of childhood but had an old face. His skin was greyish white and his Keresh didn't sound like hers. Nelo said it was because the boy spoke castle Keresh and spent his time on Embasado street where the rich people worked. He boasted that he was a messenger boy for the softfoot Ngahuru. Dica had laughed at him and said street children who saw too much and talked about it didn't live very long. She scolded him to keep his secrets close or soon he would never be able to talk again. The boy had dropped his eyes and fallen silent as he absently picked at the black glove on his hand. Oddly enough, he looked like he was smiling.

Will never held a grudge. When Nelo said to give the whispered information or the written messages to Will if the boy found her before she left her corner for the day, Dica had assumed that also meant Will would take some of her coins and food as well. But the boy had only shook his head and said to eat it herself or save the coins to buy food for the others.

Once, Will asked if she trusted Nelo.

Dica had looked at him a long time. "Nelo keeps us alive to beg for him. He does not hurt us. He does not sell us to strangers. Where do you live that a street child could be safe without a Protector?"

Will hadn't responded, only asked for any messages, gave her a small coin and left. Dica had spent a long time that day wondering where he had come from. But there were too many children drifting about the streets ready to take away her coin or corner and force her to sleep hungry to waste her thoughts on the stranger.

That had been so many seasons ago. The coin from the West Islander Ngahuru had disappeared the day Will had, and the past two years had been difficult. Nelo snapped at them to collect more coin and bread, but then he would use it to buy another child from the Orphan Master. Dica wondered what demon rode on his shoulder to try to save more little ones when he could barely feed the ones who nested with them in the warehouse.

But that was a problem for another day. Dica saw a Matasi wagon move slowly down the street. She straightened in anticipation. The missionaries never gave the street children coin, but if she was willing to listen to a story or two, they would give her something to eat. As they came abreast, she dropped her jaw in amazement. Will, the Kereki boy, was sitting in the wagon. The friend of Ngahuru, and he was sitting here in front of her. She thought Ngahuru had left Kerek City years ago, when the ambassador had been murdered in the streets.

The wagon halted in front of her.

"Dica?" The boy asked. "Do you remember me? It's Will. Can you take a ride with me?"

She scrambled into the back of the wagon and the horses pulled forward into the stream of people. Will promptly gave her some fruit and bread and fresh water.

Over the next decon, Will explained that Ngahuru was back in Kerek City but only for the day. She had an offer of freedom for any of her children that had helped her in the past. If they could meet her in front of the Vikland embasado the next day, she would take them away from the past they had known. She would be leaving the city at midday so they could not be late.

"She needs your help, Dica. She needs you to tell the others—as many as you can find. Tell the Lost Girls. Tell those who bring you the information with food and coin. Find the girl and the pretty boy from the Red Cup. Find the girl who sells flowers in Dockside under the protection of the Harbormaster. Look for a black dog and a thief who is always close by. Find the soldier who sells the schedule for the King, and the red-headed guard who follows the King's sons about when they gamble in the Sinner's District. Find the tailor at the Peacock Shop who calls herself Callis. Find the two brothers who cut away pockets and papers outside of the courts. See if you can find the boy from the ship's office and the girl named Linna who works in the import shop in the Flower District."

"Will," Dica interrupted. "They are gone. So many of them are gone."

Will fell silent. "How many?"

Dica shrugged. "I don't know. It has been so long since we have had any coin from the softfoots. I think…most of them? I don't know," she repeated.

Will glanced at the backs of the Matasi missionaries. He dropped his voice to a whisper, "Do you need coin?"

Dica nodded quickly and held out her hand.

Will opened his pocket and pulled a handful of small coins. "It's not a lot, but share them among the others. Find as many as you can, and tell them to spread the news to those that gathered information." Will grimaced. "I'll take everyone that you find, Dica.

"Ngahuru will be driving the cart as an old Kereki woman. Do you understand what I am saying? She'll have food. Wherever she takes all of you will be safer than the lives you are leading now. Say that to the others if they hesitate. Tell them to bring what they own. They will not return to Kerek City." Will grabbed Dica's forearm, and Dica looked at the hand so much lighter than her own skin. "I am trusting you. I will see you and all of the others tomorrow."

Dica looked into Will's face. It had been so long since she had seen Ngahuru and her Matasi guard, how would she know that Will was telling the truth?

"What do you gain by lying to me?" Dica questioned aloud.

"Nothing," Will replied quickly. "This is too important to question my words. I am telling you the truth by all the stars in the West Islands Constellations. Tell everyone you can find who has given you information in the past. I need all of you."

Dica nodded uncertainly. She would find Jenny and tell her what had happened. Together they could decide what to do.

***

Jenny was handing out food to the little ones when Tyra and Dica climbed up the ladder to their hiding place. Tyra started talking immediately while Dica carefully replaced the boxes and crates to hide their entrance. She slid off her boots and walked across the blankets and fabrics Nelo had spread about the floor to deaden their footsteps from the rooms below.

There had been older girls once. Jenny would tell the littlest ones stories of Aisha and Tae and Precious. Those girls had looked after them just as Jenny and Dica looked after the little ones now. But one by one they had disappeared because Nelo could not keep them all safe, not all of the time. He was only one person and not even a man full grown. Those were not the stories Jenny told the little ones.

As Tyra and Dica told Jenny of Will's visit and a promise to escape Kerek City, Jenny searched their faces for signs of disbelief. "You believed him, Dica? You believe Ngahuru can take us away from Kerek City?"

"I don't know. It was Will, I was sure of it. We haven't seen him in years, Jenny, not since the Ambassador's murder. And now he shows himself and tells us to meet Ngahuru in front of the Vikland embasado tomorrow and we can leave the city."

Jenny considered. "Why the Vikland embasado? What about the war?"

"I've thought about that. The Conrosa and West Islands embasados are deserted, and the wagon would be noted by those looking out the windows of the King's castle. The Matasi embasado still has soldiers and guards and the wagon would attract attention there as well. The deserted Vikland embasado is on the corner of a busy street. No soldiers to look us over but enough people and carts and animals on the cross street to cover the actions of children climbing into a wagon."

Jenny flicked her eyes to the little ones watching the girls talk.

"They're too young," she said succinctly.

Dica considered. "With the three of us gone, Nelo would have an easier time taking care of them. You've heard him, Jenny. You and I barely bring in enough to feed ourselves. It's the littlest ones whose tears bring coin and pity. I don't think he will care but even so, I do not plan on telling him."

Tyra's face turned stubborn. "I am going to tell him. I think Nelo can decide what to do about the little ones. I think he should know that we are gone and not taken against our will."

Dica rolled her eyes. "That's because he still likes you." She stared at Jenny. "You can do what you will, but I will be in that wagon tomorrow."

"I do not disagree, Dica, but we have to let the others know. Say again the people Will wants us to find. We can leave the little ones here to rest while we are searching about. When we return, we can tell Nelo together. I do not think he will fight us on this. But he kept us alive and without harm. The least we can do is tell him what we are doing."

"Fine." Dica told the others the list of people again. Jenny said she would go to the Red Cup. Dica knew of the Peacock Shop and would ask for the tailor called Callis. They decided it was too risky to go into Dockside for the others. Dica offered to go to the courts district and look for the cutpurses, but truthfully, none of the girls knew the other people on the list. Tyra said she would stay and wait for Nelo and see if he knew anyone else that they should warn. He had talked with Ngahuru and her Matasi guard in the past. He would know more than they would.

***

As the brass bell announced the young girl's arrival, Callis and the other tailors merely looked up and back down to their sewing. By her clothes and manner, she was nobody of importance. The girl waited by the door while the tailors mumbled at each other who would be forced to wait on her. At last, one of the newest apprentices walked to the counter.

"Whose house do you serve?"

The girl looked confused. "What do you mean?"

The apprentice smirked. "It's clear you cannot afford any of our talents. Who is your mistress? You can pay for her order and take it with you before anyone else sees you here."

Callis watched as the girl blinked rapidly at the insult. But then she had straightened and merely replied, "I am looking for Callis the tailor."

The apprentice turned slowly from the counter to the room of women and girls bending over their needlework.

"She is looking for Callis the tailor," she announced loudly. "Obviously, her trunks and all her belongings were stolen as they left the ship. May I recommend, Callis," the apprentice looked smug, "you get all her coin in advance."

Callis set down her sewing, stood up, and stretched. She didn't know the girl, although by her appearance, Callis assumed she was not from any of the Districts.

"What do you want?"

"Will sent me to find you. He had a message from Ngahuru," Dica began.

Callis approached the counter quickly. "Shush," she whispered as she pushed a paper and graphite toward the girl. "Write down your message."

Dica shook her head. "I don't know how to write."

Callis huffed and turned back to the others. "I'll take her outside so our customers in the dressing rooms will not see her. I will return soon."

Outside, Callis crossed her arms and waited. "What's your name? How do you know Ngahuru?"

"I am Dica. I don't know Ngahuru, not truly. We take messages and papers from people and give them to our Protector. He meets with Ngahuru or her Matasi guard and exchanges them for coin and food for us. Sometimes, there is a boy named Will who comes to find us. He will ask about the people who give us the papers. He is a message runner. He wears a black glove on his hand to keep the papers clean. He knows Ngahuru and can go to the West Islands embasado." Dica shrugged. "Or so he says."

"And what else does he say, this friend of Ngahuru?"

"He found me earlier today and said Ngahuru is back in Kerek City for only one day. That if anyone who has helped Ngahuru in the past would like a way to escape Kerek City to meet her on the street in front of the Vikland embasado tomorrow. She will be there at midday. If we are late, we are forgotten, Will says. She will not delay because someone cannot find their way there."

"Why are you telling me?"

"You are only one of two girls Will told me by name. These are the people he asked me to find." She recited, "Tell the Lost Girls. Tell those who bring you the information with food and coin. Find the girl and the pretty boy from the Red Cup. Find the girl who sells flowers in Dockside under the protection of the Harbormaster. Find the soldier who sells the schedule for the King and the one who follows the King's sons about when they gamble in the Sinner's District. Find the tailor at the Peacock Shop who calls herself Callis. Find the two brothers who cut away pockets and papers outside of the courts. See if you can find the boy from the ship's office and the girl named Linna who works in the import shop in the Flower District." Dica stopped to catch her breath. "Do you know any of these people?" She hesitated. "Jenny and I know next to none of them, and we do not dare go into Dockside to warn the ones we do know."

Callis looked away down the street. "Dica, my father doesn't know I have shared secrets with Ngahuru, and it will hurt him deeply to learn this. If I am on the wagon tomorrow at midday, it is because my father has asked me to leave his house and not return."

Dica considered. "Can you help us find these people even if you yourself are not on the wagon? Will said there is no second chance. We are on the wagon tomorrow at midday or we stay in Kerek City. Ngahuru will not come again to help us."

Callis blew out a hard breath. "I will look for the girl in the import shop in the Flower District. I won't go into Dockside—and you shouldn't either. I don't know the thieves and soldiers Will is talking about. I do not know if I will be on the wagon tomorrow. But I will be there before midday if my father's home is no longer mine."

Dica nodded. "If each of us can find one person, we may be able to tell most of them. Perhaps the soldiers can tell the Harbormaster's spies. They could enter Dockside with less harm than you or I could."

The bell clanged as the door opened behind them. "Have you forgotten you are working today, Callis? Or has this beautiful day convinced you that you are a woman born so wealthy you can idle away your time and ignore your responsibilities?"

Callis pasted on a smile before turning to the voice. "I was just saying goodbye to this one after convincing her that her talents are best served elsewhere. You would never take on an apprentice who does not bring coin and patronage to come."

She turned back only to see the girl running down the street and disappearing in the crowd.

***

Nelo lay on the blankets and stared at the ceiling. Tyra had just finished telling him all of Dica's story. He knew some of the people to be found. The soldiers Ngahuru wanted had been caught out as traitors and hung a season ago. The two brothers had disappeared—although the word on the street was that both of them had lost a hand for thieving first. He knew the ones working in Dockside and absently touched his scar. He had no plans to cross into their territory. If he could find others without mishap, he was fine with telling them, but he wouldn't return to Dockside.

Jenny wanted him to go with her to the Red Cup. She said she knew the ones Will had asked for. Nelo did too. He even knew their names, Falan and Josef. But the Red Cup was not for the likes of him and Jenny. He wondered how they would get close enough to give them Will's message. He didn't want Jenny dressing like one of the girls who worked there, he didn't have confidence in his knife skills that he could keep her safe enough. But if she went as a Lost Girl, they would be chased away. The owner of the Red Cup didn't like the customers to be reminded of those who didn't have enough to live on. It dampened the enthusiasm for the games with higher stakes, Nelo had been told. He also had been told that if any of his pickpockets or Lost Girls appeared again, his entire nest would be burned to the ground. Nelo believed him.

He decided Jenny would dress as a wealthy daughter looking for her wayward brother, hoping to get him home before their parents found out he had gambled away his coin. It would allow her to enter and possibly talk with Falan or Josef, and let her leave without harm. He would walk her to the door of the place and linger in the shadows. It was the best they could do.

He wondered if the boy who had helped him off the streets in Dockside all those years ago was still alive. What if Nelo could convince him to leave Kerek City? Information gatherers didn't have a long life—even if they were under the Harbormaster's protection. He wondered if he could find the street in the Sinner's District again, the alley so narrow they had to walk sideways, the door with the four West Islands locks barely waist high. If Jenny could find Falan and Josef quickly, he decided he would risk a decon and look for the boy who had saved his life six years earlier.

***

Josef heard the key in the lock and quickly sat up in bed. Falan's father walked in with a dress, underskirts, and some feathery thing over his arm. He barely looked at him as he threw the clothes on the bed. "Here's your costume for tonight. Word on the street is tonight we may have some royal guests pretending to be like the rest of us. Falan will be bringing a tub. Take a bath." He walked to the door and then turned back. "Be good, Josef. Be very good. Dance, sing, sit on the prince's lap. Just make sure he leaves more coin here than he takes home with him. You know what will happen if you fail." He pulled the door closed behind him.

Josef sighed. The owner of the Red Cup had threatened to sell him for a fancy for years now. If he wasn't funny enough with his jokes and japes, he would be sold to soldiers; if he wasn't pretty enough in those silly dresses, he would be sold to sailors; if he wasn't quick enough with signaling what cards were in the gamblers' hands, he would be sold to anybody with enough coin. Josef knew all those were possibilities, but the dagger had been at his neck for so long, sometimes he just wanted to throw himself on the blade and have it all be over.

Falan came in carrying the empty tub, her work dress already damp from heating the water.

"Papa tell you? Some soldiers wearing the king's insignia were down here earlier sniffing about. They asked about defenses and when was the last time Papa had a dance with Trouble. It seems the two Princes want to pretend they are brave enough to gamble in the Sinner's District. Papa wants to give them a show so they return. He's hired more men to follow the guards and Princes and take them safely home. You need to make sure their friends lose enough coin to pay for the extra help. Papa will make sure they do not lose so much they do not come again."

She scowled at him. "Are you just going to lay there like a princess in her bed? You need the bath, you can help me carry up the water."

***

Callis had said nothing to her father when he came to walk her home from the tailoring shop. They had eaten the evening meal quietly, talking of this and that and her mother's plans for the next day. Callis asked if her father had a man available to walk her to the Flower District to do some shopping for one of the dresses she was sewing. Her father grumbled, as she knew he would, that the tailor who owned the shop should hire the Kereki male protectors to allow the women to walk about the streets. Callis smiled, as she always did, and agreed. The grumbling was as familiar as the many evenings she spent on her tailoring errands.

Her father said he would send the boy, Beck, as soon as he got back to the tavern.

While she was waiting, Callis dressed with care. She didn't know the person in the Flower District who had given information to Ngahuru, but she thought she could guess what she would be like. Almost wealthy, but about her age and unhappy with the small lives women were forced to live in Kerek City. She doubted very much the woman would leave her comfortable life and her fine home. It was one thing to feel the frisson of excitement when passing notes and papers to a softfoot. It was quite another thing to say goodbye to a life of comfort just to test the waters of freedom.

But the Lost Girl had come to the tailor shop to find her and that had been no small thing. So now she would travel to the import shop to find this girl called Linna. Will's message had called both of them out by name. This was important enough to Ngahuru that Callis would at least try.

After a decon of wandering in and out of shops in the Flower District, Callis was not so sure of her strategy. She would wander about in the building until the Patron or someone else would ask if she needed anything in particular. She would ask for Linna. She would receive a blank look. She would excuse herself with a silly laugh saying she must have gotten the place mixed up and leave. It wasn't getting her anywhere, and there were far too many shops to test. What if Linna wasn't a shop girl? What if she was so wealthy that she would never need to work in her family's business at all? What if, since Ngahuru's information was years old, the girl had married and moved away?

"Are you finished yet?" The boy her father had sent with her was impatient.

"Why, Beck, are you so eager to get back to washing pottery and cleaning up spills?"

He scowled as only a twelve-year-old could, and Callis laughed. "I'm on a search, Beck. I am trying to find a woman and not a bit of lace. But I don't know where to look except that her family owns an import business in the Flower District. There are too many shops and I have barely begun."

"Did you ask the aunties?" He puffed up. "My mother says if you ever want to find out what a marriageable girl is up to, ask any auntie in the neighborhood."

"How do you know I am looking for a marriageable girl? Perhaps I am looking for a grandmother to box you about the ears when my father isn't around," she teased.

He shrugged and looked away. "I think you should ask the aunties," he mumbled.

Callis looked around carefully. This street didn't have any of the open-air shops where people could buy a bit of food, a cold drink, or lean on a counter and talk about the weather or their neighbors. The boy had a good idea, she just wasn't sure she should be so free with the girl's name—especially if she wasn't the type to crawl into a wagon and leave for the outlands.

"I have an idea, Beck. Could *you* ask the aunties? Tell them you are looking for your sister who went to visit her friend Linna. You have been sent to bring her home, but now you can't find the street and the shop or the house where she lives. Your father will be quite angry if you return again to ask for the directions since he said he thought you weren't paying attention."

Beck was indignant. "You make me sound like a careless boy! I would never forget a task your father set before me."

Callis tried to soothe him. "And that is why you are always the first one my father chooses to accompany his three daughters when we must venture out of our home."

Beck wasn't mollified so easily. "This will cost you a dias. My name is to be injured."

Callis reluctantly agreed. "If we find the girl named Linna whose family owns an import shop, then I will give you a dias. But I must speak to her for you to be paid so much."

Beck nodded. "Wait in that bookshop. I will return quickly." He dashed off before she could say anything. Callis sighed and walked into the bookshop. She was already regretting her bargain—a dias was an entire day's wages for her.

***

Jenny and Nelo walked confidently to the Red Cup. They had spent the better part of a decon constructing a dress and shawl that would look wealthy enough Jenny would be allowed in the gambling den yet not so wealthy, she and Nelo would be robbed on the way there or back. They walked around to the back where Nelo was going to find a safe place to wait. They were still discussing their plans when the back door opened and Falan dumped out a pail of water on the bricks.

"Falan," Nelo hissed.

She froze, and then her face contorted into a scowl. "Who are you to waste my time?"

"A friend of Will and Ngahuru. I have a message." Nelo pulled Jenny along with him.

Falan barked out a sharp laugh. "I am not a fool. Ngahuru has been gone for years."

Jenny stepped forward just as Falan stepped behind the door as if to close it.

"Wait, Falan, take a look at me. It's Jenny. I am one of the Lost Girls you would whisper your secrets to when you couldn't find Ngahuru. It's true. Will found one of the other Lost Girls today—you may know her too—and told us that Ngahuru was only in Kerek City for one day. Anyone who wants to leave Kerek City need only bring what they can carry and climb in the wagon with the others. Will specifically asked for you Falan. You and Josef. Ngahuru knew you needed to leave here. She asked for you, Falan. That must mean something."

"Yes. Obviously, it means she needs someone else to do her poking and prying for her. Has she run out of Lost Girls then?"

In spite of her words, Falan stepped out into the afternoon sun and let the door close behind her.

"No, three of us are going tomorrow. We have five that are too young. Nelo doesn't know what he is going to do about them yet. But we all know the future ahead of us in Kerek City does not include our best days."

"Did you forget there is a war? I cannot imagine your life would be better in the country where soldiers roam the roads and woods looking for tender little girls like you."

Jenny huffed. "You cannot frighten me, Falan. I know what my life is like here. I do not know what it will be like in the outlands. But truly, how much worse can it be?"

She tipped her head to the side. "Perhaps you should ask Josef if he would prefer to live in your father's house or take his chances in the outlands."

Falan scowled but said nothing.

Nelo cleared his throat. "That pretty toy is no longer a little child, Falan. I'm sure it was fun to put paint and frills on a young boy and watch him sing and say his clever bits. But then what comes next? You will someday own the Red Cup, you and your brother perhaps. Is this who you are? Are you going to bid when little children like him are on the auction block?

"Maybe you want to stay behind. No one would think lesser of you. But what about Josef? You need to tell him of Ngahuru's offer. Let him make his own decision. Tomorrow at midday in Embasado street. Tell him to look for the Lost Girls who passed his messages to Ngahuru. That's all I am asking, Falan, tell him this and let him make a decision for himself."

Falan stood still on the stone steps. Jenny and Nelo waited in front of her. No one spoke.

"I'll tell him tomorrow morning. His performance tonight has too much coin riding on it. If he is willing to give up a day's sleep to meet all of you in the Embasado street for old times' sake, that is his choice. I won't have to take care of him anymore." She jerked open the door and disappeared inside.

"Do you think she'll tell him?"

"I do, Jenny, I do." Nelo looked back at the Red Cup and then took Jenny's arm to lead her away. "What's more, I think he'll be on the wagon with you."

***

Beck was grinning as he nearly ran into the bookshop.

"Found her!" he called out. Callis quickly replaced the book to follow him out into the street.

"Are you sure this is the right one, the right Linna?"

Beck shrugged. "You can ask her. But the aunties all tsk-tsked when I asked for her. They were certainly willing to tell her story. Her papa lost a ship's goods to pirates. The Harbormaster and Tax Collector thought the captain had landed the cargo near the Salt Cliffs and the caves of the smugglers to avoid the taxes of Kerek City. So the Tax Collector still charged him for the lost cargo because the ship sailed into the harbor without any damage.

"The aunties said, everyone thought the man was ruined. But his Patron stepped forward and said he would pay the taxes and fees and secure the business until her papa could get another cargo in." Beck looked at her round-eyed. "Guess what the Patron claimed as collateral?"

Callis shook her head. "A year's receipts? A ship? The business?"

"He demanded Linna."

Callis thought her stomach would turn inside out.

"The aunties said, the parents protested she was too young. The Patron said he would wait. Now the papa has had more ships and more cargo come in and has offered to pay the man nearly double what was owed, but the man says they agreed on Linna, and she must come to his house on her next birthday." Beck shook his head. "Never did I think a man could do such a thing in Kerek." He looked up at Callis with new understanding in his eyes. "I think I am learning—a little—of what your life and your sisters' lives may be like."

Callis gave him a weak smile. "We are only protected by our fathers until someone bigger or stronger takes us away." She sighed. "Did the aunties tell you where she lives? Or are we too late already?"

"They did not know me, they said, and would not tell me where she lived. They gave me the location of her father's business and said I could deal with the man of the house." He paused. "I am not sure they believed that I had an older sister visiting Linna. Not because I was not convincing," he reassured her, "but because of what Linna's life must be like right now."

Callis put on a brave face. "Well, lead the way, Beck, I have a lady to rescue. You don't earn that dias until I actually talk to her, remember?"

***

Arden moved slowly over the rooftops. It was still too light for him to slither about, but most people didn't look up as they walked the streets. He had been sleeping when he heard his father come home and by the sounds of it, his father had brought Trouble with him.

Arden had carefully lowered Mother out the window and then quickly slipped his Sailor's Curse and daggers into his clothes before climbing out the window and reaching up to the roof. He peeked over the edge and waited until Mother spied him, and then silently moved away toward the next roof.

Mother was a scent hound and Arden's preferred method of travel was over the rooftops of Kerek City. It had been a problem until Arden had figured out that Mother could follow with only occasional glimpses, chirps, and whistles. She could wait long decons in doorways and alleys, only making a soft whine or a sharp bark when someone approached that she did not know. Once the dog and Arden had trained each other, his father and his younger brother no longer needed to go out with him on the night's thievery. Mother would wait in the shadows and alert him for a homeowner returning too soon.

Arden tried to figure out where he could go and hide for a few decons. His father never brought people to their house to conduct business, so he assumed it had to be another Spice Islander. Even so, his father had made it clear no one should ever see any of the family together. No one should ever have an opportunity to hurt or harm the Spice Islanders through their family.

And yet it hadn't kept them safe. Two years ago, when the Kerek King had thrown the country into war, his sister, Safiya, had been at the Vikland embasado selling information. Their father had walked her there and saw her pass through the gates. Although he had waited long past nightfall, she had never returned. She had disappeared "like sea smoke" his father had said.

Arden and his father, and even his younger brother Kezi, had broken into the deserted embasado more than once. But the empty building never gave up its secrets. Although Arden searched for days and even seasons, he had found no trace of her.

He would visit his brother and his mother, Arden decided. If he needed to, he and his dog could spend the night and return the next day. By then his father would have finished his business and perhaps there would be a new opportunity for coin.

It wasn't possible to travel to his mother's house by rooftop. And so, in a garbage infested alley, Arden dropped to the ground and made his way out to the street. He saw Mother down at the end huddled close to the building, paws covering her nose. She stood quickly when she caught sight of him and wagged her tail but made no attempt to approach him. He bent down and gave her a bite of food from his pocket. She turned and followed him down the street weaving in and out of the carts and people and animals toward the Sinner's District.

***

If Beck hadn't talked to the aunties, Callis would have taken one look at the business and the attached house and turned away, thinking Linna would never leave all this for a life in the outlands. She could tell by Beck's assessing gaze he was quite impressed as well. But now, knowing that even a beautiful home could be a prison, gave her a courage she didn't think she had possessed.

The man who answered the door was so cautious, so timid, Callis almost felt pity. But in her mind, she had already decided he had made a bargain with the Trickster. She was here to rescue the lady Linna.

"My name is Callis. I am here to speak with Linna. I know it is evening but I have a male protector with me," she stepped to the side so he could get a better look at Beck. "I thought she and I could take a walk together."

"I don't know you," the man said uncertainly.

"But I am not going to walk with you, I am walking with Linna." Callis bit back what she really wanted to say.

"It's fine, Papa. This is my friend from my school days. I wrote her and asked her to come visit this evening. I forgot to tell you and Mama when you came home today."

He looked from Callis and Linna and back again. Callis was sure he was going to call her out as a liar, but he merely nodded and asked her to step inside for their visit.

"Oh, do not worry, Papa. We will walk. I don't want our giggling to disturb you as you do your paperwork. And we have so much to talk about!" Linna took Callis's arm and squeezed it. She nearly pushed them both down the stairs and Beck had to scramble to keep up with them.

"Did Oro send you?" Linna asked quickly, once the door had closed behind them.

"Ah, no? A Lost Girl came to my tailoring shop and said Ngahuru is in Kerek City for one day. Anyone who wants to leave with her must be in the street of the Vikland embasado at midday tomorrow. The girl was very insistent that anyone who is not there timely will be left behind. The girl said her name was Dica. She said that you and I were called out by name by Ngahuru's messenger."

"Do you know her? Do you believe this girl?"

"I have never seen her before today. But I do believe her. I don't know what would bring Ngahuru back. I thought she had left after her ambassador had been murdered. But I started giving Ngahuru information I overheard from the wealthy that I tailored for because she gave me coin and gifts I would need to set up my own tailoring shop. She knew my plans were not to stay in Kerek City. I do not think she shared this information freely. So when Dica said that Ngahuru is here, and can take me away, and calls me by my name, then I believe this is truth and I should be on the wagon tomorrow."

Callis added gently, "Ngahuru may not know of your father's bargain, but she knew enough that she said your name too, Linna. The Lost Girls were to find you also and make sure you were on the wagon."

Linna rolled her eyes. "Does everyone in Kerek City know my father's shame?"

Callis remained silent. She wondered if Beck was listening to every word.

"How will you get there? To the Embasado street?" Linna asked.

Callis tipped her head back to Beck. "It will cost me another dias I am sure, but I have a male protector to walk me there." She paused. "Do you need someone to collect you?"

Linna's face broke into a smile. "No. You have given me enough time. If my plan works, there will be two of us on the wagon tomorrow."

***

Nelo hurried down the street. The Sinner's District wasn't in his territory, he seldom sent his Lost Girls beyond the Linen

Market, but there wasn't the sense of menace that Dockside seemed to breathe everywhere. He looked carefully down the alleys trying to remember which one the boy had dragged him down all of those years ago.

Now and again he had seen the boy, a spy for the Harbormaster, casually loitering on a corner near men talking of business. The boy dressed in clean, well-made clothes. He cut his hair close to his neck. Only those who knew how the Harbormaster gathered his information would recognize the boy as one of those hired to memorize long lists of numbers, recite entire conversations in any language, and hold so still he could be a part of the surroundings when coin and cargo was the topic of conversation.

Nelo had kept his promise. He had never tried to talk to the boy again, he had never tried to find his home again. But he felt the boy had saved his life six years ago and now he wanted to repay the debt. If Ngahuru kept her word, she could take them all to a place beyond Kerek City.

Of course, Nelo knew there was a war in greater Kerek. Everyone had heard how the Kerek King had mocked the Viklanders and told them to run like rabbits. There were even stories that Matasi was going to help the Viklanders because they too had been preyed upon by bandits and thieves on the roads to their home. But coin had soothed the Matasi Triune, and so they had sold the blood of the Viklanders for land for Matasians.

Nelo wanted to believe that there was a place where all of the children hiding in warehouses in Dockside and Lowertown and the Sinner's District would not have to run faster than their pursuers, or have a Protector take half their begged coin, instead of the bully down the street taking all of it. And that was why he was hurrying down alley after alley looking for a door with four West Islands locks.

There was not enough time.

Nelo slowed, realizing there were too many streets, and he had no idea which one could be the right one. He had been nearly out of his head that night from the pain from the beating. He remembered crossing from Dockside into the Sinner's District. He remembered the oil lights and candle lights of the taverns and gambling dens flickering, but he didn't remember a street or a landmark. He didn't remember anything more than the too thin shoulder underneath him as the boy had struggled to drag him out of danger.

He started walking back towards the Linen Market and his own nest. He still didn't know what he was going to do. He wanted to be on the wagon tomorrow at midday. But the truth was only the three oldest of his own Lost Girls would be able to make their way with Ngahuru. The youngest five were far too little to sleep rough and survive the outlands. More than toddlers, less than the clever girls he needed to keep them all safe. He wondered what would become of them if he had to care for them alone.

Nelo wasn't sure what had caught his eye. It could have been the dog—calm and well-mannered when most dogs from the dogfights had to be restrained with chains and thick collars. The boy beside the dog was lean, plain-faced, watchful. The two stood casually at the edge of a decrepit building. Doors and windows boarded up. Suddenly, the dog slipped behind him and vanished. The boy lingered a little longer and then walked away.

Nelo waited for the dog to return from between the buildings. When nothing happened, he walked to where the dog disappeared. He looked down an opening so narrow, he doubted he would fit. But the space dead-ended and there was no dog hiding in the shadows. He thought he saw an indentation in the wall.

Of course! He had grown taller and broader since the boy had helped him. The space would be narrower, the door locks would be even lower and less shiny then six years ago. He looked at the opening and wondered if he had found it.

Nelo turned sideways and started to creep forward through the narrow space. Walls on both sides touched him and he imagined leaving a smudge of his passing on the building. It would be a clever way to mark if someone had been there while they were out.

Before he reached the indentation in the wall, a dagger flew through the air and stuck in the ground just a hands' width in front of him. He froze.

"That's far enough. There is nothing there that would interest you. If you are hiding from the soldiers walking down the street, they have passed by. It is only because I thought you needed somewhere to hide, that my dagger did not part your hair for you. Thieves must stick together. Is that not so? Now if you would like to leave a token of appreciation, just drop it beside my dagger as you back your way out."

Nelo turned his head to the street but there was no one there. He looked up and saw nothing but sky.

"Who are you?" Nelo directed his question to the roof.

"I could ask you the same." A pause. "In fact I will. What are you doing here?"

"Not hiding from soldiers." Nelo wondered how much he should say to a stranger. "I was looking for someone. I thought I could find him again. I have news for him."

"This sounds promising. Is he a rich man? Should he die of Kereki metal poisoning and we split his purse?"

"No, he was just a boy six years ago. He saved my life and brought me to his home. I gave my word I would never try to find him again, but this is important. I have news to get him out of Kerek City."

There was a pause. "Does this boy have a name?"

Nelo shook his head. "I never knew it. The woman was a Spice Islander—an indigo dyer—she only called him 'the boy.' He broke her rule, she said, to save my life."

"And this is why you are standing beside a building that will topple on top of you if you turn the wrong way?"

"You are hiding on the roof, aren't you? You sent the dog to the door because it could not climb. But you are no longer slender enough to slide your way through and have to find another way." Nelo knew that wasn't true. The boy had been thinner than Nelo.

He heard a chuckle. "I have another dagger. I will not miss. Tell me why I should not drop this one as well."

"If you are this boy, if you know this boy, tell him Nelo, the man with the scar on his face, came to find him today with news of Ngahuru. I will leave this small space and stand across the street for half a decon. Send the boy out to me and I can tell him what he needs to know to be free of the Harbormaster forever."

"Kereki metal poisoning would free the boy from the grasp of the Harbormaster, is this what you are planning?"

Nelo grunted in frustration. "No! I had been beaten in Dockside and left on the street to die. He found me. He was just a boy, and he said he couldn't carry me. He was too small. He took me to his home, a woman kept me there overnight, she said it was too late to get me back to Lowertown. Are you this boy?"

There was a long pause. "No. Stand on your corner across the street. Give me one decon. If the boy appears, keep your hands out where they can be seen. I will be watching. If the boy does not appear, it is because your story is not true."

"The story is true."

There was no answer.

Nelo edged his way out into the street. He saw someone at a vegetable cart eyeing him, and he pretended to tighten the rope around his pants. He wiped his sweaty hands on his shirt and tried to casually cross the street. He looked about him and realized he was the only Kereki. Everyone about him was either a Spice Islander or from the West Islands. He wondered how he had not noticed this before.

He jumped when a voice behind him spoke, "Are you looking for me?"

Nelo spun about and saw a youth about fourteen years or so. He had the same lean look as the one with the dog. This one was much better dressed and wore his hair short. Nelo looked closely but wasn't sure if this was the same one who had rescued him. That boy had been so young.

"Do I look familiar to you? Six years is a long time."

"You do. I am sorry my mother could not sew your face. But I think it is the white hair which draws everyone's eye." He paused. "You said your name is Nelo. Do you still run Lost Girls and Lost Boys?"

Nelo nodded. "I still do not sell them. I remember that was the reason you said you stopped to help me."

"It was." The boy didn't say anything more.

"Look, one of my girls was found by Will, the friend of Ngahuru. The softfoot is back in Kerek City, he says, but only for one day. If anyone who helped Ngahuru would like to leave the city for another place to call home, they need to be in front of the Vikland embasado tomorrow at midday. There will be a wagon there. We are to bring only what we can carry, a travel cloak, a few clothes. She will have food for us. Dica says there are no second chances. If we are not there at midday, we will be forgotten."

"Will you have all your children there?"

Nelo shook his head. "Only the three oldest. The youngest ones are too little."

"And you are just going to abandon these children to the streets?"

"No. I must stay behind. They are too young to be on their own."

"Would you go if you could?"

Nelo chuffed. "Escape this? Have enough food? Not have to worry about having enough coin every time the Orphan Master has an auction so the littlest ones are not sold to those who would harm them? Of course, I would be on that wagon."

The boy smiled. "How many do you have that are too little?"

"Five. All girls. None older than six or so."

Nelo watched the boy. He was so still. It was like he was barely breathing. The boy's eyes flicked behind him, and Nelo whirled expecting a knife in his ribs.

It was the indigo dyer. She was no longer beautiful, but she must not have worked making the dyes very long. The poisons from the vats, the fumes from the fires had coarsened her skin but not ruined her face. She smiled at Nelo.

"I am glad to see you are still alive. I heard your words. Even if the boy goes with you, he must go to the Harbormaster tomorrow morning and begin his work. He must not appear to be missing until he is out of the city, and it will be too late to search for him. Bring your littlest girls here in the morning, we will find a home for them amongst all of us. No harm will come to them. Go, Nelo. Go on the wagon with the others and find a new home. You have earned it more than most."

"Thank you for bringing this news." The boy smiled. "You can call me Kid."

***

As Ngahuru hid in the refugee camp at the edges of the city, she wondered what of her network would still be intact. Which children would be found in time? She wished she could have looked for everyone herself, but she didn't know who was still alive after two years. Where would they have gone? What would they look like?

She had been dismayed at Dica's belief that they were 'all gone.' However, she thought the girl had been frightened often enough by her Protector, she would not disobey the command to find the others—if they could be found.

Ngahuru got up from the fire and walked restlessly among the tents and makeshift spaces people called their homes. This is where the people came who had no friends or coin when they first arrived to Kerek City. Some walked long decons to find work, some searched for their communities and friends who had traveled ahead of them, some lost hope and spent days and nights regretting their decision to leave everything they had known.

When she had decided to answer Zren's call for help she knew what he needed. To keep his people safe at Manumina, they didn't need an army. They could call on Vikland for that and the Empress would be happy to garrison soldiers there.

Instead, she had spent time with her King asking for a chance to return and search for those who had murdered her ambassador and his wife—the King's sister. He had shaken his head and said no one blamed her, and she needed to forgive herself. But Ngahuru's ears were stopped up against his words and she spent her days planning her return to Kerek.

She hadn't told the children that, had merely said she could take them away from their lives they were living now. Some she thought would come quickly: the Lost Girls who grew too old for their role and were forced to become fancies or thieves, Linna who was facing marriage to a man to pay her father's debts. Years ago, the daughter of the owner of the Red Cup had offered to give her information in exchange for the boy's freedom, but Ngahuru wasn't convinced Falan would be so selfless in the end. Still, she hoped Josef would be there tomorrow.

Ngahuru wanted soldiers and softfoots and men with coin. But the chances of any of them climbing into the wagon only meant they had lost their ability and connections in Kerek City to help her. She couldn't count on them.

She hoped the children wouldn't regret their choices.

There was a shadow ahead of her and she recognized a boy she had seen earlier. Angry voices chased him away from the fire, and she was intrigued. West Islanders cherished children. Who would chase one away from a bit of light and comfort? She called out as she hurried up to the boy.

He gave her a skeptical look, but he had stopped.

"Are you looking for food? I have some to share with you." She held out her hand with a meat pie. "Come take a walk with me…" The boy grabbed the pie and ran between the closely pitched tents.

"Don't waste your time with that one. He's a thief who plagues us all." The voice came out of the twilight.

"His mother must quite despair of him," Ngahuru said lightly.

"He has no family that we know of. We think he begs or steals in Lowertown during the day. It's a fair distance to walk out here each night. That tells me, he has no one there he can trust for shelter."

Ngahuru nodded and asked to approach the fire. The woman who spoke was careworn, but not all that old. She was bundled in Kereki clothes and huddled under a dingy greyish brown traveler's cloak.

"Have you eaten?" Ngahuru asked politely. "I have one more meat pie."

"I have not, but I don't like to take a gift for pity's sake."

"I will trade you my meat pie for that traveler's cloak. There. No pity is involved, it is a business transaction." Ngahuru smiled.

"I am getting the better end of the bargain. You think you only have to wash it to restore it to beauty. I have tried and this is what remains. I have decided that only a blind tailor could make this cloak and call it beautiful."

Ngahuru reached forward and took the dirt-colored cloak. She gave the woman the food.

"I have decided that 'dirt' is a color and it will suit me very well." She smiled, twirled the cloak about her, and went in search of the boy who stole the meat pie.

***

Josef panted himself awake from a nightmare. He realized he was in his own bed and alone. He carefully turned back the covers, got up, and tested the door. Locked. His dream was only a dream.

He had been fondled and groped by the Princes and all the soldiers who had come to the gambling tables last night. He had danced and sang to distract the players as they lost their coin. They had laughed and drank and called for Falan's father to raise the stakes for more than gold and silver. "My horse for the singer," the Prince had shouted. "One ride is as good as another. What say you?"

Falan's father had joked and said not this time. But perhaps if the Prince liked gambling at the Red Cup he would like to come again. Who knows what stakes would be acceptable in the Sinner's District the next time? The men had roared in laughter.

Josef felt like the bottom had fallen out of his world. He had looked at Falan and her face was furious. He didn't know if she was angry at him, her father, or the two Princes and their friends. Probably all of them. He didn't remember much of the rest of the night. The soldiers had lost a lot of coin, the two Princes even more. Miraculously, most of the soldiers in the last hands regained some of their coin.

The Princes had laughed at that as well.

When all the drunken men had found their horses, and the hired men had taken the reins and began walking the fools slowly back to castle, Falan and her brother began locking up the place. Falan's father smiled and told them they did well and to enjoy sleeping late the next day. They had earned it.

Nothing was said about the words of the Prince.

But Josef had dreamed the next time had come, and he had not been able to fight his way free.

He stepped back to his bed, but couldn't make himself crawl back in it.

The lock on his door slowly turned. Falan slipped in and closed the door quickly.

"I saw Jenny. She was one of the Lost Girls we gave our names of people who gambled and how much they lost. It was for the softfoot Ngahuru. Do you remember her?"

"I remember the Lost Girls. I am not sure I could tell them apart," Josef offered.

"It doesn't matter. Ngahuru is in town. If you want to be free of this life you must be in front of the Vikland embasado at midday. Midday, Josef. That means you need to pack your things now and hide about Embasado street until then. My family is still sleeping but will be awake soon. If you leave now, I will lock the door to your room, and no one will suspect you are missing until it is time to get ready for tonight."

Josef thought he was dreaming. He had wanted to escape for so long. Now Falan was just casually giving him the instructions as if she was complaining about how he made his bed.

"Will you come with me?"

"What? And give up all this? I count coins with my father, Josef, I know how rich I will be someday. You think just because you are gone, this place will go to ruin?"

Josef fell silent. He had thought Falan was his friend. Listening to her words made him feel like he had been nothing but another thing on her never-ending list of chores.

"Could you walk me to Embasado street? I don't know if I could find it by myself."

"Oh, like that won't tell my father something is wrong. He will wake and find his house is not clean, his food is not cooked, and the shopping is not done. Then he will see the door is locked from the outside and realize we are both gone. Who will he blame? My brother? Hardly. He'll still be lying in bed."

Josef started to smile. "If I am gone, and my door is locked from the outside, you will be blamed anyway. Wouldn't it be better to go on this grand adventure with Ngahuru than to remain here and be beaten for giving me my freedom?"

"There's a war out there, Josef. There are militia and soldiers and crimpers. You will be stolen for a soldier, and I will be nothing more than lump of clothes when they finish with me."

Josef looked at her steadily. "And this is different from my future how?"

Falan blew out a hard breath. "You should go. After last night, I no longer believe my father loves anyone or anything but the coin in his pocket. Pack your belongings. I'll walk you to Embasado street." She reached behind her skirts and pulled out a battered traveling bag. "I put some of my brother's clothes in here. Try them to be sure they fit. I don't know how you got so tall. I'll find you a pair of boots and something to eat. When I come back, you must be ready. My family won't sleep much longer."

She dropped the bag on the floor, walked out the door, and locked it.

Josef grinned. She had brought clothes, she had brought a pack, she had planned all along that he should have his freedom. He scrambled for the bag and the clothes within.

****

Kid opened his eyes when the first of the four locks clicked. It had been daylight for a decon, but his house had been quiet. Arden was still sleeping beside him. They had talked late into the night of Ngahuru's plan and what it would mean for their family.

Arden had thought he and Kid should be on the wagon. With only half the family, there would be enough coin saved that their parents could sail back to the Spice Island. Perhaps Safiya had convinced the Viklanders to help her return to their home, and she was even now waiting for them to join her.

They reminded their mother that Ngahuru was a wealthy and influential West Islander. Both boys thought they could join Ngahuru out of the city and then once she had finished her plans, it would be nothing for her to take them with her when she sailed for home. From there, the Spice Island was so close any *kapene* or even a fishing boat could take them the rest of the way. This would be the best way to return them all to the Spice Island and the life they had left behind.

Kid thought he should be on the wagon but was worried Ngahuru knew that Arden softfooted for the Viklanders as well as the West Islands. He wondered aloud if the West Islander would know their father resold other things that found their way into Arden's pockets. His brother had not been cautious about only selecting the items the softfoots had requested.

Their mother worried about the war. "Are you leaving your father and I only to walk into a greater trouble? We thought to go to Matasi to rebuild a life. They waved their hands at us like we were chickens in the garden and sent us on to Kerek. Do you boys even remember our home in the Spice Island before the sea storm? And now. What if I am sending you into a war where someone looks you up and down and decides you both will make fine soldiers?"

Arden glanced at his brother. "A long dagger is bigger than Kezi. They will not confuse him for a soldier. But if he does not remember to move, they may mistake him for a sapling."

"That's another thing. I do not think you should use your true names. I do not think you should let anyone find out you are brothers. If you find yourself in trouble, you can make for the nearest port and sail for home while people are still looking and talking about two Kereki boys. I must find your traveling papers for you."

Kid interrupted, "My older brother has a name different from Arden? Did I ever know this?" He gave his brother a cheeky grin.

Both reassured their mother, no one seeing them could threaten harm to one with the other. Since they had been children, they had known to protect the family was to protect themselves as Spice Islanders. They would not forget so easily. Arden joked that once his father and mother had split their house, he had forgotten he had a younger brother. Kid had added, claiming to be Kereki was only an excuse for Arden to forget to cut his hair—again.

But that had been last night.

As the final lock snicked open, Kid felt Arden tense beside him. He felt his brother's hand move under the blanket and knew he had a knife in his hand.

"*Wahine?*" A pause. "*Taku tama?*"

"Papa?" Kid whispered.

The door opened and their father slipped in. He visibly relaxed when he saw Arden on the sleeping mats next to Kid.

"I came here first. I thought I had heard Arden leave my house yesterday, but I could not call out and say it was not necessary. I did not want to alert our visitor that I did not live alone. I thought you would all be here."

"Papa, we have news."

Kid spoke first. He told of Nelo's visit. Then since he had never told his father what had happened six years ago, he had to tell that story as well. Kid reassured him Arden had not been seen by Nelo, although the white-haired boy may have seen Mother. Kid said they would join Ngahuru for all of her journey and travel back with her to the West Islands. From there they could find a *kapene* who would take them home on the strength of a Spice Islander's word.

"Without the two of us, you and mama have enough coin to sail home now. You could see if Safiya is there already. It is much more likely she would travel there than to return here, where she cannot move about freely," Kid reasoned.

"What good were all those decons you made us learn to read and write if you are not home in the Spice Island to receive our news that we are on our way there?" Arden grinned.

The boys' father sighed. "I do not like the idea of parting again. I feel each decision I have made since leaving our home after the sea storm has only made our situation worse."

"Shush." Their mother patted him on his shoulder. "You were Adah's age the first time you came to my father and said you wanted to build me the finest house on the island. When he sent you away—'for seasoning' he said—you did not pout by your mother's fire. You went out on your brother's boat, you traveled to Matasi to learn to be a carpenter. You built your house, invited my father to a meal, and asked again.

"We did what we did here in Kerek to survive. Now your sons want to test their strength. We need to go home and rebuild our house and plant our gardens. Adah is right. Safiya may be there waiting for us. How would we know unless we sail? The boys will travel with the West Islander and come home as soon as she does. I have listened as they have talked it out. Adah and Kezi will be able to watch out for each other. We have taught them to be young men, now they must show us what they have learned."

"This is what you want?"

Kid nodded and Arden grinned.

"When do you leave?"

"Midday. We are to bring a travel pack and meet in front of the Vikland embasado."

"So soon." Their father took a deep breath. "I will be nearby and see there is no trickery. If I call out that you must run, do not question me. Split up and do not return here until after dark. It means I have seen soldiers or trouble that you cannot see from where you stand. Promise me. I will not give my blessing otherwise."

The boys agreed quickly.

"You should not leave this house destitute. We have not yet sold all our gold." Their father looked to their mother. She nodded.

"Earrings, I think. I have small leather pockets you can hide them in. You can wear them on the ship to the West Islands with Ngahuru. She will know how to convert them into a passage home."

Arden grinned. "After today, the next time we meet will be in the Spice Island."

"To home," Kid said solemnly.

"To home," they all repeated.

***

Ngahuru carefully hitched the horses to the wagon. The Matasi missionaries had been grateful for the coin she had given them to drive her about yesterday, but today she would be leaving Kerek City and heading to Manumina. She blew out a hard breath wondering what the days ahead of her would be like. She had never traveled the Northern Track, but Zren's letter had not downplayed the dangers she would face. She hoped some of the soldiers and guards who had sold her information during her time in Kerek City would be waiting with the children in front of the Vikland embasado.

She grumbled to herself. She was stiff and sore from sleeping on top of the crates of West Islands steel Raumati's family had sent. The West Islands boy she had talked with last night had returned this morning. He said his name was Ross, and he would like to go on this journey she had told him about. She had warned him this was no small adventure she was asking him to join her on. But she said there were others who would join them. She had assured him they were mostly strangers to each other and he would not be one standing against many.

He had only asked if she had food to give him.

***

Falan and Josef waited in the shadow of the Vikland embasado gate. Josef looked down the street and noticed the

Matasi guards watching them. He gave a little wave with his fingers and Falan swatted them down.

"You aren't at the Red Cup, Josef. Try to be invisible," she hissed.

"How will Ngahuru see us if we are invisible? Perhaps that was her Matasi guard that followed her about when she was in the marketplaces. He should know we are here before her."

Falan huffed but said nothing. Josef watched as her eyes seemed to dart everywhere at once. He knew she was looking for her father's men. But she had taken such a twisted way here he doubted anyone could have followed. He knew he couldn't have found his way back.

As he had carefully tiptoed behind her down the stairs and out the door, he had glanced about the house. The rooms were gleaming, and he could smell a soup cooking on a low flame in the spotless kitchen. She must have stayed up after everyone else went to bed to get all of her tasks done before her family woke. Now they would only think she had taken a servant and gone to the market. No one would look for her for decons.

She had planned all along to come with him. He had almost tripped over his feet his eyes had filled with tears so quickly.

"Who else should we be watching for? Did Jenny say anyone else we might have met before?" He looked down the busy street with wagons and carts and people traveling.

Falan shook her head. "The Lost Girls, I think. But I do not know which ones are still alive. I saw Nelo. He no longer looks like a boy, but I do not believe he could have kept all of them safe from harm. Once Ngahuru and her coin deserted us two years ago, he would have had a much harder time keeping them alive."

"I remember him. The white-blond hair, the scarred face. He didn't talk much."

"No one can get a word in sideways when you are around, Josef. I'm sure the Lost Girls will tell you lots of stories of what he said when they didn't bring enough from their begging."

Josef said nothing and continued to watch the street with her.

***

Callis and Beck walked in and out of the shops in the Linen Market. "I don't know why you want to shop here," Beck sniffed, "the shops near the Peacock are so much nicer."

"But the other tailors and I shop there all the time. I wanted something unusual for this latest dress. Let's walk to the shops near the embasados. They will have something unique enough even for my fussiest client."

Beck sighed but followed her without any further comment.

A decon and another handful of shops later and Beck started complaining about missing midday. Callis listened absently as she looked for the wagon with Ngahuru and her Matasi guard.

Callis had only written down her gossip and news and pushed them to the West Islander when she came into the shop. She wasn't sure who else would be on Embasado street waiting and ready to leave the city. She had been too startled yesterday to ask the girl for details. Would there be other women? Children like the girl who had come to the shop yesterday? Men or soldiers? She clutched her tailoring bag with her clothes and coin and wondered again if she was making the right decision. She still hadn't decided how she was going to convince Beck to leave her. At least she wasn't going to make him tell her father what she had done. The letter on her bed would tell her family she was going to make a new life for herself on the frontier. That part was true anyway.

She didn't see Linna. She wondered if the girl had decided to stay or if she had been unable to leave. Callis thought perhaps she should have offered again to have her and Beck walk with her so she could escape her father's house. But Linna had been quick to say she already had a plan and she would be there. It was too late to do anything about it now.

***

Kid made another slow scan of the area. He was casually standing against the wall just behind a cart laden with kindling. The owner twisted about to look at him and Kid made eye contact. He had deliberately worn his best shirt and new Kereki pants so he would not be marked as a potential thief and watched.

Instead, he wanted to be the one watching. He made another long sweep up the street. There was a girl and a tall boy standing near the gates of the Vikland embasado. Kid didn't know them, but he guessed they were part of the ones waiting for Ngahuru's wagon. Both had battered traveling bags. Her hair was cropped short. She wore a cloak even though the day was mild. He watched her shift from foot to foot and her eyes dart about. Kid guessed there would be trouble when the two of them were found missing.

He looked to Mother laying quietly in the doorway across the street and risked a glance upward to see if he could catch a glimpse of Arden. His father was standing opposite the Matasi embasado. If this was a trap, if there was trouble, his father would call out in Mata for help. The Matasian soldiers might not run to assist, but the cry would definitely draw their attention and help provide the interference needed for Arden and him to flee a dance with Trouble.

Arden had assured everyone he could watch the streets for the wagon, look for soldiers or the Harbormaster's thugs, and still climb down and jump in the wagon before it had turned the corner and start its way to freedom.

"It's the last time I will look out for you, little brother," Arden had teased. "After you are on the wagon, you are a stranger to me."

"You are already strange," Kid had responded drily. "Are you wearing that? I know Mama packed better clothes for you."

Arden had ignored him, grabbed his traveling pack, and begun climbing the stone steps on the outside wall to the rooftop.

Kid made another survey of the area.

There was a solidly built woman and her male protector. Although Kid thought the boy was younger than he was, he was sturdy and well-fed. He carried a cudgel with some size to it. It was obvious the woman and boy knew each other well, and he was not a hire boy for the morning. Kid wondered if one or both would climb on to the wagon.

Kid straightened suddenly as he saw Nelo hurry down the street. It had been so long since Kid had seen the Lost Girls, he barely recognized the three older girls. Jenny, Dica, and Tyra all held tightly to the hands of the five little ones—all strangers to him. Everyone was carrying a pack. He heard a sharp chirp and Mother rose on all fours. Arden must have given some other commands that Kid didn't hear because the dog turned and bounded up the street to his father. This had not been part of their plans. Why had Nelo brought the little ones here?

Kid slipped back into the shadows. He knew the white-haired boy hadn't seen him; he had been too distracted. He watched silently as Nelo waited with the Lost Girls. Papa and the dog walked leisurely towards them.

"You were supposed to leave the littlest ones with my wife. She told me about it this morning." Kid's father was abrupt.

"I don't know you." Nelo reached inside his cloak. Kid quickly stepped out between them.

"Nelo, its me. Kid." Out of the corner of his eye, he saw his father scowl. "What happened?"

"Your mother wasn't there. She didn't answer my knock. I didn't know what else to do," Nelo began. "I explained to the little ones they would have a new home with food to eat and not have to beg on the streets. We went to your house, but no one opened the door to our knock. There was a man at a cart who said he knew me from the day before. He said he knew your parents and he was to wait and take the girls with him. I had never seen this man before. I am not just going to hand over five children to a stranger."

Kid nodded. "I am sorry. The man was not a stranger to us. We thought you would have been earlier when my papa and I were still there." He raised his shoulders and dropped them. "I am sorry. I didn't think it through. I was in a hurry to get away from the Harbormaster and come here. I had an opportunity much earlier than any of us expected. We told our friend to meet you there when we had to leave." He repeated, "I am sorry."

"So am I," Nelo said heavily, "I'll have to stay behind."

Jenny twisted about and looked down the street. "The wagon isn't here. Could you take the little ones back and we tell Ngahuru where to find you?"

"No!" Kid and his father said together.

"I'll take the girls back with me. My wife and I agreed they will be safe with us."

"I have kept so many of them alive because I trust no one," Nelo retorted. "I don't know you, either."

"This is my father. Truly, Nelo. The girls are safe with them. Do not throw this chance away to give them a better life because you do not trust me." Kid paused. "You did not have to look for me yesterday. But you did. Come on the wagon with me, Nelo. Let the littlest ones have a home with those who can give them one."

Kid watched as the emotions played over Nelo's face. He knew whatever decision Nelo made, it wouldn't be an easy one.

Nelo took the Lost Girls aside. The conversation was low and soothing, but Kid couldn't make out any of the words.

***

It is midday.

Ngahuru looks at the sun once more and decides it is time. She steps out of the shade cast by the empty Conrosan embasado and climbs up on the wagon seat. Ross quickly climbs over the seat and sits down hard beside her. He gives her another look and sniffs.

Ngahuru has changed from her Kereki pants and shirt and tunic to a worn and patched dress. Her white hair is only partially covered by a rag.

"Call me Tiju Tia. That is my name no matter what you hear from others today."

Ross narrows his eyes at her before he suddenly smiles. "If you feed me every day, I will call you the King of Kerek if you wish."

Tiju Tia chuckles. She picks up the reins and slowly turns the wagon down Embasado street. There are no guards with horses, no soldiers with wagons waiting to join her. There are a few children. There is no one else. She drives the length of the street so anyone who is hiding can see her. She hopes there are many more hiding. She turns the wagon into the busy street and stops. She doesn't step down and neither does Ross. She waits.

***

Jenny looks at Dica, "Is that the wagon? Why else would it stop there? Where is Will? Where is Ngahuru and her guard?"

Dica shakes her head. "I don't know. Will didn't say anything yesterday. He just said an old Kereki woman would be in the wagon at midday and not to be late."

"Look!" Tyra hisses.

The tall boy and the girl cross the street and talk to the old woman. The girl turns and looks at them for a long time. She turns back to the old woman. After another conversation, the two crawl in the back of the wagon.

An argument breaks out between the woman carrying the tailoring bag and the sturdy boy with the cudgel. He grabs her arm, but she shakes him off and walks to the wagon. She talks to the old woman and then goes around to the back. Jenny assumes she is talking to the boy and girl, unless there are others already hiding. The woman comes back to the boy with the cudgel and says a few words. She gives him a coin. He takes the coin but folds his arms and waits.

"We need to go."

Jenny runs to the little girls and gives them each a quick hug. She grabs Dica's hand and the two run across the street. The little girls start crying and Tyra hugs them goodbye. She looks to Nelo. He shoos her to the wagon.

"Trust me, Nelo," Kid pleads. "Trust me."

Nelo finally nods and hugs each of the girls. The anguish is plain on his face. Kid touches his father's hand, "Family is family," and hurries across the street. He and the woman on the wagon bench only nod to each other before he climbs into the back. The woman smiles.

The girls cling to Nelo but he peels off their hands and picks up his traveling bag. He crosses the street. He talks to the old woman for a long time and then walks around to the back. He sits so he faces up Embasado street and cannot see the crying girls.

Arden casually walks down the street with Mother by his side and a traveling bag over his shoulder. He grins at the old woman on the wagon seat and walks to the back.

Falan shouts, "Not a dog!" and pulls her skirts in close.

Arden calls to Ngahuru. "A thief from a family of thieves might be a good person to have on this adventure of yours. I am interested in traveling with you. But I will not travel without my Mother." He waits for her decision.

Tiju Tia sighs. "Falan, come ride on the wagon bench with me. I want Arden and his dog, and you must accept that. Ross, you can ride in the wagon bed."

"I will not. I was here first," he protests.

Josef laughs. "I have heard that every adventure has trouble along the way, but truly I thought it was going to be after we actually started on the journey."

The others smile or chuckle quietly, and Falan knows she cannot win this one. She steps up and over, so she is sitting between the back of the wagon seat and Josef.

Tiju Tia tells Arden to climb in, it is time to go. There is no more lingering about. She tells them from this moment forward to call her Tiju Tia. She asks them to introduce themselves to each other.

"It will be several decons before we stop for the night. You might as well make friends." She gives Falan a stern look.

Tiju Tia asks if any of them can ride a horse. They will purchase one in Vingt so they will have an outrider. The children look at her like she is speaking another language. She sighs and picks up the reins.

There is a shout and two people come running down the street towards the wagon.

"It's Linna!" Callis calls out. Then she frowns, "But I do not know the man running behind her."

Josef asks nobody in particular if they think the man is chasing the girl and if so, should they jump out and help her?

"What would a Viklander be doing in Kerek City?" Kid asks. Nelo and Arden each reach for a hidden knife in their boot. They look at each other and smile.

Linna starts talking as soon as Tiju Tia stops the horses. "You can see by his face, he is not safe in Kerek City." She turns to those in the wagon, "Oro was born in the West Islands, he can shoot a short bow. He would be a good person to have with us on the frontier." She turns back to the woman on the wagon seat and waits.

Ngahuru nods and the two walk around to the back of the wagon and crowd in.

Falan looks Linna up and down and remarks, "I guess those who have enough coin can make midday be whatever time they want."

Linna snaps back, "When one is under lock and key, it takes time to escape a prison."

Josef looks Linna in the face and says he understands completely.

He tells Falan, "Obviously, her hero isn't as fierce as mine."

Tiju Tia blows out a hard breath. These were not the ones she would have chosen. There are no soldiers, no guards, no men who can defend them on the Northern Track. They are children with brutal pasts and damaged lives.

Last night about the campfire, she had decided they could not be called boys and girls, their history had stolen their childhood from them. Instead she had chosen the name, "The Wrens."

The horses begin the journey to Manumina.